DARK COMPANY

DARK COMPANY

THE TEN GREATEST GHOST STORIES

Edited by Lincoln Child

St. Martin's Press
New York

To M.

ACKNOWLEDGMENTS

"The Mezzotint" by M. R. James from *The Ghost Stories of M. R. James,* Second Edition (1974), Edward Arnold (Publishers) Ltd., London. Reprinted by permission.
"The Shadow Out of Time" by H. P. Lovecraft. Reprinted by permission of Arkham House Publishers, Inc., Sauk City, Wisconsin.

Library of Congress Cataloging in Publication Data
Main entry under title: Dark company.
Bibliography: p.
Contents: The fall of the House of Usher / Edgar Allan Poe—Green tea / J. Sheridan LeFanu—The jolly corner / Henry James—[etc.]
1. Ghost stories, English. 2. Ghost stories, American.
I. Child, Lincoln.
PR1309.G5D37 1984 823'.0872'08 83-13759
ISBN 0-312-18231-7
First Edition
10 9 8 7 6 5 4 3 2 1

Contents

Introduction

The ghost story as literature has led a curiously double life. On the one hand, it has always been immensely successful as entertainment —from early gothic romances such as *The Mysteries of Udolpho* and *The Monk,* to the recent novels of Peter Straub and Stephen King. On the other, it has rarely if ever received the critical attention it deserves. Many in fact don't consider the ghost story to be a branch of "serious" fiction at all, and consign it to the gray regions at the periphery of literature—a zone inhabited by mystery, science fiction, and other indulgences base and sensational.

The reasons why supernatural literature has been such a critical pariah are numerous and vague. Perhaps it is due in part to the genre's vulnerability to exploitation—think of crude cinematic monsters, and pulp magazines. Or perhaps it is because of some critical sense that anything "fun" to read, hence popular, is beneath examination. Whatever the cause, the gap between the influential role the ghost story has played and any real recognition of this role has always been unfairly wide.

It is in part to help bridge this gap that the following collection has been assembled. Within these covers are perhaps the ten best reasons why supernatural literature should be taken more seriously: a careful assembly of what in this editor's opinion are the ten greatest stories of ghostly horror written in the English language, the classics that have endured time's fell hand and now comprise the foundation of the genre.

The works that follow are indeed great ghost stories. But they are also great fiction. The ghost story has lured many renowned literary figures: Henry James, Hawthorne, Yeats, Kipling, Conrad, and others have dabbled in the art, and elevated it in the process. Some of them are found in these pages. But the realm of the ghost story claims as well its own peculiar masters—writers who chose it as their medium and remained faithful always. Few readers, however well versed in standard literature, may have heard such names as Sheridan Le Fanu or Oliver Onions. But these artists, and the others included here, have crafted works of fiction that—for enduring appeal and power, subtle development of atmosphere and character, and sheer technical virtuosity—rank with the best in our literary tradition.

It is not enough, however, for great ghost stories to qualify simply as fine literature. They must also be scary. The stories here are that, and more: mysterious, perverse, sometimes profoundly unsettling. All ten provide, at the very least, frissons of anxiety. Many have moments of genuine terror—terror not forced upon the reader by repulsive images, but developed by restrained and artful orchestration. "The Willows," for example, is the masterpiece of Algernon Blackwood, leader of the genre's "visionary" tradition. In this story, the horror that overtakes two explorers deep inside Hungary seems benign enough in retelling: it is simply the darker side of nature, manifesting itself in the malefic influences of the willow bushes and the black waters of the Danube that surround the travelers. But Blackwood's skill in slowly constructing the framework of his story around us as we read, and in subtly convincing us of the strangeness inherent in the ordinary, makes "The Willows" one of the most unnerving stories ever written.

Ghost stories—and the fears of death and the unknown that first motivated them—have been in existence for as long as there have been people to relate and people to listen. But modern supernatural fiction had its birth two centuries ago, when Horace Walpole's slim novel *The Castle of Otranto* appeared in 1764. The history of macabre literature since then has been a long and complex one, embodying within its traditions many distinct stylistic schools. The stories in this volume represent the finest work from many of these ghostly traditions. "The Jolly Corner" by Henry James is an admirable example of the psychological school—"psychological" being a common if inadequate label for ghost stories whose apparitions *appear* to have their origins within the mind of the protagonist. "Green Tea," by the influential Victorian writer Joseph Sheridan Le Fanu, can also be considered a tale in the psychological mold—if one explains away the hideous apparition that confronts the protagonist, Mr. Jennings, as the manifestation of his repressed sexual desires. But "Green Tea" strongly resists classification, and (like most great stories in the genre) leaves its conclusion open to more than one disturbing interpretation. Oliver Onions's "The Beckoning Fair One"—which is an absolutely perfect work of fiction, ghostly or otherwise—is another that falls into the psychological classification while transcending it simultaneously.

The mystical, anti-scientific "visionary" school has already been mentioned. Besides Blackwood, another exponent of this tradition is Arthur Machen, almost forgotten today despite such works as "The White People" and "The Novel of the White Powder." "The Great God Pan," his greatest story, is a highly lyrical example of the strange and menacing world of the visionary tale: a world of forces that exist beyond the veil of ordinary perception. Characters in tales of this sort find all too often that, when this veil is torn aside, the forces that emerge are neither benign nor (worse) controllable.

M. R. James was master and chief patron of the "antiquarian" ghost story, of which "The Mezzotint" is a justly famous paradigm. Subtle, spare, elegantly restrained—usually featuring a scholarly setting and an erudite, retiring hero (victim)—the antiquarian tale unfolds in such a cool and measured fashion that the reader is wholely unprepared for the horror that inevitably comes. In explaining the principles of his own ghostly poetics, James once wrote, with his habitual terseness, that it is quite acceptable "to leave a loophole for a natural explanation, but I would say, let the loophole be so narrow as not to be quite practicable."

The most contemporary writer in our collection (in period if not in style) is H. P. Lovecraft, who is almost singlehandedly responsible for directing the course of supernatural fiction over the last half-century. By drawing freely from many predecessors and fusing the elements of disparate schools, Lovecraft in his Cthulhu mythos pioneered the "cosmic" tradition of ghostly literature. The tradition hinges on an elaborate mythology, created by Lovecraft and greatly elaborated on since. This mythology has at its core a race of highly sophisticated beings who once inhabited the planet and now lurk in remote corners of earth and space, waiting to be resurrected by evil or unsuspecting humans. "The Shadow Out of Time" focuses (as does much of his best work) on a single aspect of the mythology, elaborating upon it with horrifying effectiveness.

These stories, then, and the others that make up this fat volume, are the best of a genre that is historically important as well as uniquely compelling. I present them as their own most eloquent defense. One final note before urging the reader onward: in earlier ghostly anthologies, editors have sometimes found themselves in the grip of two preoccupations. The first is with justifying the term "ghost story" itself; and the second is with investigating the reasons why people deliberately seek out tales that will frighten them. I won't spend time on the shortcomings of the first; terms like *horror, macabre,* and *grotesque* are all partly right and partly wrong, and *ghost story* is an acceptable compromise (since, as one critic put it, the stories in the genre are all "apparitional in one way or another"). In particular, I have chosen not to examine the instinct that prompts one to *read* such a story. It is as obscure and fundamentally human as the tradition itself; and to poke or probe at either the stories or the reader's motivation too closely is to diffuse the magic.

Better to throw aside such considerations and to accept the stories as they are, on their own enigmatic terms. Well into one of Machen's tales, a character recalls the old phrase *Omnia exeunt in mysterium,* which translates happily (if not quite correctly) as "everything recedes into mystery." More than anything else, ghost stories bring us closer to the mystery.

So turn the page, and get closer.

Lincoln Child
St. Martin's Press

I can readily believe that there are more invisible than visible beings in the universe.

—Thomas Burnet
Archaelogiae Philosophical

I wants to make your flesh creep.

—Charles Dickens
The Pickwick Papers

DARK COMPANY

The Fall of the House of Usher

EDGAR ALLAN POE

[1809–1849]

Poe, a preeminent American man of letters and the true father of the modern supernatural tale, ironically languished in obscurity in his own country for many years after his death. Abroad, however, Poe was much admired, especially by French symbolists such as Mallarmé and Baudelaire. Although drink and his mysterious death cut short his achievement, Poe produced an extraordinary amount of fine material. Above all else, Poe considered himself a poet. Yet today he is revered chiefly for such prose works as his novel The Narrative of A. Gordon Pym *and his many fine stories, including of course the unforgettable* "The Fall of the House of Usher."

Son coeur est un luth suspendu;
Sitôt qu'on le touche il résonne.
DE BÉRANGER

During the whole of a dull, dark, and soundless day in the autumn of the year, when the clouds hung oppressively low in the heavens, I had been passing alone, on horseback, through a singularly dreary tract of country; and at length found myself, as the shades of the evening drew on, within view of the melancholy House of Usher. I knew not how it was—but, with the first glimpse of the building, a sense of insufferable gloom pervaded my spirit. I say insufferable; for the feeling was unrelieved by any of that half-pleasurable, because poetic, sentiment with which the mind usually receives even the sternest natural images of the desolate or terrible. I looked upon the scene before me—upon the mere house, and the simple landscape features of the domain, upon the bleak walls, upon the vacant eye-like windows, upon a few rank sedges, and upon a few white trunks of decayed trees—with an utter depression of soul which I can compare to no earthly sensation more properly than to the afterdream of the reveler upon opium; the bitter lapse into everyday life, the hideous dropping off of the veil. There was an iciness, a sinking, a sickening of the heart, an unredeemed dreariness of thought which no goading of the imagination could torture into aught of the sublime. What was it—I paused to think—what was it that so unnerved me in the contemplation of the House of Usher? It was a mystery all insoluble; nor could I grapple with the shadowy fancies that crowded upon me as I pondered. I was forced to fall back upon the unsatisfactory conclusion, that while, beyond doubt, there *are* combinations of very simple natural objects which have the power of thus affecting us, still the analysis of this power lies among considerations beyond our depth. It was possible, I reflected, that a mere different arrangement of the particulars of the scene, of the details of the picture, would be sufficient to modify, or perhaps to annihilate, its capacity for sorrowful impression; and, acting upon this idea, I reined my horse to the precipitous brink of a black and lurid tarn that lay in unruffled luster by the dwelling, and gazed down—but with a shudder even more thrilling than before—upon the remodeled and inverted images of the gray sedge, and the ghastly tree stems, and the vacant and eye-like windows.

Nevertheless, in this mansion of gloom I now proposed to myself a sojourn of some weeks. Its proprietor, Roderick Usher, had been one of my boon companions in boyhood; but many years had elapsed since our last meeting. A letter, however, had lately reached me in a distant part of the country—a letter from him—which in its wildly importunate nature had admitted of no other than a personal reply. The MS. gave evidence of nervous agitation. The writer spoke of acute bodily illness, of a mental disorder which oppressed him, and of an earnest desire to see me, as his best and indeed his only personal friend, with a view of attempting, by the cheerfulness of my society, some alleviation of his malady. It was the manner in which all this, and much more, was said—it was the apparent *heart* that went with his request—which allowed me no room for hesitation; and I accordingly obeyed forthwith what I still considered a very singular summons.

Although as boys we had been even intimate associates, yet I really knew little of my friend. His reserve had been always excessive and habitual. I was aware, however, that his very ancient family had been noted, time out of mind, for a peculiar sensibility of temperament, displaying itself, through long ages, in many works of exalted art, and manifested of late in repeated deeds of munificent yet unobtrusive charity, as well as in a passionate devotion of the intricacies, perhaps even more than to the orthodox and easily recognizable beauties, of musical science. I had learned, too, the very remarkable fact that the stem of the Usher race, all time-honored as it was, had put forth at no period any enduring branch; in other words, that the entire family lay in the direct line of descent, and had always, with very trifling and very temporary variation, so lain. It was this deficiency, I considered, while running over in thought the perfect keeping of the character of the premises with the accredited character of the people, and while speculating upon the possible influence which the one, in the long lapse of centuries, might have exercised upon the other—it was this deficiency, perhaps, of collateral issue, and the consequent undeviating transmission from sire to son of the patrimony with the name, which had, at length, so identified the two as to merge the original title of the estate in the quaint and equivocal appellation of the "House of Usher"—an appellation which seemed to include, in the minds of the peasantry who used it, both the family and the family mansion.

I have said that the sole effect of my somewhat childish experiment, that of looking down within the tarn, had been to deepen the first singular impression. There can be no doubt that the consciousness of the rapid increase of my superstition—for why should I not so term it?—served mainly to accelerate the increase itself. Such, I have long known, is the paradoxical law of all sentiments having terror as a basis. And it might have been for this reason only, that, when I again uplifted my eyes to the house itself, from its image in the pool, there grew in my mind a strange fancy—a fancy so ridiculous, indeed, that I but mention it to show the vivid force of the sensations which oppressed me. I had so worked upon my imagination as really to believe that about the whole mansion and domain there hung an atmosphere peculiar to themselves and their immediate vicinity: an atmosphere which had no affinity with the air of heaven, but which had reeked up from the decayed trees, and the gray wall, and the silent tarn: a pestilent and mystic vapor, dull, sluggish, faintly discernible, and leaden-hued.

Shaking off from my spirit what *must* have been a dream, I scanned more narrowly the real aspect of the building. Its principal feature seemed to be that of an excessive antiquity. The discoloration of ages had been great. Minute fungi overspread the whole exterior, hanging in a fine tangled webwork from the eaves. Yet all this was apart from any extraordinary dilapidation. No portion of the masonry had fallen; and there appeared to be a wild inconsistency between its still perfect adaptation of parts and the crumbling condition of the individual stones. In this there was much that reminded me of the specious totality of old woodwork which has rotted for long years in some neglected vault, with no disturbance from the breath of the external air. Beyond this indication of excessive decay, however, the fabric gave little token of instability. Perhaps the eye of a scrutinizing observer might have discovered a barely perceptible fissure, which, extending from the roof of the building in front, made its way down the wall in a zigzag direction, until it became lost in the sullen waters of the tarn.

Noticing these things, I rode over a short causeway to the house. A servant in waiting took my horse, and I entered the Gothic archway of the hall. A valet, of stealthy step, thence conducted me, in silence, through many dark and intricate passages in my progress to the studio of his master. Much that I encountered on the way contributed, I know not how, to heighten the vague sentiments of which I have already spoken. While the objects around me—while the carvings of the ceilings, the somber tapestries of the walls, the ebon blackness of the floors, and the phantasmagoric armorial trophies which rattled as I strode, were but matters to which, or to such as which, I had been accustomed from my infancy—while I hesitated not to acknowledge how familiar was all this—I still wondered to find how unfamiliar were the fancies which ordinary images were stirring up. On one of the staircases, I met the physician of the family. His countenance, I thought, wore a mingled expression of low cunning and perplexity. He accosted me with trepidation and passed on. The valet now threw open a door and ushered me into the presence of his master.

The room in which I found myself was very large and lofty. The windows were long, narrow, and pointed, and at so vast a distance from the black oaken floor as to be altogether inaccessible from within. Feeble gleams of encrimsoned light made their way through the trellised panes, and served to render sufficiently distinct the more prominent objects around; the eye, however, struggled in vain to reach the remoter angles of the chamber, or the recesses of the vaulted and fretted ceiling. Dark draperies hung upon the walls. The general furniture was profuse, comfortless, antique, and tattered. Many books and musical instruments lay scattered about, but failed to give any vitality to the scene. I felt that I breathed an atmosphere of sorrow. An air of stern, deep, and irredeemable gloom hung over and pervaded all.

Upon my entrance, Usher arose from a sofa on which he had been lying at full length, and greeted me with a vivacious warmth which had much in it, I at first thought, of an overdone cordiality—of the constrained effort of the *ennuyé* man of the world. A glance, however, at his countenance, convinced me of his perfect sincerity. We sat down; and for some moments, while he spoke not, I gazed upon him with a feeling half of pity, half of awe. Surely man had never before so terribly altered in so brief a period as had Roderick Usher! It was with difficulty that I could bring myself to admit the identity of the wan being before me with the companion of my boyhood. Yet the character of his face had been at all times remarkable. A cadaverousness of complexion; an eye large, liquid, and luminous beyond comparison; lips somewhat thin and very pallid, but of a surpassingly beautiful curve; a nose of a delicate Hebrew model, but with a breadth of nostril unusual in similar formations; a finely molded chin, speaking, in its want of prominence, of a want of moral energy; hair of a more than weblike softness and tenuity; these features, with an inordinate expansion above the regions of the temple, made up altogether a countenance not easily to be forgotten. And now in the mere exaggeration of the prevailing character of these features, and of the expression they were wont to convey, lay so much of change that I doubted to whom I spoke. The now ghostly pallor of the skin, and the now miraculous luster of the eye, above all things startled and even awed me. The silken hair, too, had been suffered to grow all unheeded, and as, in its wild gossamer texture, it floated rather than fell about the face, I could not, even with effort, connect its arabesque expression with any idea of simple humanity.

In the manner of my friend I was at once struck with an incoherence, an inconsistency; and I soon found this to arise from a series of feeble and futile struggles to overcome an habitual trepidancy, an excessive nervous agitation. For something of this nature I had indeed been prepared, no less by his letter than by reminiscences of certain boyish traits, and by conclusions deduced from his peculiar physical conformation and temperament. His action was alternatively vivacious and sullen. His voice varied rapidly from a tremulous indecision (when the animal spirits seemed utterly in abeyance) to that species of energetic concision—that abrupt, weighty, unhurried, and hollow-sounding enunciation—that leaden, self-balanced and perfectly modulated guttural utterance—which may be observed in the lost drunkard, or the irreclaimable eater of opium, during the periods of his most intense excitement.

It was thus that he spoke of the object of my visit, of his earnest desire to see me, and of the solace he expected me to afford him. He entered, at some length, into what he conceived to be the nature of his malady. It was, he said, a constitutional and a family evil, and one for which he despaired to find a remedy—a mere nervous affection, he immediately added, which would undoubtedly soon pass off. It displayed itself in a host of unnatural sensations. Some of these, as he detailed them, interested and bewildered me: although, perhaps, the terms and the general manner of the narration had their weight. He suffered much from a morbid acuteness of the senses; the most insipid food was alone endurable; he could wear only garments of a certain texture; the odors of all flowers were oppressive; his eyes were tortured by even a faint light; and there were but peculiar sounds, and these from stringed instruments, which did not inspire him with horror.

To an anomalous species of terror I found him a bounden slave. "I shall perish," said he, "I *must* perish in this deplorable folly. Thus, thus, and not otherwise, shall I be lost. I dread the events of the future, not in themselves, but in their results. I shudder at the thought of any, even the most trivial, incident, which may operate upon this intolerable agitation of soul. I have, indeed, no abhorrence of danger, except in its absolute effect—in terror. In this unnerved—in this pitiable condition—I feel that the period will sooner or later arrive when I must abandon life and reason together, in some struggle with the grim phantasm, FEAR."

I learned moreover at intervals, and through broken and equivocal hints, another singular feature of his mental condition. He was enchained by certain superstitious impressions in regard to the dwelling which he tenanted, and whence, for many years, he had never ventured forth—in regard to an influence whose suppositious force was conveyed in terms too shadowy here to be restated—an influence which some peculiarities in the mere form and substance of his family mansion, had, by dint of long sufferance, he said, obtained over his spirit—an effect which the physique of the gray walls and turrets, and of the dim tarn into which they all looked down, had, at length, brought about upon the morale of his existence.

He admitted, however, although with hesitation, that much of the peculiar gloom which thus afflicted him could be traced to a more natural and far more palpable origin—to the severe and long-continued illness, indeed to the evidently approaching dissolution, of a tenderly beloved sister—his sole companion for long years, his last and only relative on earth. "Her decease," he said, with a bitterness which I can never forget, "would leave him (him the hopeless and the frail) the last of the ancient race of the Ushers." While he spoke, the lady Madeline (for so was she called) passed slowly through a remote portion of the apartment, and, without having noticed my presence, disappeared. I regarded her with an utter astonishment not unmingled with dread, and yet I found it impossible to account for such feelings. A sensation of stupor oppressed me, as my eyes followed her retreating steps. When a door, at length, closed upon her, my glance sought instinctively and eagerly the countenance of the brother, but he had buried his face in his hands, and I could only perceive that a far more than ordinary wanness had overspread the emaciated fingers through which trickled many passionate tears.

The disease of the lady Madeline had long baffled the skill of her physicians. A settled apathy, a gradual wasting away of the person, and frequent although transient affections of a partially cataleptical character, were the unusual diagnosis. Hitherto she had steadily borne up against the pressure of her malady, and had not betaken herself finally to bed; but, on the closing in of the evening of my arrival at the house, she succumbed (as her brother told me at night with inexpressible agitation) to the prostrating power of the destroyer; and I learned that the glimpse I had obtained of her person would thus probably be the last I should obtain—that the lady, at least while living, would be seen by me no more.

For several days ensuing, her name was unmentioned by either Usher or myself; and during this period I was busied in earnest endeavors to alleviate the melancholy of my friend. We painted and read together; or I listened, as if in a dream, to the wild improvisation of his speaking guitar. And thus, as a closer and still closer intimacy admitted me more unreservedly into the recesses of his spirit, the more bitterly did I perceive the futility of all attempt at cheering a mind from which darkness, as if an inherent positive quality, poured forth upon all objects of the moral and physical universe, in one unceasing radiation of gloom.

I shall ever bear about me a memory of the many solemn hours I thus spent alone with the master of the House of Usher. Yet I should fail in any attempt to convey an idea of the exact character of the studies, or of the occupations, in which he involved me, or led me the way. An excited and highly distempered ideality threw a sulphurous luster over all. His long improvised dirges will ring forever in my ears. Among other things, I hold painfully in mind a certain singular perversion and amplification of the wild air of the last waltz of Von Weber. From the paintings over which his elaborate fancy brooded, and which grew, touch by touch, into vagueness at which I shuddered the more thrillingly because I shuddered knowing not why;—from these paintings (vivid as their images now are before me) I would in vain endeavor to enduce more than a small portion which should lie within the compass of merely written words. By the utter simplicity, by the nakedness of his designs, he arrested and overawed attention. If ever mortal painted an idea, that mortal was Roderick Usher. For me at least, in the circumstances then surrounding me, there arose, out of the pure abstractions which the hypochondriac contrived to throw upon his canvas, an intensity of intolerable awe, no shadow of which felt I ever yet in the contemplation of the certainly glowing yet too concrete reveries of Fuseli.

One of the phantasmagoric conceptions of my friend, partaking not so rigidly of the spirit of abstraction, may be shadowed forth, although feebly, in words. A small picture presented the interior of an immensely long and rectangular vault or tunnel, with low walls, smooth, white, and without interruption or device. Certain accessory points of the design served well to convey the idea that this excavation lay at an exceeding depth below the surface of the earth. No outlet was observed in any portion of its vast extent, and no torch or other artificial source of light was discernible; yet a flood of intense rays rolled throughout, and bathed the whole in a ghastly and inappropriate splendor.

I have just spoken of that morbid condition of the auditory nerve which rendered all music intolerable to the sufferer, with the exception of certain effects of stringed instruments. It was, perhaps, the narrow limits to which he thus confined himself upon the guitar, which gave birth, in great measure, to the fantastic character of his performances. But the fervid *facility* of his *impromptus* could not be so accounted for. They must have been, and were, in the notes, as well as in the words of his wild fantasias (for he not unfrequently accompanied himself with rhymed verbal improvisations), the result of that intense mental collectedness and concentration to which I have previously alluded as observable only in particular moments of the highest artificial excitement. The words of one of these rhapsodies I have easily remembered. I was, perhaps, the more forcibly impressed with it, as he gave it, because, in the under or mystic current of its meaning, I fancied that I perceived, and for the first time, a full consciousness, on the part of Usher, of the tottering of his lofty reason upon her throne. The verses, which were entitled "The Haunted Palace," ran very nearly, if not accurately, thus:

In the greenest of our valleys,
By good angels tenanted,
Once a fair and stately palace—
Radiant palace—reared its head.
In the monarch Thought's dominion,
It stood there!
Never seraph spread a pinion
Over fabric half so fair.

Banners yellow, glorious, golden,
On its roof did float and flow,
(This—all this—was in the olden
Time long ago)
And every gentle air that dallied,
In that sweet day,
Along the ramparts plumed and pallid,
A wingèd odor went away.

Wanderers in that happy valley
Through two luminous windows saw
Spirits moving musically
To a lute's well-tunèd law,
Round about a throne where, sitting,
(Porphyrogene!)
In state his glory well befitting,
The ruler of the realm was seen.

And all with pearl and ruby glowing
Was the fair palace door,
Through which came flowing, flowing, flowing,
And sparkling evermore,
A troop of Echoes whose sweet duty
Was but to sing
In voices of surpassing beauty,
The wit and wisdom of their king.

But evil things, in robes of sorrow,
Assailed the monarch's high estate;
(Ah, let us mourn, for never morrow
Shall dawn upon him, desolate!)
And round about his home the glory
That blushed and bloomed
Is but a dim-remembered story
Of the old time entombed.

And travellers now within that valley
Through the red-litten windows see
Vast forms that move fantastically
To a discordant melody;
While, like a rapid ghastly river,
Through the pale door,
A hideous throng rush out forever,
And laugh—but smile no more.

I well remember that suggestions arising from this ballad led us into a train of thought, wherein there became manifest an opinion of Usher's which I mention not so much on account of its novelty (for other men have thought thus) as on account of the pertinacity with which he maintained it. This opinion, in its general form, was that of the sentience of all vegetable things. But in his disordered fancy the idea had assumed a more daring character, and trespassed, under certain conditions, upon the kingdom of inorganization. I lack words to express the full extent, or the earnest *abandon* of his persuasion. The belief, however, was connected (as I have previously hinted) with the gray stones of the home of his forefathers. The conditions of the sentience had been here, he imagined, fulfilled in the method of collocation of these stones—in the order of their arrangement, as well as in that of the many fungi which overspread them, and of the decayed trees which stood around—above all, in the long undisturbed endurance of this arrangement, and in its reduplication in the still waters of the tarn. Its evidence—the evidence of the sentience—was to be seen, he said (and I here started as he spoke), in the gradual yet certain condensation of an atmosphere of their own about the waters and the walls. The result was discoverable, he added, in that silent, yet importunate and terrible influence which for centuries had molded the destinies of his family, and which made *him* what I now saw him—what he was. Such opinions need no comment, and I will make none.

Our books—the books which, for years, had formed no small portion of the mental existence of the invalid—were, as might be supposed, in strict keeping with this character of phantasm. We pored together over such works as the Ververt and Chartreuse of Gresset; the Belphegor of Machiavelli; the Heaven and Hell of Swedenborg; the Subterranean Voyage of Nicholas Klimm by Holberg; the Chiromancy of Robert Flud, of Jean D'Indaginé, and of De la Chambre; the Journey into the Blue Distance of Tieck; and the City of the Sun of Campanella. One favorite volume was a small octavo edition of the *Directorium Inquisitorium,* by the Dominican Eymeric de Gironne; and there were passages in Pomponius Mela, about the old African Satyrs and Ægipans, over which Usher would sit dreaming for hours. His chief delight, however, was found in the perusal of an exceedingly rare and curious book in quarto Gothic—the manual of a forgotten church—the *Vigiliæ Mortuorum Secundum Chorum Ecclesiæ Maguntinæ.*

I could not help thinking of the wild ritual of this work, and of its probable influence upon the hypochondriac, when one evening, having informed me abruptly that the lady Madeline was no more, he stated his intention of preserving her corpse for a fortnight (previously to its final interment) in one of the numerous vaults within the main walls of the building. The worldly reason, however, assigned for this singular proceeding was one which I did not feel at liberty to dispute. The brother had been led to his resolution (so he told me) by consideration of the unusual character of the malady of the deceased, of certain obtrusive and eager inquiries on the part of her medical men, and of the remote and exposed situation of the burial ground of the family. I will not deny that when I called to mind the sinister countenance of the person whom I met upon the staircase, on the day of my arrival at the house, I had no desire to oppose what I regarded as at best but a harmless, and by no means an unnatural, precaution.

At the request of Usher, I personally aided him in the arrangements for the temporary entombment. The body having been encoffined, we two alone bore it to its rest. The vault in which we placed it (and which had been so long unopened that our torches, half smothered in its oppressive atmosphere, gave us little opportunity for investigation) was small, damp, and entirely without means of admission for light; lying, at great depth, immediately beneath that portion of the building in which was my own sleeping apartment. It had been used, apparently, in remote feudal times, for the worst purposes of a donjon-keep, and in later days as a place of deposit for powder, or some other highly combustible substance, as a portion of its floor, and the whole interior of a long archway through which we reached it, were carefully sheathed with copper. The door, of massive iron, had been also similarly protected. Its immense weight caused an unusually sharp grating sound, as it moved upon its hinges.

Having deposited our mournful burden upon trestles within this region of horror, we partially turned aside the yet unscrewed lid of the coffin, and looked upon the face of the tenant. A striking similitude between the brother and sister now first arrested my attention; and Usher divining, perhaps, my thoughts, murmured out some few words from which I learned that the deceased and himself had been twins, and that sympathies of a scarcely intelligible nature had always existed between them. Our glances, however, rested not long upon the dead—for we could not regard her unawed. The disease which had thus entombed the lady in the maturity of youth, had left, as usual in all maladies of a strictly cataleptical character, the mockery of a faint blush upon the bosom and the face, and that suspiciously lingering smile upon the lip which is so terrible in death. We replaced and screwed down the lid, and, having secured the door of iron, made our way, with toil, into the scarcely less gloomy apartments of the upper portion of the house.

And now, some days of bitter grief having elapsed, an observable change came over the features of the mental disorder of my friend. His ordinary manner had vanished. His ordinary occupations were neglected or forgotten. He roamed from chamber to chamber with hurried, unequal, and objectless step. The pallor of his countenance had assumed, if possible, a more ghastly hue—but the luminousness of his eye had utterly gone out. The once occasional huskiness of his tone was heard no more; and a tremulous quaver, as if of extreme terror, habitually characterized his utterance. There were times, indeed, when I thought his unceasingly agitated mind was laboring with some oppressive secret, to divulge which he struggled for the necessary courage. At times, again, I was obliged to resolve all into the mere inexplicable vagaries of madness, for I beheld him gazing upon vacancy for long hours, in an attitude of the profoundest attention, as if listening to some imaginary sound. It was no wonder that his condition terrified—that it infected me. I felt creeping upon me, by slow yet certain degrees, the wild influences of his own fantastic yet impressive superstitions.

It was, especially, upon retiring to bed late in the night of the seventh or eighth day after the placing of the lady Madeline within the donjon, that I experienced the full power of such feelings. Sleep came not near my couch, while the hours waned and waned away. I struggled to reason off the nervousness which had dominion over me. I endeavored to believe that much, if not all, of what I felt was due to the bewildering influence of the gloomy furniture of the room —of the dark and tattered draperies which, tortured into motion by the breath of a rising tempest, swayed fitfully to and fro upon the walls, and rustled uneasily about the decorations of the bed. But my efforts were fruitless. An irrepressible tremor gradually pervaded my frame; and at length there sat upon my very heart an incubus of utterly causeless alarm. Shaking this off with a gasp and a struggle, I uplifted myself upon the pillows, and, peering earnestly within the intense darkness of the chamber, hearkened—I know not why, except that an instinctive spirit prompted me—to certain low and indefinite sounds which came, through the pauses of the storm, at long intervals, I knew not whence. Overpowered by an intense sentiment of horror, unaccountable yet unendurable, I threw on my clothes with haste (for I felt that I should sleep no more during the night) and endeavored to arouse myself from the pitiable condition into which I had fallen, by pacing rapidly to and fro through the apartment.

I had taken but few turns in this manner, when a light step on an adjoining staircase arrested my attention. I presently recognized it as that of Usher. In an instant afterward he rapped with a gentle touch at my door, and entered, bearing a lamp. His countenance was, as usual, cadaverously wan—but, moreover, there was a species of mad hilarity in his eyes—an evidently restrained *hysteria* in his whole demeanor. His air appalled me—but anything was preferable to the solitude which I had so long endured, and I even welcomed his presence as a relief.

"And you have not seen it?" he said abruptly, after having stared about him for some moments in silence—"you have not then seen it? —but, stay! you shall." Thus speaking, and having carefully shaded his lamp, he hurried to one of the casements, and threw it freely open to the storm.

The impetuous fury of the entering gust nearly lifted us from our feet. It was, indeed, a tempestuous yet sternly beautiful night, and one wildly singular in its terror and its beauty. A whirlwind had apparently collected its force in our vicinity; for there were frequent and violent alterations in the direction of the wind; and the exceeding density of the clouds (which hung so low as to press upon the turrets of the house) did not prevent our perceiving the lifelike velocity with which they flew careening from all points against each other, without passing away into the distance. I say that even their exceeding density did not prevent our perceiving this; yet we had no glimpse of the moon or stars, nor was there any flashing forth of the lightning. But the under surfaces of the huge masses of agitated vapor, as well as all terrestrial objects immediately around us, were glowing in the unnatural light of a faintly luminous and distinctly visible gaseous exhalation which hung about and enshrouded the mansion.

"You must not—you shall not behold this!" said I, shudderingly, to Usher, as I led him with a gentle violence from the window to a seat. "These appearances, which bewilder you, are merely electrical phenomena not uncommon—or it may be that they have their ghastly origin in the rank miasma of the tarn. Let us close this casement; the air is chilling and dangerous to your frame. Here is one of your favorite romances. I will read, and you shall listen;—and so we will pass away this terrible night together."

The antique volume which I had taken up was the *Mad Trist* of Sir Launcelot Canning; but I had called it a favorite of Usher's more in sad jest than in earnest; for, in truth, there is little in its uncouth and unimaginative prolixity which could have had interest for the lofty and spiritual ideality of my friend. It was, however, the only book immediately at hand; and I indulged a vague hope that the excitement which now agitated the hypochondriac might find relief (for the history of mental disorder is full of similar anomalies) even in the extremeness of the folly which I should read. Could I have judged, indeed, by the wild overstrained air of vivacity with which he hearkened, or apparently hearkened, to the words of the tale, I might well have congratulated myself upon the success of my design.

I had arrived at that well-known portion of the story where Ethelred, the hero of the Trist, having sought in vain for peaceable admission into the dwelling of the hermit, proceeds to make good an entrance by force. Here, it will be remembered, the words of the narrative run thus:

> And Ethelred, who was by nature of a doughty heart, and who was now mighty withal, on account of the powerfulness of the wine which he had drunken, waited no longer to hold parley with the hermit, who, in sooth, was of an obstinate and maliceful turn, but, feeling the rain upon his shoulders, and fearing the rising of the tempest, uplifted his mace outright, and, with blows, made quickly room in the plankings of the door for his gauntleted hand; and now pulling therewith sturdily, he so cracked, and ripped, and tore all asunder, that the noise of the dry and hollow-sounding wood alarummed and reverberated throughout the forest.

At the termination of this sentence I started, and for a moment paused; for it appeared to me (although I at once concluded that my excited fancy had deceived me)—it appeared to me that from some very remote portion of the mansion there came, indistinctly, to my ears, what might have been, in its exact similarity of character, the echo (but a stifled and dull one certainly) of the very cracking and ripping sound which Sir Launcelot had so particularly described. It was, beyond doubt, the coincidence alone which had arrested my attention; for, amid the rattling of the sashes of the casements, and the ordinary commingled noises of the still increasing storm, the sound, in itself, had nothing, surely, which should have interested or disturbed me. I continued the story:

> But the good champion Ethelred, now entering within the door, was sore enraged and amazed to perceive no signal of the maliceful hermit; but, in the stead thereof, a dragon of a scaly and prodigious demeanor, and of a fiery tongue, which sate in guard before a palace of gold, with a floor of silver; and upon the wall there hung a shield of shining brass with this legend enwritten—
>
> *Who entereth herein, a conqueror hath bin;*
> *Who slayeth the dragon, the shield he shall win*
>
> And Ethelred uplifted his mace, and struck upon the head of the dragon, which fell before him, and gave up his pesty breath, with a shriek so horrid and harsh, and withal so piercing, that Ethelred had fain to close his ears with his hands against the dreadful noise of it, the like whereof was never before heard.

Here again I paused abruptly, and now with a feeling of wild amazement; for there could be no doubt whatever that, in this instance, I did actually hear (although from what direction it proceeded I found it impossible to say) a low and apparently distant, but harsh, protracted, and most unusual screaming or grating sound—the exact counterpart of what my fancy had already conjured up for the dragon's unnatural shriek as described by the romancer.

Oppressed, as I certainly was, upon the occurrence of this second and most extraordinary coincidence, by a thousand conflicting sensations, in which wonder and extreme terror were predominant, I still retained sufficient presence of mind to avoid exciting, by any observation, the sensitive nervousness of my companion. I was by no means certain that he had noticed the sounds in question; although, assuredly, a strange alteration had during the last few minutes taken place in his demeanor. From a position fronting my own, he had gradually brought round his chair, so as to sit with his face to the door of the chamber; and thus I could but partially perceive his features, although I saw that his lips trembled as if he were murmuring inaudibly. His head had dropped upon his breast—yet I knew that he was not asleep, from the wide and rigid opening of the eye as I caught a glance of it in profile. The motion of his body, too, was at variance with this idea—for he rocked from side to side with a gentle yet constant and uniform sway. Having rapidly taken notice of all this, I resumed the narrative of Sir Launcelot, which thus proceeded:

> And now, the champion having escaped from the terrible fury of the dragon, bethinking himself of the brazen shield, and of the breaking up of the enchantment which was upon it, removed the carcass from out of the way before him, and approached valorously over the silver pavement of the castle to where the shield was upon the wall; which in sooth tarried not for his full coming, but fell down at his feet upon the silver floor, with a mighty great and terrible ringing sound.

No sooner had these syllables passed my lips, than—as if a shield of brass had indeed, at the moment, fallen heavily upon a floor of silver—I became aware of a distinct, hollow, metallic and clangorous, yet apparently muffled reverberation. Completely unnerved, I leaped to my feet; but the measured rocking movement of Usher was undisturbed. I rushed to the chair in which he sat. His eyes were bent fixedly before him, and throughout his whole countenance there reigned a stony rigidity. But, as I placed my hand upon his shoulder, there came a strong shudder over his whole person; a sickly smile quivered about his lips; and I saw that he spoke in a low, hurried, and gibbering murmur, as if unconscious of my presence. Bending closely over him, I at length drank in the hideous import of his words.

"Not hear it?—yes, I hear it, and *have* heard it. Long—long—long—many minutes, many hours, many days, have I heard it—yet I dared not—oh, pity me, miserable wretch that I am!—I dared not—*I dared not speak! We have put her living in the tomb!* Said I not that my senses were acute? I *now* tell you that I heard her first feeble movements in the hollow coffin. I heard them—many, many days ago—yet I dared not—*I dared not speak!* And now—tonight—Ethelred—ha! ha!—the breaking of the hermit's door, and the death-cry of the dragon, and the clangor of the shield!—say, rather, the rending of her coffin, and the grating of the iron hinges of her prison, and her struggles within the coppered archway of the vault! Oh, whither shall I fly? Will she not be here anon? Is she not hurrying to upbraid me for my haste? Have I not heard her footsteps on the stair? Do I not distinguish that heavy and horrible beating of her heart? Madman!"—here he sprang furiously to his feet, and shrieked out his syllables, as if in the effort he were giving up his soul—*"Madman! I tell you that she now stands without the door!"*

As if in the superhuman energy of his utterance there had been found the potency of a spell, the huge antique panels to which the speaker pointed drew slowly back, upon the instant, their ponderous and ebony jaws. It was the work of the rushing gust—but then without the doors there *did* stand the lofty and enshrouded figure of the lady Madeline of Usher. There was blood upon her white robes, and the evidence of some bitter struggle upon every portion of her emaciated frame. For a moment she remained trembling and reeling to and fro upon the threshold—then, with a low moaning cry, fell heavily inward upon the person of her brother, and, in her violent and now final death-agonies, bore him to the floor a corpse, and a victim to the terrors he had anticipated.

From that chamber, and from that mansion, I fled aghast. The storm was still abroad in all its wrath as I found myself crossing the old causeway. Suddenly there shot along the path a wild light, and I turned to see whence a gleam so unusual could have issued; for the vast house and its shadows were alone behind me. The radiance was that of the full, setting, and blood-red moon, which now shone vividly through that once barely discernible fissure, of which I have before spoken as extending from the roof of the building, in a zigzag direction, to the base. While I gazed, this fissure rapidly widened—

there came a fierce breath of the whirlwind—the entire orb of the satellite burst at once upon my sight—my brain reeled as I saw the mighty walls rushing asunder—there was a long tumultuous shouting sound like the voice of a thousand waters—and the deep and dank tarn at my feet closed sullenly and silently over the fragments of the House of Usher.

Green Tea

JOSEPH SHERIDAN LE FANU

[1814–1873]

Joseph Sheridan Le Fanu, an Irish writer of mysteries and supernatural tales, was a descendant of the Augustan playwright Richard Sheridan (The School for Scandal). *The greatest Victorian to write ghost stories, Le Fanu exercised a tremendous influence on M. R. James and many others. Included in Le Fanu's large body of work are such neglected novels as* The House by the Churchyard *and* Uncle Silas, *as well as stories like* "Carmilla," *one of the earliest and most horrific tales of vampirism. Until recently,* "Green Tea" *(which has been called "the archetypal ghost story") was practically Le Fanu's only story to reach a large audience. It remains his greatest and perhaps most disturbing tale.*

Prologue: Martin Hesselius, the German Physician

Though carefully educated in medicine and surgery, I have never practised either. The study of each continues, nevertheless, to interest me profoundly. Neither idleness nor caprice caused my secession from the honourable calling which I had just entered. The cause was a very trifling scratch inflicted by a dissecting knife. This trifle cost me the loss of two fingers, amputated promptly, and the more painful loss of my health, for I have never been quite well since, and have seldom been twelve months together in the same place.

In my wanderings I became acquainted with Dr. Martin Hesselius, a wanderer like myself, like me a physician, and like me an enthusiast in his profession. Unlike me in this, that his wanderings were voluntary, and he a man, if not of fortune, as we estimate fortune in England, at least in what our forefathers used to term "easy circumstances." He was an old man when I first saw him; nearly five-and-thirty years my senior.

In Dr Martin Hesselius, I had found my master. His knowledge was immense, his grasp of a case was an intuition. He was the very man to inspire a young enthusiast, like me, with awe and delight. My admiration has stood the test of time and survived the separation of death. I am sure it was well-founded.

For nearly twenty years I acted as his medical secretary. His immense collection of papers he has left in my care, to be arranged, indexed and bound. His treatment of some of these cases is curious. He writes in two distinct characters. He describes what he saw and heard as an intelligent layman might, and when in his style of narrative he had seen the patient either through his own halldoor, to the light of day, or through the gates of darkness to the caverns of the dead, he returns upon the narrative, and in the terms of his art and with all the force of originality of genius, proceeds to the work of analysis, diagnosis and illustration.

Here and there a case strikes me as of a kind to amuse or horrify a lay reader with an interest quite different from the peculiar one which it may possess for an expert. With slight modifications, chiefly of language, and of course a change of names, I copy the following. The narrator is Dr Martin Hesselius. I find it among the voluminous notes of cases which he made during a tour in England about sixty-four years ago.

It is related in series of letters to his friend Professor Van Loo of Leyden. The professor was not a physician, but a chemist, and a man who read history and metaphysics and medicine, and had, in his day, written a play.

The narrative is therefore, if somewhat less valuable as a medical record, necessarily written in a manner more likely to interest an unlearned reader.

These letters, from a memorandum attached, appear to have been returned on the death of the professor, in 1819, to Dr Hesselius. They are written, some in English, some in French, but the greater part in German. I am a faithful, though I am conscious, by no means a graceful translator, and although here and there I omit some passages, and shorten others, and disguise names, I have interpolated nothing.

1 Dr. Hesselius Relates How He Met the Rev Mr Jennings

The Rev Mr. Jennings is tall and thin. He is middle-aged, and dresses with a natty, old-fashioned, high church precision. He is naturally a little stately, but not at all stiff. His features, without being handsome, are well formed, and their expression extremely kind, but also shy.

I met him one evening at Lady Mary Heyduke's. The modesty and benevolence of his countenance are extremely prepossessing.

We are but a small party, and he joined agreeably enough in the conversation. He seems to enjoy listening very much more than contributing to the talk; but what he says is always to the purpose and well said. He is a great favourite of Lady Mary's, who it seems, consults him upon many things, and thinks him the most happy and blessed person on earth. Little knows she about him.

The Rev Mr Jennings is a bachelor, and has, they say sixty thousand pounds in the funds. He is a charitable man. He is most anxious to be actively employed in his sacred profession, and yet though always tolerably well elsewhere, when he goes down to his vicarage in Warwickshire, to engage in the actual duties of his sacred calling, his health soon fails him, and in a very strange way. So says Lady Mary.

There is no doubt that Mr Jennings' health does break down in, generally, a sudden and mysterious way, sometimes in the very act of officiating in his old and pretty church at Kenlis. It may be his heart, it may be his brain. But so it has happened three or four times, or oftener, that after proceeding a certain way in the service, he has on a sudden stopped short, and after a silence, apparently quite unable to resume, he has fallen into solitary, inaudible prayer, his hands and his eyes uplifted, and then pale as death, and in the agitation of a strange shame and horror, descended trembling, and got into the vestry-room, leaving his congregation, without explanation, to themselves. This occurred when his curate was absent. When he goes down to Kenlis now, he always takes care to provide a clergyman to share his duty, and to supply his place on the instant should he become thus suddenly incapacitated.

When Mr Jennings breaks down quite, and beats a retreat from the vicarage, and returns to London, where, in a dark street off Piccadilly, he inhabits a very narrow house, Lady Mary says that he is always perfectly well. I have my own opinion about that. There are degrees of course. We shall see.

Mr Jennings is a perfectly gentlemanlike man. People, however, remark something odd. There is an impression a little ambiguous. One thing which certainly contributes to it, people I think don't remember; or, perhaps, distinctly remark. But I did, almost immediately. Mr Jennings has a way of looking sidelong upon the carpet, as if his eye followed the movements of something there. This, of course, not always. It occurs now and then. But often enough to give a certain oddity, as I have said, to his manner, and in this glance travelling along the floor there is something both shy and anxious.

A medical philosopher, as you are good enough to call me, elaborating theories by the aid of cases sought out by himself, and by him watched and scrutinised with more time at command, and consequently infinitely more minuteness than the ordinary practitioner can afford, falls insensibly into habits of observation, which accompany him everywhere, and are exercised, as some people would say, impertinently, upon every subject that presents itself with the least likelihood of rewarding inquiry.

There was a promise of this kind in the slight, timid, kindly, but reserved gentleman, whom I met for the first time at this agreeable little evening gathering. I observed, of course, more than I here set down; but I reserve all that borders on the technical for a strictly scientific paper.

I may remark, that when I here speak of medical science, I do so, as I hope some day to see it more generally understood, in a much more comprehensive sense than its generally material treatment would warrant. I believe the entire natural world is but the ultimate expression of that spiritual world from which, and in which alone, it has its life. I believe that the essential man is a spirit, that the spirit is an organised substance, but as different in point of material from what we ordinarily understand by matter, as light or electricity is; that the material body is, in the most literal sense, a vesture, and death consequently no interruption of the living man's existence, but simply his extrication from the natural body—a process which commences at the moment of what we term death, and the completion of which, at further a few days later, is the resurrection "in power".

The person who weighs the consequences of these positions will probably see their practical bearing upon medical science. This is, however, by no means the proper place for displaying the proofs and discussing the consequences of this too generally unrecognised state of facts.

In pursuit of my habit, I was covertly observing Mr Jennings, with all my caution—I think he perceived it—and I saw plainly that he was as cautiously observing me. Lady Mary happening to address me by my name, as Dr Hesselius, I saw that he glanced at me more sharply, and then became thoughtful for a few minutes.

After this, as I conversed with a gentleman at the other end of the room, I saw him look at me more steadily, and with an interest which I thought I understood. I then saw him take an opportunity of chatting with Lady Mary, and was, as one always is, perfectly aware of being the subject of a distant inquiry and answer.

This tall clergyman approached me by-and-by; and in a little time we had got into conversation. When two people, who like reading, and know books and places, having travelled, wish to converse, it is very strange if they can't find topics. It was not accident that brought him near me, and led him into conversation. He knew German and had read my Essays on Metaphysical Medicine which suggest more than they actually say.

This courteous man, gentle, shy, plainly a man of thought and reading, who moving and talking among us, was not altogether of us, and whom I already suspected of leading a life whose transactions and alarms were carefully concealed, with an impenetrable reserve from, not only the world, but his best beloved friends—was cautiously weighing in his own mind the idea of taking a certain step with regard to me.

I penetrated his thoughts without his being aware of it, and was careful to say nothing which could betray to his sensitive vigilance my suspicions respecting his position, or my surmises about his plans respecting myself.

We chatted upon indifferent subjects for a time; but at last he said:

"I was very much interested by some papers of yours, Dr Hesselius, upon what you term Metaphysical Medicine—I read them in German, ten or twelve years ago—have they been translated?"

"No, I'm sure they have not—I should have heard. They would have asked my leave, I think."

"I asked the publishers here, a few months ago, to get the book for me in the original German; but they tell me it is out of print."

"So it is, and has been for some years; but it flatters me as an author to find that you have not forgotten my little book, although," I added, laughing, "ten or twelve years is a considerable time to have managed without it; but I suppose you have been turning the subject over again in your mind, or something has happened lately to revive your interest in it."

At this remark, accompanied by a glance of inquiry, a sudden embarrassment disturbed Mr Jennings, analogous to that which makes a young lady blush and look foolish. He dropped his eyes, and folded his hands together uneasily, and looked oddly, and you would have said, guiltily, for a moment.

I helped him out of his awkwardness in the best way, by appearing not to observe it, and going straight on, I said: "Those revivals of interest in a subject happen to me often; one book suggests another, and often sends me back on a wild-goose chase over an interval of twenty years. But if you will care to possess a copy, I shall be only too happy to provide you; I have still got two or three by me—and if you allow me to present one I shall be very much honoured."

"You are very good indeed," he said, quite at his ease again, in a moment: "I almost despaired—I don't know how to thank you."

"Pray don't say a word; the thing is really so little worth that I am only ashamed of having offered it, and if you thank me any more I shall throw it into the fire in a fit of modesty."

Mr Jennings laughed. He inquired where I was staying in London, and after a little more conversation on a variety of subjects, he took his departure.

2 The Doctor Questions Lady Mary, and She Answers

"I like your vicar so much, Lady Mary," said I, as soon as he was gone. "He has read, travelled, and thought, and having also suffered, he ought to be an accomplished companion."

"So he is, and, better still, he is a really good man," said she. "His advice is invaluable about my schools, and all my little undertakings at Dawlbridge, and he's so painstaking, he takes so much trouble—you have no idea—wherever he thinks he can be of use; he's so good-natured and so sensible."

"It is pleasant to hear so good an account of his neighbourly virtues. I can only testify to his being an agreeable and gentle companion, and in addition to what you have told me, I think I can tell you two or three things about him," said I.

"Really!"

"Yes, to begin with, he's unmarried."

"Yes, that's right—go on."

"He has been writing, that is he *was,* but two or three years perhaps he has not gone on with his work, and the book was upon some rather abstract subject—perhaps theology."

"Well, he was writing a book, as you say; I'm not quite sure what it was about, but only that it was nothing that I cared for; very likely you are right, and he certainly did stop—yes."

"And although he only drank a little coffee here tonight, he likes tea, at least, did like it extravagantly."

"Yes, that's *quite* true."

"He drank green tea, a good deal, didn't he?" I pursued.

"Well, that's very odd! Green tea was a subject on which we used almost to quarrel."

"But he has quite given that up," said I.

"So he has."

"And, now, one more fact. His mother or his father, did you know them?"

"Yes, both; his father is only ten years dead, and their place is near Dawlbridge. We knew them very well," she answered.

"Well, either his mother or his father—I should rather think his father, saw a ghost," said I.

"Well, you really are a conjuror, Dr Hesselius."

"Conjuror or no, haven't I said right?" I answered merrily.

"You certainly have, and it *was* his father; he was a silent, whimsical man, and he used to bore my father about his dreams, and at last he told him a story about a ghost he had seen and talked with, and a very odd story it was. I remember it particularly, because I was so afraid of him. This story was long before he died—when I was quite a child—and his ways were so silent and moping, and he used to drop in sometimes, in the dusk, when I was alone in the drawing-room, and I used to fancy there were ghosts about him."

I smiled and nodded.

"And now, having established my character as a conjuror, I think I must say good-night," said I.

"But how *did* you find it out?"

"By the planets, of course, as the gipsies do," I answered, and so, gaily, we said goodnight.

Next morning I sent the little book he had been inquiring after, and a note to Mr Jennings, and on returning late that evening, I found that he had called at my lodgings, and left his card. He asked whether I was at home, and asked at what hour he would be most likely to find me.

Does he intend opening his case, and consulting me "professionally," as they say? I hope so. I have already conceived a theory about him. It is supported by Lady Mary's answers to my parting questions. I should like much to ascertain from his own lips. But what can I do consistently with good breeding to invite a confession? Nothing. I rather think he meditates one. At all events, my dear Van L., I shan't make myself difficult of access; I mean to return his visit tomorrow. It will be only civil in return for his politeness, to ask to see him. Perhaps something may come of it. Whether much, little, or nothing, my dear Van L, you shall hear.

3 Dr Hesselius Picks Up Something in Latin Books

Well, I have called at Blank Street.

On inquiring at the door, the servant told me that Mr Jennings was engaged very particularly with a gentleman, a clergyman from Kenlis, his parish in the country. Intending to reserve my privilege, and to call again, I merely intimated that I should try another time, and had turned to go, when the servant begged my pardon, and asked me, looking at me a little more attentively than well-bred persons of his order usually do, whether I was Dr Hesselius; and, on learning that I was, he said, "Perhaps then, sir, you would allow me to mention it to Mr Jennings, for I am sure he wishes to see you."

The servant returned in a moment, with a message from Mr Jennings, asking me to go into his study, which was in effect his back drawing-room, promising to be with me in a very few minutes.

This was really a study—almost a library. The room was lofty, with two tall slender windows, and rich dark curtains. It was much larger than I had expected, and stored with books on every side, from floor to the ceiling. The upper carpet—for to my tread it felt that there were two or three—was a Turkey carpet. My steps fell noiselessly. The bookcases standing out, placed the windows, particularly narrow ones, in deep recesses. The effect of the room was, although extremely comfortable, and even luxurious, decidedly gloomy, and aided by the silence, almost oppressive. Perhaps, however, I ought to have allowed something for association. My mind had connected peculiar ideas with Mr Jennings. I stepped into this perfectly silent room, of a very silent house, with a peculiar foreboding; and its darkness, and solemn clothing of books, for except where two narrow looking-glasses were set in the wall, they were everywhere, helped this sombre feeling.

While awaiting Mr Jennings' arrival, I amused myself by looking into some of the books with which his shelves were laden. Not among these, but immediately under them, with their backs upward, on the floor, I lighted upon a complete set of Swedenborg's *Arcana Cælestia,* in the original Latin, a very fine folio set, bound in the natty livery which theology affects, pure vellum, namely, gold letters, and carmine edges. There were paper markers in several of these volumes. I raised and placed them, one after the other upon the table, and opening where these papers were placed, I read in the solemn Latin phraseology, a series of sentences indicated by a pencilled line at the margin. Of these I copy here a few, translating them into English.

"When man's interior sight is opened, which is that of his spirit, then there appears the things of another life, which cannot possibly be made visible to the bodily sight . . ."

"By the internal sight it has been granted to me to see the things that are in the other life, more clearly than I see those that are in the world. From these considerations, it is evident that external vision exists from interior vision, and this from a vision still more interior, and so on . . ."

"There are with every man at least two evil spirits . . ."

"With wicked genii there is also a fluent speech, but harsh and grating. There is also among them a speech which is not fluent, wherein the dissent of the thoughts is perceived as something secretly creeping along within it . . ."

"The evil spirits associated with man are indeed from the hells, but when with man they are not then in hell, but are taken out thence. The place where they then are, is in the midst between heaven and hell, and is called the world of spirits—when the evil spirits who are with man, are in that world, they are not in any infernal torment, but in every thought and affection of man, and so, in all that the man himself enjoys. But when they are remitted into their hell, they return to their former state . . ."

"If evil spirits could perceive that they were associated with man, and yet that they were spirits separate from him, and if they could flow in into the things of his body, they would attempt by a thousand means to destroy him; for they hate man with a deadly hatred . . ."

"Knowing, therefore, that I was a man in the body, they were continually striving to destroy me, not as to the body only, but especially as to the soul; for to destroy any man or spirit is the very delight of the life of all who are in hell; but I have been continually protected by the Lord. Hence it appears how dangerous it is for man to be in a living consort with spirits unless he be in the good of faith . . ."

"Nothing is more carefully guarded from the knowledge of associate spirits than their being thus conjoint with a man, for if they knew it they would speak to him, with the intention to destroy him . . ."

"The delight of hell is to do evil to man, and to hasten his eternal ruin."

A long note, written with a very sharp and fine pencil, in Mr Jennings' neat hand, at the foot of the page, caught my eye. Expecting his criticism upon the text, I read a word or two, and stopped, for it was something quite different, and began with these words, *Deus misereatur mei*—"May God compassionate me". Thus warned of its private nature, I averted my eyes, and shut the book, replacing all the volumes as I had found them, except one which interested me, and in which, as men studious and solitary in their habits will do, I grew so absorbed as to take no cognisance of the outer world, nor to remember where I was.

I was reading some pages which refer to "representatives" and "correspondents," in the technical language of Swedenborg, and had arrived at a passage, the substance of which is, that evil spirits, when seen by other eyes than those of their infernal associates, present themselves, by "correspondence," in the shape of the beast *(fera)* which represents their particular lust and life, in aspect direful and atrocious. This is a long passage, and particularises a number of those bestial forms.

4 Four Eyes Were Reading the Passage

I was running the head of my pencil-case along the line as I read it, and something caused me to raise my eyes.

Directly before me was one of the mirrors I have mentioned, in which I saw reflected the tall shape of my friend, Mr Jennings, leaning over my shoulder, and reading the page at which I was busy, and with a face so dark and wild that I should hardly have known him.

I turned and rose. He stood erect also, and with an effort laughed a little, saying:

"I came in and asked you how you did, but without succeeding in awaking you from your book; so I could not restrain my curiosity, and very impertinently, I'm afraid, peeped over your shoulder. This is not the first time of looking into those pages. You have looked into Swedenborg, no doubt, long ago?"

"Oh dear, yes! I owe Swedenborg a great deal; you will discover traces of him in the little book on Metaphysical Medicine, which you were so good as to remember."

Although my friend affected a gaiety of manner, there was a slight flush in his face, and I could perceive that he was inwardly much perturbed.

"I'm scarcely yet qualified, I know so little of Swedenborg. I've only had them a fortnight," he answered, "and I think they are rather likely to make a solitary man nervous—that is, judging from the very little I have read—I don't say that they have made me so," he laughed; "and I'm so very much obliged for the book. I hope you got my note?"

I made all proper acknowledgments and modest disclaimers.

"I never read a book that I go with, so entirely, as that of yours," he continued. "I saw at once there is more in it than is quite unfolded. Do you know Dr Harley?" he asked, rather abruptly.

In passing, the editor remarks that the physician here named was one of the most eminent who had ever practised in England.

I did, having had letters to him, and had experienced from him great courtesy and considerable assistance during my visit to England.

"I think that man one of the very greatest fools I ever met in my life," said Mr Jennings.

This was the first time I had ever heard him say a sharp thing of anybody, and such a term applied to so high a name a little startled me.

"Really! and in what way?" I asked.

"In his profession," he answered.

I smiled.

"I mean this," he said: "he seems to me, one half, blind—I mean one half of all he looks at is dark—preternaturally bright and vivid all the rest; and the worst of it is, it seems *wilful.* I can't get him—I mean he won't—I've had some experience of him as a physician, but I look on him as, in that sense, no better than a paralytic mind, an intellect half dead. I'll tell you—I know I shall some time—all about it," he said, with a little agitation. "You stay some months longer in England. If I should be out of town during your stay for a little time, would you allow me to trouble you with a letter?"

"I should be only too happy," I assured him.

"Very good of you. I am so utterly dissatisfied with Harley."

"A little leaning to the materialistic school," I said.

"A *mere* materialist," he corrected me; "you can't think how that sort of thing worries one who knows better. You won't tell anyone

—any of my friends you know—that I am hippish; now, for instance, no one knows—not even Lady Mary—that I have seen Dr Harley, or any other doctor. So pray don't mention it; and, if I should have any threatening of an attack, you'll kindly let me write, or, should I be in town, have a little talk with you."

I was full of conjecture, and unconsciously I found I had fixed my eyes gravely on him, for he lowered his for a moment, and he said:

"I see you think I might as well tell you now, or else you are forming a conjecture; but you may as well give it up. If you were guessing all the rest of your life, you will never hit on it."

He shook his head smiling, and over that wintry sunshine a black cloud suddenly came down, and he drew his breath in, through his teeth as men do in pain.

"Sorry, of course, to learn that you apprehend occasion to consult any of us; but, command me when and how you like, and I need not assure you that your confidence is sacred."

He then talked of quite other things, and in a comparatively cheerful way and after a little time, I took my leave.

5 Dr Hesselius Is Summoned to Richmond

We parted cheerfully, but he was not cheerful, nor was I. There are certain expressions of that powerful organ of spirit—the human face —which, although I have seen them often, and possess a doctor's nerve, yet disturb me profoundly. One look of Mr Jennings' haunted me. It had seized my imagination with so dismal a power that I changed my plans for the evening, and went to the opera, feeling that I wanted a change of ideas.

I heard nothing of or from him for two or three days, when a note in his hand reached me. It was cheerful, and full of hope. He said that he had been for some little time so much better—quite well, in fact—that he was going to make a little experiment, and run down for a month or so to his parish, to try whether a little work might not quite set him up. There was in it a fervent religious expression of gratitude for his restoration, as he now almost hoped he might call it.

A day or two later I saw Lady Mary, who repeated what his note had announced, and told me that he was actually in Warwickshire, having resumed his clerical duties at Kenlis; and she added, "I begin to think that he is really perfectly well, and that there never was anything the matter, more than nerves and fancy; we are all nervous, but I fancy there is nothing like a little hard work for that kind of weakness, and he has made up his mind to try it. I should not be surprised if he did not come back for a year."

Notwithstanding all this confidence, only two days later I had this note, dated from his house off Piccadilly:

> DEAR SIR, I have returned disappointed. If I should feel at all able to see you, I shall write to ask you kindly to call. At present, I am too low, and, in fact, simply unable to say all I wish to say. Pray don't mention my name to my friends. I can see no one. By-and-by, please God, you shall hear from me. I mean to take a run into Shropshire, where some of my people are. God bless you! May we, on my return, meet more happily than I can now write.

About a week after this I saw Lady Mary at her own house, the last person, she said, left in town, and just on the wing for Brighton, for the London season was quite over. She told me that she had heard from Mr Jennings' niece, Martha, in Shropshire. There was nothing to be gathered from her letter, more than that he was low and nervous. In those words, of which healthy people think so lightly, what a world of suffering is sometimes hidden!

Nearly five weeks had passed without any further news of Mr Jennings. At the end of that time I received a note from him. He wrote:

> I have been in the country, and have had change of air, change of scene, change of faces, change of everything—and in everything—but *myself.* I have made up my mind, so far as the most irresolute creature on earth can do it, to tell my case fully to you. If your engagements will permit, pray come to me today, tomorrow, or the next day; but, pray defer as little as possible. You know not how much I need help. I have a quiet house at Richmond, where I now am. Perhaps you can manage to come to dinner, or to luncheon, or even to tea. You shall have no trouble in finding me out. The servant at Blank Street, who takes this note, will have a carriage at your door at any hour you please; and I am always to be found. You will say that I ought not to be alone. I have tried everything. Come and see.

I called up the servant, and decided on going out the same evening, which accordingly I did.

He would have been much better in a lodging-house, or hotel, I thought, as I drove up through a short double row of sombre elms to a very old-fashioned brick house, darkened by the foliage of these trees, which overtopped, and nearly surrounded it. It was a perverse choice, for nothing could be imagined more triste and silent. The house, I found, belonged to him. He had stayed for a day or two in town, and, finding it for some cause insupportable, had come out here, probably because being furnished and his own, he was relieved of the thought and delay of selection, by coming here.

The sun had already set, and the red reflected light of the western sky illuminated the scene with the peculiar effect with which we are all familiar. The hall seemed very dark, but, getting to the back drawing-room, whose windows command the west, I was again in the same dusky light.

I sat down, looking out upon the richly-wooded landscape that glowed in the grand and melancholy light which was every moment fading. The corners of the room were already dark; all was growing dim, and the gloom was insensibly toning my mind, already prepared for what was sinister. I was waiting alone for his arrival, which soon took place. The door communicating with the front room opened, and the tall figure of Mr Jennings, faintly seen in the ruddy twilight, came, with quiet stealthy steps, into the room.

We shook hands, and, taking a chair to the window, where there was still light enough to enable us to see each other's faces, he sat down beside me, and, placing his hand upon my arm, with scarcely a word of preface began his narrative.

6 How Mr Jennings Met His Companion

The faint glow of the west, the pomp of the then lonely woods of Richmond, were before us, behind and about us the darkening room, and on the stony face of the sufferer—for the character of his face, though still gentle and sweet, was changed—rested that dim, odd glow which seems to descend and produce, where it touches, lights, sudden though faint, which are lost, almost without gradation, in darkness. The silence, too, was utter: not a distant wheel, or bark, or whistle from without; and within, the depressing stillness of an invalid bachelor's house.

I guessed well the nature, though not even vaguely the particulars of the revelations I was about to receive, from that fixed face of suffering that so oddly flushed stood out, like a portrait of Schalken's, before its background of darkness.

"It began," he said, "on the 15th of October, three years and eleven weeks ago, and two days—I keep very accurate count, for every day is torment. If I leave anywhere a chasm in my narrative, tell me.

"About four years ago I began a work, which had cost me very much thought and reading. It was upon the religious metaphysics of the ancients."

"I know," said I, "the actual religion of educated and thinking paganism, quite apart from symbolic worship? A wide and very interesting field."

"Yes, but not good for the mind—the Christian mind, I mean. Paganism is all bound together in essential unity, and, with evil sympathy, their religion involves their art, and both their manners, and the subject is a degrading fascination and the Nemesis sure. God forgive me!

"I wrote a great deal; I wrote late at night. I was always thinking on the subject, walking about, wherever I was, everywhere. It thoroughly infected me. You are to remember that all the material ideas connected with it were more or less of the beautiful, the subject itself delightfully interesting, and I, then, without a care."

He sighed heavily.

"I believe that every one who sets about writing in earnest does his work, as a friend of mine phrased it, *on* something—tea, or coffee, or tobacco. I suppose there is a material waste that must be hourly supplied in such occupations, or that we should grow too abstracted, and the mind, as it were, pass out of the body, unless it were reminded often enough of the connection by actual sensation. At all events, I felt the want, and I supplied it. Tea was my companion—at first the ordinary black tea, made in the usual way, not too strong; but I drank a good deal, and increased its strength as I went on. I never experienced an uncomfortable symptom from it.

"I began to take a little green tea. I found the effect pleasanter, it cleared and intensified the power of thought so, I had come to take it frequently, but not stronger than one might take it for pleasure. I wrote a great deal out here, it was so quiet, and in this room. I used to sit up very late, and it became a habit with me to sip my tea—green tea—every now and then as my work proceeded. I had a little kettle on my table, that swung over a lamp, and made tea two or three times between eleven o'clock and two or three in the morning, my hours of going to bed.

"I used to go into town every day. I was not a monk, and,

although I spent an hour or two in a library, hunting up authorities and looking out lights upon my theme, I was in no morbid state as far as I can judge. I met my friends pretty much as usual and enjoyed their society, and, on the whole, existence had never been, I think, so pleasant before.

"I had met with a man who had some odd old books, German editions in mediæval Latin, and I was only too happy to be permitted access to them. This obliging person's books were in the City, a very out-of-the-way part of it. I had rather out-stayed my intended hour, and, on coming out, seeing no cab near, I was tempted to get into the omnibus which used to drive past this house. It was darker than this by the time the 'bus had reached an old house, you may have remarked, with four poplars at each side of the door, and there the last passenger but myself got out. We drove along rather faster. It was twilight now. I leaned back in my corner next the door ruminating pleasantly.

"The interior of the omnibus was nearly dark. I had observed in the corner opposite to me at the other side, and at the end next the horses, two small circular reflections, as it seemed to me of a reddish light. They were about two inches apart, and about the size of those small brass buttons that yachting men used to put upon their jackets. I began to speculate, as listless men will, upon this trifle, as it seemed. From what centre did that faint but deep red light come, and from what—glass beads, buttons, toy decorations—was it reflected? We were lumbering along gently, having nearly a mile still to go. I had not solved the puzzle, and it became in another minute more odd, for these two luminous points, with a sudden jerk descended nearer and nearer the floor, keeping still their relative distance and horizontal position, and then, as suddenly they rose to the level of the seat on which I was sitting and I saw them no more.

"My curiosity was now really excited, and, before I had time to think, I saw again these two dull lamps, again together near the floor; again they disappeared, and again in their old corner I saw them.

"So, keeping my eyes upon them, I edged quietly up my own side, towards the end at which I still saw these tiny discs of red.

"There was very little light in the 'bus. It was nearly dark. I leaned forward to aid my endeavour to discover what these little circles really were. They shifted position a little as I did so. I began now to perceive an outline of something black, and I soon saw, with tolerable distinctiveness, the outline of a small black monkey, pushing its face forward in mimicry to meet mine; those were its eyes, and I now dimly saw its teeth grinning at me.

"I drew back, not knowing whether it might not meditate a spring. I fancied that one of the passengers had forgot this ugly pet, and wishing to ascertain something of its temper, though not caring to trust my fingers to it, I poked my umbrella softly towards it. It remained immovable—up to it—*through* it! For through it, and back and forward it passed, without the slightest resistance.

"I can't, in the least, convey to you the kind of horror I felt. When I had ascertained that the thing was an illusion, as I then supposed, there came a misgiving about myself and a terror that fascinated me in impotence to remove my gaze from the eyes of the brute for some moments. As I looked, it made a little skip back, quite into the corner, and I, in a panic found myself at the door, having put my head out, drawing deep breaths of the outer air, and staring at the lights and trees we were passing, too glad to reassure myself of reality.

"I stopped the 'bus and got out. I perceived the man look oddly at me as I paid him. I dare say there was something unusual in my looks and manner, for I had never felt so strangely before."

7 The Journey: First Stage

"When the omnibus drove on, and I was alone upon the road, I looked carefully round to ascertain whether the monkey had followed me. To my indescribable relief I saw it nowhere. I can't describe easily what a shock I had received, and my sense of genuine gratitude on finding myself, as I supposed, quite rid of it.

"I had got out a little before we reached this house, two or three hundred steps. A brick wall runs along the footpath, and inside the wall is a hedge of yew, or some dark evergreen of that kind, and within that again the row of fine trees which you may have remarked as you came.

"This brick wall is about as high as my shoulder, and happening to raise my eyes I saw the monkey, with that stooping gait, on all fours, walking or creeping, close beside me, on top of the wall. I stopped, looking at it with a feeling of loathing and horror. As I stopped so did it. It sat up on the wall with its long hands on its knees looking at me. There was not light enough to see it much more than in outline, nor was it dark enough to bring the peculiar light of its eyes into strong relief. I still saw, however, that red foggy light plainly enough. It did not show its teeth, nor exhibit any sign of irritation, but seemed jaded and sulky, and was observing me steadily.

"I drew back into the middle of the road. It was an unconscious recoil, and there I stood, still looking at it; it did not move.

"With an instinctive determination to try something—anything, I turned about and walked briskly towards town with askance look, all the time, watching the movements of the beast. It crept swiftly along the wall, at exactly my pace.

"Where the wall ends, near the turn of the road, it came down, and with a wiry spring or two brought itself close to my feet, and continued to keep up with me, as I quickened my pace. It was at my left side, so close to my leg that I felt every moment as if I should tread upon it.

"The road was quite deserted and silent, and it was darker every moment. I stopped dismayed and bewildered, turning as I did so, the other way—I mean, towards this house, away from which I had been walking. When I stood still, the monkey drew back to a distance of, I suppose, about five or six yards, and remained stationary, watching me.

"I had been more agitated than I have said. I had read, of course, as everyone has, something about 'spectral illusions,' as you physicians term the phenomena of such cases. I considered my situation, and looked my misfortune in the face.

"These affections, I had read, are sometimes transitory and sometimes obstinate. I had read of cases in which the appearance, at first harmless, had, step by step, degenerated into something direful and insupportable, and ended by wearing its victim out. Still as I stood there, but for my bestial companion, quite alone, I tried to comfort myself by repeating again and again the assurance, 'the thing is purely disease, a well-known physical affection, as distinctly as small-pox or neuralgia. Doctors are all agreed on that, philosophy demonstrates it. I must not be a fool. I've been sitting up too late, and I daresay my digestion is quite wrong, and, with God's help, I shall be all right, and this is but a symptom of nervous dyspepsia.' Did I believe all this? Not one word of it, no more than any other miserable being ever did who is once seized and riveted in this satanic captivity. Against my convictions, I might say my knowledge, I was simply bullying myself into a false courage.

"I now walked homeward. I had only a few hundred yards to go.

I had forced myself into a sort of resignation, but I had not got over the sickening shock and the flurry of the first certainty of my misfortune.

"I had made up my mind to pass the night at home. The brute moved close beside me, and I fancied there was the sort of anxious drawing toward the house, which one sees in tired horses or dogs, sometimes as they come toward home.

"I was afraid to go into town. I was afraid of anyone's seeing and recognising me. I was conscious of an irrepressible agitation in my manner. Also, I was afraid of any violent change in my habits, such as going to a place of amusement, or walking from home in order to fatigue myself. At the hall door it waited till I mounted the steps, and when the door was opened entered with me.

"I drank no tea that night. I got cigars and some brandy-and-water. My idea was that I should act upon my material system, and by living for a while in sensation apart from thought, send myself forcibly, as it were, into a new groove. I came up here to this drawing-room. I sat just there. The monkey then got upon a small table that then stood *there.* It looked dazed and languid. An irrepressible uneasiness as to its movements kept my eyes always upon it. Its eyes were half closed, but I could see them glow. It was looking steadily at me. In all situations, at all hours, it is awake and looking at me. That never changes.

"I shall not continue in detail my narrative of this particular night. I shall describe, rather, the phenomena of the first year, which never varied, essentially. I shall describe the monkey as it appeared in daylight. In the dark, as you shall presently hear, there are peculiarities. It is a small monkey, perfectly black. It had only one peculiarity—a character of malignity—unfathomable malignity. During the first year it looked sullen and sick. But this character of intense malice and vigilance was always underlying that surly languor. During all that time it acted as if on a plan of giving me as little trouble as was consistent with watching me. Its eyes were never off me. I have never lost sight of it, except in my sleep, light or dark, day or night, since it came here, excepting when it withdraws for some weeks at a time, unaccountably.

"In total dark it is visible as in daylight. I do not mean merely its eyes. It is *all* visible distinctly in a halo that resembles a glow of red embers, and which accompanies it in all its movements.

"When it leaves me for a time, it is always at night, in the dark, and in the same way. It grows at first uneasy, and then furious, and then advances towards me, grinning and shaking, its paws clenched, and, at the same time, there comes the appearance of fire in the grate. I never have any fire. I can't sleep in the room where there is any, and it draws nearer and nearer to the chimney, quivering, it seems, with rage, and when its fury rises to the highest pitch, it springs into the grate, and up the chimney, and I see it no more.

"When first this happened, I thought I was released. I was now a new man. A day passed—a night—and no return, and a blessed week—a week—another week. I was always on my knees, Dr Hesselius, always, thanking God and praying. A whole month passed of liberty, but on a sudden, it was with me again."

8 The Second Stage

"It was with me, and the malice which before was torpid under a sullen exterior, was now active. It was perfectly unchanged in every other aspect. This new energy was apparent in its activity and its looks, and soon in other ways.

"For a time, you will understand, the change was shown only in an increased vivacity, and an air of menace, as if it were always brooding over some atrocious plan. Its eyes, as before, were never off me."

"Is it here now?" I asked.

"No," he replied, "it has been absent exactly a fortnight and a day—fifteen days. It has sometimes been away so long as nearly two months, once for three. Its absence always exceeds a fortnight, although it may be but by a single day. Fifteen days having past since I saw it last, it may return now at any moment."

"Is its return," I asked, "accompanied by any peculiar manifestation?"

"Nothing—no," he said. "It is simply with me again. On lifting my eyes from a book, or turning my head, I see it, as usual, looking at me, and then it remains, as before, for its appointed time. I have never told so much and so minutely before to any one."

I perceived that he was agitated, and looking like death, and he repeatedly applied his handkerchief to his forehead; I suggested that he might be tired, and told him that I would call, with pleasure, in the morning, but he said:

"No, if you don't mind hearing it all now. I have got so far, and I should prefer making one effort of it. When I spoke to Dr Harley,

I had nothing like so much to tell. You are a philosophic physician. You give spirit its proper rank. If this thing is real—"

He paused, looking at me with agitated inquiry.

"We can discuss it by-and-by, and very fully. I will give you all I think," I answered, after an interval.

"Well—very well. If it is anything real, I say, it is prevailing, little by little, and drawing me more interiorly into hell. Optic nerves, he talked of. Ah! well—there are other nerves of communication. May God Almighty help me! You shall hear.

"Its power of action, I tell you, had increased. Its malice became, in a way, aggressive. About two years ago, some questions that were pending between me and the bishop having been settled, I went down to my parish in Warwickshire, anxious to find occupation in my profession. I was not prepared for what happened, although I have since thought I might have apprehended something like it. The reason of my saying so is that—"

He was beginning to speak with a great deal more effort and reluctance, and sighed often, and seemed at times nearly overcome. But at this time his manner was not agitated. It was more like that of a sinking patient, who has given himself up.

"Yes, but I will first tell you about Kenlis, my parish.

"It was with me when I left this place for Dawlbridge. It was my silent travelling companion, and it remained with me at the vicarage. When I entered on the discharge of my duties, another change took place. The thing exhibited an atrocious determination to thwart me. It was with me in the church—in the reading-desk—in the pulpit—within the communion rails. At last, it reached this extremity, that while I was reading to the congregation, it would spring upon the book and squat there, so that I was unable to see the page. This happened more than once.

"I left Dawlbridge for a time. I placed myself in Dr Harley's hands. I did everything he told me. He gave my case a great deal of thought. It interested him, I think. He seemed successful. For nearly three months I was perfectly free from a return. I began to think I was safe. With his full assent I returned to Dawlbridge.

"I travelled in a chaise. I was in good spirits. I was more—I was happy and grateful. I was returning, as I thought, delivered from a dreadful hallucination, to the scene of duties which I longed to enter upon. It was a beautiful sunny evening, everything looked serene and cheerful, and I was delighted. I remember looking out of the window to see the spire of my church at Kenlis among the trees, at the point where one has the earliest view of it. It is exactly where the little stream that bounds the parish passes under the road by a culvert, and where it emerges at the roadside, a stone with an old inscription is placed. As we passed this point, I drew my head in and sat down, and in the corner of the chaise was the monkey.

"For a moment I felt faint, and then quite wild with despair and horror. I called to the driver, and got out, and sat down at the road-side, and prayed to God silently for mercy. A despairing resignation supervened. My companion was with me as I re-entered the vicarage. The same persecution followed. After a short struggle I submitted, and soon I left the place.

"I told you," he said, "that the beast had before this become in certain ways aggressive. I will explain a little. It seemed to be actuated by intense and increasing fury, whenever I said my prayers, or even meditated prayer. It amounted at last to a dreadful interruption. You will ask, how could a silent immaterial phantom effect that? It was thus, whenever I meditated praying; it was always before me, and nearer and nearer.

"It used to spring on a table, on the back of a chair, on the chimney-piece, and slowly to swing itself from side to side, looking at me all the time. There is in its motion an indefinable power to dissipate thought, and to contract one's attention to that monotony, till the ideas shrink, as it were, to a point, and at last to nothing—and unless I had started up, and shook off the catalepsy I have felt as if my mind were on the point of losing itself. There are other ways," he sighed heavily; "thus, for instance, while I pray with my eyes closed, it comes closer and closer, and I see it. I know it is not to be accounted for physically, but I do actually see it, though my lids are closed, and so it rocks my mind, as it were, and overpowers me, and I am obliged to rise from my knees. If you had ever yourself known this, you would be acquainted with desperation."

9 The Third Stage

"I see, Dr Hesselius, that you don't lose one word of my statement. I need not ask you to listen specially to what I am now going to tell you. They talk of the optic nerves, and of spectral illusions, as if the organ of sight was the only point assailable by the influences that have fastened upon me—I know better. For two years in my direful case that limitation prevailed. But as food is taken in softly at the lips, and then brought under the teeth, as the tip of the little finger caught in a mill crank will draw in the hand, and the arm, and the whole body, so the miserable mortal who has been once caught firmly by the end of the finest fibre of his nerve, is drawn in and in, by the enormous machinery of hell, until he is as I am. Yes, Doctor, as *I* am, for while I talk to you, and implore relief, I feel that my prayer is for the impossible, and my pleading with the inexorable."

I endeavoured to calm his visibly increasing agitation, and told him that he must not despair.

While we talked the night had overtaken us. The filmy moonlight was wide over the scene which the window commanded, and I said:

"Perhaps you would prefer having candles. This light, you know, is odd. I should wish you, as much as possible, under your usual conditions while I make my diagnosis, shall I call it—otherwise I don't care."

"All lights are the same to me," he said; "except when I read or write, I care not if night were perpetual. I am going to tell you what happened about a year ago. The thing began to speak to me."

"Speak! How do you mean—speak as a man does, do you mean?"

"Yes; speak in words and consecutive sentences, with perfect coherence and articulation; but there is a peculiarity. It is not like the tone of a human voice. It is not by my ears it reaches me—it comes like a singing through my head.

"This faculty, the power of speaking to me, will be my undoing. It won't let me pray, it interrupts me with dreadful blasphemies. I dare not go on, I could not. Oh! Doctor, can the skill, and thought, and prayers of man avail me nothing!"

"You must promise me, my dear sir, not to trouble yourself with unnecessarily exciting thoughts; confine yourself strictly to the narrative of *facts;* and recollect, above all, that even if the thing that infests you be, you seem to suppose, a reality with an actual independent life and will, yet it can have no power to hurt you, unless it be given from above: its access to your senses depends mainly upon your physical condition—this is, under God, your comfort and reliance: we are all alike environed. It is only that in your case, the *paries,* the veil of the flesh, the screen, is a little out of repair, and sights and sounds are transmitted. We must enter on a new course, sir—be encouraged. I'll give tonight to the careful consideration of the whole case."

"You are very good, sir; you think it worth trying, you don't give me quite up; but, sir, you don't know, it is gaining such an influence over me; it orders me about, it is such a tyrant, and I'm growing so helpless. May God deliver me!"

"It orders you about—of course you mean by speech?"

"Yes, yes; it is always urging me to crimes, to injure others, or myself. You see, Doctor, the situation is urgent, it is indeed. When I was in Shropshire, a few weeks ago" (Mr Jennings was speaking rapidly and trembling now, holding my arm with one hand, and looking in my face), "I went out one day with a party of friends for a walk: my persecutor, I tell you, was with me at the time. I lagged behind the rest: the country near the Dee, you know, is beautiful. Our path happened to lie near a coal mine, and at the verge of the wood is a perpendicular shaft, they say, a hundred and fifty feet deep. My niece had remained behind with me—she knows, of course, nothing of the nature of my sufferings. She knew, however, that I had been ill, and was low, and she remained to prevent my being quite alone. As we loitered slowly on together, the brute that accompanied me was urging me to throw myself down the shaft.

"I tell you now—oh, sir, think of it!—the one consideration that saved me from that hideous death was the fear lest the shock of witnessing the occurrence should be too much for the poor girl. I asked her to go on and walk with her friends, saying that I could go no further. She made excuses, and the more I urged her the firmer she became. She looked doubtful and frightened. I suppose there was something in my looks or manner that alarmed her; but she would not go, and that literally saved me. You had no idea, sir, that a living man could be made so abject a slave of Satan," he said, with a ghastly groan and shudder.

There was a pause here, and I said, "You *were* preserved nevertheless. It was the act of God. You are in His hands and in the power of no other being: be therefore confident for the future."

10 Home

I made him have candles lighted, and saw the room looking cheery and inhabited before I left him. I told him that he must regard his illness strictly as one dependent on physical, though *subtle* physical causes. I told him that he had evidence of God's care and love in the deliverance which he had just described, and that I had perceived with pain that he seemed to regard its peculiar features as indicating that he had been delivered over to spiritual reprobation. Than such a conclusion nothing could be, I insisted, less warranted; and not only so, but more contrary to facts, as disclosed in his mysterious deliverance from that murderous influence during his Shropshire excursion. First, his niece had been retained by his side without his intending to keep her near him; and, secondly, there had been infused into his mind an irresistible repugnance to execute the dreadful suggestion in her presence.

As I reasoned this point with him, Mr Jennings wept. He seemed comforted. One promise I exacted, which was that should the monkey at any time return, I should be sent for immediately; and, repeating my assurance that I would give neither time nor thought to any other subject until I had thoroughly investigated his case, and that tomorrow he should hear the result, I took my leave.

Before getting into the carriage I told the servant that his master was far from well, and that he should make a point of frequently looking into his room.

My own arrangements I made with a view to being quite secure from interruption.

I merely called at my lodgings, and with a travelling-desk and carpet-bag, set off in a hackney-carriage for an inn about two miles out of town, called The Horns, a very quiet and comfortable house, with good thick walls. And there I resolved, without the possibility of intrusion or distraction, to devote some hours of the night, in my comfortable sitting-room, to Mr Jennings' case, and so much of the morning as it might require.

(There occurs here a careful note of Dr Hesselius' opinion upon the case, and of the habits, dietary, and medicines which he prescribed. It is curious—some persons would say mystical. But, on the whole, I doubt whether it would sufficiently interest a reader of the kind I am likely to meet with, to warrant its being here reprinted. The whole letter was plainly written at the inn where he had hid himself for the occasion. The next letter is dated from his town lodgings.)

I left town for the inn where I slept last night at half-past nine, and did not arrive at my room in town until one o'clock this afternoon. I found a letter in Mr Jennings' hand upon my table. It had not come by post, and, on inquiry, I learned that Mr Jennings' servant had brought it, and on learning that I was not to return until today, and that no one could tell him my address, he seemed very uncomfortable, and said his orders from his master were that he was not to return without an answer.

I opened the letter and read:

DEAR DR HESSELIUS.—It is here. You had not been an hour gone when it returned. It is speaking. It knows all that has happened. It knows everything—it knows you, and is frantic and atrocious. It reviles. I send you this. It knows every word I have written—I write. This I promised, and I therefore write, but, I fear, very confused, very incoherently. I am so interrupted, disturbed.

Ever yours, sincerely yours,
ROBERT LYNDER JENNINGS.

"When did this come?" I asked.

"About eleven last night: the man was here again, and has been here three times today. The last time is about an hour since."

Thus answered, and with the notes I had made upon his case in my pocket, I was in a few minutes driving towards Richmond, to see Mr Jennings.

I by no means, as you perceive, despaired of Mr Jennings' case. He had himself remembered and applied, though quite in a mistaken way, the principle which I lay down in my Metaphysical Medicine, and which governs all such cases. I was about to apply it in earnest. I was profoundly interested, and very anxious to see and examine him while the 'enemy' was actually present.

I drove up to the sombre house, and ran up the steps, and knocked. The door, in a little time, was opened by a tall woman in black silk. She looked ill, and as if she had been crying. She curtseyed, and heard my question, but she did not answer. She turned her face away, extending her hand towards two men who were coming downstairs; and thus having, as it were, tacitly made me over to them, she passed through a side-door hastily and shut it.

The man who was nearest the hall, I at once accosted, but being now close to him, I was shocked to see that both his hands were covered in blood.

I drew back a little, and the man, passing downstairs, merely said in a low tone, "Here's the servant, sir."

The servant had stopped on the stairs, confounded and dumb at seeing me. He was rubbing his hands in a handkerchief, and it was steeped in blood.

"Jones, what is it? what has happened?" I asked, while a sickening suspicion overpowered me.

The man asked me to come up to the lobby. I was beside him in a moment, and, frowning and pallid, with contracted eyes, he told me the horror which I already half guessed.

His master had made away with himself.

I went upstairs with him to the room—what I saw there I won't tell you. He had cut his throat with his razor. It was a frightful gash. The two men had laid him on the bed, and composed his limbs. It had happened, as the immense pool of blood on the floor declared, at some distance between the bed and the window. There was carpet round his bed, and a carpet under his dressing-table, but none on the rest of the floor, for the man said he did not like a carpet in his bedroom. In this sombre and now terrible room, one of the great elms that darkened the house was slowly moving the shadow of one of its great boughs upon this dreadful floor.

I beckoned to the servant, and we went downstairs together. I turned off the hall into an old-fashioned panelled room, and there standing, I heard all the servant had to tell. It was not a great deal.

"I concluded, sir, from your words, and looks, sir, as you left last night, that you thought my master was seriously ill. I thought it might be that you were afraid of a fit, or something. So I attended very close to your directions. He sat up late, till past three o'clock. He was not writing or reading. He was talking a great deal to himself, but that was nothing unusual. At about that hour I assisted him to undress, and left him in his slippers and dressing-gown. I went back softly in about half-an-hour. He was in his bed, quite undressed, and a pair of candles lighted on the table beside his bed. He was leaning on his elbow, and looking out at the other side of the bed when I came in. I asked him if he wanted anything, and he said no.

"I don't know whether it was what you said to me, sir, or something a little unusual about him, but I was uneasy, uncommon uneasy about him last night.

"In another half hour, or it might be a little more, I went up again. I did not hear him talking as before. I opened the door a little. The candles were both out, which was not usual. I had a bedroom candle, and I let the light in, a little bit, looking softly round.

"I saw him sitting in that chair beside the dressing-table with his clothes on again. He turned round and looked at me. I thought it strange he should get up and dress, and put out the candles to sit in the dark, that way. But I only asked him again if I could do anything for him. He said no, rather sharp, I thought. I asked him if I might light the candles and he said, 'Do as you like, Jones.' So I lighted them, and I lingered about the room, and he said, 'Tell me truth,

Jones; why did you come again—you did not hear anyone cursing?' 'No, sir,' I said, wondering what he could mean.

"'No,' said he, after me, 'of course, no'; and I said to him, 'Wouldn't it be well, sir, you went to bed? It's just five o'clock', and he said nothing, but, 'Very likely; good-night, Jones.' So I went, sir, but in less than an hour I came again. The door was fast, and he heard me, and called as I thought from the bed to know what I wanted, and he desired me not to disturb him again. I lay down and slept for a little.

"It must have been between six and seven when I went up again. The door was still fast, and he made no answer, so I did not like to disturb him, and thinking he was asleep, I left him till nine. It was his custom to ring when he wished me to come, and I had no particular hour for calling him. I tapped very gently, and getting no answer, I stayed away a good while, supposing he was getting some rest then. It was not till eleven o'clock I grew really uncomfortable about him—for at the latest he was never, that I could remember, later than half-past ten. I got no answer. I knocked and called, and still no answer. So not being able to force the door, I called Thomas from the stables, and together we forced it, and found him in the shocking way you saw."

Jones had no more to tell. Poor Mr Jennings was very gentle, and very kind. All his people were fond of him. I could see that the servant was very much moved.

So, dejected and agitated, I passed from that terrible house, and its dark canopy of elms, and I hope I shall never see it more. While I write to you I feel like a man who has but half waked from a frightful and monotonous dream. My memory rejects the picture with incredulity and horror. Yet I know it is true. It is the story of the process of a poison, a poison which excites the reciprocal action of spirit and nerve, and paralyses the tissue that separates those cognate functions of the senses, the external and the interior. Thus we find strange bed-fellows, and the mortal and immortal prematurely make acquaintance.

Conclusion: A Word for Those Who Suffer

My dear Van L—, you have suffered from an affection similar to that which I have just described. You twice complained of a return of it.

Who, under God, cured you? Your humble servant, Martin Hesselius. Let me rather adopt the more emphasised piety of a certain good old French surgeon of three hundred years ago: "I treated, and God cured you."

Come, my friend, you are not to be hippish. Let me tell you a fact.

I have met with, and treated, as my book shows, fifty-seven cases of this kind of vision, which I term indifferently "sublimated", "precocious", and "interior".

There is another class of affections which are truly termed—though commonly confounded with those which I describe—spectral illusions. These latter I look upon as being no less simply curable than a cold in the head or a trifling dyspepsia.

It is those which rank in the first category that test our promptitude of thought. Fifty-seven such cases have I encountered, neither more nor less. And in how many of these have I failed? In no single instance.

There is no one affliction of mortality more easily and certainly reducible, with a little patience, and a rational confidence in the physician. With these simple conditions, I look upon the cure as absolutely certain.

You are to remember that I had not even commenced to treat Mr Jennings' case. I have not any doubt that I should have cured him perfectly in eighteen months, or possibly it might have extended to two years. Some cases are very rapidly curable, others extremely tedious. Every intelligent physician who will give thought and diligence to the task, will effect a cure.

You know my tract on The Cardinal Functions of the Brain. I there, by the evidence of innumerable facts, prove, as I think, the high probability of a circulation arterial and venous in its mechanism, through the nerves. Of this system, thus considered, the brain is the heart. The fluid, which is propagated hence through one class of nerves, returns in an altered state through another, and the nature of that fluid is spiritual, though not immaterial, any more than, as I before remarked, light or electricity are so.

By various abuses, among which the habitual use of such agents as green tea is one, this fluid may be affected as to its quality, but it is more frequently disturbed as to equilibrium. This fluid being that which we have in common with spirits, a congestion found upon the masses of brain or nerve, connected with the interior sense, forms a surface unduly exposed, on which disembodied spirits may operate: communication is thus more or less effectually established. Between this brain circulation and the heart circulation there is an intimate sympathy. The seat, or rather the instrument of exterior vision, is the eye. The seat of interior vision is the nervous tissue and brain, immediately about and above the eyebrow.

You remember how effectually I dissipated your pictures by the simple application of iced eau-de-cologne. Few cases, however, can be treated exactly alike with anything like rapid success. Cold acts powerfully as a repellant of the nervous fluid. Long enough continued it will even produce that permanent insensibility which we call numbness, and a little longer, muscular as well as sensational paralysis.

I have not, I repeat, the slightest doubt that I should have first dimmed and ultimately sealed that inner eye which Mr Jennings had inadvertently opened. The same senses are opened in delirium tremens, and entirely shut up again when the overaction of the cerebral heart, and the prodigious nervous congestions that attend it, are terminated by a decided change in the state of the body. It is by acting steadily upon the body by a simple process, that this result is produced—and inevitably produced—I have never yet failed.

Poor Mr Jennings made away with himself. But that catastrophe was the result of a totally different malady, which, as it were, projected itself upon the disease which was established. His case was in the distinctive manner a complication, and the complaint under which he really succumbed, was a hereditary suicidal mania. Poor Mr Jennings I cannot call a patient of mine, for I had not even begun to treat his case, and he had not yet given me, I am convinced, his full and unreserved confidence. If the patient do not array himself on the side of the disease, his cure is certain.

The Jolly Corner

HENRY JAMES

[1843–1916]

Little need be said of so famous a literary figure as Henry James—author of such brilliant novels as The Portrait of a Lady*—save that James in fact wrote a large number of ghost stories beyond his famous novel in the tradition,* The Turn of the Screw. "The Jolly Corner," *which belongs to James's great final period that also produced* The Ambassadors *and* The Golden Bowl, *is perhaps the most sophisticated and complex ghost story ever written. Unlike* The Turn of the Screw, *whose manifold interpretations have sparked a controversy that still smolders,* "The Jolly Corner" *is undisguisedly supernatural in content. Yet, as the reader will discover, it is hardly less formidable for being so.*

I

"Everyone asks me what I 'think' of everything," said Spencer Brydon; "and I make answer as I can—begging or dodging the question, putting them off with any nonsense. It wouldn't matter to any of them really," he went on, "for, even were it possible to meet in that stand-and-deliver way so silly a demand on so big a subject, my 'thoughts' would still be almost altogether about something that concerns only myself." He was talking to Miss Staverton, with whom for a couple of months now he had availed himself of every possible occasion to talk; this disposition and this resource, this comfort and support, as the situation in fact presented itself, having promptly enough taken the first place in the considerable array of rather unattenuated surprises attending his so strangely belated return to America. Everything was somehow a surprise; and that might be natural when one had so long and so consistently neglected everything, taken pains to give surprises so much margin for play. He had given them more than thirty years—thirty-three, to be exact; and they now seemed to him to have organized their performance quite on the scale of that license. He had been twenty-three on leaving New York—he was fifty-six today: unless indeed he were to reckon as he had sometimes, since his repatriation, found himself feeling; in which case he would have lived longer than is often allotted to man. It would have taken a century, he repeatedly said to himself, and said also to Alice Staverton, it would have taken a longer absence and a more averted mind than those even of which he had been guilty, to pile up the differences, the newnesses, the queernesses, above all the bignesses, for the better or the worse, that at present assaulted his vision wherever he looked.

The great fact all the while however had been the incalculability; since he *had* supposed himself, from decade to decade, to be allowing, and in the most liberal and intelligent manner, for brilliancy of change. He actually saw that he had allowed for nothing; he missed what he would have been sure of finding, he found what he would never have imagined. Proportions and values were upside-down; the ugly things he had expected, the ugly things of his faraway youth, when he had too promptly waked up to a sense of the ugly—these uncanny phenomena placed him rather, as it happened, under the charm; whereas the "swagger" things, the modern, the monstrous, the famous things, those he had more particularly, like thousands of ingenuous inquirers every year, come over to see, were exactly his sources of dismay. They were as so many set traps for displeasure, above all for reaction, of which his restless tread was constantly pressing the spring. It was interesting, doubtless, the whole show, but it would have been too disconcerting hadn't a certain finer truth saved the situation. He had distinctly not, in this steadier light, come over *all* for the monstrosities; he had come, not only in the last analysis but quite on the face of the act, under an impulse with which they had nothing to do. He had come—putting the thing pompously—to look at his "property," which he had thus for a third of a century not been within four thousand miles of; or, expressing it less sordidly, he had yielded to the humor of seeing again his house on the jolly corner, as he usually, and quite fondly, described it—the one in which he had first seen the light, in which various members of his family had lived and had died, in which the holidays of his overschooled boyhood had been passed and the few social flowers of his chilled adolescence gathered, and which, alienated then for so long a period, had, through the successive deaths of his two brothers and the termination of old arrangements, come wholly into his hands. He was the owner of another, not quite so "good"—the jolly corner having been, far from back, superlatively extending and consecrated; and the value of the pair represented his main capital, with an income consisting, in these later years, of their respective rents which (thanks precisely to their original excellent type) had never been depressingly low. He could live in "Europe," as he had been in the habit of living, on the product of these flourishing New York leases, and all the better since, that of the second structure, the mere number in its long row, having within a twelvemonth fallen in, renovation at a high advance had proved beautifully possible.

These were items of property indeed, but he had found himself since his arrival distinguishing more than ever between them. The house within the street, two bristling blocks westward, was already in course of reconstruction as a tall mass of flats; he had acceded, some time before, to overtures for this conversion—in which, now that it was going forward, it had been not the least of his astonishments to find himself able, on the spot, and though without a previous ounce of such experience, to participate with a certain intelligence, almost with a certain authority. He had lived his life with his back so turned to such concerns and his face addressed to those of so different an order that he scarce knew what to make of this lively stir, in a compartment of his mind never yet penetrated, of a capacity for business and a sense for construction. These virtues, so common all round him now, had been dormant in his own organism—where it might be said of them perhaps that they had slept the sleep of the just. At present, in the splendid autumn weather—the autumn at least was a pure boon in the terrible place—he loafed about his "work" undeterred, secretly agitated; not in the least "minding" that the whole proposition, as they said, was vulgar and sordid, and ready to climb ladders, to walk the plank, to handle materials and look wise about them, to ask questions, in fine, and challenge explanations and really "go into" figures.

It amused, it verily quite charmed him; and, by the same stroke, it amused, and even more, Alice Staverton, though perhaps charming her perceptibly less. She wasn't however going to be better off for it, as *he* was—and so astonishingly much: nothing was now likely, he knew, even to make her better off than she found herself, in the afternoon of life, as the delicately frugal professor and tenant of the small house in Irving Place to which she had subtly managed to cling through her almost unbroken New York career. If he knew the way to it now better than to any other address among the dreadful multiplied numberings which seemed to him to reduce the whole place to some vast ledger page, overgrown, fantastic, of ruled and crisscrossed lines and figures—if he had formed, for his consolation, that habit, it was really not a little because of the charm of his having encountered and recognized, in the vast wilderness of the wholesale, breaking through the mere gross generalization of wealth and force and success, a small still scene where items and shades, all delicate things, kept the sharpness of the notes of a high voice perfectly trained, and where economy hung about like the scent of a garden. His old friend lived with one maid and herself dusted her relics and trimmed her lamps and polished her silver; she stood off, in the awful modern crush, when she could, but she sallied forth and did battle when the challenge was really to "spirit," the spirit she after all confessed to, proudly and a little shyly, as to that of the better time, that of *their* common, their quite far away and antediluvian social period and order. She made use of the street cars when need be, the terrible things that people scrambled for as the panic-stricken at sea scramble for the boats; she affronted, inscrutably, under stress, all the public concussions and ordeals; and yet, with that slim mystifying grace of her appearance, which defied you to say if she were a fair young woman who looked older through trouble, or fine smooth older one who looked young through successful indifference; with her precious reference, above all, to memories and histories into which he could enter, she was as exquisite for him as some pale pressed flower (a rarity to begin with), and, failing other sweetnesses, she was a sufficient reward of his effort. They had communities of knowledge, "their" knowledge (this discriminating possessive was always on her lips) of presences of the other age, presences all overlaid, in his case, by the experience of a man and the freedom of a wanderer, overlaid by pleasure, by infidelity, by passages of life that were strange and dim to her, just by "Europe" in short, but still unobscured, still exposed and cherished, under that pious visitation of the spirit from which she had never been diverted.

She had come with him one day to see how his "apartment house" was rising; he had helped her over gaps and explained to her plans, and while they were there had happened to have, before her, a brief but lively discussion with the man in charge, the representative of the building firm that had undertaken his work. He had found himself quite "standing-up" to this personage over a failure on the latter's part to observe some detail of one of their noted conditions, and had so lucidly argued his case that, besides ever so prettily flushing, at the time, for sympathy in his triumph, she had afterwards said to him (though to a slightly greater effect of irony) that he had clearly for too many years neglected a real gift. If he had but stayed at home he would have anticipated the inventor of the skyscraper. If he had but stayed at home he would have discovered his genius in time really to start some new variety of awful architectual hare and run it till it burrowed in the gold mine. He was to remember these words, while the weeks elapsed, for the small silver ring they had sounded over the queerest and deepest of his own lately most disguised and most muffled vibrations.

It had begun to be present to him after the first fortnight, it had broken out with the oddest abruptness, this particular wanton wonderment: it met him there—and this was the image under which he himself judged the matter, or at least, not a little, thrilled and flushed with it—very much as he might have been met by some strange figure, some unexpected occupant, at a turn of one of the dim passages of an empty house. The quaint analogy quite hauntingly remained with him, when he didn't indeed rather improve it by a still intenser form: that of his opening a door behind which he would have made sure of finding nothing, a door into a room shuttered and void, and yet so coming, with a great suppressed start, on some quite erect confronting presence, sometimes planted in the middle of the place and facing him through the dusk. After that visit to the house in construction he walked with his companion to see the other and always so much the better one, which in the eastward direction formed one of the corners, the "jolly" one precisely, of the street now so generally dishonored and disfigured in its westward reaches, and of the comparatively conservative avenue. The avenue still had pretensions, as Miss Staverton said, to decency; the old people had mostly gone, the old names were unknown, and here and there an old association seemed to stray, all vaguely, like some very aged person, out too late, whom you might meet and feel the impulse to watch or follow, in kindness, for safe restoration to shelter.

They went in together, our friends; he admitted himself with his key, as he kept no one there, he explained, preferring, for his reasons, to leave the place empty, under a simple arrangement with a good woman living in the neighborhood and who came for a daily hour to open windows and dust and sweep. Spencer Brydon had his reasons and was growingly aware of them; they seemed to him better each time he was there, though he didn't name them all to his companion, any more than he told her as yet how often, how quite absurdly often, he himself came. He only let her see for the present, while they walked through the great blank rooms, that absolute vacancy reigned and that, from top to bottom, there was nothing but Mrs. Muldoon's broomstick, in the corner, to tempt the burglar. Mrs. Muldoon was then on the premises, and she loquaciously attended the visitors, preceding them from room to room and pushing back shutters and throwing up sashes—all to show them, as she remarked, how little there was to see. There was little indeed to see in the great gaunt shell where the main dispositions and the general apportionment of space, the style of an age of ampler allowances, had nevertheless for its master their honest pleading message, affecting him as some good old servant's, some lifelong retainer's appeal for a character, or even for a retiring pension; yet it was also a remark of Mrs. Muldoon's that, glad as she was to oblige him by her noonday round, there was a request she greatly hoped he would never make of her. If he should wish her for any reason to come in after dark she would just tell him, if he "plased," that he must ask it of somebody else.

The fact that there was nothing to see didn't militate for the worthy woman against what one *might* see, and she put it frankly to Miss Staverton that no lady could be expected to like, could she? "craping up to thim top storys in the ayvil hours." The gas and electric light were off the house, and she fairly evoked a gruesome vision of her march through the great gray rooms—so many of them as there were too!—with her glimmering taper. Miss Staverton met her honest glare with a smile and the profession that she herself certainly would recoil from such an adventure. Spencer Brydon meanwhile held his peace—for the moment; the question of the "evil" hours in his old home had already become too grave for him. He had begun some time since to "crape," and he knew just why a packet of candles addressed to that pursuit had been stowed by his own hand, three weeks before, at the back of a drawer of the fine old sideboard that occupied, as a "fixture," the deep recess in the dining room. Just now he laughed at his companions—quickly however changing the subject; for the reason that, in the first place, his laugh struck him even at that moment as starting the odd echo, the conscious human resonance (he scarce knew how to qualify it) that sounds made while he was there alone sent back to his ear or his fancy; and that, in the second, he imagined Alice Staverton for the instant on the point of asking him, with a divination, if he ever so prowled. There were divinations he was unprepared for, and he had at all events averted inquiry by the time Mrs. Muldoon had left them, passing on to other parts.

There was happily enough to say, on so consecrated a spot, that could be said freely and fairly; so that a whole train of declarations was precipitated by his friend's having herself broken out, after a yearning look round: "But I hope you don't mean they want you to pull *this* to pieces!" His answer came, promptly, with his reawakened wrath: it was of course exactly what they wanted, and what they were "at" him for, daily, with the iteration of people who couldn't for their life understand a man's liability to decent feelings. He had found the place, just as it stood and beyond that he could express, an interest and a joy. There were values other than the beastly rent values, and in short, in short—! But it was thus Miss Staverton took him up. "In short you're to make so good a thing of your skyscraper that, living in luxury on *those* ill-gotten gains, you can afford for a while to be sentimental here!" Her smile had for him, with the words, the particular mild irony with which he found half her talk suffused; an irony without bitterness and that came, exactly, from her having so much imagination—not, like the cheap sarcasms with which one heard most people, about the world of "society," bid for the reputation of cleverness, from nobody's really having any. It was agreeable to him at this very moment to be sure that when he had answered, after a brief demur, "Well yes: so, precisely, you may put it!" her imagination would still do him justice. He explained that even if never a dollar were to come to him from the other house he would nevertheless cherish this one; and he dwelt, further, while they lingered and wandered, on the fact of the stupefaction he was already exciting, the positive mystification he felt himself create.

He spoke of the value of all he read into it, into the mere sight of the walls, mere shapes of the rooms, mere sound of the floors, mere feel, in his hand, of the old silverplated knobs of the several mahogany doors, which suggested the pressure of the palms of the dead; the seventy years of the past in fine that these things represented, the annals of nearly three generations, counting his grandfather's, the one that had ended there, and the impalpable ashes of his long-extinct youth, afloat in the very air like microscopic motes. She listened to everything; she was a woman who answered intimately but who utterly didn't chatter. She scattered abroad therefore no cloud of words; she could assent, she could agree, above all she could encourage, without doing that. Only at the last she went a little further than he had done himself. "And then how do you know? You may still, after all, want to live here." It rather indeed pulled him up, for it wasn't what he had been thinking, at least in her sense of the words. "You mean I may decide to stay on for the sake of it?"

"Well, *with* such a home—!" But, quite beautifully, she had too much tact to dot so monstrous an *i,* and it was precisely an illustration of the way she didn't rattle. How could any one—of any wit—insist on anyone else's "wanting" to live in New York?

"Oh," he said, "I *might* have lived here (since I had my opportunity early in life); I might have put in here all these years. Then everything would have been different enough—and, I dare say, 'funny' enough. But that's another matter. And then the beauty of it—I mean of my perversity, of my refusal to agree to a 'deal'—is just in the total absence of a reason. Don't you see that if I had a reason about the matter at all it would *have* to be the other way, and would then be inevitably a reason of dollars? There are no reasons here *but* of dollars. Let us therefore have none whatever—not the ghost of one."

They were back in the hall then for departure, but from where they stood the vista was large, through an open door, into the great square main saloon, with its almost antique felicity of brave spaces between windows. Her eyes came back from that reach and met his own a moment. "Are you very sure the 'ghost' of one doesn't, much rather, serve—?"

He had a positive sense of turning pale. But it was as near as they were then to come. For he made answer, he believed, between a glare and a grin: "Oh ghosts—of course the place must swarm with them! I should be ashamed of it if it didn't. Poor Mrs. Muldoon's right, and it's why I haven't asked her to do more than look in."

Miss Staverton's gaze again lost itself, and things she didn't utter, it was clear, came and went in her mind. She might even for the minute, off there in the fine room, have imagined some element dimly gathering. Simplified like the death mask of a handsome face, it perhaps produced for her just then an effect akin to the stir of an expression in the "set" commemorative plaster. Yet whatever her impression may have been she produced instead a vague platitude. "Well, if it were only furnished and lived in—!"

She appeared to imply that in case of its being still furnished he might have been a little less opposed to the idea of a return. But she passed straight into the vestibule, as if to leave her words behind her, and the next moment he had opened the house door and was standing with her on the steps. He closed the door and, while he repocketed his key, looking up and down, they took in the comparatively harsh actuality of the avenue, which reminded him of the assault of the outer light of the desert on the traveler emerging from an Egyptian tomb. But he risked before they stepped into the street his gathered answer to her speech. "For me it *is* lived in. For me it *is* furnished." At which it was easy for her to sigh "Ah yes—!" all vaguely and discreetly; since his parents and his favorite sister, to say nothing of other kin, in numbers, had run their course and met their end there. That represented, within the walls, ineffaceable life.

It was a few days after this that, during an hour passed with her again, he had expressed his impatience of the too flattering curiosity—among the people he met—about his appreciation of New York. He had arrived at none at all that was socially producible, and as for that matter of his "thinking" (thinking the better or the worse of anything there) he was wholly taken up with one subject of thought. It was mere vain egoism, and it was moreover, if she liked, a morbid obsession. He found all things come back to the question of what he personally might have been, how he might have led his life and "turned out," if he had not so, at the outset, given it up. And confessing for the first time to the intensity within him of this absurd speculation—which but proved also, no doubt, the habit of too selfishly thinking—he affirmed the impotence there of any other source of interest, any other native appeal. "What would it have made of me, what would it have made of me? I keep forever wondering, all idiotically; as if I could possibly know! I see what it has made of dozens of others, those I meet, and it positively aches within me, to the point of exasperation, that it would have made something of me as well. Only I can't make out *what,* and the worry of it, the small rage of curiosity never to be satisfied, brings back what I remember to have felt, once or twice, after judging best, for reasons, to burn some important letter unopened. I've been sorry, I've hated it—I've never known what was in the letter. You may of course say it's a trifle—!"

"I don't say it's a trifle," Miss Staverton gravely interrupted.

She was seated by her fire, and before her, on his feet and

restless, he turned to and fro between this intensity of his idea and a fitful and unseeing inspection, through his single eyeglass, of the dear little old objects on her chimney-piece. Her interruption made him for an instant look at her harder. "I shouldn't care if you did!" he laughed, however; "and it's only a figure, at any rate, for the way I now feel. Not to have followed my perverse young course—and almost in the teeth of my father's curse, as I may say; not to have kept it up, so, 'over there,' from that day to this, without a doubt or a pang; not, above all, to have liked it, to have loved it, so much, loved it, no doubt, with such an abysmal conceit of my own preference: some variation from *that,* I say, must have produced some different effect for my life and for my 'form.' I should have stuck here—if it had been possible; and I was too young, at twenty-three, to judge, *pour deux sous,* whether it *were* possible. If I had waited I might have seen it was, and then I might have been, by staying here, something nearer to one of these types who have been hammered so hard and made so keen by their conditions. It isn't that I admire them so much—the question of any charm in them, or of any charm, beyond that of the rank money passion, exerted by their conditions *for* them, has nothing to do with the matter: it's only a question of what fantastic, yet perfectly possible, development of my own nature I mayn't have missed. It comes over me that I had then a strange *alter ego* deep down somewhere within me, as the full-blown flower is in the small tight bud, and that I just took the course, I just transferred him to the climate, that blighted him for once and forever."

"And you wonder about the flower," Miss Staverton said. "So do I, if you want to know; and so I've been wondering these several weeks. I believe in the flower," she continued, "I felt it would have been quite splendid, quite huge and monstrous."

"Monstrous above all!" her visitor echoed; "and I imagine, by the same stroke, quite hideous and offensive."

"You don't believe that," she returned; "if you did you wouldn't wonder. You'd know, and that would be enough for you. What you feel—and what I feel *for* you—is that you'd have had power."

"You'd have liked me that way?" he asked.

She barely hung fire. "How should I not have liked you?"

"I see. You'd have liked me, have preferred me, a billionaire!"

"How should I not have liked you?" she simply again asked.

He stood before her still—her question kept him motionless. He took it in, so much there was of it; and indeed his not otherwise meeting it testified to that. "I know at least what I am," he simply went on; "the other side of the medal's clear enough. I've not been edifying—I believe I'm thought in a hundred quarters to have been barely decent. I've followed strange paths and worshipped strange gods; it must have come to you again and again—in fact you've admitted to me as much—that I was leading, at any time these thirty years, a selfish frivolous scandalous life. And you see what it has made of me."

She just waited, smiling at him. "You see what it has made of *me.*"

"Oh you're a person whom nothing can have altered. You were born to be what you are, anywhere, anyway: you've the perfection nothing else could have blighted. And don't you see how, without my exile, I shouldn't have been waiting till now—?" But he pulled up for the strange pang.

"The great thing to see," she presently said, "seems to me to be that it has spoiled nothing. It hasn't spoiled your being here at last. It hasn't spoiled this. It hasn't spoiled your speaking—" She also however faltered.

He wondered at everything her controlled emotion might mean. "Do you believe then—too dreadfully!—that I *am* as good as I might ever have been?"

"Oh no! Far from it!" With which she got up from her chair and was nearer to him. "But I don't care," she smiled.

"You mean I'm good enough?"

She considered a little. "Will you believe it if I say so? I mean will you let that settle your question for you?" And then as if making out in his face that he drew back from this, that he had some idea which, however absurd, he couldn't yet bargain away: "Oh you don't care either—but very differently: you don't care for anything but yourself."

Spencer Brydon recognized it—it was in fact what he had absolutely professed. Yet he importantly qualified. "*He* isn't myself. He's the just so totally other person. But I do want to see him," he added. "And I can. And I shall."

Their eyes met for a minute while he guessed from something in hers that she divined his strange sense. But neither of them otherwise expressed it, and her apparent understanding, with no protesting shock, no easy derision, touched him more deeply than anything yet, constituting for his stifled perversity, on the spot, an element that was like breathable air. What she said however was unexpected. "Well, *I've* seen him."

"You—?"

"I've seen him in a dream."

"Oh a 'dream'—!" It let him down.

"But twice over," she continued. "I saw him as I see you now."

"You've dreamed the same dream—?"

"Twice over," she repeated. "The very same."

This did somehow a little speak to him, as it also gratified him. "You dream about me at that rate?"

"Ah, about *him!*" she smiled.

His eyes again sounded her. "Then you know all about him." And as she said nothing more: "What's the wretch like?"

She hesitated, and it was as if he were pressing her so hard that, resisting for reasons of her own, she had to turn away. "I'll tell you some other time!"

II

It was after this that there was most of a virtue for him, most of a cultivated charm, most of a preposterous secret thrill, in the particular form of surrender to his obsession and of address to what he more and more believed to be his privilege. It was what in these weeks he was living for—since he really felt life to begin but after Mrs. Muldoon had retired from the scene and, visiting the ample house from attic to cellar, making sure he was alone, he knew himself in safe possession and, as he tacitly expressed it, let himself go. He sometimes came twice in the twenty-four hours; the moments he liked best were those of gathering dusk, of the short autumn twilight; this was the time of which, again and again, he found himself hoping most. Then he could, as seemed to him, most intimately wander and wait, linger and listen, feel his fine attention, never in his life before so fine, on the pulse of the great vague place: he preferred the lampless hour and only wished he might have prolonged each day the deep crepuscular spell. Later—rarely much before midnight, but then for a considerable vigil—he watched with his glimmering light; moving slowly, holding it high, playing it far, rejoicing above all, as much as he might, in open vistas, reaches of communication between rooms and by passages; the long straight chance or show, as he would have called it, for the revelation he pretended to invite. It was a practice he found he could perfectly "work" without exciting remark; no one was in the least the wiser for it; even Alice Staverton, who was moreover a well of discretion, didn't quite fully imagine.

He let himself in and let himself out with the assurance of calm proprietorship; and accident so far favored him that, if a fat avenue "officer" had happened on occasion to see him entering at eleven-thirty, he had never yet, to the best of his belief, been noticed as emerging at two. He walked there on the crisp November nights, arrived regularly at the evening's end; it was as easy to do this after dining out as to take his way to a club or to his hotel. When he left his club, if he hadn't been dining out, it was ostensibly to go to his hotel; and when he left his hotel, if he had spent a part of the evening there, it was ostensibly to go to his club. Everything was easy in fine; everything conspired and promoted: there was truly even in the strain of his experience something that glossed over, something that salved and simplified, all the rest of consciousness. He circulated, talked, renewed, loosely and pleasantly, old relations—met indeed, so far as he could, new expectations and seemed to make out on the whole that in spite of the career, of such different contacts, which he had spoken of to Miss Staverton as ministering so little, for those who might have watched it, to edification, he was positively rather liked than not. He was a dim secondary social success—and all with people who had truly not an idea of him. It was all mere surface sound, this murmur of their welcome, this popping of their corks—just as his gestures of response were the extravagant shadows, emphatic in proportion as they meant little, of some game of *ombres chinoises.* He projected himself all day, in thought, straight over the bristling line of hard unconscious heads and into the other, the real, the waiting life; the life that, as soon as he had heard behind him the click of his great house door, began for him, on the jolly corner, as beguilingly as the slow opening bars of some rich music follows the tap of the conductor's wand.

He always caught the first effect of the steel point of his stick on the old marble of the hall pavement, large black-and-white squares that he remembered as the admiration of his childhood and that had then made in him, as he now saw, for the growth of an early conception of style. This effect was the dim reverberating tinkle as of some far-off bell hung who should say where?—in the depths of the house, of the past, of that mystical other world that might have flourished for him had he not, for weal or woe, abandoned it. On this impression he did ever the same thing; he put his stick noiselessly away in a corner—feeling the place once more in the likeness of some great glass bowl, all precious concave crystal, set delicately humming by the play of a moist finger round its edge. The concave crystal held, as it were, this mystical other world, and the indescribably fine murmur of its rim was the sign there, the scarce audible pathetic wail to his strained ear, of all the old baffled forsworn possibilities. What he did therefore by this appeal of his hushed presence was to wake them into such measure of ghostly life as they might still enjoy. They were shy, all but unappeasably shy, but they weren't really sinister; at least they weren't as he had hitherto felt them—before they had taken the Form he so yearned to make them take, the Form he at moments saw himself in the light of fairly hunting on tiptoe, the points of his evening shoes, from room to room and from story to story.

That was the essence of his vision—which was all rank folly, if one would, while he was out of the house and otherwise occupied, but which took on the last verisimilitude as soon as he was placed and posted. He knew what he meant and what he wanted; it was as clear as the figure on a check presented in demand for cash. His *alter ego* "walked"—that was the note of his image of him, while his image of his motive for his own odd pastime was the desire to waylay him and meet him. He roamed, slowly, warily, but all restlessly, he himself did—Mrs. Muldoon had been right, absolutely, with her figure of their "craping;" and the presence he watched for would roam restlessly too. But it would be as cautious and as shifty; the conviction of its probable, in fact its already quite sensible, quite audible evasion of pursuit grew for him from night to night, laying on him finally a rigor to which nothing in his life had been comparable. It had been the theory of many superficially judging persons, he knew, that he was wasting that life in a surrender to sensations, but he had tasted of no pleasure so fine as his actual tension, had been introduced to no sport that demanded at once the patience and the nerve of this stalking of a creature more subtle, yet at bay perhaps more formidable, than any beast of the forest. The terms, the comparisons, the very practices of the chase positively came again into play; there were even moments when passages of his occasional experience as a sportsman, stirred memories, from his younger time, of moor and mountain and desert, revived for him—and to the increase of his keenness—by the tremendous force of analogy. He found himself at moments—once he had placed his single light on some mantel shelf or in some recess—stepping back into shelter or shade, effacing himself behind a door or in an embrasure, as he had sought of old the vantage of rock and tree; he found himself holding his breath and living in the joy of the instant, the supreme suspense created by big game alone.

He wasn't afraid (though putting himself the question as he believed gentlemen on Bengal tiger shoots or in close quarters with the great bear of the Rockies had been known to confess to having put it); and this indeed—since here at least he might be frank!—because of the impression, so intimate and so strange, that he himself produced as yet a dread, produced certainly a strain, beyond the liveliest he was likely to feel. They fell for him into categories, they fairly became familiar, the signs, for his own perception, of the alarm his presence and his vigilance created; though leaving him always to remark, portentously, on his probably having formed a relation, his probably enjoying a consciousness, unique in the experience of man. People enough, first and last, had been in terror apparitions, but who had ever before so turned the tables and become himself, in the apparitional world, an incalculable terror? He might have found this sublime had he quite dared to think of it; but he didn't too much insist, truly, on that side of his privilege. With habit and repetition he gained to an extraordinary degree the power to penetrate the dusk of distances and the darkness of corners, to resolve back into their innocence the treacheries of uncertain light, the evil-looking forms taken in the gloom by mere shadows, by accidents of the air, by shifting effects of perspective; putting down his dim luminary he could still wander on without it, pass into other rooms and, only knowing it was there behind him in case of need, see his way about, visually project for his purpose a comparative clearness. It made him feel, this acquired faculty, like some monstrous stealthy cat; he wondered if he would have glared at these moments with large shining yellow eyes, and what it mightn't verily be, for the poor hard-pressed *alter ego,* to be confronted with such a type.

He liked however the open shutters; he opened everywhere those Mrs. Muldoon had closed, closing them as carefully afterwards, so that she shouldn't notice: he liked—oh this he did like, and above all in the upper rooms!—the sense of the hard silver of the autumn stars through the window panes, and scarcely less the flare of the street lamps below, the white electric luster which it would have taken curtains to keep out. This was human actual social; this was of the world he had lived in, and he was more at his ease certainly for the countenance, coldly general and impersonal, that all the while and in spite of his detachment it seemed to give him. He had support of course mostly in the rooms at the wide front and the prolonged side; it failed him considerably in the central shades and the parts at the back. But if he sometimes, on his rounds, was glad of his optical reach, so none the less often the rear of the house affected him as the very jungle of his prey. The place was there more subdivided; a large "extension" in particular, where small rooms for servants had been multiplied, abounded in nooks and corners, in closets and passages, in the ramifications especially of an ample back staircase over which he leaned, many a time, to look far down—not deterred from his gravity even while aware that he might, for a spectator, have figured some solemn simpleton playing at hide-and-seek. Outside in fact he might himself make that ironic *rapprochement;* but within the walls, and in spite of the clear windows, his consistency was proof against the cynical light of New York.

It had belonged to the idea of the exasperated consciousness of his victim to become a real test for him; since he had quite put it to himself from the first that, oh distinctly! he could "cultivate" his whole perception. He had felt it as above all open to cultivation—which indeed was but another name for his manner of spending his time. He was bringing it on, bringing it to perfection, by practice; in consequence of which it had grown so fine that he was now aware of impressions, attestations of his general postulate, that couldn't have broken upon him at once. This was the case more specifically with a phenomenon at last quite frequent for him in the upper rooms, the recognition—absolutely unmistakable, and by a turn dating from a particular hour, his resumption of his campaign after a diplomatic drop, a calculated absence of three nights—of his being definitely followed, tracked at a distance carefully taken and to the express end that he should the less confidently, less arrogantly, appear to himself merely to pursue. It worried, it finally quite broke him up, for it proved, of all the conceivable impressions, the one least suited to his book. He was kept in sight while remaining himself—as regards the essence of his position—sightless, and his only recourse then was in abrupt turns, rapid recoveries of ground. He wheeled about, retracing his steps, as if he might so catch in his face at least the stirred air of some other quick revolution. It was indeed true that his fully dislocalized thought of these maneuvers recalled to him Pantaloon, at the Christmas farce, buffeted and tricked from behind by ubiquitous

Harlequin; but it left intact the influence of the conditions themselves each time he was reexposed to them, so that in fact this association, had he suffered it to become constant, would on a certain side have but ministered to his intenser gravity. He had made, as I have said, to create on the premises the baseless sense of a reprieve, his three absences; and the result of the third was to confirm the aftereffect of the second.

On his return, that night—the night succeeding his last intermission—he stood in the hall and looked up the staircase with a certainty more intimate than any he had yet known. "He's *there,* at the top, and waiting—not, as in general, falling back for disappearance. He's holding his ground, and it's the first time—which is a proof, isn't it? that something has happened for him." So Brydon argued with his hand on the banister and his foot on the lowest stair; in which position he felt as never before the air chilled by his logic. He himself turned cold in it, for he seemed of a sudden to know what now was involved. "Harder pressed?—yes, he takes it in, with its thus making clear to him that I've come, as they say, 'to stay.' He finally doesn't like and can't bear it, in the sense, I mean, that his wrath, his menaced interest, now balances with his dread. I've hunted him till he has 'turned': that, up there, is what has happened—he's the fanged or the antlered animal brought at last to bay." There came to him, as I say—but determined by an influence beyond my notation!—the acuteness of this certainty; under which however the next moment he had broken into a sweat that he would as little have consented to attribute to fear as he would have dared immediately to act upon it for enterprise. It marked nonetheless a prodigious thrill, a thrill that represented sudden dismay, no doubt, but also represented, and with the self-same throb, the strangest, the most joyous, possibly the next minute almost the proudest, duplication of consciousness.

"He has been dodging, retreating, hiding, but now, worked up to anger, he'll fight"—this intense impression made a single mouthful, as it were, of terror and applause. But what was wondrous was that the applause, for the felt fact, was so eager, since, if it was his other self he was running to earth, this ineffable identity was thus in the last resort not unworthy of him. It bristled there—somewhere near at hand, however unseen still—as the hunted thing, even as the trodden worm of the adage *must* at last bristle; and Brydon at this instant tasted probably of a sensation more complex than had ever before found itself consistent with sanity. It was as if it would have shamed him that a character so associated with his own should triumphantly succeed in just skulking, should to the end not risk the open, so that the drop of this danger was, on the spot, a great lift of the whole situation. Yet with another rare shift of the same subtlety he was already trying to measure by how much more he himself might now be in peril of fear; so rejoicing that he could, in another form, actively inspire that fear, and simultaneously quaking for the form in which he might passively know it.

The apprehension of knowing it must after a little have grown in him, and the strangest moment of his adventure perhaps, the most memorable or really most interesting, afterwards, of his crisis, was the lapse of certain instants of concentrated conscious *combat,* the sense of a need to hold on to something, even after the manner of a man slipping and slipping on some awful incline; the vivid impulse, above all, to move, to act, to charge, somehow and upon something —to show himself, in a word, that he wasn't afraid. The state of "holding on" was thus the state to which he was momentarily reduced; if there had been anything, in the great vacancy, to seize, he would presently have been aware of having clutched it as he might under a shock at home have clutched the nearest chair back. He had been surprised at any rate—of this he *was* aware—into something unprecedented since his original appropriation of the place; he had closed his eyes, held them tight, for a long minute, as with that instinct of dismay and that terror of vision. When he opened them the room, the other contiguous rooms, extraordinarily, seemed lighter—so light, almost, that at first he took the change for day. He stood firm, however that might be, just where he had paused; his resistance had helped him—it was as if there were something he had tided over. He knew after a little what this was—it had been in the imminent danger of flight. He had stiffened his will against going; without this he would have made for the stairs, and it seemed to him that, still with his eyes closed, he would have descended them, would have known how, straight and swiftly, to the bottom.

Well, as he had held out, here he was—still at the top, among the more intricate upper rooms and with the gauntlet of the others, of all the rest of the house, still to run when it should be his time to go. He would go at his time—only at his time: didn't he go every night very much at the same hour? He took out his watch—there was light for that: it was scarcely a quarter past one, and he had never withdrawn so soon. He reached his lodgings for the most part at two

—with his walk of a quarter of an hour. He would wait for the last quarter—he wouldn't stir till then; and he kept his watch there with his eyes on it, reflecting while he held it that this deliberate wait, a wait with an effort, which he recognized, would serve perfectly for the attestation he desired to make. It would prove his courage—unless indeed the latter might most be proved by his budging at last from his place. What he mainly felt now was that, since he hadn't scuttled, he had his dignities—which had never in his life seemed so many—all to preserve and to carry aloft. This was before him in truth as a physical image, an image almost worthy of an age of greater romance. That remark indeed glimmered for him only to glow the next instant with a finer light; since what age of romance, after all, could have matched either the state of his mind or, "objectively," as they said, the wonder of his situation? The only difference would have been that, brandishing his dignities over his head as in a parchment scroll, he might then—that is in the heroic time—have proceeded downstairs with a drawn sword in his other grasp.

At present, really, the light he had set down on the mantel of the next room would have to figure his sword; which utensil, in the course of a minute, he had taken the requisite number of steps to possess himself of. The door between the rooms was open, and from the second another door opened to a third. These rooms, as he remembered, gave all three upon a common corridor as well, but there was a fourth, beyond them, without issue save through the preceding. To have moved, to have heard his step again, was appreciably a help; though even in recognizing this he lingered once more a little by the chimney-piece on which his light had rested. When he next moved, just hesitating where to turn, he found himself considering a circumstance that, after his first and comparatively vague apprehension of it, produced in him the start that often attends some pang of recollection, the violent shock of having ceased happily to forget. He had come into sight of the door in which the brief chain of communication ended and which he now surveyed from the nearer threshold, the one not directly facing it. Placed at some distance to the left of this point, it would have admitted him to the last room of the four, the room without other approach or egress, had it not, to his intimate conviction, been closed *since* his former visitation, the matter probably of a quarter of an hour before. He stared with all his eyes at the wonder of the fact, arrested again where he stood and again holding his breath while he sounded its sense. Surely it had been *subsequently* closed—that is it had been on his previous passage indubitably open!

He took it full in the face that something had happened between—that he couldn't not have noticed before (by which he meant on his original tour of all the rooms that evening) that such a barrier had exceptionally presented itself. He had indeed since that moment undergone an agitation so extraordinary that it might have muddled for him any earlier view; and he tried to convince himself that he might perhaps then have gone into the room and, inadvertently, automatically, on coming out, have drawn the door after him. The difficulty was that this exactly was what he never did; it was against his whole policy, as he might have said, the essence of which was to keep vistas clear. He had them from the first, as he was well aware, quite on the brain: the strange apparition, at the far end of one of them, of his baffled "prey" (which had become by so sharp an irony so little the term now to apply!) was the form of success his imagination had most cherished, projecting into it always a refinement of beauty. He had known fifty times the start of perception that had afterwards dropped; had fifty times gasped to himself "There!" under some fond brief hallucination. The house, as the case stood, admirably lent itself; he might wonder at the taste, the native architecture of the particular time, which could rejoice so in the multiplication of doors—the opposite extreme to the modern, the actual almost complete proscription of them; but it had fairly contributed to provoke this obsession of the presence encountered telescopically, as he might say, focused and studied in diminishing perspective and as by a rest for the elbow.

It was with these considerations that his present attention was charged—they perfectly availed to make what he saw portentous. He *couldn't,* by any lapse, have blocked that aperture; and if he hadn't, if it was unthinkable, why what else was clear but that there had been another agent? Another agent?—he had been catching, as he felt, a moment back, the very breath of him; but when had he been so close as in this simple, this logical, this completely personal act? It was so logical, that is, that one might have *taken* it for personal; yet for what did Brydon take it, he asked himself, while, softly panting, he felt his eyes almost leave their sockets. Ah this time at last they *were,* the two, the opposed projections of him, in presence; and this time, as much as one would, the question of danger loomed. With it rose, as not before, the question of courage—for what he knew the blank face of the door to say to him was "Show us how much you have!" It stared, it glared back at him with that challenge; it put to him the two alternatives: should he just push it open or not? Oh to have this consciousness was to *think*—and to think, Brydon knew, as he stood there, was, with the lapsing moments, not to have acted! Not to have acted—that was the misery and the pang—was even still not to act; was in fact *all* to feel the thing in another, in a new and terrible way. How long did he pause and how long did he debate? There was presently nothing to measure it; for his vibration had already changed—as just by the effect of its intensity. Shut up there, at bay, defiant, and with the prodigy of the thing palpably provably *done,* thus giving notice like some stark signboard—under that accession of accent the situation itself had turned; and Brydon at last remarkably made up his mind on what it had turned to.

It had turned altogether to a different admonition; to a supreme hint, for him, of the value of discretion! This slowly dawned, no doubt—for it could take its time; so perfectly, on his threshold, had he been stayed, so little as yet had he either advanced or retreated. It was the strangest of all things that now when, by his taking ten steps and applying his hand to the latch, or even his shoulder and his knee, if necessary, to a panel, all the hunger of his prime need might have been met, his high curiosity crowned, his unrest assuaged—it was amazing, but it was also exquisite and rare, that insistence should have, at a touch, quite dropped from him. Discretion—he jumped at that; and yet not, verily, at such a pitch, because it saved his nerves or his skin, but because, much more valuably, it saved the situation. When I say he "jumped" at it I feel the consonance of this term with the fact that—at the end indeed of I know not how long—he did move again, he crossed straight to the door. He wouldn't touch it—it seemed now that he might *if* he would: he would only just wait there a little, to show, to prove, that he wouldn't. He had thus another station, close to the thin partition by which revelation was denied him; but with his eyes bent and his hands held off in a mere intensity of stillness. He listened as if there had been something to hear, but this attitude, while it lasted, was his own communication. "If you won't then—good: I spare you and I give up. You affect me as by the appeal positively for pity: you convince me that for reasons rigid and sublime—what do I know?—we both of us should have suffered. I respect them then, and, though moved and privileged as, I believe, it has never been given to man, I retire, I renounce—never, on my honor, to try again. So rest forever—and let *me!*"

That, for Brydon was the deep sense of this last demonstration—solemn, measured, directed, as he felt it to be. He brought it to a close, he turned away; and now verily he knew how deeply he had been stirred. He retraced his steps, taking up his candle, burnt, he observed, well-nigh to the socket, and marking again, lighten it as he would, the distinctness of his footfall; after which, in a moment, he knew himself at the other side of the house. He did here what he had not yet done at these hours—he opened half a casement, one of those in the front, and let in the air of the night; a thing he would have taken at any time previous for a sharp rupture of his spell. His spell was broken now, and it didn't matter—broken by his concession and his surrender, which made it idle henceforth that he should ever come back. The empty street—it's other life so marked even by the great lamplit vacancy—was within call, within touch; he stayed there as to be in it again, high above it though he was still perched; he watched as for some comforting common fact, some vulgar human note, the passage of a scavenger or a thief, some nightbird however base. He would have blessed that sign of life; he would have welcomed positively the slow approach of his friend the policeman, whom he had hitherto only sought to avoid, and was not sure that if the patrol had come into sight he mightn't have felt the impulse to get into relation with it, to hail it, on some pretext, from his fourth floor.

The pretext that wouldn't have been too silly or too compromising, the explanation that would have saved his dignity and kept his name, in such a case, out of the papers, was not definite to him: he was so occupied with the thought of recording his discretion—as an effect of the vow he had just uttered to his intimate adversary—that the importance of this loomed large and something had overtaken all ironically his sense of proportion. If there had been a ladder applied to the front of the house, even one of the vertiginous perpendiculars employed by painters and roofers and sometimes left standing overnight, he would have managed somehow, astride of the windowsill, to compass by outstretched leg and arm that mode of descent. If there had been some such uncanny thing as he had found in his room at hotels, a workable fire-escape in the form of notched cable or a canvas shoot, he would have availed himself of it as a proof—well, of his present delicacy. He nursed that sentiment, as the question stood, a little in vain, and even—at the end of he scarcely knew, once more, how long—found it, as by the action on his mind of the failure of response of the outer world, sinking back to vague anguish. It seemed to him he had waited an age for some stir of the great grim hush; the life of the town was itself under a spell—so unnaturally, up and down the whole prospect of known and rather ugly objects, the blankness and the silence lasted. Had they ever, he asked himself, the hard-faced houses, which had begun to look livid in the dim dawn, had they ever spoken so little to any need of his spirit? Great builded voids, great crowded stillnesses put on, often, in the heart of cities, for the small hours, a sort of sinister mask, and it was of this large collective negation that Brydon presently became conscious—all the more that the break of day was, almost incredibly, now at hand, proving to him what a night he had made of it.

He looked again at his watch, saw what had become of his time values (he had taken hours for minutes—not, as in other tense situations, minutes for hours) and the strange air of the streets was but the weak, the sullen flush of a dawn in which everything was still locked up. His choked appeal from his own open window had been the sole note of life, and he could not break off at last as for a worse despair. Yet while so deeply demoralized he was capable again of an impulse denoting—at least by his present measure—extraordinary resolution; of retracing his steps to the spot where he had turned cold with the extinction of his last pulse of doubt as to there being in the place another presence than his own. This required an effort strong enough to sicken him; but he had his reason, which overmastered for the moment everything else. There was the whole of the rest of the house to traverse, and how should he screw himself to that if the door he had seen closed were at present open? He could hold to the idea that the closing had practically been for him an act of mercy, a chance offered him to descend, depart, get off the ground and never again profane it. This conception held together, it worked; but what it meant for him depended now clearly on the amount of forbearance his recent action, or rather his recent inaction, had engendered. The image of the "presence," whatever it was, waiting there for him to go—this image had not yet been so concrete for his nerves as when he stopped short of the point at which certainty would have come to him. For, with all his resolution, or more exactly with all his dread, he did stop short—he hung back from really seeing. The risk was too great and his fear too definite: it took at this moment an awful specific form.

He knew—yes, as he had never known anything—that, *should* he see the door open, it would all too abjectly be the end of him. It would mean that the agent of his shame—for his shame was the deep abjection—was once more at large and in general possession; and what glared him thus in the face was the act that this would determine for him. It would send him straight about to the window he had left open, and by that window, be long ladder and dangling rope as absent as they would, he saw himself uncontrollably insanely fatally take his way to the street. The hideous chance of this he at least could avert; but he could only avert it by recoiling in time from assurance. He had the whole house to deal with, this fact was still there; only he now knew that uncertainty alone could start him. He stole back from where he had checked himself—merely to do so was suddenly like safety—and, making blindly for the greater staircase, left gaping rooms and sounding passages behind. Here was the top of the stairs, with a fine large dim descent and three spacious landings to mark off. His instinct was all for mildness, but his feet were harsh on the floors, and strangely, when he had in a couple of minutes become aware of this, it counted somehow for help. He couldn't have spoken, the tone of his voice would have scared him, and the common conceit or resource of "whistling in the dark" (whether literally or figuratively) have appeared basely vulgar; yet he liked nonetheless to hear himself go, and when he had reached his first landing—taking it all with no rush, but quite steadily—that stage of success drew from him a gasp of relief.

The house, withal, seemed immense, the scale of space again inordinate; the open rooms, to no one of which his eyes deflected, gloomed in their shuttered state like mouths of caverns; only the high skylight that formed the crown in the deep well created for him a medium in which he could advance, but which might have been, for queerness of color, some watery underworld. He tried to think of something noble, as that his property was really grand, a splendid possession; but this nobleness took the form too of the clear delight with which he was finally to sacrifice it. They might come in now, the builders, the destroyers—they might come as soon as they would. At the end of two flights he had dropped to another zone, and from the middle of the third, with only one more left, he recognized the influence of the lower windows, of half-drawn blinds, of the occasional gleam of street lamps, of the glazed spaces of the vestibule. This was the bottom of the sea, which showed an illumination of its own and which he even saw paved—when at a given moment he drew up to sink a long look over the banisters—with the marble squares of his childhood. By that time indubitably he felt, as he might have said in a commoner cause, better; it had allowed him to stop and draw breath, and the ease increased with the sight of the old black-and-white slabs. But what he most felt was that now surely, with the element of impunity pulling him as by hard firm hands, the case was settled for what he might have seen above had he dared that last look. The closed door, blessedly remote now, was still closed—and he had only in short to reach that of the house.

He came down further, he crossed the passage forming the access to the last flight; and if here again he stopped an instant it was almost for the sharpness of the thrill of assured escape. It made him shut his eyes—which opened again to the straight slope of the remainder of the stairs. Here was impunity still, but impunity almost excessive; inasmuch as the side lights and the high fan tracery of the entrance were glimmering straight into the hall; an appearance produced, he the next instant saw, by the fact that the vestibule gaped wide, that the hinged halves of the inner door had been thrown far back. Out of that again the *question* sprang at him, making his eyes, as he felt, half-start from his head, as they had done, at the top of the house, before the sign of the other door. If he had left that one open, hadn't he left this one closed, and wasn't he now in *most* immediate presence of some inconceivable occult activity? It was as sharp, the question, as a knife in his side, but the answer hung fire still and seemed to lose itself in the vague darkness to which the thin admitted dawn, glimmering archwise over the whole outer door, made a semicircular margin, a cold silvery nimbus that seemed to play a little as he looked —to shift and expand and contract.

It was as if there had been something within it, protected by indistinctness and corresponding in extent with the opaque surface behind, the painted panels of the last barrier to his escape, of which the key was in his pocket. The indistinctness mocked him even while he stared, affected him as somehow shrouding or challenging certitude, so that after faltering an instant on his step he let himself go with the sense that here *was* at last something to meet, to touch, to take, to know—something all unnatural and dreadful, but to advance upon which was the condition for him either of liberation or of supreme defeat. The penumbra, dense and dark, was the virtual screen of a figure which stood in it as still as some image erect in a niche or as some black-vizored sentinel guarding a treasure. Brydon was to know afterwards, was to recall and make out, the particular thing he had believed during the rest of his descent. He saw, in its great gray glimmering margin, the central vagueness diminish, and he felt it to be taking the very form toward which, for so many days, the passion of his curiosity had yearned. It gloomed, it loomed, it was something, it was somebody, the prodigy of a personal presence.

Rigid and conscious, spectral yet human, a man of his own substance and stature waited there to measure himself with his power to dismay. This only could it be—this only till he recognized, with his advance, that what made the face dim was the pair of raised hands that covered it and in which, so far from being offered in defiance, it was buried as for dark deprecation. So Brydon, before him, took him in; with every fact of him now, in the higher light, hard and acute—his planted stillness, his vivid truth, his grizzled bent head and white masking hands, his queer actuality of evening dress, of dangling double eyeglass, of gleaming silk lappet and white linen, of pearl button and gold watch guard and polished shoe. No portrait by a great modern master could have presented him with more intensity, thrust him out of his frame with more art, as if there had been "treatment," of the consummate sort, in his every shade and salience. The revulsion, for our friend, had become, before he knew it, immense—this drop, in the act of apprehension, to the sense of his adversary's inscrutable maneuver. That meaning at least, while he gaped, it offered him; for he could but gape at his other self in this other anguish, gape as a proof that *he,* standing there for the achieved, the enjoyed, the triumphant life, couldn't be faced in his triumph. Wasn't the proof in the splendid covering hands, strong and completely spread?—so spread and so intentional that, in spite of a special verity that surpassed every other, the fact that one of these hands had lost two fingers, which were reduced to stumps, as if accidentally shot away, the face was effectually guarded and saved.

"Saved," though, *would* it be?—Brydon breathed his wonder till the very impunity of his attitude and the very insistence of his eyes produced, as he felt, a sudden stir which showed the next instant as a deeper portent, which the head raised itself, the betrayal of a braver purpose. The hands, as he looked, began to move, to open; then, as if deciding in a flash, dropped from the face and left it uncovered and presented. Horror, with the sight, had leaped into Brydon's throat, gasping there in a sound he couldn't utter; for the bared identity was too hideous as *his,* and his glare was the passion of his protest. The face, *that* face, Spencer Brydon's?—he searched it still, but looking away from it in dismay and denial, falling straight from his height of sublimity. It was unknown, inconceivable, awful, disconnected from any possibility—! He had been "sold," he inwardly moaned, stalking such game as this: the presence before him was a presence, the horror within him a horror, but the waste of his nights had been only grotesque and the success of his adventure an irony. Such an identity fitted his at *no* point, made its alternative monstrous. A thousand times yes, as it came upon him nearer now—the face was the face of a stranger. It came upon him nearer now, quite as one of those expanding fantastic images projected by the magic lantern of childhood; for the stranger, whoever he might be, evil, odious, blatant, vulgar, had advanced as for aggression, and he knew himself give ground. Then harder pressed still, sick with the force of his shock, and falling back as under the hot breath and the roused passion of a life larger than his own, a rage of personality before which his own collapsed, he felt the whole vision turn to darkness and his very feet give way. His head went round; he was going; he had gone.

III

What had next brought him back, clearly—though after how long?—was Mrs. Muldoon's voice, coming to him from quite near, from so near that he seemed presently to see her as kneeling on the ground before him while he lay looking up at her; himself not wholly on the ground, but half-raised and upheld—conscious, yes, of tenderness of support and, more particularly, of a head pillowed in extraordinary softness and faintly refreshing fragrance. He considered, he wondered, his wit but half at his service; then another face intervened, bending more directly over him, and he finally knew that Alice Staverton had made her lap an ample and perfect cushion to him, and that she had to this end seated herself on the lowest degree of the staircase, the rest of his long person remaining stretched on his old black-and-white slabs. They were cold, these marble squares of his youth; but *he* somehow was not, in this rich return of consciousness—the most wonderful hour, little by little, that he had ever known, leaving him, as it did, so gratefully, so abysmally passive, and yet as with a treasure of intelligence waiting all round him for quiet appropriation; dissolved, he might call it, in the air of the place and producing the golden glow of a late autumn afternoon. He had come back, yes—come back from further away than any man but himself had ever traveled; but it was strange how with this sense what he had come back *to* seemed really the great thing, and as if his prodigious journey had been all for the sake of it. Slowly but surely his consciousness grew, his vision of his state thus completing itself: he had been miraculously *carried* back—lifted and carefully borne as from where he had been picked up, the uttermost end of an interminable gray passage. Even with this he was suffered to rest, and what had now brought him to knowledge was the break in the long mild motion.

It had brought him to knowledge, to knowledge—yes, this was the beauty of his state; which came to resemble more and more that of a man who has gone to sleep on some news of a great inheritance, and then, after dreaming it away, after profaning it with matters strange to it, has waked up again to serenity of certitude and has only to lie and watch it grow. This was the drift of his patience—that he had only to let it shine on him. He must moreover, with intermissions, still have been lifted and borne; since why and how else should he have known himself, later on, with the afternoon glow intenser, no longer at the foot of his stairs—situated as these now seemed at that dark other end of his tunnel—but on a deep windowbench of his high saloon, over which had been spread, couch fashion, a mantle of soft stuff lined with gray fur that was familiar to his eyes and that one of his hands kept fondly feeling as for its pledge of truth. Mrs. Muldoon's face had gone, but the other, the second he had recognized, hung over him in a way that showed how he was still propped and pillowed. He took it all in, and the more he took it the more it seemed to suffice: he was as much at peace as if he had had food and drink. It was the two women who had found him, on Mrs. Muldoon's having plied, at her usual hour, her latchkey—and on her having above all arrived while Miss Staverton still lingered near the house. She had been turning away, all anxiety, from worrying the vain bell-handle—her calculation having been of the hour of the good woman's visit; but the latter, blessedly, had come up while she was still there, and they had entered together. He had then lain, beyond the vestibule, very much as he was lying now—quite, that is, as he appeared to have fallen, but all so wondrously without bruise or gash; only in a depth of stupor. What he most took in, however, at present, with the steadier clearance, was that Alice Staverton had for a long unspeakable moment not doubted he was dead.

"It must have been that I *was.*" He made it out as she held him. "Yes—I can only have died. You brought me literally to life. Only," he wondered, his eyes rising to her, "only, in the name of all the benedictions, how?"

It took her but an instant to bend her face and kiss him, and something in the manner of it, and in the way her hands clasped and locked his head while he felt the cool charity and virtue of her lips, something in all this beatitude somehow answered everything. "And now I keep you," she said.

"Oh keep me, keep me!" he pleaded while her face still hung over him: in response to which it dropped again and stayed close, clingingly close. It was the seal of their situation—of which he tasted the impress for a long blissful moment in silence. But he came back. "Yet how did you know—?"

"I was uneasy. You were to have come, you remember—and you had sent no word."

"Yes, I remember—I was to have gone to you at one today." It caught on to their "old" life and relation—which were so near and so far. "I was still out there in my strange darkness—where was it, what was it? I must have stayed there so long." He could but wonder at the depth and the duration of his swoon.

"Since last night?" she asked with a shade of fear for her possible indiscretion.

"Since this morning—it must have been; the cold dim dawn of today. Where have I been," he vaguely wailed, "where have I been?" He felt her hold him close, and it was if this helped him now to make in all security his mild moan. "What a long dark day!"

All in her tenderness she had waited a moment. "In the cold dim dawn?" she quavered.

But he had already gone on piecing together the parts of the whole prodigy. "As I didn't turn up you came straight—?"

She barely cast about. "I went first to your hotel—where they told me of your absence. You had dined out last evening and hadn't been back since. But they appeared to know you had been at your club."

"So you had the idea of *this—?*"

"Of what?" she asked in a moment.

"Well—of what has happened."

"I believed at least you'd have been here. I've known, all along," she said, "that you've been coming."

"'Known' it—?"

"Well, I've believed it. I said nothing to you after that talk we had a month ago—but I felt sure. I knew you *would,*" she declared.

"That I'd persist, you mean?"

"That you'd see him."

"Ah, but I didn't!" cried Brydon with his long wail. "There's somebody—an awful beast; whom I brought, too horribly, to bay. But it's not me."

At this she bent over him again, and her eyes were in his eyes. "No—it's not you." And it was as if, while her face hovered, he might have made out in it, hadn't it been so near, some particular meaning blurred by a smile. "No, thank heaven," she repeated—"it's not you! Of course it wasn't to have been."

"Ah but it *was,*" he gently insisted. And he stared before him now as he had been staring for so many weeks. "I was to have known myself."

"You couldn't!" she returned consolingly. And then reverting, and as if to account further for what she had herself done, "But it wasn't only *that,* that you hadn't been at home," she went on. "I waited till the hour at which we had found Mrs. Muldoon that day of my going with you; and she arrived, as I've told you, while, failing to bring anyone to the door, I lingered in my despair on the steps. After a little, if she hadn't come, by such a mercy, I should have found means to hunt her up. But it wasn't," said Alice Staverton, as if once more with her fine intention—"it wasn't only that."

His eyes, as he lay, turned back to her. "What more then?"

She met it, the wonder she had stirred. "In the cold dim dawn, you say? Well, in the cold dim dawn of this morning I too saw you."

"Saw *me—?*"

"Saw *him,*" said Alice Staverton. "It must have been at the same moment."

He lay an instant taking it in—as if he wished to be quite reasonable. "At the same moment?"

"Yes—in my dream again, the same one I've named to you. He came back to me. Then I knew it for a sign. He had come to you."

At this Brydon raised himself; he had to see her better. She helped him when she understood his movement, and he sat up, steadying himself beside her there on the windowbench and with his right hand grasping her left. "*He* didn't come to me."

"You came to yourself," she beautifully smiled.

"Ah, I've come to myself now—thanks to you, dearest. But this brute, with his awful face—this brute's a black stranger. He's none of *me,* even as I *might* have been," Brydon sturdily declared.

But she kept the clearness that was like the breath of infallibility. "Isn't the whole point that you'd have been different?"

He almost scowled for it. "As different as *that—?"*

Her look again was more beautiful to him than the things of this world. "Haven't you exactly wanted to know *how* different? So this morning," she said, "you appeared to me."

"Like *him?"*

"A black stranger!"

"Then how did you know it was I?"

"Because, as I told you weeks ago, my mind, my imagination, had worked so over what you might, what you mightn't have been—to show you, you see, how I've thought of you. In the midst of that you came to me—that my wonder might be answered. So I knew," she went on; "and believed that, since the question held you too so fast, as you told me that day, you too would see for yourself. And when this morning I again saw I knew it would be because you had—and also then, from the first moment, because you somehow wanted me. *He* seemed to tell me of that. So why," she strangely smiled, "shouldn't I like him?"

It brought Spencer Brydon to his feet. "You 'like' that horror—?"

"I *could* have liked him. And to me," she said, "he was no horror. I had accepted him."

" 'Accepted'—?" Brydon oddly sounded.

"Before, for the interest of his difference—yes. And as *I* didn't disown him, as *I* knew him—which you at last, confronted with him in his difference, so cruelly didn't, my dear—well, he must have been, you see, less dreadful to me. And it may have pleased him that I pitied him."

She was beside him on her feet, but still holding his hand—still with her arm supporting him. But though it all brought for him thus a dim light, "You 'pitied' him?" he grudgingly, resentfully asked.

"He has been unhappy; he has been ravaged," she said.

"And haven't I been unhappy? Am not I—you've only to look at me!—ravaged?"

"Ah I don't say I like him *better,"* she granted after a thought. "But he's grim, he's worn—and things have happened to him. He doesn't make shift, for sight, with your charming monocle."

"No"—it struck Brydon: "I couldn't have sported mine 'downtown.' They'd have guyed me there."

"His great convex pince-nez—I saw it, I recognized the kind—is for his poor ruined sight. And his poor right hand—!"

"Ah!" Brydon winced—whether for his proved identity or for his lost fingers. Then, "He has a million a year," he lucidly added. "But he hasn't you."

"And he isn't—no, he isn't—*you!*" she murmured as he drew her to his breast.

The Mezzotint

M. R. JAMES

[1862–1936]

Born in Kent, England, M. R. James was a distinguished medieval scholar as well as Provost at King's College and Eton. He is, however, chiefly remembered today for his understated but insidiously effective ghost stories. In the thirty-three years during which he wrote supernatural fiction, James produced a body of work singular in both style and accomplishment. Stories such as "Count Magnus," "An Episode of Cathedral History," *and our selection,* "The Mezzotint," *have kept James a favorite among fans of the genre for almost a century.*

Some time ago I believe I had the pleasure of telling you the story of an adventure which happened to a friend of mine by the name of Dennistoun, during his pursuit of objects of art for the museum at Cambridge.

He did not publish his experiences very widely upon his return to England; but they could not fail to become known to a good many of his friends, and among others to the gentleman who at that time presided over an art museum at another University. It was to be expected that the story should make a considerable impression on the mind of a man whose vocation lay in lines similar to Dennistoun's, and that he should be eager to catch at any explanation of the matter which tended to make it seem improbable that he should ever be called upon to deal with so agitating an emergency. It was, indeed, somewhat consoling to him to reflect that he was not expected to acquire ancient MSS. for his institution; that was the business of the Shelburnian Library. The authorities of that might, if they pleased, ransack obscure corners of the Continent for such matters. He was glad to be obliged at the moment to confine his attention to enlarging the already unsurpassed collection of English topographical drawings and engravings possessed by his museum. Yet, as it turned out, even a department so homely and familiar as this may have its dark corners, and to one of these Mr. Williams was unexpectedly introduced.

Those who have taken even the most limited interest in the acquisition of topographical pictures are aware that there is one London dealer whose aid is indispensable to their researchers. Mr. J. W. Britnell publishes at short intervals very admirable catalogues of a large and constantly changing stock of engravings, plans, and old sketches of mansions, churches, and towns in England and Wales. These catalogues were, of course, the ABC of his subject to Mr. Williams: but as his museum already contained an enormous accumulation of topographical pictures, he was a regular, rather than a copious, buyer; and he rather looked to Mr. Britnell to fill up gaps in the rank and file of his collection than to supply him with rarities.

Now, in February of last year there appeared upon Mr. Williams's desk at the museum a catalogue from Mr. Britnell's emporium, and accompanying it was a typewritten communication from the dealer himself. This latter ran as follows:

Dear Sir,—

We beg to call your attention to No. 978 in our accompanying catalogue, which we shall be glad to send on approval.

Yours faithfully,
J. W. Britnell.

To turn to No. 978 in the accompanying catalogue was with Mr. Williams (as he observed to himself) the work of a moment, and in the place indicated he found the following entry:

"978.—*Unknown.* Interesting mezzotint: View of a manor-house, early part of the century. 15 by 10 inches; black frame. £2 2*s.*"

It was not specially exciting, and the price seemed high. However, as Mr. Britnell, who knew his business and his customer, seemed to set store by it, Mr. Williams wrote a postcard asking for the article to be sent on approval, along with some other engravings and sketches which appeared in the same catalogue. And so he passed without much excitement of anticipation to the ordinary labours of the day.

A parcel of any kind always arrives a day later than you expect it, and that of Mr. Britnell proved, as I believe the right phrase goes, no exception to the rule. It was delivered at the museum by the afternoon post of Saturday, after Mr. Williams had left his work, and it was accordingly brought round to his rooms in college by the attendant, in order that he might not have to wait over Sunday before looking through it and returning such of the contents as he did not propose to keep. And here he found it when he came in to tea, with a friend.

The only item with which I am concerned was the rather large, black-framed mezzotint of which I have already quoted the short description given in Mr. Britnell's catalogue. Some more details of it will have to be given, though I cannot hope to put before you the look of the picture as clearly as it is present to my own eye. Very nearly the exact duplicate of it may be seen in a good many old inn parlours, or in the passages of undisturbed country mansions at the present moment. It was a rather indifferent mezzotint, and an indifferent mezzotint is, perhaps, the worst form of engraving known. It presented a full-face view of a not very large manor-house of the last century, with three rows of plain sashed windows with rusticated masonry about them, a parapet with balls or vases at the angles, and a small portico in the centre. On either side were trees, and in front a considerable expanse of lawn. The legend "A.W.F. sculpsit" was engraved on the narrow margin; and there was no further inscription. The whole thing gave the impression that it was the work of an amateur. What in the world Mr. Britnell could mean by affixing the price of £2 2*s.* to such an object was more than Mr. Williams could imagine. He turned it over with a good deal of contempt; upon the back was a paper label, the left-hand half of which had been torn off. All that remained were the ends of two lines of writing: the first had the letters *—ngley Hall;* the second, *—ssex.*

It would, perhaps, be just worth while to identify the place represented, which he could easily do with the help of a gazetteer, and then he would send it back to Mr. Britnell, with some remarks reflecting upon the judgment of that gentleman.

He lighted the candles, for it was now dark, made the tea, and supplied the friend with whom he had been playing golf (for I believe the authorities of the University I write of indulge in that pursuit by way of relaxation); and tea was taken to the accompaniment of a discussion which golfing persons can imagine for themselves, but which the conscientious writer has no right to inflict upon any non-golfing persons.

The conclusion arrived at was that certain strokes might have been better, and that in certain emergencies neither player had experienced that amount of luck which a human being has a right to expect. It was now that the friend—let us call him Professor Binks—took up the framed engraving, and said:

"What's this place, Williams?"

"Just what I am going to try to find out," said Williams, going to the shelf for a gazetteer. "Look at the back. Somethingley Hall, either in Sussex or Essex. Half the name's gone, you see. You don't happen to know it, I suppose?"

"It's from that man Britnell, I suppose, isn't it?" said Binks. "Is it for the museum?"

"Well, I think I should buy it if the price was five shillings," said Williams; "but for some unearthly reason he wants two guineas for it. I can't conceive why. It's a wretched engraving, and there aren't even any figures to give it life."

"It's not worth two guineas, I should think," said Binks; "but I don't think it's so badly done. The moonlight seems rather good to me; and I should have thought there *were* figures, or at least a figure, just on the edge in front."

"Let's look," said Williams. "Well, it's true the light is rather cleverly given. Where's your figure? Oh yes! Just the head, in the very front of the picture."

And indeed there was—hardly more than a black blot on the extreme edge of the engraving—the head of a man or woman, a good deal muffled up, the back turned to the spectator, and looking towards the house.

Williams had not noticed it before.

"Still," he said, "though it's a cleverer thing than I thought, I can't spend two guineas of museum money on a picture of a place I don't know."

Professor Binks had his work to do, and soon went; and very nearly up to Hall time Williams was engaged in a vain attempt to identify the subject of his picture. "If the vowel before the *ng* had only been left, it would have been easy enough," he thought; "but as it is, the name may be anything from Guestingley to Langley, and there are many more names ending like this than I thought; and this rotten book has no index of terminations."

Hall in Mr. Williams's college was at seven. It need not be dwelt upon; the less so as he met there colleagues who had been playing golf during the afternoon, and words with which we have no concern were freely bandied across the table—merely golfing words, I would hasten to explain.

I suppose an hour or more to have been spent in what is called common-room after dinner. Later in the evening some few retired to Williams's rooms, and I have little doubt that whist was played and tobacco smoked. During a lull in these operations Williams picked up the mezzotint from the table without looking at it, and handed it to a person mildly interested in art, telling him where it had come from, and the other particulars which we already know.

The gentleman took it carelessly, looked at it, then said, in a tone of some interest:

"It's really a very good piece of work, Williams; it has quite a feeling of the romantic period. The light is admirably managed, it seems to me, and the figure, though it's rather too grotesque, is somehow very impressive."

"Yes, isn't it?" said Williams, who was just then busy giving whisky-and-soda to others of the company, and was unable to come across the room to look at the view again.

It was by this time rather late in the evening, and the visitors were on the move. After they went Williams was obliged to write a letter or two and clear up some odd bits of work. At last, some time past midnight, he was disposed to turn in, and he put out his lamp after lighting his bedroom candle. The picture lay face upwards on the table where the last man who looked at it had put it, and it caught his eye as he turned the lamp down. What he saw made him very nearly drop the candle on the floor, and he declares now that if he had been left in the dark at that moment he would have had a fit. But, as that did not happen, he was able to put down the light on the table and take a good look at the picture. It was indubitable—rankly impossible, no doubt, but absolutely certain. In the middle of the lawn in front of the unknown house there was a figure where no figure had been at five o'clock that afternoon. It was crawling on all-fours towards the house, and it was muffled in a strange black garment with a white cross on the back.

I do not know what is the ideal course to pursue in a situation of this kind. I can only tell you what Mr. Williams did. He took the picture by one corner and carried it across the passage to a second set of rooms which he possessed. There he locked it up in a drawer, sported the doors of both sets of rooms, and retired to bed; but first he wrote out and signed an account of the extraordinary change which the picture had undergone since it had come into his possession.

Sleep visited him rather late; but it was consoling to reflect that the behaviour of the picture did not depend upon his own unsupported testimony. Evidently the man who had looked at it the night before had seen something of the same kind as he had, otherwise he might have been tempted to think that something gravely wrong was happening either to his eyes or his mind. This possibility being fortunately precluded, two matters awaited him on the morrow. He must take stock of the picture very carefully, and call in a witness for the purpose, and he must make a determined effort to ascertain what house it was that was represented. He would therefore ask his neighbour Nisbet to breakfast with him, and he would subsequently spend a morning over the gazetteer.

Nisbet was disengaged, and arrived about 9:30. His host was not quite dressed, I am sorry to say, even at this late hour. During breakfast nothing was said about the mezzotint by Williams, save that he had a picture on which he wished for Nisbet's opinion. But those who are familiar with University life can picture for themselves the wide and delightful range of subjects over which the conversation of two Fellows of Canterbury College is likely to extend during a Sunday morning breakfast. Hardly a topic was left unchallenged, from golf to lawn-tennis. Yet I am bound to say that Williams was rather distraught; for his interest naturally centred in that very strange picture which was now reposing, face downwards, in the drawer in the room opposite.

The morning pipe was at last lighted, and the moment had arrived for which he looked. With very considerable—almost tremulous—excitement, he ran across, unlocked the drawer, and, extracting the picture—still face downwards—ran back, and put it into Nisbet's hands.

"Now," he said, "Nisbet, I want you to tell me exactly what you see in that picture. Describe it, if you don't mind, rather minutely. I'll tell you why afterwards."

"Well," said Nisbet, "I have here a view of a country-house—English, I presume—by moonlight."

"Moonlight? You're sure of that?"

"Certainly. The moon appears to be on the wane, if you wish for details, and there are clouds in the sky."

"All right. Go on. I'll swear," added Williams in an aside, "there was no moon when I saw it first."

"Well, there's not much more to be said," Nisbet continued. "The house has one—two—three rows of windows, five in each row, except at the bottom, where there's a porch instead of the middle one, and—"

"But what about figures?" said Williams, with marked interest.

"There aren't any," said Nisbet; "but—"

"What! No figure on the grass in front?"

"Not a thing."

"You'll swear to that?"

"Certainly I will. But there's just one other thing."

"What?"

"Why, one of the windows on the ground-floor—left of the door —is open."

"Is it really? My goodness! he must have got in," said Williams, with great excitement; and he hurried to the back of the sofa on which Nisbet was sitting, and, catching the picture from him, verified the matter for himself.

It was quite true. There was no figure, and there was the open window. Williams, after a moment of speechless surprise, went to the writing-table and scribbled for a short time. Then he brought two papers to Nisbet, and asked him first to sign one—it was his own description of the picture, which you have just heard—and then to read the other which was Williams's statement written the night before.

"What can it all mean?" said Nisbet.

"Exactly," said Williams. "Well, one thing I must do—or three things, now I think of it. I must find out from Garwood"—this was his last night's visitor—"what he saw, and then I must get the thing photographed before it goes further, and then I must find out what the place is."

"I can do the photographing myself," said Nisbet, "and I will. But, you know, it looks very much as if we were assisting at the working out of a tragedy somewhere. The question is, Has it happened already, or is it going to come off? You must find out what the place is. Yes," he said, looking at the picture again, "I expect you're right: he has got in. And if I don't mistake there'll be the devil to pay in one of the rooms upstairs."

"I'll tell you what," said Williams: "I'll take the picture across to old Green" (this was the senior Fellow of the College, who had been Bursar for many years). "It's quite likely he'll know it. We have property in Essex and Sussex, and he must have been over the two counties a lot in his time."

"Quite likely he will," said Nisbet; "but just let me take my photograph first. But look here, I rather think Green isn't up to-day. He wasn't in Hall last night, and I think I heard him say he was going down for the Sunday."

"That's true, too," said Williams; "I know he's gone to Brighton. Well, if you'll photograph it now, I'll go across to Garwood and get his statement, and you keep an eye on it while I'm gone. I'm beginning to think two guineas is not a very exorbitant price for it now."

In a short time he had returned, and brought Mr. Garwood with him. Garwood's statement was to the effect that the figure, when he had seen it, was clear of the edge of the picture, but had not got far across the lawn. He remembered a white mark on the back of its drapery, but could not have been sure it was a cross. A document to this effect was then drawn up and signed, and Nisbet proceeded to photograph the picture.

"Now what do you mean to do?" he said. "Are you going to sit and watch it all day?"

"Well, no, I think not," said Williams. "I rather imagine we're meant to see the whole thing. You see, between the time I saw it last night and this morning there was time for lots of things to happen, but the creature only got into the house. It could easily have got through its business in the time and gone to its own place again; but the fact of the window being open, I think, must mean that it's in there now. So I feel quite easy about leaving it. And, besides, I have a kind of idea that it wouldn't change much, if at all, in the daytime. We might go out for a walk this afternoon, and come in to tea, or whenever it gets dark. I shall leave it out on the table here, and sport the door. My skip can get in, but no one else."

The three agreed that this would be a good plan; and, further, that if they spent the afternoon together they would be less likely to talk about the business to other people; for any rumour of such a transaction as was going on would bring the whole of the Phasmatological Society about their ears.

We may give them a respite until five o'clock.

At or near that hour the three were entering Williams's staircase: They were at first slightly annoyed to see that the door of his rooms was unsported; but in a moment it was remembered that on Sunday the skips came for orders an hour or so earlier than on week-days. However, a surprise was awaiting them. The first thing they saw was the picture leaning up against a pile of books on the table, as it had been left, and the next thing was Williams's skip, seated on a chair opposite, gazing at it with undisguised horror. How was this? Mr. Filcher (the name is not my own invention) was a servant of considerable standing, and set the standard of etiquette to all his own college and to several neighbouring ones, and nothing could be more alien to his practice than to be found sitting on his master's chair, or appearing to take any particular notice of his master's furniture or pictures. Indeed, he seemed to feel this himself. He started violently when the three men came into the room, and got up with a marked effort. Then he said:

"I ask your pardon, sir, for taking such a freedom as to set down."

"Not at all, Robert," interposed Mr. Williams. "I was meaning to ask you some time what you thought of that picture."

"Well, sir, of course I don't set up my opinion again yours, but it ain't the pictur I should 'ang where my little girl could see it, sir."

"Wouldn't you, Robert? Why not?"

"No, sir. Why, the pore child, I recollect once she see a Door Bible, with pictures not 'alf what that is, and we 'ad to set up with her three or four nights afterwards, if you'll believe me; and if she was to ketch a sight of this skelinton here, or whatever it is, carrying off the pore baby, she would be in a taking. You know 'ow it is with children; 'ow nervish they git with a little thing and all. But what I should say, it don't seem a right pictur to be laying about, sir, not where anyone that's liable to be startled could come on it. Should you be wanting anything this evening, sir? Thank you, sir."

With these words the excellent man went to continue the round of his masters, and you may be sure the gentlemen whom he left lost no time in gathering round the engraving. There was the house, as before, under the waning moon and the drifting clouds. The window that had been open was shut, and the figure was once more on the lawn: but not this time crawling cautiously on hands and knees. Now it was erect and stepping swiftly, with long strides, towards the front of the picture. The moon was behind it, and the black drapery hung down over its face so that only hints of that could be seen, and what was visible made the spectators profoundly thankful that they could see no more than a white dome-like forehead and a few straggling hairs. The head was bent down, and the arms were tightly clasped over an object which could be dimly seen and identified as a child, whether dead or living it was not possible to say. The legs of the appearance alone could be plainly discerned, and they were horribly thin.

From five to seven the three companions sat and watched the picture by turns. But it never changed. They agreed at last that it would be safe to leave it, and that they would return after Hall and await further developments.

When they assembled again, at the earliest possible moment, the engraving was there, but the figure was gone, and the house was quiet under the moonbeams. There was nothing for it but to spend the evening over gazetteers and guide-books. Williams was the lucky one at last, and perhaps he deserved it. At 11:30 P.M. he read from Murray's *Guide to Essex* the following lines:

"16½ miles, *Anningley.* The church has been an interesting building of Norman date, but was extensively classicized in the last century. It contains the tombs of the family of Francis, whose mansion, Anningley Hall, a solid Queen Anne house, stands immediately beyond the churchyard in a park of about 80 acres. The family is now extinct, the last heir having disappeared mysteriously in infancy in the year 1802. The father, Mr. Arthur Francis, was locally known as a talented amateur engraver in mezzotint. After his son's disappearance he lived in complete retirement at the Hall, and was found dead in his studio on the third anniversary of the disaster, having just completed an engraving of the house, impressions of which are of considerable rarity."

This looked like business, and, indeed, Mr. Green on his return at once identified the house as Anningley Hall.

"Is there any kind of explanation of the figure, Green?" was the question which Williams naturally asked.

"I don't know, I'm sure, Williams. What used to be said in the place when I first knew it, which was before I came up here, was just this: old Francis was always very much down on these poaching fellows, and whenever he got a chance he used to get a man whom he suspected of it turned off the estate, and by degrees he got rid of them all but one. Squires could do a lot of things then that they daren't think of now. Well, this man that was left was what you find pretty often in that country—the last remains of a very old family.

I believe they were Lords of the Manor at one time. I recollect just the same thing in my own parish."

"What, like the man in *Tess of the D'Urbervilles?*" Williams put in.

"Yes, I dare say; it's not a book I could ever read myself. But this fellow could show a row of tombs in the church there that belonged to his ancestors, and all that went to sour him a bit; but Francis, they said, could never get at him—he always kept just on the right side of the law—until one night the keepers found him at it in a wood right at the end of the estate. I could show you the place now; it marches with some land that used to belong to an uncle of mine. And you can imagine there was a row; and this man Gawdy (that was the name, to be sure—Gawdy; I thought I should get it—Gawdy), he was unlucky enough, poor chap! to shoot a keeper. Well, that was what Francis wanted, and grand juries—you know what they would have been then—and poor Gawdy was strung up in double-quick time; and I've been shown the place he was buried in, on the north side of the church—you know the way in that part of the world: anyone that's been hanged or made away with themselves, they bury them that side. And the idea was that some friend of Gawdy's—not a relation, because he had none, poor devil! he was the last of his line: kind of *spes ultima gentis*—must have planned to get hold of Francis's boy and put an end to *his* line, too. I don't know—it's rather an out-of-the-way thing for an Essex poacher to think of—but, you know, I should say now it looks more as if old Gawdy had managed the job himself. Booh! I hate to think of it! have some whisky, Williams!"

The facts were communicated by Williams to Dennistoun, and by him to a mixed company, of which I was one, and the Sadducean Professor of Ophiology another. I am sorry to say that the latter, when asked what he thought of it, only remarked: "Oh, those Bridgeford people will say anything"—a sentiment which met with the reception it deserved.

I have only to add that the picture is now in the Ashleian Museum; that it has been treated with a view to discovering whether sympathetic ink has been used in it, but without effect; that Mr. Britnell knew nothing of it save that he was sure it was uncommon; and that, though carefully watched, it has never been known to change again.

The Monkey's Paw

W. W. JACOBS

[1863–1943]

Had he written nothing else, W. W. Jacobs would be immortalized for "The Monkey's Paw." *And justly so; it is one of the best-known of all stories, ghostly or otherwise. Jacobs did, in fact, publish several works —mostly collections of sea stories—around the turn of the century. None, however, match the elemental force of* "The Monkey's Paw." *The manner in which Jacobs takes the mundane, fairy-tale concept of the three wishes and places it in a sinister new light is one of the most brilliant twists ever put on paper.*

I

Without, the night was cold and wet, but in the small parlour of Laburnum Villa the blinds were drawn and the fire burned brightly. Father and son were at chess; the former, who possessed ideas about the game involving radical changes, putting his king into such sharp and unnecessary perils that it even provoked comment from the white-haired old lady knitting placidly by the fire.

"Hark at the wind," said Mr. White, who, having seen a fatal mistake after it was too late, was amiably desirous of preventing his son from seeing it.

"I'm listening," said the latter, grimly surveying the board as he stretched out his hand. "Check."

"I should hardly think that he'd come to-night," said his father, with his hand poised over the board.

"Mate," replied the son.

"That's the worst of living so far out," bawled Mr. White, with sudden and unlooked-for violence; "of all the beastly, slushy, out-of-the-way places to live in, this is the worst. Path's a bog, and the road's a torrent. I don't know what people are thinking about. I suppose because only two houses in the road are let, they think it doesn't matter."

"Never mind, dear," said his wife soothingly; "perhaps you'll win the next one."

Mr. White looked up sharply, just in time to intercept a knowing glance between mother and son. The words died away on his lips, and he hid a guilty grin in his thin gray beard.

"There he is," said Herbert White, as the gate banged to loudly and heavy footsteps came toward the door.

The old man rose with hospitable haste, and opening the door, was heard condoling with the new arrival. The new arrival also condoled with himself, so that Mrs. White said, "Tut tut!" and coughed gently as her husband entered the room, followed by a tall, burly man, beady of eye and rubicund of visage.

"Sergeant-Major Morris," he said, introducing him.

The sergeant-major shook hands, and taking the proffered seat by the fire, watched contentedly while his host got out whisky and tumblers and stood a small copper kettle on the fire.

At the third glass his eyes got brighter, and he began to talk, the little family circle regarding with eager interest this visitor from distant parts, as he squared his broad shoulders in the chair, and spoke of wild scenes and doughty deeds; of wars and plagues, and strange peoples.

"Twenty-one years of it," said Mr. White, nodding at his wife and son. "When he went away he was a slip of a youth in the warehouse. Now look at him."

"He don't look to have taken much harm," said Mrs. White politely.

"I'd like to go to India myself," said the old man, "just to look around a bit, you know."

"Better where you are," said the sergeant-major, shaking his head. He put down the empty glass, and sighing softly, shook it again.

"I should like to see those old temples and fakirs and jugglers," said the old man. "What was that you started telling me the other day about a monkey's paw or something, Morris?"

"Nothing," said the soldier hastily. "Leastways nothing worth hearing."

"Monkey's paw?" said Mrs. White curiously.

"Well, it's just a bit of what you might call magic, perhaps," said the sergeant-major off-handedly.

His three listeners leaned forward eagerly. The visitor absent-mindedly put his empty glass to his lips and then set it down again. His host filled it for him.

"To look at," said the sergeant-major, fumbling in his pocket, "it's just an ordinary little paw, dried to a mummy."

He took something out of his pocket and proffered it. Mrs. White drew back with a grimace, but her son, taking it, examined it curiously.

"And what is there special about it?" inquired Mr. White as he took it from his son, and having examined it, placed it upon the table.

"It had a spell put on it by an old fakir," said the sergeant-major, "a very holy man. He wanted to show that fate ruled people's lives, and that those who interfered with it did so to their sorrow. He put a spell on it so that three separate men could each have three wishes from it."

His manner was so impressive that his hearers were conscious that their light laughter jarred somewhat.

"Well, why don't you have three, sir?" said Herbert White cleverly.

The soldier regarded him in the way that middle age is wont to regard presumptuous youth. "I have," he said quietly, and his blotchy face whitened.

"And did you really have the three wishes granted?" asked Mrs. White.

"I did," said the sergeant-major, and his glass tapped against his strong teeth.

"And has anybody else wished?" persisted the old lady.

"The first man had his three wishes. Yes," was the reply; "I don't know what the first two were, but the third was for death. That's how I got the paw."

His tones were so grave that a hush fell upon the group.

"If you've had your three wishes, it's no good to you now then, Morris," said the old man at last. "What do you keep it for?"

The soldier shook his head. "Fancy, I suppose," he said slowly. "I did have some idea of selling it, but I don't think I will. It has caused enough mischief already. Besides, people won't buy. They think it's a fairy tale, some of them; and those who do think anything of it want to try it first and pay me afterward."

"If you could have another three wishes," said the old man, eyeing him keenly, "would you have them?"

"I don't know," said the other. "I don't know."

He took the paw, and dangling it between his forefinger and thumb, suddenly threw it upon the fire. White, with a slight cry, stooped down and snatched it off.

"Better let it burn," said the soldier solemnly.

"If you don't want it, Morris," said the other, "give it to me."

"I won't," said his friend doggedly. "I threw it on the fire. If you keep it, don't blame me for what happens. Pitch it on the fire again like a sensible man."

The other shook his head and examined his new possession closely. "How do you do it?" he inquired.

"Hold it up in your right hand and wish aloud," said the sergeant-major, "but I warn you of the consequences."

"Sounds like the *Arabian Nights,*" said Mrs. White, as she rose and began to set the supper. "Don't you think you might wish for four pairs of hands for me?"

Her husband drew the talisman from his pocket, and then all three burst into laughter as the sergeant-major, with a look of alarm on his face, caught him by the arm.

"If you must wish," he said gruffly, "wish for something sensible."

Mr. White dropped it back in his pocket, and placing chairs, motioned his friend to the table. In the business of supper the talisman was partly forgotten, and afterward the three sat listening in an enthralled fashion to a second installment of the soldier's adventures in India.

"If the tale about the monkey's paw is not more truthful than those he has been telling us," said Herbert, as the door closed behind their guest, just in time to catch the last train, "we shan't make much out of it."

"Did you give him anything for it, father?" inquired Mrs. White, regarding her husband closely.

"A trifle," said he, colouring slightly. "He didn't want it, but I made him take it. And he pressed me again to throw it away."

"Likely," said Herbert, with pretended horror. "Why, we're going to be rich, and famous, and happy. Wish to be an emperor, father, to begin with; then you can't be henpecked."

He darted round the table, pursued by the maligned Mrs. White armed with an antimacassar.

Mr. White took the paw from his pocket and eyed it dubiously.

"I don't know what to wish for, and that's a fact," he said slowly. "It seems to me I've got all I want."

"If you only cleared the house, you'd be quite happy, wouldn't you!" said Herbert, with his hand on his shoulder. "Well, wish for two hundred pounds, then; that'll just do it."

His father, smiling shamefacedly at his own credulity, held up the talisman, as his son, with a solemn face, somewhat marred by a wink at his mother, sat down at the piano and struck a few impressive chords.

"I wish for two hundred pounds," said the old man distinctly.

A fine crash from the piano greeted the words, interrupted by a shuddering cry from the old man. His wife and son ran toward him.

"It moved," he cried, with a glance of disgust at the object as it lay on the floor. "As I wished, it twisted in my hand like a snake."

"Well, I don't see the money," said his son, as he picked it up and placed it on the table, "and I bet I never shall."

"It must have been your fancy, father," said his wife, regarding him anxiously.

He shook his head. "Never mind, though; there's no harm done, but it gave me a shock all the same."

They sat down by the fire again while the two men finished their pipes. Outside, the wind was higher than ever, and the old man started nervously at the sound of a door banging upstairs. A silence unusual and depressing settled upon all three, which lasted until the old couple rose to retire for the night.

"I expect you'll find the cash tied up in a big bag in the middle of your bed," said Herbert, as he bade them good night, "and something horrible squatting up on top of the wardrobe watching you pocket your ill-gotten gains."

He sat alone in the darkness, gazing at the dying fire, and seeing faces in it. The last face was so horrible and so simian that he gazed at it with amazement. It got so vivid that, with a little uneasy laugh, he felt on the table for a glass containing a little water to throw over it. His hand grasped the monkey's paw, and with a little shiver he wiped his hand on his coat and went up to bed.

II

In the brightness of the wintery sun next morning as it streamed over the breakfast table he laughed at his fears. There was an air of prosaic wholesomeness about the room which it had lacked on the previous night, and the dirty, shrivelled little paw was pitched on the sideboard with a carelessness which betokened no great belief in its virtues.

"I suppose all old soldiers are the same," said Mrs. White. "The idea of our listening to such nonsense! How could wishes be granted in these days? And if they could, how could two hundred pounds hurt you, father?"

"Might drop on his head from the sky," said the frivolous Herbert.

"Morris said the things happened so naturally," said his father, "that you might if you so wished attribute it to coincidence."

"Well, don't break into the money before I come back," said Herbert as he rose from the table. "I'm afraid it'll turn you into a mean, avaricious man, and we will have to disown you."

His mother laughed, and following him to the door, watched him down the road; and returning to the breakfast table, was very happy at the expense of her husband's credulity. All of which did not prevent her from scurrying to the door at the postman's knock, nor prevent her from referring somewhat shortly to retired sergeant-majors of bibulous habits when she found that the post brought a tailor's bill.

"Herbert will have some more of his funny remarks, I expect, when he comes home," she said, as they sat at dinner.

"I dare say," said Mr. White, pouring himself out some beer; "but for all that, the thing moved in my hand; that I'll swear to."

"You thought it did," said the old lady soothingly.

"I say it did," replied the other. "There was no thought about it; I had just—What's the matter?"

His wife made no reply. She was watching the mysterious movements of a man outside, who, peering in an undecided fashion at the house, appeared to be trying to make up his mind to enter. In mental connection with the two hundred pounds, she noticed that the stranger was well dressed, and wore a silk hat of glossy newness. Three times he paused at the gate, and then walked on again. The fourth time he stood with his hand upon it, and then with a sudden resolution flung it open and walked up the path. Mrs. White at the same moment placed her hands behind her, and hurriedly unfastening the strings on her apron, put that useful article of apparel beneath the cushion of her chair.

She brought the stranger, who seemed ill at ease, into the room.

He gazed at her furtively, and listened in a preoccupied fashion as the old lady apologized for the appearance of the room, and her husband's coat, a garment he usually reserved for the garden. She then waited as patiently as her sex would permit, for him to broach his business, but he was at first strangely silent.

"I—was asked to call," he said at last, and stooped and picked a piece of cotton from his trousers. "I come from Maw and Meggins."

The old lady started. "Is anything the matter?" she asked breathlessly. "Has anything happened to Herbert? What is it? What is it?"

Her husband interposed. "There, there, mother," he said hastily. "Sit down, and don't jump to conclusions. You've not brought bad news, I'm sure, sir;" and he eyed the other wistfully.

"I'm sorry—" began the visitor.

"Is he hurt?" demanded the mother wildly.

The visitor bowed in assent. "Badly hurt," he said quietly, "but he is not in any pain."

"Oh, thank God!" said the old woman, clasping her hands. "Thank God for that! Thank—"

She broke off suddenly as the sinister meaning of the assurance dawned upon her, and she saw the awful confirmation of her fears in the other's averted face. She caught her breath, and turning to her slower-witted husband, laid her trembling old hand upon his. There was a long silence.

"He was caught in the machinery," said the visitor at length in a low voice.

"Caught in the machinery," repeated Mr. White, in a dazed fashion, "yes."

He sat staring blankly out at the window, and taking his wife's hand between his own, pressed it as he had been wont to do in their old courting days nearly forty years before.

"He was the only one left to us," he said, turning gently to the visitor. "It is hard."

The other coughed, and rising, walked slowly to the window.

"The firm wished me to convey their sincere sympathy with you in your great loss," he said, without looking round. "I beg that you will understand I am only their servant and merely obeying orders."

There was no reply; the old woman's face was white, her eyes staring, and her breath inaudible; on the husband's face was a look such as his friend the sergeant might have carried into his first action.

"I was to say that Maw and Meggins disclaim all responsibility," continued the other. "They admit no liability at all, but in consideration of your son's services, they wish to present you with a certain sum as compensation."

Mr. White dropped his wife's hand, and rising to his feet, gazed with a look of horror at his visitor. His dry lips shaped the words, "How much?"

"Two hundred pounds," was the answer.

Unconscious of his wife's shriek, the old man smiled faintly, put out his hands like a sightless man, and dropped, a senseless heap, to the floor.

III

In the huge new cemetery, some two miles distant, the old people buried their dead, and came back to the house steeped in shadow and silence. It was all over so quickly that at first they could hardly realise it, and remained in a state of expectation as though of something else to happen—something else which was to lighten this load, too heavy for old hearts to bear.

But the days passed, and expectation gave place to resignation—the hopeless resignation of the old, sometimes miscalled apathy. Sometimes they hardly exchanged a word, for now they had nothing to talk about, and their days were long to weariness.

It was about a week after, that the old man, waking suddenly in the night, stretched out his hand and found himself alone. The room was in darkness, and the sound of subdued weeping came from the window. He raised himself in bed and listened.

"Come back," he said tenderly. "You will be cold."

"It is colder for my son," said the old woman, and wept afresh.

The sound of her sobs died away on his ears. The bed was warm, and his eyes heavy with sleep. He dozed fitfully, and then slept until a sudden wild cry from his wife awoke him with a start.

"The paw!" she cried wildly. "The monkey's paw!"

He started up in alarm. "Where? Where is it? What's the matter?"

She came stumbling across the room toward him. "I want it," she said quietly. "You've not destroyed it?"

"It's in the parlour, on the bracket," he replied, marvelling. "Why?"

She cried and laughed together, and bending over, kissed his cheek.

"I only just thought of it," she said hysterically. "Why didn't I think of it before? Why didn't *you* think of it?"

"Think of what?" he questioned.

"The other two wishes," she replied rapidly. "We've only had one."

"Was not that enough?" he demanded fiercely.

"No," she cried triumphantly; "we'll have one more. Go down and get it quickly, and wish our boy alive again."

The man sat up in bed and flung the bedclothes from his quaking limbs. "Good God, you are mad!" he cried, aghast.

"Get it," she panted; "get it quickly, and wish—Oh, my boy, my boy!"

Her husband struck a match and lit the candle. "Get back to bed," he said unsteadily. "You don't know what you are saying."

"We had the first wish granted," said the old woman feverishly; "why not the second?"

"A coincidence," stammered the old man.

"Go and get it and wish," cried his wife, quivering with excitement.

The old man turned and regarded her, and his voice shook. "He has been dead ten days, and besides he—I would not tell you else, but—I could only recognize him by his clothing. If he was too terrible for you to see then, how now?"

"Bring him back," cried the old woman, and dragged him toward the door. "Do you think I fear the child I have nursed?"

He went down in the darkness, and felt his way to the parlour, and then to the mantelpiece. The talisman was in its place, and a horrible fear that the unspoken wish might bring his mutilated son before him ere he could escape from the room seized upon him, and he caught his breath as he found that he had lost the direction of the door. His brow cold with sweat, he felt his way round the table, and groped along the wall until he found himself in the small passage with the unwholesome thing in his hand.

Even his wife's face seemed changed as he entered the room. It was white and expectant, and to his fears seemed to have an unnatural look upon it. He was afraid of her.

"Wish!" she cried, in a strong voice.

"It is foolish and wicked," he faltered.

"Wish!" repeated his wife.

He raised his hand. "I wish my son alive again."

The talisman fell to the floor, and he regarded it fearfully. Then he sank trembling into a chair as the old woman, with burning eyes, walked to the window and raised the blind.

He sat until he was chilled with the cold, glancing occasionally at the figure of the old woman peering through the window. The candle-end, which had burned below the rim of the china candlestick, was throwing pulsating shadows on the ceiling and walls, until, with a flicker larger than the rest it expired. The old man, with an unspeakable sense of relief at the failure of the talisman, crept back to his bed, and a minute or two afterward the old woman came silently and apathetically beside him.

Neither spoke, but lay silently listening to the ticking of the clock. A stair creaked, and a squeaky mouse scurried noisily through the wall. The darkness was oppressive, and after lying for some time screwing up his courage, he took the box of matches, and striking one, went downstairs for a candle.

At the foot of the stairs the match went out, and he paused to strike another; and at the same moment a knock, so quiet and stealthy as to be scarcely audible, sounded on the front door.

The matches fell from his hand and spilled in the passage. He stood motionless, his breath suspended until the knock was repeated. Then he turned and fled swiftly back to his room, and closed the door behind him. A third knock sounded through the house.

"What's that?" cried the old woman, starting up.

"A rat," said the old man in shaking tones—"a rat. It passed me on the stairs."

His wife sat up in bed listening. A loud knock resounded through the house.

"It's Herbert!" she screamed. "It's Herbert!"

She ran to the door, but her husband was before her, and catching her by the arm, held her tightly.

"What are you going to do?" he whispered hoarsely.

"It's my boy; it's Herbert!" she cried, struggling mechanically. "I forgot it was two miles away. What are you holding me for? Let go. I must open the door."

"For God's sake don't let it in," cried the old man, trembling.

"You're afraid of your own son," she cried, struggling. "Let me go. I'm coming, Herbert; I'm coming."

There was another knock, and another. The old woman with a sudden wrench broke free and ran from the room. Her husband followed to the landing, and called after her appealingly as she hurried downstairs. He heard the chain rattle back and the bottom bolt drawn slowly and stiffly from the socket. Then the old woman's voice strained and panting.

"The bolt," she cried loudly. "Come down. I can't reach it."

But her husband was on his hands and knees groping wildly on the floor in search of the paw. If he could only find it before the thing outside got in. A perfect fusillade of knocks reverberated through the house, and he heard the scraping of a chair as his wife put it down in the passage against the door. He heard the creaking of the bolt as it came slowly back, and at the same moment he found the monkey's paw, and frantically breathed his third and last wish.

The knocking ceased suddenly, although the echoes of it were still in the house. He heard the chair drawn back, and the door opened. A cold wind rushed up the staircase, and a long loud wail of disappointment and misery from his wife gave him courage to run down to her side, and then to the gate beyond. The street lamp flickering opposite shone on a quiet and deserted road.

The Great God Pan

ARTHUR MACHEN

[1863–1947]

The novels and stories of Welsh writer Arthur Machen demonstrate the visionary tradition of ghostly literature in one of its most perfect states. In such novels as The Hill of Dreams *and such shorter works as* "The White People," *Machen's elegant prose is woven in such a way that, in the words of critic Jack Sullivan, it produces "a trancelike sense of rhythm and imagery." At its best moments, it "strikes a highly original note of dissonance, in which beauty and horror ring out at precisely the same moment."* "The Great God Pan," *which scandalized critics when it first appeared, is still as shocking and provocative close to seventy years later.*

I. The Experiment

"I am glad you came, Clarke; very glad indeed. I was not sure you could spare the time."

"I was able to make arrangements for a few days; things are not very lively just now. But have you no misgivings, Raymond? Is it absolutely safe?"

The two men were slowly pacing the terrace in front of Dr. Raymond's house. The sun still hung above the western mountain line, but it shone with a dull red glow that cast no shadows, and all the air was quiet; a sweet breath came from the great wood on the hillside above, and with it, at intervals, the soft murmuring call of the wild doves. Below, in the long lovely valley, the river wound in and out between the lonely hills, and, as the sun hovered and vanished into the west, a faint mist, pure white, began to rise from the banks. Dr. Raymond turned sharply to his friend.

"Safe? Of course it is. In itself the operation is a perfectly simple one; any surgeon could do it."

"And there is no danger at any other stage?"

"None; absolutely no physical danger whatever, I give you my word. You are always timid, Clarke, always; but you know my history. I have devoted myself to transcendental medicine for the last twenty years. I have heard myself called quack and charlatan and impostor, but all the while I knew I was on the right path. Five years ago I reached the goal, and since then every day has been a preparation for what we shall do tonight."

"I should like to believe it is all true." Clarke knit his brows, and looked doubtfully at Dr. Raymond. "Are you perfectly sure, Raymond, that your theory is not a phantasmagoria—a splendid vision, certainly, but a mere vision after all?"

Dr. Raymond stopped in his walk and turned sharply. He was a middle-aged man, gaunt and thin, of a pale yellow complexion, but as he answered Clarke and faced him, there was a flush on his cheek.

"Look about you, Clarke. You see the mountain, and hill following after hill, as wave on wave, you see the woods and orchards, the fields of ripe corn, and the meadows reaching to the reed beds by the river. You see me standing here beside you, and hear my voice; but I tell you that all these things—yes, from that star that has just shone out in the sky to the solid ground beneath our feet—I say that all these are but dreams and shadows: the shadows that hide the real world from our eyes. There *is* a real world, but it is beyond this glamour and this vision, beyond these 'chases in Arras, dreams in a career,' beyond them all as beyond a veil. I do not know whether any human being has ever lifted that veil; but I do know, Clarke, that you and I shall see it lifted this very night from before another's eyes. You may think all this strange nonsense; it may be strange, but it is true, and the ancients knew what lifting the veil means. They called it seeing the god Pan."

Clarke shivered; the white mist gathering over the river was chilly.

"It is wonderful indeed," he said. "We are standing on the brink of a strange world, Raymond, if what you say is true. I suppose the knife is absolutely necessary?"

"Yes; a slight lesion in the grey matter, that is all; a trifling rearrangement of certain cells, a microscopical alteration that would escape the attention of ninety-nine brain specialists out of a hundred. I don't want to bother you with 'shop,' Clarke; I might give you a mass of technical detail which would sound very imposing, and would leave you as enlightened as you are now. But I suppose you have read, casually, in out-of-the-way corners of your paper, that immense strides have been made recently in the physiology of the brain. I saw a paragraph the other day about Digby's theory, and Browne Faber's discoveries. Theories and discoveries! Where they are standing now, I stood fifteen years ago, and I need not tell you that I have not been standing still for the last fifteen years. It will be enough if I say that five years ago I made the discovery to which I alluded when I said that then I reached the goal. After years of labour, after years of toiling and groping in the dark, after days and nights of disappointment and sometimes of despair, in which I used now and then to tremble and grow cold with the thought that perhaps there were others seeking for what I sought, at last, after so long, a pang of sudden joy thrilled my soul, and I knew the long journey was at an end. By what seemed then and still seems a chance, the suggestion of a moment's idle thought followed up upon familiar lines and paths that I had tracked a hundred times already, the great truth burst upon me, and I saw, mapped out in lines of light, a whole world, a sphere unknown; continents and islands, and great oceans in which no ship has sailed (to my belief) since Man first lifted up his eyes and beheld the sun, and the stars of heaven, and the quiet earth beneath. You will think all this high-flown language, Clarke, but it is hard to be literal. And yet; I do not know whether what I am hinting at cannot be set forth in plain and homely terms. For instance, this world of ours is pretty well girded now with the telegraph wires and cables; thought, with something less than the speed of thought, flashes from sunrise to sunset, from north to south, across the floods and the desert places. Suppose that an electrician of today were suddenly to perceive that he and his friends have merely been playing with pebbles and mistaking them for the foundations of the world; suppose that such a man saw uttermost space lie open before the current, and words of men flash forth to the sun and beyond the sun into the systems beyond, and the voices of articulate-speaking men echo in the waste void that bounds our thought. As analogies go, that is a pretty good analogy of what I have done; you can understand now a little of what I felt as I stood here one evening; it was a summer evening, and the valley looked much as it does now; I stood here, and saw before me the unutterable, the unthinkable gulf that yawns profound between two worlds, the world of matter and the world of spirit; I saw the great empty deep stretch dim before me, and in that instant a bridge of light leapt from the earth to the unknown shore, and the abyss was spanned. You may look in Browne Faber's book, if you like, and you will find that to the present day men of science are unable to account for the presence, or to specify the functions of a certain group of nerve-cells in the brain. That group is, as it were, land to let, a mere waste place for fanciful theories. I am not in the position of Browne Faber and the specialists, I am perfectly instructed as to the possible functions of those nerve-centres in the scheme of things. With a touch I can bring them into play, with a touch, I say, I can set free the current, with a touch I can complete the communication between this world of sense and—we shall be able to finish the sentence later on. Yes, the knife is necessary; but think what that knife will effect. It will level utterly the solid wall of sense, and probably, for the first time since man was made, a spirit will gaze on a spirit world. Clarke, Mary will see the god Pan!"

"But you remember what you wrote to me? I thought it would be requisite that she—"

He whispered the rest into the doctor's ear.

"Not at all, not at all. That is nonsense, I assure you. Indeed, it is better as it is; I am quite certain of that."

"Consider the matter well, Raymond. It's a great responsibility. Something might go wrong; you would be a miserable man for the rest of your days."

"No, I think not, even if the worst happened. As you know, I rescued Mary from the gutter, and from almost certain starvation, when she was a child; I think her life is mine, to use as I see fit. Come, it is getting late; we had better go in."

Dr. Raymond led the way into the house, through the hall, and down a long dark passage. He took a key from his pocket and opened a heavy door, and motioned Clarke into his laboratory. It had once been a billiard-room, and was lighted by a glass dome in the centre of the ceiling, whence there still shone a sad grey light on the figure of the doctor as he lit a lamp with a heavy shade and placed it on a table in the middle of the room.

Clarke looked about him. Scarcely a foot of wall remained bare; there were shelves all around laden with bottles and phials of all shapes and colours, and at one end stood a little Chippendale book-case. Raymond pointed to this.

"You see that parchment Oswald Crollius? He was one of the first to show me the way, though I don't think he ever found it himself. That is a strange saying of his: 'In every grain of wheat there lies hidden the soul of a star.' "

There was not much of furniture in the laboratory. The table in the centre, a stone slab with a drain in one corner, the two armchairs on which Raymond and Clarke were sitting; that was all, except an odd-looking chair at the furthest end of the room. Clarke looked at it, and raised his eyebrows.

"Yes, that is the chair," said Raymond. "We may as well place it in position." He got up and wheeled the chair to the light, and began raising and lowering it, letting down the seat, setting the back at various angles, and adjusting the foot-rest. It looked comfortable enough, and Clarke passed his hand over the soft green velvet, as the doctor manipulated the levers.

"Now, Clarke, make yourself quite comfortable. I have a couple of hours' work before me; I was obliged to leave certain matters to the last."

Raymond went to the stone slab, and Clarke watched him drearily as he bent over a row of phials and lit the flame under the crucible. The doctor had a small hand-lamp, shaded as the larger one, on a ledge above his apparatus, and Clarke, who sat in the shadows, looked down the great dreary room, wondering at the bizarre effects of brilliant light and undefined darkness contrasting with one another. Soon he became conscious of an odd odour, at first the merest suggestion of odour, in the room; and as it grew more decided he felt surprised that he was not reminded of the chemist's shop or the surgery. Clarke found himself idly endeavouring to analyse the sensation, and half conscious, he began to think of a day, fifteen years ago, that he had spent in roaming through the woods and meadows near his old home. It was a burning day at the beginning of August, the heat had dimmed the outlines of all things and all distances with a faint mist, and people who observed the thermometer spoke of an abnormal register, of a temperature that was almost tropical. Strangely that wonderful hot day of the 'fifties rose up in Clarke's imagination; the sense of dazzling all-pervading sunlight seemed to blot out the shadows and the lights of the laboratory, and he felt again the heated air beating in gusts about his face, saw the shimmer rising from the turf, and heard the myriad murmur of the summer.

"I hope the smell doesn't annoy you, Clarke; there's nothing unwholesome about it. It may make you a bit sleepy, that's all."

Clarke heard the words quite distinctly, and knew that Raymond was speaking to him, but for the life of him he could not rouse himself from his lethargy. He could only think of the lonely walk he had taken fifteen years ago; it was his last look at the fields and woods he had known since he was a child, and now it all stood out in brilliant light, as a picture, before him. Above all there came to his nostrils the scent of summer, the smell of flowers mingled, and the odour of the woods, of cool shaded places, deep in the green depths, drawn forth by the sun's heat; and the scent of the good earth, lying as it were with arms stretched forth, and smiling lips, overpowered all. His fancies made him wander, as he had wandered long ago, from the fields into the wood, tracking a little path between the shining undergrowth of beechtrees; and the trickle of water dropping from the limestone rock sounded as a clear melody in the dream. Thoughts began to go astray and to mingle with other recollections; the beech alley was transformed to a path beneath ilex-trees, and here and there a vine climbed from bough to bough, and sent up waving tendrils and drooped with purple grapes, and the sparse grey-green leaves of a wild olive-tree stood out against the dark shadows of the ilex. Clarke, in the deep folds of dream, was conscious that the path from his father's house had led him into an undiscovered country, and he was wondering at the strangeness of it all, when suddenly, in place of the hum and murmur of the summer, an infinite silence seemed to fall on all things, and the wood was hushed, and for a moment of time he stood face to face there with a presence, that was neither man nor beast, neither the living nor the dead, but all things mingled, the form of all things but devoid of all form. And in that moment, the sacrament of body and soul was dissolved, and a voice seemed to cry, "Let us go hence," and then the darkness of darkness beyond the stars, the darkness of everlasting.

When Clarke woke up with a start he saw Raymond pouring a few drops of some oily fluid into a green phial, which he stoppered tightly.

"You have been dozing," he said: "the journey must have tired you out. It is done now. I am going to fetch Mary; I shall be back in ten minutes."

Clarke lay back in his chair and wondered. It seemed as if he had but passed from one dream into another. He half expected to see the walls of the laboratory melt and disappear, and to awake in London, shuddering at his own sleeping fancies. But at last the door opened, and the doctor returned, and behind him came a girl of about seventeen, dressed all in white. She was so beautiful that Clarke did not wonder at what the doctor had written to him. She was blushing now over face and neck and arms, but Raymond seemed unmoved.

"Mary," he said, "the time has come. You are quite free. Are you willing to trust yourself to me entirely?"

"Yes, dear."

"You hear that, Clarke? You are my witness. Here is the chair, Mary. It is quite easy. Just sit in it and lean back. Are you ready?"

"Yes, dear, quite ready. Give me a kiss before you begin."

The doctor stooped and kissed her mouth, kindly enough. "Now shut your eyes," he said. The girl closed her eyelids, as if she were tired, and longed for sleep, and Raymond held the green phial to her nostrils. Her face grew white, whiter than her dress; she struggled faintly, and then with the feeling of submission strong within her, crossed her arms upon her breast as a little child about to say her prayers. The bright light of the lamp beat full upon her, and Clarke watched changes fleeting over that face as the changes of the hills when the summer clouds float across the sun. And then she lay all white and still, and the doctor turned up one of her eyelids. She was quite unconscious. Raymond pressed hard on one of the levers and the chair instantly sank back. Clarke saw him cutting away a circle, like a tonsure, from her hair, and the lamp moved nearer. Raymond took a small glittering instrument from a little case, and Clarke turned away shuddering. When he looked again the doctor was binding up the wound he had made.

"She will awake in five minutes." Raymond was still perfectly cool. "There is nothing more to be done; we can only wait."

The minutes passed slowly; they could hear a slow, heavy ticking. There was an old clock in the passage. Clarke felt sick and faint; his knees shook beneath him, he could hardly stand.

Suddenly, as they watched, they heard a long-drawn sigh, and suddenly did the colour that had vanished return to the girl's cheeks, and suddenly her eyes opened. Clarke quailed before them. They shone with an awful light, looking far away, and a great wonder fell upon her face, and her hands stretched out as if to touch what was invisible; but in an instant the wonder faded, and gave place to the most awful terror. The muscles of her face were hideously convulsed, she shook from head to foot; the soul seemed struggling and shuddering within the house of flesh. It was a horrible sight, and Clarke rushed forward, as she fell shrieking to the floor.

Three days later Raymond took Clarke to Mary's bedside. She was lying wide-awake, rolling her head from side to side, and grinning vacantly.

"Yes," said the doctor, still quite cool, "it is a great pity; she is a hopeless idiot. However, it could not be helped; and, after all, she has seen the Great God Pan."

2. Mr. Clarke's Memoirs

Mr. Clarke, the gentleman chosen by Dr. Raymond to witness the strange experiment of the god Pan, was a person in whose character caution and curiosity were oddly mingled; in his sober moments he thought of the unusual and the eccentric with undisguised aversion, and yet, deep in his heart, there was a wide-eyed inquisitiveness with respect to all the more recondite and esoteric elements in the nature of men. The latter tendency had prevailed when he accepted Raymond's invitation, for though his considered judgment had always repudiated the doctor's theories as the wildest nonsense, yet he secretly hugged a belief in fantasy, and would have rejoiced to see that belief confirmed. The horrors that he witnessed in the dreary laboratory were to a certain extent salutary; he was conscious of being involved in an affair not altogether reputable, and for many years afterwards he clung bravely to the commonplace, and rejected all occasions of occult investigation. Indeed, on some homoeopathic principle, he for some time attended the séances of distinguished mediums, hoping that the clumsy tricks of these gentlemen would make him altogether disgusted with mysticism of every kind, but the remedy, though caustic, was not efficacious. Clarke knew that he still pined for the unseen, and little by little, the old passion began to reassert itself, as the face of Mary, shuddering and convulsed with an unknowable terror, faded slowly from his memory. Occupied all day in pursuits both serious and lucrative, the temptation to relax in the evening was too great, especially in the winter months, when the fire cast a warm glow over his snug bachelor apartment, and a bottle of some choice claret stood ready by his elbow. His dinner digested, he would make a brief pretence of reading the evening paper, but the mere catalogue of news soon palled upon him, and Clarke would find himself casting glances of warm desire in the direction of an old Japanese bureau, which stood at a pleasant distance from the hearth. Like a boy before a jam-closet, for a few minutes he would hover indecisive, but lust always prevailed, and Clarke ended by drawing up his chair, lighting a candle, and sitting down before the bureau. Its pigeon-holes and drawers teemed with documents on the most morbid subjects, and in the well reposed a large manuscript volume, in which he had painfully entered the gems of his collection. Clarke had a fine contempt for published literature; the most ghostly story ceased to interest him if it happened to be printed; his sole pleasure was in the reading, compiling, and rearranging what he called his "Memoirs to Prove the Existence of the Devil," and engaged in this pursuit the evening seemed to fly and the night appeared too short.

On one particular evening, an ugly December night, black with fog, and raw with frost, Clarke hurried over his dinner, and scarcely deigned to observe his customary ritual of taking up the paper and laying it down again. He paced two or three times up and down the room, and opened the bureau, stood still a moment, and sat down. He leant back, absorbed in one of those dreams to which he was subject, and at length drew out his book, and opened it at the last entry. There were three or four pages densely covered with Clarke's round, set penmanship, and at the beginning he had written in a somewhat larger hand:

> *Singular Narrative told me by my Friend, Dr. Phillips. He assures me that all the facts related therein are strictly and wholly True, but refuses to give either the Surnames of the Persons concerned, or the Place where these Extraordinary Events occurred.*

Mr. Clarke began to read over the account for the tenth time, glancing now and then at the pencil notes he had made when it was told him by his friend. It was one of his humours to pride himself on a certain literary ability; he thought well of his style, and took pains in arranging the circumstances in dramatic order. He read the following story:

The persons concerned in this statement are Helen V., who, if she is still alive, must now be a woman of twenty-three. Rachel M., since deceased, who was a year younger than the above, and Trevor W., an imbecile, aged eighteen. These persons were at the period of the story inhabitants of a village on the borders of Wales, a place of some importance in the time of the Roman occupation, but now a scattered hamlet, of not more than five hundred souls. It is situated on rising ground, about six miles from the sea, and is sheltered by a large and picturesque forest.

Some eleven years ago, Helen V. came to the village under rather peculiar circumstances. It is understood that she, being an orphan, was adopted in her infancy by a distant relative, who brought her up in his own house till she was twelve years old. Thinking, however, that it would be better for the child to have playmates of her own age, he advertised in several local papers for a good home in a comfortable farmhouse for a girl of twelve, and this advertisement was answered by Mr. R., a well-to-do farmer in the above-mentioned village. His references proving satisfactory, the gentleman sent his adopted daughter to Mr. R., with a letter, in which he stipulated that the girl should have a room to herself, and stated that her guardians need be at no trouble in the matter of education, as she was already sufficiently educated for the position in life which she would occupy. In fact, Mr. R. was given to understand that the girl was to be allowed to find her own occupations, and to spend her time almost as she liked. Mr. R. duly met her at the nearest station, at town some seven miles away from his house, and seems to have remarked nothing extraordinary about the child, except that she was reticent as to her former life and her adopted father. She was, however, of a very different type from the inhabitants of the village; her skin was a pale, clear olive, and her features were strongly marked, and of a somewhat foreign character. She appears to have settled down easily enough into farmhouse life, and became a favourite with the children, who sometimes went with her on her rambles in the forest, for this was her amusement. Mr. R. states that he has known her to go out by herself directly after their early breakfast, and not return till after dusk, and that, feeling uneasy at a young girl being out alone for so many hours, he communicated with her adopted father, who replied in a brief note that Helen must do as she chose. In the winter, when the forest paths are impassable, she spent most of her time in her bedroom, where she slept alone, according to the instructions of her relative. It was on one of these expeditions to the forest that the first of the singular incidents with which this girl is connected occurred, the date being about a year after her arrival at the village. The preceding winter had been remarkably severe, the snow drifting to a great depth, and the frost continuing for an unexampled period, and the summer following was as noteworthy for its extreme heat. On one of the very hottest days in this summer, Helen V. left the farmhouse for one of her long rambles in the forest, taking with her, as usual, some bread and meat for lunch. She was seen by some men in the fields making for the old Roman Road, a green causeway which traverses the highest part of the wood, and they were astonished to observe that the girl had taken off her hat, though the heat of the sun was already almost tropical. As it happened, a labourer, Joseph W. by name, was working in the forest near the Roman Road, and at twelve o'clock his little son, Trevor, brought the man his dinner of bread and cheese. After the meal, the boy, who was about seven years old at the time, left his father at work, and, as he said, went to look for flowers in the wood, and the man, who could hear him shouting with delight over his discoveries, felt no uneasiness. Suddenly, however, he was horrified at hearing the most dreadful screams, evidently the result of great terror, proceeding from the direction in which his son had gone, and he hastily threw down his tools and ran to see what had happened. Tracing his path by the sound, he met the little boy, who was running headlong, and was evidently terribly frightened, and on questioning him the man at last elicited that after picking a posy of flowers he felt tired, and lay down on the grass and fell asleep. He was suddenly awakened, as he stated, by a peculiar noise, a sort of singing he called it, and on peeping through the branches he saw Helen V. playing on the grass with a "strange naked man," whom he seemed unable to describe more fully. He said he felt dreadfully frightened, and ran away crying for his father. Joseph W. proceeded in the direction indicated by his son, and found Helen V. sitting on the grass in the middle of a glade or open space left by charcoal burners. He angrily charged her with frightening his little boy, but she entirely denied the accusation and laughed at the child's story of a "strange man," to which he himself did not attach much credence. Joseph W. came to the conclusion that the boy had woke up with a sudden fright, as children sometimes do, but Trevor persisted in his story, and continued in such evident distress that at last his father took him home, hoping that his mother would be able to soothe him. For many weeks, however, the boy gave his parents much anxiety; he became nervous and strange in his manner, refusing to leave the cottage by himself, and constantly alarming the household by waking in the night with cries of "The man in the wood! Father! Father!"

In course of time, however, the impression seemed to have worn off, and about three months later he accompanied his father to the house of a gentleman in the neighbourhood, for whom Joseph W. occasionally did work. The man was shown into the study, and the little boy was left sitting in the hall, and a few minutes later, while the gentleman was giving W. his instructions, they were both horrified by a piercing shriek and the sound of a fall, and rushing out they found the child lying senseless on the floor, his face contorted with terror. The doctor was immediately summoned, and after some examination he pronounced the child to be suffering from a kind of fit, apparently produced by a sudden shock. The boy was taken to one of the bedrooms, and after some time recovered consciousness, but only to pass into a condition described by the medical man as one of violent hysteria. The doctor exhibited a strong sedative, and in the course of two hours pronounced him fit to walk home, but in passing through the hall the paroxysms of fright returned and with additional violence. The father perceived that the child was pointing at some object and heard the old cry, "The man in the wood," and looking in the direction indicated saw a stone head of grotesque appearance, which had been built into the wall above one of the doors. It seems that the owner of the house had recently made alterations in his premises, and on digging the foundation for some offices, the men had found a curious head, evidently of the Roman period, which had been placed in the hall in the manner described. The head is pronounced by the most experienced archaeologists of the district to be that of a faun or satyr.[1]

From whatever cause arising, this second shock seemed too severe for the boy Trevor, and at the present date he suffers from a weakness of intellect, which gives but little promise of amending. The matter caused a good deal of sensation at the time, and the girl Helen was closely questioned by Mr. R., but to no purpose, she steadfastly denying that she had frightened or in any way molested Trevor.

The second event with which this girl's name is connected took place about six years ago, and is of a still more extraordinary character.

At the beginning of the summer of 1882 Helen contracted a friendship of a peculiarly intimate character with Rachel M., the daughter of a prosperous farmer in the neighbourhood. This girl, who was a year younger than Helen, was considered by most people to

[1]Dr. Phillips tells me that he has seen the head in question, and assures me that he has never received such a vivid presentment of intense evil.

be the prettier of the two, though Helen's features had to a great extent softened as she became older. The two girls, who were together on every available opportunity, presented a singular contrast, the one with her clear, olive skin and almost Italian appearance, and the other of the proverbial red and white of our rural districts. It must be stated that the payments made to Mr. R. for the maintenance of Helen were known in the village for their excessive liberality, and the impression was general that she would one day inherit a large sum of money from her relative. The parents of Rachel were therefore not averse from their daughter's friendship with the girl, and even encouraged the intimacy, though they now bitterly regret having done so. Helen still retained her extraordinary fondness for the forest, and on several occasions Rachel accompanied her, the two friends setting out early in the morning, and remaining in the wood till dusk. Once or twice after these excursions Mrs. M. thought her daughter's manner rather peculiar; she seemed languid and dreamy, and as it has been expressed, "different from herself," but these peculiarities seem to have been thought too trifling for remark. One evening, however, after Rachel had come home, her mother heard a noise which sounded like suppressed weeping in the girl's room, and on going in found her lying, half undressed, upon the bed, evidently in the greatest distress. As soon as she saw her mother, she exclaimed, 'Ah, Mother, Mother, why did you let me go to the forest with Helen?' Mrs. M. was astonished at so strange a question, and proceeded to make inquiries. Rachel told her a wild story. She said—

Clarke closed the door with a snap, and turned his chair towards the fire. When his friend sat one evening in that very chair, and told his story, Clarke had interrupted him at a point a little subsequent to this, had cut short his words in a paroxysm of horror. "My God!" he had exclaimed, "think, think what you are saying. It is too incredible, too monstrous; such things can never be in this quiet world, where men and women live and die, and struggle, and conquer, or maybe fail, and fall down under sorrow, and grieve and suffer strange fortunes for many a year; but not this, Phillips, not such things as this. There must be some explanation, some way out of the terror. Why, man, if such a case were possible, our earth would be a nightmare."

But Phillips had told his story to the end, concluding:

"Her flight remains a mystery to this day; she vanished in broad sunlight; they saw her walking in a meadow, and a few moments later she was not there."

Clarke tried to conceive the thing again, as he sat by the fire, and again his mind shuddered and shrank back, appalled before the sight of such awful, unspeakable elements enthroned as it were, and triumphant in human flesh. Before him stretched the long dim vista of the green causeway in the forest, as his friend had described it; he saw the swaying leaves and the quivering shadows on the grass, he saw the sunlight and the flowers, and far away, far in the long distance, the two figures moved towards him. One was Rachel, but the other?

Clarke had tried his best to disbelieve it all, but at the end of the account, as he had written it in his book, he had placed the inscription:

ET DIABOLUS INCARNATUS EST. ET HOMO FACTUS EST.

3. The City of Resurrections

"Herbert! Good God! Is it possible?"

"Yes, my name's Herbert. I think I know your face too, but I don't remember your name. My memory is very queer."

"Don't you recollect Villiers of Wadham?"

"So it is, so it is. I beg your pardon, Villiers, I didn't think I was begging of an old college friend. Good-night."

"My dear fellow, this haste is unnecessary. My rooms are close by, but we won't go there just yet. Suppose we walk up Shaftesbury Avenue a little way? But how in heaven's name have you come to this pass, Herbert?"

"It's a long story, Villiers, and a strange one, too, but you can hear it if you like."

"Come on, then. Take my arm, you don't seem very strong."

The ill-assorted pair moved slowly up Rupert Street; the one in dirty, evil-looking rags, and the other attired in the regulation uniform of a man about town, trim, glossy, and eminently well-to-do. Villiers had emerged from his restaurant after an excellent dinner of many courses, assisted by an ingratiating little flask of Chianti, and, in that frame of mind which was with him almost chronic, had delayed a moment by the door, peering round in the dimly lighted street in search of those mysterious incidents and persons with which the streets of London teem in every quarter and at every hour. Villiers prided himself as a practised explorer of such obscure mazes and byways of London life, and in this unprofitable pursuit he displayed an assiduity which was worthy of more serious employment. Thus he stood beside the lamp-post surveying the passers-by with undisguised curiosity, and with that gravity only known to the systematic diner, had just enunciated in his mind the formula: "London has been called the city of encounters; it is more than that, it is the city of resurrections," when these reflections were suddenly interrupted by a piteous whine at his elbow, and a deplorable appeal for alms. He looked around in some irritation, and with a sudden shock found himself confronted with the embodied proof of his somewhat stilted fancies. There, close beside him, his face altered and disfigured by poverty and disgrace, his body barely covered by greasy ill-fitting rags, stood his old friend Charles Herbert, who had matriculated on the same day as himself, with whom he had been merry and wise for twelve revolving terms. Different occupations and varying interests had interrupted the friendship, and it was six years since Villiers had seen Herbert; and now he looked upon this wreck of a man with grief and dismay, mingled with a certain inquisitiveness as to what dreary chain of circumstances had dragged him down to such a doleful pass. Villiers felt together with compassion all the relish of the amateur in mysteries, and congratulated himself on his leisurely speculations outside the restaurant.

They walked on in silence for some time, and more than one passer-by stared in astonishment at the unaccustomed spectacle of a well-dressed man with an unmistakable beggar hanging on to his arm, and observing this, Villiers led the way to an obscure street in Soho. Here he repeated his question.

"How on earth has it happened, Herbert? I always understood you would succeed to an excellent position in Dorsetshire. Did your father disinherit you? Surely not?"

"No, Villiers; I came into all the property at my poor father's death; he died a year after I left Oxford. He was a very good father to me, and I mourned his death sincerely enough. But you know what young men are; a few months later I came up to town and went a good deal into society. Of course I had excellent introductions, and I managed to enjoy myself very much in a harmless sort of way. I played a little, certainly, but never for heavy stakes, and the few bets I made on races brought me in money—only a few pounds, you know, but enough to pay for cigars and such petty pleasures. It was in my second season that the tide turned. Of course you have heard of my marriage?"

"No, I never heard anything about it."

"Yes, I married, Villiers. I met a girl, a girl of the most wonderful and most strange beauty, at the house of some people whom I knew. I cannot tell you her age; I never knew it, but, so far as I can guess, I should think she must have been about nineteen when I made her acquaintance. My friends had come to know her as Florence; she told them she was an orphan, the child of an English father and an Italian mother, and she charmed them as she charmed me. The first time I saw her was at an evening party. I was standing by the door talking to a friend, when suddenly above the hum and babble of conversation I heard a voice which seemed to thrill to my heart. She was singing an Italian song. I was introduced to her that evening, and in three months I married Helen. Villiers, that woman, if I can call her 'woman,' corrupted my soul. The night of the wedding I found myself sitting in her bedroom in the hotel, listening to her talk. She was sitting up in bed, and I listened to her as she spoke in her beautiful voice, spoke of things which even now I would not dare whisper in blackest night, though I stood in the midst of a wilderness. You, Villiers, you may think you know life, and London, and what goes on day and night in this dreadful city; for all I can say you may have heard the talk of the vilest, but I tell you you can have no conception of what I know, not in your most fantastic, hideous dreams can you have imaged forth the faintest shadow of what I have heard—and seen. Yes, seen. I have seen the incredible, such horrors that even I myself sometimes stop in the middle of the street, and ask whether it is possible for a man to hold such things and live. In a year, Villiers, I was a ruined man, in body and soul—in body and soul."

"But your property, Herbert? You had land in Dorset."

"I sold it all; the fields and woods, the dear old house—everything."

"And the money?"

"She took it all from me."

"And then left you?"

"Yes; she disappeared one night. I don't know where she went, but I am sure if I saw her again it would kill me. The rest of my story is of no interest; sordid misery, that is all. You may think, Villiers, that I have exaggerated and talked for effect; but I have not told you half. I could tell you certain things which would convince you, but you would never know a happy day again. You would pass the rest of your life, as I pass mine, a haunted man, a man who has seen hell."

Villiers took the unfortunate man to his rooms, and gave him a meal. Herbert could eat little, and scarcely touched the glass of wine set before him. He sat moody and silent by the fire, and seemed relieved when Villiers sent him away with a small present of money.

"By the way, Herbert," said Villiers, as they parted at the door, "what was your wife's name? You said Helen, I think? Helen what?"

"The name she passed under when I met her was Helen Vaughan, but what her real name was I can't say. I don't think she had a name. No, no, not in that sense. Only human beings have names, Villiers; I can't say any more. Good-bye; yes, I will not fail to call if I see any way in which you can help me. Good-night."

The man went out into the bitter night, and Villiers returned to his fireside. There was something about Herbert which shocked him inexpressibly; not his poor rags nor the marks which poverty had set upon his face, but rather an indefinite terror which hung about him like a mist. He had acknowledged that he himself was not devoid of blame; the woman, he had avowed, had corrupted him body and soul, and Villiers felt that this man, once his friend, had been an actor in scenes evil beyond the power of words. His story needed no confirmation: he himself was the embodied proof of it. Villiers mused curiously over the story he had heard, and wondered whether he had heard both the first and the last of it. "No," he thought, "certainly not the last, probably only the beginning. A case like this is like a nest of Chinese boxes; you open one after another and find a quainter workmanship in every box. Most likely poor Herbert is merely one of the outside boxes; there are stranger ones to follow."

Villiers could not take his mind away from Herbert and his story, which seemed to grow wilder as the night wore on. The fire began to burn low, and the chilly air of the morning crept into the room; Villiers got up with a glance over his shoulder, and shivering slightly, went to bed.

A few days later he saw at his club a gentleman of his acquaintance, named Austin, who was famous for his intimate knowledge of London life, both in its tenebrous and luminous phases. Villiers, still full of his encounter in Soho and its consequences, thought Austin might possibly be able to shed some light on Herbert's history, and so after some casual talk he suddenly put the question:

"Do you happen to know anything of a man named Herbert—Charles Herbert?"

Austin turned round sharply and stared at Villiers with some astonishment.

"Charles Herbert? Weren't you in town three years ago? No; then you have not heard of the Paul Street case? It caused a good deal of sensation at the time."

"What was the case?"

"Well, a gentleman, a man of very good position, was found dead, stark dead, in the area of a certain house in Paul Street, off Tottenham Court Road. Of course the police did not make the discovery; if you happen to be sitting up all night and have a light in your window, the constable will ring the bell, but if you happen to be lying dead in somebody's area, you will be left alone. In this instance as in many others the alarm was raised by some kind of vagabond; I don't mean a common tramp, or a public-house loafer, but a gentleman, whose business or pleasure, or both, made him a spectator of the London streets at five o'clock in the morning. This individual was, as he said, 'going home,' it did not appear whence or whither, and had occasion to pass through Paul Street between four and five A.M. Something or other caught his eye at Number 20; he said, absurdly enough, that the house had the most unpleasant physiognomy he had ever observed, but, at any rate, he glanced down the area, and was a good deal astonished to see a man lying on the stones, his limbs all huddled together, and his face turned up. Our gentleman thought his face looked peculiarly ghastly, and so set off at a run in search of the nearest policeman. The constable was at first inclined to treat the matter lightly, suspecting common drunkenness; however, he came, and after looking at the man's face, changed his tone, quickly enough. The early bird, who had picked up this fine worm, was sent off for a doctor, and the policeman rang and knocked at the door till a slatternly servant girl came down looking more than half asleep. The constable pointed out the contents of the area to the maid, who screamed loudly enough to wake up the street, but she knew nothing of the man; had never seen him at the house, and so forth. Meanwhile the original discoverer had come back with a medical man, and the next thing was to get into the area. The gate was open, so the whole quartet stumped down the steps. The doctor hardly needed a moment's examination; he said the poor fellow had been dead for several hours, and it was then the case began to get interesting. The dead man had not been robbed, and in one of his pockets were papers identifying him as—well, as a man of good family and means, a favourite in society, and nobody's enemy, so far as could be known. I don't give his name, Villiers, because it has nothing to do with the story, and because it's no good raking up these affairs about the dead when there are no relations living. The next curious point was that the medical men couldn't agree as to how he met his death. There were some slight bruises on his shoulders, but they were so slight that it looked as if he had been pushed roughly out of the kitchen door, and not thrown over the railings from the street or even dragged down the steps. But there were positively no other marks of violence about him, certainly none that would account for his death; and when they came to the autopsy there wasn't a trace of poison of any kind. Of course the police wanted to know all about the people at Number 20, and here again, so I have heard from private sources, one or two other very curious points came out. It appears that the occupants of the house were a Mr. and Mrs. Charles Herbert; he was said to be a landed proprietor, though it struck most people that Paul Street was not exactly the place to look for country gentry. As for Mrs. Herbert, nobody seemed to know who or what she was, and, between ourselves, I fancy the divers after her history found themselves in rather strange waters. Of course they both denied knowing anything about the deceased, and in default of any evidence against them they were discharged. But some very odd things came out about them. Though it was between five and six in the morning when the dead man was removed, a large crowd had collected, and several of the neighbours ran to see what was going on. They were pretty free with their comments, by all accounts, and from these it appeared that Number 20 was in very bad odour in Paul Street. The detectives tried to trace down these rumours to some solid foundation of fact, but could not get hold of anything. People shook their heads and raised their eyebrows and thought the Herberts rather 'queer,' 'would rather not be seen going into their house,' and so on, but there was nothing tangible. The authorities were morally certain that the man met his death in some way or another in the house and was thrown out by the kitchen door, but they couldn't prove it, and the absence of any indications of violence or poisoning left them helpless. An odd case, wasn't it? But curiously enough, there's something more that I haven't told you. I happened to know one of the doctors who was consulted as to the cause of death, and some time after the inquest I met him, and asked him about it. 'Do you really mean to tell me,' I said, 'that you were baffled by the case, that you actually don't know what the man died of?' 'Pardon me,' he replied, 'I know perfectly well what caused death. Blank died of fright, of sheer, awful terror; I never saw features so hideously contorted in the entire course of my practice, and I have seen the faces of a whole host of dead.' The doctor was usually a cool customer enough, and a certain vehemence in his manner struck me, but I couldn't get anything more out of him. I suppose the Treasury didn't see their way to prosecuting the Herberts for frightening a man to death; at any rate, nothing was done, and the case dropped out of men's minds. Do you happen to know anything of Herbert?"

"Well," replied Villiers, "he was an old college friend of mine."

"You don't say so? Have you ever seen his wife?"

"No, I haven't. I have lost sight of Herbert for many years."

"It's queer, isn't it, parting with a man at the college gate or at Paddington, seeing nothing of him for years, and then finding him pop up his head in such an odd place. But I should like to have seen Mrs. Herbert; people said extraordinary things about her."

"What sort of things?"

"Well, I hardly know how to tell you. Everyone who saw her at the police court said she was at once the most beautiful woman and the most repulsive they had ever set eyes on. I have spoken to a man who saw her, and I assure you he positively shuddered as he tried to describe the woman, but he couldn't tell why. She seems to have been a sort of enigma; and I expect if that one dead man could have told tales, he would have told some uncommonly queer ones. And there you are again in another puzzle; what could a respectable country gentleman like Mr. Blank (we'll call him that if you don't mind) want in such a very queer house as Number 20? It's altogether a very odd case, isn't it?"

"It is indeed, Austin; an extraordinary case. I didn't think, when I asked you about my old friend, I should strike on such strange metal. Well, I must be off; good-day."

Villiers went away, thinking of his own conceit of the Chinese boxes; here was quaint workmanship indeed.

4. The Discovery in Paul Street

A few months after Villiers's meeting with Herbert, Mr. Clarke was sitting, as usual, by his after-dinner hearth, resolutely guarding his fancies from wandering in the direction of the bureau. For more than a week he had succeeded in keeping away from the "Memoirs," and he cherished hopes of a complete self-reformation; but, in spite of his endeavours, he could not hush the wonder and the strange curiosity that that last case he had written down had executed within him. He had put the case, or rather the outline of it, conjecturally to a scientific friend, who shook his head, and thought Clarke getting queer, and on this particular evening Clarke was making an effort to rationalise the story, when a sudden knock at this door roused him from his meditations.

"Mr. Villiers to see you, sir."

"Dear me, Villiers, it is very kind of you to look me up; I have not seen you for many months; I should think nearly a year. Come in, come in. And how are you, Villiers? Want any advice about investments?"

"No, thanks. I fancy everything I have in that way is pretty safe. No, Clarke, I have really come to consult you about a rather curious matter that has been brought under my notice of late. I am afraid you will think it all rather absurd when I tell my tale. I sometimes think so myself, and that's just why I made up my mind to come to you, as I know you're a practical man."

Mr. Villiers was ignorant of the "Memoirs to Prove the Existence of the Devil."

"Well, Villiers, I shall be happy to give you my advice, to the best of my ability. What is the nature of the case?"

"It's an extraordinary thing, altogether. You know my ways; I always keep my eyes open in the streets, and in my time I have chanced upon some queer customers, and queer cases too, but this, I think, beats all. I was coming out of a restaurant one nasty winter night about three months ago; I had had a capital dinner and a good bottle of Chianti, and I stood for a moment on the pavement, thinking what a mystery there is about London streets and the companies that pass along them. A bottle of red wine encourages these fancies, Clarke, and I dare say I should have thought a page of small type, but I was cut short by a beggar who had come behind me, and was making the usual appeals. Of course I looked round, and this beggar turned out to be what was left of an old friend of mine, a man named Herbert. I asked him how he had come to such a wretched pass, and he told me. We walked up and down one of those long dark Soho streets, and there I listened to his story. He said he had married a beautiful girl, some years younger than himself, and, as he put it, she had corrupted him body and soul. He wouldn't go into details; he said he dare not, that what he had seen and heard haunted him by night and day, and when I looked in his face I knew he was speaking the truth. There was something about the man that made me shiver. I don't know why, but it was there. I gave him a little money and sent him away, and I assure you that when he was gone I gasped for breath. His presence seemed to chill one's blood."

"Isn't all this just a little fanciful, Villiers? I suppose the poor fellow had made an imprudent marriage, and, in plain English, gone to the bad."

"Well, listen to this." Villiers told Clarke the story he had heard from Austin.

"You see," he concluded, "there can be but little doubt that this Mr. Blank, whoever he was, died of sheer terror; he saw something so awful, so terrible, that it cut short his life. And what he saw, he most certainly saw in that house, which, somehow or other, had got a bad name in the neighbourhood. I had the curiosity to go and look at the place for myself. It's a saddening kind of street; the houses are old enough to be mean and dreary, but not old enough to be quaint. As far as I could see most of them are let in lodgings, furnished and unfurnished, and almost every door has three bells to it. Here and there ground floors have been made into shops of the commonest kind; it's a dismal street in every way. I found Number 20 was to let, and I went to the agent's and got the key. Of course I should have heard nothing of the Herberts in that quarter, but I asked the man, fair and square, how long they had left the house, and whether there had been other tenants in the meanwhile. He looked at me queerly for a minute, and told me the Herberts had left immediately after the unpleasantness, as he called it, and since then the house had been empty."

Mr. Villiers paused for a moment.

"I have always been rather fond of going over empty houses; there's a sort of fascination about the desolate empty rooms, with the nails sticking in the walls, and the dust thick upon the window-sills. But I didn't enjoy going over Number 20, Paul Street. I had hardly put my foot inside the passage before I noticed a queer, heavy feeling about the air of the house. Of course all empty houses are stuffy, and so forth, but this was something quite different; I can't describe it to you, but it seemed to stop the breath. I went into the front room and the back room, and the kitchens downstairs; they were all dirty and dusty enough, as you would expect, but there was something strange about them all. I couldn't define it to you, I only know I felt queer. It was one of the rooms on the first floor, though, that was the worst. It was a largish room, and once on a time the paper must have been cheerful enough, but when I saw it, paint, paper, and everything were most doleful. But the room was full of horror; I felt my teeth grinding as I put my hand on the door, and when I went in, I thought I should have fallen fainting to the floor. However, I pulled myself together, and stood against the end wall, wondering what on earth there could be about the room to make my limbs tremble, and my heart beat as if I were at the hour of death. In one corner there was a pile of newspapers littered about on the floor, and I began looking at them; they were papers of three or four years ago, some of them half torn, and some crumpled as if they had been used for packing. I turned the whole pile over, and among them I found a curious drawing; I will show it you presently. But I couldn't stay in the room; I felt it was overpowering me. I was thankful to come out, safe and sound, into the open air. People stared at me as I walked along the street, and one man said I was drunk. I was staggering about from one side of the pavement to the other, and it was as much as I could do to take the key back to the agent and get home. I was in bed for a week, suffering from what my doctor called nervous shock and exhaustion. One of those days I was reading the evening paper, and happened to notice a paragraph headed: "Starved to Death." It was the usual style of thing; a model lodging-house in Marylebone, a door locked for several days, and a dead man in his chair when they broke in. 'The deceased,' said the paragraph, 'was known as Charles Herbert, and is believed to have been once a prosperous country gentleman. His name was familiar to the public three years ago in connection with the mysterious death in Paul Street, Tottenham Court Road, the deceased being the tenant of the house Number 20, in the area of which a gentleman of good position was found dead under circumstances not devoid of suspicion.' A tragic ending, wasn't it? But after all, if what he told me were true, which I am sure it was, the man's life was all a tragedy, and a tragedy of a stranger sort than they put on the boards."

"And that is the story, is it?" said Clarke musingly.

"Yes, that is the story."

"Well, really, Villiers, I scarcely know what to say about it.

There are, no doubt, circumstances in the case which seem peculiar, the finding of the dead man in the area of Herbert's house, for instance, and the extraordinary opinion of the physician as to the cause of death; but, after all, it is conceivable that the facts may be explained in a straightforward manner. As to your own sensations, when you went to see the house, I would suggest that they were due to a vivid imagination; you must have been brooding, in a semi-conscious way, over what you had heard. I don't exactly see what more can be said or done in the matter; you evidently think there is a mystery of some kind, but Herbert is dead; where then do you propose to look?"

"I propose to look for the woman; the woman whom he married. *She* is the mystery."

The two men sat silent by the fireside; Clarke secretly congratulating himself on having successfully kept up the character of advocate of the commonplace, and Villiers wrapt in his gloomy fancies.

"I think I will have a cigarette," he said at last, and put his hand in his pocket to feel for the cigarette-case.

"Ah!" he said, starting slightly, "I forgot I had something to show you. You remember my saying that I had found a rather curious sketch among the pile of old newspapers at the house in Paul Street? Here it is."

Villiers drew out a small thin parcel from his pocket. It was covered with brown paper, and secured with string, and the knots were troublesome. In spite of himself Clarke felt inquisitive; he bent forward on his chair as Villiers painfully undid the string, and unfolded the outer covering. Inside was a second wrapping of tissue, and Villiers took it off and handed the small piece of paper to Clarke without a word.

There was dead silence in the room for five minutes or more; the two men sat so still that they could hear the ticking of the tall old-fashioned clock that stood outside in the hall, and in the mind of one of them the slow monotony of sound woke up a far, far memory. He was looking intently at the small pen-and-ink sketch of the woman's head; it had evidently been drawn with great care, and by a true artist, for the woman's soul looked out of the eyes, and the lips were parted with a strange smile. Clarke gazed still at the face; it brought to his memory one summer evening long ago; he saw again the long lovely valley, the river winding between the hills, the meadows and the cornfields, the dull red sun, and the cold white mist rising from the water. He heard a voice speaking to him across the waves of many years, and saying: "Clarke, Mary will see the God Pan!" and then he was standing in the grim room beside the doctor, listening to the heavy ticking of the clock, waiting and watching, watching the figure lying on the green chair beneath the lamp-light. Mary rose up, and he looked into her eyes, and his heart grew cold within him.

"Who is this woman?" he said at last. His voice was dry and hoarse.

"That is the woman whom Herbert married."

Clarke looked again at the sketch; it was not Mary after all. There certainly was Mary's face, but there was something else, something he had not seen on Mary's features when the white-clad girl entered the laboratory with the doctor, nor at her terrible awakening, nor when she lay grinning on the bed. Whatever it was, the glance that came from those eyes, the smile on the full lips, or the expression of the whole face, Clarke shuddered before it in his inmost soul, and thought, unconsciously, of Dr. Phillips's words, "the most vivid presentment of evil I have ever seen." He turned the paper over mechanically in his hand and glanced at the back.

"Good God! Clarke, what is the matter? You are as white as death."

Villiers had started wildly from his chair, as Clarke fell back with a groan, and let the paper drop from his hands.

"I don't feel very well, Villiers, I am subject to these attacks. Pour me out a little wine; thanks, that will do. I shall feel better in a few minutes."

Villiers picked up the fallen sketch and turned it over as Clarke had done.

"You saw that?" he said. "That's how I identified it as being a portrait of Herbert's wife, or I should say his widow. How do you feel now?"

"Better, thanks, it was only a passing faintness. I don't think I quite catch your meaning. What did you say enabled you to identify the picture?"

"This word—'Helen'—written on the back. Didn't I tell you her name was Helen? Yes; Helen Vaughan."

Clarke groaned; there could be no shadow of doubt.

"Now, don't you agree with me," said Villiers, "that in the story

I have told you tonight, and in the part this woman plays in it, there are some very strange points?"

"Yes, Villiers," Clarke muttered, "it is a strange story indeed; a strange story indeed. You must give me time to think it over; I may be able to help you or I may not. Must you be going now? Well, good-night, Villiers, good-night. Come and see me in the course of a week."

5. The Letter of Advice

"Do you know, Austin," said Villiers, as the two friends were pacing sedately along Piccadilly one pleasant morning in May, "do you know I am convinced that what you told me about Paul Street and the Herberts is a mere episode in an extraordinary history? I may as well confess to you that when I asked you about Herbert a few months ago I had just seen him."

"You had seen him? Where?"

"He begged of me in the street one night. He was in the most pitiable plight, but I recognised the man, and I got him to tell me his history, or at least the outline of it. In brief, it amounted to this—he had been ruined by his wife."

"In what manner?"

"He would not tell me; he would only say that she had destroyed him, body and soul. The man is dead now."

"And what has become of his wife?"

"Ah, that's what I should like to know, and I mean to find her sooner or later. I know a man named Clarke, a dry fellow, in fact a man of business, but shrewd enough. You understand my meaning; not shrewd in the mere business sense of the word, but a man who really knows something about men and life. Well, I laid the case before him, and he was evidently impressed. He said it needed consideration, and asked me to come again in the course of a week. A few days later I received this extraordinary letter."

Austin took the envelope, drew out the letter, and read it curiously. It ran as follows:

> My dear Villiers—I have thought over the matter on which you consulted me the other night, and my advice to you is this. Throw the portrait into the fire, blot out the story from your mind. Never give it another thought, Villiers, or you will be sorry. You will think, no doubt, that I am in possession of some secret information, and to a

certain extent that is the case. But I only know a little; I am like a traveller who has peered over an abyss, and has drawn back in terror. What I know is strange enough and horrible enough, but beyond my knowledge there are depths and horrors more frightful still, more incredible than any tale told of winter nights about the fire. I have resolved, and nothing shall shake that resolve, to explore no whit further, and if you value your happiness you will make the same determination.

Come and see me by all means; but we will talk on more cheerful topics than this.

Austin folded the letter methodically, and returned it to Villiers.

"It is certainly an extraordinary letter," he said, "what does he mean by the portrait?"

"Ah! I forgot to tell you I have been to Paul Street and have made a discovery."

Villiers told his story as he had told it to Clarke, and Austin listened in silence. He seemed puzzled.

"How very curious that you should experience such an unpleasant sensation in that room!" he said at length. "I hardly gather that it was a mere matter of the imagination; a feeling of repulsion, in short."

"No, it was more physical than mental. It was as if I were inhaling at every breath some deadly fume, which seemed to penetrate to every nerve and bone and sinew of my body. I felt racked from head to foot, my eyes began to grow dim; it was like the entrance of death."

"Yes, yes, very strange, certainly. You see, your friend confesses that there is some very black story connected with this woman. Did you notice any particular emotion in him when you were telling your tale?"

"Yes, I did. He became very faint, but he assured me that it was a mere passing attack to which he was subject."

"Did you believe him?"

"I did at the time, but I don't now. He heard what I had to say with a good deal of indifference, till I showed him the portrait. It was then he was seized with the attack of which I spoke. He looked ghastly, I assure you."

"Then he must have seen the woman before. But there might be another explanation; it might have been the name, and not the face, which was familiar to him. What do you think?"

"I couldn't say. To the best of my belief it was after turning the portrait in his hands that he nearly dropped from his chair. The name, you know, was written on the back."

"Quite so. After all, it is impossible to come to any resolution in a case like this. I hate melodrama, and nothing strikes me as more commonplace and tedious than the ordinary ghost story of commerce; but really, Villiers, it looks as if there were something very queer at the bottom of all this."

The two men had, without noticing it, turned up Ashley Street, leading northward from Piccadilly. It was a long street, and rather a gloomy one, but here and there a brighter taste had illuminated the dark houses with flowers, and gay curtains, and a cheerful paint on the doors. Villiers glanced up as Austin stopped speaking, and looked at one of these houses, geraniums, red and white, drooped from every sill, and daffodil-coloured curtains were draped back from each window.

"It looks cheerful, doesn't it?" he said.

"Yes, and the inside is still more cheery. One of the pleasantest houses of the season, so I have heard. I haven't been there myself, but I've met several men who have, and they tell me it's uncommonly jovial."

"Whose house is it?"

"A Mrs. Beaumont's."

"And who is she?"

"I couldn't tell you. I have heard she comes from South America, but, after all, who she is is of little consequence. She is a very wealthy woman, there's no doubt of that, and some of the best people have taken her up. I heard she has some wonderful claret, really marvellous wine, which must have cost a fabulous sum. Lord Argentine was telling me about it; he was there last Sunday evening. He assures me he has never tasted such a wine, and Argentine, as you know, is an expert. By the way, that reminds me, she must be an oddish sort of woman, this Mrs. Beaumont. Argentine asked her how old the wine was, and what do you think she said? 'About a thousand years, I believe.' Lord Argentine thought she was chaffing him, you know, but when he laughed she said she was speaking quite seriously, and offered to show him the jar. Of course, he couldn't say anything more after that; but it seems rather antiquated for a beverage, doesn't it? Why, here we are at my rooms. Come in, won't you?"

"Thanks, I think I will. I haven't seen the curiosity-shop for some time."

It was a room furnished richly, yet oddly, where every chair and bookcase and table, and every rug and jar and ornament seemed to be a thing apart, preserving each its own individuality.

"Anything fresh lately?" said Villiers after a while.

"No; I think not; you saw those queer jugs, didn't you? I thought so. I don't think I have come across anything for the last few weeks."

Austin glanced round the room from cupboard to cupboard, from shelf to shelf, in search of some new oddity. His eyes fell at last on an old chest, pleasantly and quaintly carved, which stood in a dark corner of the room.

"Ah," he said, "I was forgetting, I have got something to show you." Austin unlocked the chest, drew out a thick quarto volume, laid it on the table, and resumed the cigar he had put down.

"Did you know Arthur Meyrick the painter, Villiers?"

"A little; I met him two or three times at the house of a friend of mine. What has become of him? I haven't heard his name mentioned for some time."

"He's dead."

"You don't say so! Quite young, wasn't he?"

"Yes; only thirty when he died."

"What did he die of?"

"I don't know. He was an intimate friend of mine, and a thoroughly good fellow. He used to come here and talk to me for hours, and he was one of the best talkers I have met. He could even talk about painting, and that's more than can be said of most painters. About eighteen months ago he was feeling rather overworked, and partly at my suggestion he went off on a sort of roving expedition, with no very definite end or aim about it. I believe New York was to be his first port, but I never heard from him. Three months ago I got this book, with a very civil letter from an English doctor practising in Buenos Aires, stating that he had attended the late Mr. Meyrick during his illness, and that the deceased had expressed an earnest wish that the enclosed packet should be sent to me after his death. That was all."

"And haven't you written for further particulars?"

"I have been thinking of doing so. You would advise me to write to the doctor?"

"Certainly. And what about the book?"

"It was sealed up when I got it. I don't think the doctor had seen it."

"It is something very rare? Meyrick was a collector, perhaps?"

"No, I think not, hardly a collector. Now, what do you think of those Ainu jugs?"

"They are peculiar, but I like them. But aren't you going to show me poor Meyrick's legacy?"

"Yes, yes, to be sure. The fact is, it's rather a peculiar sort of thing, and I haven't shown it to anyone. I wouldn't say anything about it if I were you. There it is."

Villiers took the book, and opened it haphazard.

"It isn't a printed volume then?" he said.

"No. It's a collection of drawings in black and white by my poor friend Meyrick."

Villiers turned to the first page, it was blank; the second bore a brief inscription, which he read:

> Silet per diem universus, nec sine horrore secretus est; lucet nocturnis ignibus, chorus Aegipanum undique personatur; audiuntur et cantus tibiarum, et tinnitus cymbalorum per oram maritiman.

On the third page was a design which made Villiers start and look up at Austin; he was gazing abstractedly out of the window. Villiers turned page after page, absorbed, in spite of himself, in the frightful Walpurgis-night of evil, strange monstrous evil, that the dead artist had set forth in hard black and white. The figures of fauns and satyrs and Ægipans danced before his eyes, the darkness of the thicket, the dance on the mountain-top, the scenes by lonely shores, in green vineyards, by rocks and desert places, passed before him: a world before which the human soul seemed to shrink back and shudder. Villiers whirled over the remaining pages; he had seen enough, but the picture on the last leaf caught his eye, as he almost closed the book.

"Austin!"

"Well, what is it?"

"Do you know who that is?"

It was a woman's face, alone on the white page.

"Know who it is? No, of course not."

"I do."

"Who is it?"

"It is Mrs. Herbert."

"Are you sure?"

"I am perfectly certain of it. Poor Meyrick! He is one more chapter in her history."

"But what do you think of the designs?"

"They are frightful. Lock the book up again, Austin. If I were you I would burn it; it must be a terrible companion even though it be in a chest."

"Yes, they are singular drawings. But I wonder what connection there could be between Meyrick and Mrs. Herbert, or what link between her and these designs?"

"Ah, who can say? It is possible that the matter may end here, and we shall never know, but in my own opinion this Helen Vaughan, or Mrs. Herbert, is only the beginning. She will come back to London, Austin; depend upon it, she will come back, and we shall hear more about her then. I don't think it will be very pleasant news."

6. The Suicides

Lord Argentine was a great favourite in London society. At twenty he had been a poor man, decked with the surname of an illustrious family, but forced to earn a livelihood as best he could, and the most speculative of money-lenders would not have entrusted him with fifty pounds on the chance of his ever changing his name for a title, and his poverty for a great fortune. His father had been near enough to the fountain of good things to secure one of the family livings, but the son, even if he had taken orders, would scarcely have obtained so much as this, and moreover felt no vocation for the ecclesiastical estate. Thus he fronted the world with no better armour than the bachelor's gown and the wit of a younger son's grandson, with which equipment he contrived in some way to make a very tolerable fight of it. At twenty-five Mr. Charles Aubernoun saw himself still a man of struggles and of warfare with the world, but out of the seven who stood between him and the high places of his family three only remained. These three, however, were "good lives," but yet not proof against the Zulu assegais and typhoid fever, and so one morning Aubernoun woke up and found himself Lord Argentine, a man of thirty who had faced the difficulties of existence, and had conquered. The situation amused him immensely, and he resolved that riches should be as pleasant to him as poverty had always been. Argentine, after some little consideration, came to the conclusion that dining, regarded as a fine art, was perhaps the most amusing pursuit open to fallen humanity and thus his dinners became famous in London and an invitation to his table a thing covetously desired. After ten years of lordship and dinners Argentine still declined to be jaded, still persisted in enjoying life, and by a kind of infection had become recognised as the cause of joy in others, in short, as the best of company. His sudden and tragical death therefore caused a wide and deep sensation. People could scarce believe it, even though the newspaper was before their eyes, and the cry of "Mysterious Death of a Nobleman" came ringing up from the street. But there stood the brief paragraph: "Lord Argentine was found dead this morning by his valet under distressing circumstances. It is stated that there can be no doubt that his lordship committed suicide, though no motive can be assigned for the act. The deceased nobleman was widely known in society, and much liked for his genial manner and sumptuous hospitality. He is succeeded by," etc., etc.

By slow degrees the details came to light, but the case still remained a mystery. The chief witness at the inquest was the dead nobleman's valet, who said that the night before his death Lord Argentine had dined with a lady of good position, whose name was suppressed in the newspaper reports. At about eleven o'clock Lord Argentine had returned, and informed his man that he should not require his services till the next morning. A little later the valet had occasion to cross the hall and was somewhat astonished to see his master quietly letting himself out at the front door. He had taken off his evening clothes, and was dressed in a Norfolk coat and knickerbockers, and wore a low brown hat. The valet had no reason to suppose that Lord Argentine had seen him, and though his master rarely kept late hours, thought little of the occurrence till the next morning, when he knocked at the bedroom door at a quarter to nine as usual. He received no answer, and, after knocking two or three times, entered the room, and saw Lord Argentine's body leaning forward at an angle from the bottom of the bed. He found that his master had tied a cord securely to one of the short bedposts, and, after making a running noose and slipping it round his neck, the unfortunate man must have resolutely fallen forward, to die by slow strangulation. He was dressed in the light suit in which the valet had seen him go out, and the doctor who was summoned pronounced that life had been extinct for more than four hours. All papers, letters, and so forth seemed in perfect order, and nothing was discovered which pointed in the most remote way to any scandal either great or small.

Here the evidence ended; nothing more could be discovered. Several persons had been present at the dinner-party at which Lord Argentine had assisted, and to all these he seemed in his usual genial spirits. The valet, indeed, said he thought his master appeared a little excited when he came home, but he confessed that the alteration in his manner was very slight, hardly noticeable, indeed. It seemed hopeless to seek for any clue, and the suggestion that Lord Argentine had been suddenly attacked by acute suicidal mania was generally accepted.

It was otherwise, however, when within three weeks, three more gentlemen, one of them a nobleman, and the two others men of good position and ample means, perished miserably in almost precisely the same manner. Lord Swanleigh was found one morning in his dressing-room, hanging from a peg affixed to the wall, and Mr. Collier-Stuart and Mr. Herries had chosen to die as Lord Argentine. There was no explanation in either case; a few bald facts; a living man in the evening, and a dead body with a black swollen face in the morning. The police had been forced to confess themselves powerless to arrest or to explain the sordid murders of Whitechapel; but before the horrible suicides of Piccadilly and Mayfair they were dumbfounded, for not even the mere ferocity which did duty as an explanation of the crimes of the East End, could be of service in the West. Each of these men who had resolved to die a tortured shameful death was rich, prosperous, and to all appearances in love with the world, and not the acutest research could ferret out any shadow of a lurking motive in either case. There was a horror in the air, and men looked at one another's faces when they met, each wondering whether the other was to be the victim of the fifth nameless tragedy. Journalists sought in vain in their scrapbooks for materials whereof to concoct reminiscent articles; and the morning paper was unfolded in many a house with a feeling of awe; no man knew when or where the blow would next light.

A short while after the last of these terrible events, Austin came to see Mr. Villiers. He was curious to know whether Villiers had succeeded in discovering any fresh traces of Mrs. Herbert, either through Clarke or by other sources, and he asked the question soon after he had sat down.

"No," said Villiers. "I wrote to Clarke, but he remains obdurate, and I have tried other channels, but without any result. I can't find out what became of Helen Vaughan after she left Paul Street, but I think she must have gone abroad. But to tell the truth, Austin, I haven't paid very much attention to the matter for the last few weeks; I knew poor Herries intimately, and his terrible death has been a great shock to me, a great shock."

"I can well believe it," answered Austin gravely; "you know Argentine was a friend of mine. If I remember rightly, we were speaking of him that day you came to my rooms."

"Yes; it was in connection with the house in Ashley Street, Mrs. Beaumont's house. You said something about Argentine's dining there."

"Quite so. Of course you know it was there Argentine dined the night before—before his death."

"No, I haven't heard that."

"Oh yes; the name was kept out of the papers to spare Mrs. Beaumont. Argentine was a great favourite of hers, and it is said she was in a terrible state for some time after."

A curious look came over Villiers's face; he seemed undecided whether to speak or not. Austin began again.

"I never experienced such a feeling of horror as when I read the account of Argentine's death. I didn't understand it at the time, and I don't now. I knew him well, and it completely passes my understanding for what possible cause he—or any of the others for the matter of that—could have resolved in cold blood to die in such an awful manner. You know how men babble away each other's characters in London, you may be sure any buried scandal or hidden skeleton would have been brought to light in such a case as this; but nothing of the sort has taken place. As for the theory of mania, that is very well, of course, for the coroner's jury, but everybody knows that it's all nonsense. Suicidal mania is not smallpox."

Austin relapsed into gloomy silence. Villiers sat silent also, watching his friend. The expression of indecision still fleeted across his face; he seemed as if weighing his thoughts in the balance, and the considerations he was revolving left him still silent. Austin tried to shake off the remembrance of tragedies as hopeless and perplexed as the labyrinth of Daedalus, and began to talk in an indifferent voice of the more pleasant incidents and adventures of the season.

"That Mrs. Beaumont," he said, "of whom we were speaking, is a great success; she has taken London almost by storm. I met her the other night at Fulham's; she is really a remarkable woman."

"You have met Mrs. Beaumont?"

"Yes; she had quite a court around her. She would be called very handsome, I suppose, and yet there is something about her face which I didn't like. The features are exquisite, but the expression is strange. And all the time I was looking at her, and afterwards, when I was going home, I had a curious feeling that that very expression was in some way or other familiar to me."

"You must have seen her in the Row."

"No, I am sure I never set eyes on the woman before; it is that which makes it puzzling. And to the best of my belief I have never seen anybody like her; what I felt was a kind of dim far-off memory, vague but persistent. The only sensation I can compare it to, is that odd feeling one sometimes has in a dream, when fantastic cities and wondrous lands and phantom personages appear familiar and accustomed."

Villiers nodded and glanced aimlessly round the room, possibly in search of something on which to turn the conversation. His eyes fell on an old chest somewhat like that in which the artist's strange legacy lay hid beneath a Gothic scutcheon.

"Have you written to the doctor about poor Meyrick?" he asked.

"Yes; I wrote asking for full particulars as to his illness and death. I don't expect to have an answer for another three weeks or a month. I thought I might as well inquire whether Meyrick knew an Englishwoman named Herbert, and if so, whether the doctor could give me any information about her. But it's very possible that Meyrick fell in with her at New York, or Mexico, or San Francisco; I have no idea as to the extent or direction of his travels."

"Yes, and it's very possible that the woman may have more than one name."

"Exactly. I wish I had thought of asking you to lend me the portrait of her which you possess. I might have enclosed it in my letter to Dr. Matthews."

"So you might; that never occurred to me. We might send it now. Hark! what are those boys calling?"

While the two men had been talking together a confused noise of shouting had been gradually growing louder. The noise rose from the eastward and swelled down Piccadilly, drawing nearer and nearer, a very torrent of sound; surging up streets usually quiet, and making every window a frame for a face, curious or excited. The cries and voices came echoing up the silent street where Villiers lived, growing more distinct as they advanced, and, as Villiers spoke, an answer rang up from the pavement:

THE WEST END HORRORS; ANOTHER AWFUL SUICIDE; FULL DETAILS!

Austin rushed down the stairs and bought a paper and read out the paragraph to Villiers as the uproar in the street rose and fell. The window was open and the air seemed full of noise and terror.

> Another gentleman has fallen a victim to the terrible epidemic of suicide which for the last month has prevailed in the West End. Mr. Sidney Crashaw, of Stoke House, Fulham, and King's Pomeroy, Devon, was found, after a prolonged search, hanging from the branch of a tree in his garden at one o'clock today. The deceased gentleman dined last night at the Carlton Club and seemed in his usual health and spirits. He left the Club at about ten o'clock, and was seen walking leisurely up St. James's Street a little later. Subsequent to this his movements cannot be traced. On the discovery of the body medical aid was at once summoned, but life had evidently been long extinct. So far as is known, Mr. Crashaw had no trouble or anxiety of any kind. This painful suicide, it will be remembered, is the fifth of the kind in the last month. The authorities at Scotland Yard are unable to suggest any explanation of these terrible occurrences.

Austin put down the paper in mute horror.

"I shall leave London tomorrow," he said, "it is a city of nightmares. How awful this is, Villiers!"

Mr. Villiers was sitting by the window quietly looking out into the street. He had listened to the newspaper report attentively, and the hint of indecision was no longer on his face.

"Wait a moment, Austin," he replied, "I have made up my mind to mention a little matter that occurred last night. It is stated, I think, that Crashaw was last seen alive in St. James's Street shortly after ten?"

"Yes, I think so. I will look again. Yes, you are quite right."

"Quite so. Well, I am in a position to contradict that statement at all events. Crashaw was seen after that; considerably later indeed."

"How do you know?"

"Because I happened to see Crashaw myself at about two o'clock this morning."

"You saw Crashaw? You, Villiers?"

"Yes, I saw him quite distinctly; indeed, there were but a few feet between us."

"Where, in Heaven's name, did you see him?"

"Not far from here. I saw him in Ashley Street. He was just leaving a house."

"Did you notice what house it was?"

"Yes. It was Mrs. Beaumont's."

"Villiers! Think what you are saying; there must be some mistake. How could Crashaw be in Mrs. Beaumont's house at two o'clock in the morning? Surely, surely, you must have been dreaming, Villiers, you were always rather fanciful."

"No; I was wide awake enough. Even if I had been dreaming as you say, what I saw would have roused me effectually."

"What you saw? What did you see? Was there anything strange about Crashaw? But I can't believe it; it is impossible."

"Well, if you like I will tell you what I saw, or if you please, what I think I saw, and you can judge for yourself."

"Very good, Villiers."

The noise and clamour of the street had died away, though now and then the sound of shouting still came from the distance, and the dull, leaden silence seemed like the quiet after an earthquake or a storm. Villiers turned from the window and began speaking.

"I was at a house near Regent's Park last night, and when I came away the fancy took me to walk home instead of taking a hansom. It was a clear pleasant night enough, and after a few minutes I had the streets pretty much to myself. It's a curious thing, Austin, to be alone in London at night, the gas-lamps stretching away in perspective, and the dead silence, and then perhaps the rush and clatter of a hansom on the stones, and the fire starting up under the horse's hoofs. I walked along pretty briskly, for I was feeling a little tired of being out in the night, and as the clocks were striking two I turned down Ashley Street, which, you know, is on my way. It was quieter than ever there, and the lamps were fewer; altogether, it looked as dark and gloomy as a forest in winter. I had done about half the length of the street when I heard a door closed very softly, and naturally I looked up to see who was abroad like myself at such an hour. As it happens, there is a street lamp close to the house in question, and I saw a man standing on the step. He had just shut the door and his face was towards me, and I recognised Crashaw directly. I never knew him to speak to, but I had often seen him, and I am positive that I was not mistaken in my man. I looked into his face for a moment, and then—I will confess the truth—I set off at a good run, and kept it up till I was within my own door."

"Why?"

"Why? Because it made my blood run cold to see that man's face. I could never have supposed that such an infernal medley of passions could have glared out of any human eyes; I almost fainted as I looked. I knew I had looked into the eyes of a lost soul, Austin, the man's outward form remained, but all hell was within it. Furious lust, and hate that was like fire, and the loss of all hope and horror that seemed to shriek aloud to the night, though his teeth were shut; and the utter blackness of despair. I am sure he did not see me; he saw nothing that you or I can see, but he saw what I hope we never shall. I do not know when he died; I suppose in an hour, perhaps two, but when I passed down Ashley Street and heard the closing door, that man no longer belonged to this world; it was a devil's face I looked upon."

There was an interval of silence in the room when Villiers ceased speaking. The light was failing, and all the tumult of an hour ago was quite hushed. Austin had bent his head at the close of the story, and his hand covered his eyes.

"What can it mean?" he said at length.

"Who knows, Austin, who knows? It's a black business, but I think we had better keep it to ourselves, for the present at any rate. I will see if I cannot learn anything about that house through private channels of information, and if I do light upon anything I will let you know."

7. The Encounter in Soho

Three weeks later Austin received a note from Villiers, asking him to call either that afternoon or the next. He chose the nearer date, and found Villiers sitting as usual by the window, apparently lost in meditation on the drowsy traffic of the street. There was a bamboo table by his side, a fantastic thing, enriched with gilding and queer painted scenes, and on it lay a little pile of papers arranged and cocketed as neatly as anything in Mr. Clarke's office.

"Well, Villiers, have you made any discoveries in the last three weeks?"

"I think so; I have here one or two memoranda which struck me as singular, and there is a statement to which I shall call your attention."

"And these documents relate to Mrs. Beaumont? It was really Crashaw whom you saw that night standing on the doorstep of the house in Ashley Street?"

"As to that matter my belief remains unchanged, but neither my inquiries nor their results have any special relation to Crashaw. But my investigations have had a strange issue. I have found out who Mrs. Beaumont is!"

"Who is she? In what way do you mean?"

"I mean that you and I know her better under another name."

"What name is that?"

"Herbert."

"Herbert!" Austin repeated the word, dazed with astonishment.

"Yes, Mrs. Herbert of Paul Street, Helen Vaughan of earlier adventures unknown to me. You had reason to recognise the expression of her face; when you go home look at the the face in Meyrick's book of horrors, and you will know the sources of your recollection."

"And you have proof of this?"

"Yes, the best of proof; I have seen Mrs. Beaumont, or shall we say Mrs. Herbert?"

"Where did you see her?"

"Hardly in a place where you would expect to see a lady who lives in Ashley Street, Piccadilly. I saw her entering a house in one of the meanest and most disreputable streets in Soho. In fact, I had made an appointment, though not with her, and she was precise both to time and place."

"All this seems very wonderful, but I cannot call it incredible. You must remember, Villiers, that I have seen this woman, in the ordinary adventure of London society, talking and laughing, and sipping her coffee in a commonplace drawing-room with commonplace people. But you know what you are saying?"

"I do; I have not allowed myself to be led by surmises or fancies. It was with no thought of finding Helen Vaughan that I searched for Mrs. Beaumont in the dark waters of the life of London, but such has been the issue."

"You must have been in strange places, Villiers."

"Yes, I have been in very strange places. It would have been useless, you know, to go to Ashley Street, and ask Mrs. Beaumont to give me a short sketch of her previous history. No; assuming, as I had to assume, that her record was not of the cleanest, it would be pretty certain that at some previous time she must have moved in circles not quite so refined as her present ones. If you see mud on the top of a stream, you may be sure that it was once at the bottom. I went to the bottom. I have always been fond of diving into Queer Street for my amusement, and I found my knowledge of that locality and its inhabitants very useful. It is, perhaps, needless to say that my friends had never heard the name of Beaumont, and as I had never seen the lady, and was quite unable to describe her, I had to set to work in an indirect way. The people there know me; I have been able to do some of them a service now and again, so they made no difficulty about giving their information; they were aware I had no communication direct or indirect with Scotland Yard. I had to cast out a good many lines, though, before I got what I wanted, and when I landed the fish I did not for a moment suppose it was my fish. But I listened to what I was told out of a constitutional liking for useless information, and I found myself in possession of a very curious story, though, as I imagined, not the story I was looking for. It was to this effect. Some five or six years ago, a woman named Raymond suddenly made her appearance in the neighbourhood to which I am referring. She was described to me as being quite young, probably not more than seventeen or eighteen, very handsome, and looking as if she came from the country. I should be wrong in saying that she found her level in going to this particular quarter, or associating with these people, for from what I was told, I should think the worst den in London far too good for her. The person from whom I got my information, as you may suppose, no great Puritan, shuddered and grew sick in telling me of the nameless infamies which were laid to her charge. After living there for a year, or perhaps a little more, she disappeared as suddenly as she came, and they saw nothing of her till about the time of the Paul Street case. At first she came to her old haunts only occasionally, then more frequently, and finally took up her abode there as before, and remained for six or eight months. It's of no use my going into details as to the life that woman led; if you want particulars you can look at Meyrick's legacy. Those designs were not drawn from his imagination. She again disappeared, and the people of the place saw nothing of her till a few months ago. My informant told me that she had taken some rooms in a house which he pointed out, and these rooms she was in the habit of visiting two or three times a week and always at ten in the morning. I was led to expect that one of these visits would be paid on a certain day about a week ago, and I accordingly managed to be on the look-out in company with my cicerone at a quarter to ten, and the hour and the lady came with equal punctuality. My friend and I were standing under an archway, a little way back from the street, but she saw us, and gave me a glance that I shall be long in forgetting. That look was quite enough for me; I knew Miss Raymond to be Mrs. Herbert; as for Mrs. Beaumont she had quite gone out of my head. She went into the house, and I watched it till four o'clock, when she came out, and then I followed her. It was a long chase, and I had to be very careful to keep a long way in the background, and yet not lose sight of the woman. She took me down to the Strand, and then to Westminster, and then up St. James's Street, and along Piccadilly. I felt queerish when I saw her turn up Ashley Street; the thought that Mrs. Herbert was Mrs. Beaumont came into my mind, but it seemed too improbable to be true. I waited at the corner, keeping my eye on her all the time, and I took particular care to note the house at which she stopped. It was the house with the gay curtains, the house of flowers, the house out of which Crashaw came the night he hanged himself in his garden. I was just going away with my discovery, when I saw an empty carriage come round and draw up in front of the house, and I came to the conclusion that Mrs. Herbert was going out for a drive, and I was right. I took a hansom and followed the carriage into the Park. There, as it happened, I met a man I know, and we stood talking together a little distance from the carriage-way, to which I had my back. We had not been there for ten minutes when my friend took off his hat, and I glanced round and saw the lady I had been following all day. "Who is that?" I said, and his answer was, "Mrs. Beaumont; lives in Ashley Street." Of course there could be no doubt after that. I don't know whether she saw me, but I don't think she did. I went home at once, and, in consideration, I thought that I had a sufficiently good case with which to go to Clarke."

"Why to Clarke?"

"Because I am sure that Clarke is in possession of facts about this woman, facts of which I know nothing."

"Well, what then?"

Mr. Villiers leaned back in his chair and looked reflectively at Austin for a moment before he answered:

"My idea was that Clarke and I should call on Mrs. Beaumont."

"You would never go into such a house as that? No, no, Villiers, you cannot do it. Besides, consider; what result. . . ."

"I will tell you soon. But I was going to say that my information does not end here; it has been completed in an extraordinary manner.

"Look at this neat little packet of manuscript; it is paginated, you see, and I have indulged in the civil coquetry of a ribbon of red tape. It has almost a legal air, hasn't it? Run your eye over it, Austin. It is an account of the entertainment Mrs. Beaumont provided for her choicer guests. The man who wrote this escaped with his life, but I do not think he will live many years. The doctors tell him he must have sustained some severe shock to the nerves."

Austin took the manuscript, but never read it. Opening the neat pages at haphazard his eye was caught by a word and a phrase that followed it; and, sick at heart, with white lips and a cold sweat pouring like water from his temples, he flung the paper down.

"Take it away, Villiers, never speak of this again. Are you made of stone, man? Why, the dread and horror of death itself, the thoughts of the man who stands in the keen morning air on the black platform, bound, the bell tolling in his ears, and waits for the harsh rattle of the bolt, are as nothing compared to this. I will not read it; I should never sleep again."

"Very good. I can fancy what you saw. Yes; it is horrible enough; but after all, it is an old story, an old mystery played in our day, and in dim London streets instead of amidst the vineyards and the olive gardens. We know what happened to those who chanced to meet the Great God Pan, and those who are wise know that all symbols are symbols of something, not of nothing. It was, indeed, an exquisite symbol beneath which men long ago veiled their knowledge of the most awful, most secret forces which lie at the heart of all things; forces before which the souls of men must wither and die and blacken, as their bodies blacken under the electric current. Such forces cannot be named, cannot be spoken, cannot be imagined except under a veil and a symbol, a symbol to the most of us appearing a quaint, poetic fancy, to some a foolish tale. But you and I, at all events, have known something of the terror that may dwell in the secret place of life, manifested under human flesh; that which is without form taking to itself a form. Oh, Austin, how can it be? How is it that the very sunlight does not turn to blackness before this thing, the hard earth melt and boil beneath such a burden?"

Villiers was pacing up and down the room, and the beads of sweat stood out on his forehead. Austin sat silent for a while, but Villiers saw him make a sign upon his breast.

"I say again, Villiers, you will surely never enter such a house as that? You would never pass out alive."

"Yes, Austin, I shall go out alive—I, and Clarke with me."

"What do you mean? You cannot, you would not dare. . . ."

"Wait a moment. The air was very pleasant and fresh this morning; there was a breeze blowing, even through this dull street, and I thought I would take a walk. Piccadilly stretched before me a clear, bright vista, and the sun flashed on the carriages and on the quivering leaves in the park. It was a joyous morning, and men and women looked at the sky and smiled as they went about their work or their pleasure, and the wind blew as blithely as upon the meadows and the scented gorse. But somehow or other I got out of the bustle and the gaiety, and found myself walking slowly along a quiet, dull street, where there seemed to be no sunshine and no air, and where the few foot-passengers loitered as they walked, and hung indecisively about corners and archways. I walked along, hardly knowing where I was going or what I did there, but feeling impelled, as one sometimes is, to explore still further, with a vague idea of reaching some unknown goal. Thus I forged up the street, noting the small traffic in the milk-shop, and wondering at the incongruous medley of penny pipes, black tobacco, sweets, newspapers, and comic songs which here and there jostled one another in the short compass of a single window. I think it was a cold shudder that suddenly passed through me that first told me that I had found what I wanted. I looked up from the pavement and stopped before a dusty shop, above which the lettering had faded, where the red bricks of two hundred years ago had grimed to black; where the windows had gathered to themselves the fog and the dirt of winters innumerable. I saw what I required; but I think it was five minutes before I had steadied myself and could walk in and ask for it in a cool voice and with a calm face. I think there must even then have been a tremor in my words, for the old man who came out from his back parlour, and fumbled slowly among his goods, looked oddly at me as he tied the parcel. I paid what he asked, and stood leaning by the counter, with a strange reluctance to take up my goods and go. I asked about the business, and learnt that trade was bad and the profits cut down sadly; but then the street was not what it was before traffic had been diverted, but that was done forty years ago, 'just before my father died,' he said. I got away at last, and walked along sharply; it was a dismal street indeed, and I was glad to return to the bustle and the noise. Would you like to see my purchase?"

Austin said nothing, but nodded his head slightly; he still looked white and sick. Villiers pulled out a drawer in the bamboo table, and showed Austin a long coil of cord, hard and new; and at one end was a running noose.

"It is the best hempen cord," said Villiers, "just as it used to be made for the old trade, the man told me. Not an inch of jute from end to end."

Austin set his teeth hard, and stared at Villiers, growing whiter as he looked.

"You would not do it," he murmured at last. "You would not have blood on your hands. My God!" he exclaimed, with sudden vehemence, "you cannot mean this, Villiers, that you will make yourself a hangman?"

"No. I shall offer a choice, and leave Helen Vaughan alone with this cord in a locked room for fifteen minutes. If when we go in it is not done, I shall call the nearest policeman. That is all."

"I must go now. I cannot stay here any longer; I cannot bear this. Good-night."

"Good-night, Austin."

The door shut, but in a moment it was opened again, and Austin stood, white and ghastly, in the entrance.

"I was forgetting," he said, "that I too have something to tell. I have received a letter from Dr. Harding of Buenos Aires. He says that he attended Meyrick for three weeks before his death."

"And does he say what carried him off in the prime of life? It was not fever?"

"No, it was not fever. According to the doctor, it was an utter collapse of the whole system, probably caused by some severe shock. But he states that the patient would tell him nothing, and that he was consequently at some disadvantage in treating the case."

"Is there anything more?"

"Yes. Dr. Harding ends his letter by saying: 'I think this is all the information I can give you about your poor friend. He had not been long in Buenos Aires, and knew scarcely anyone, with the exception of a person who did not bear the best of characters, and has since left—a Mrs. Vaughan.' "

8. The Fragments

Among the papers of the well-known physician, Dr. Robert Matheson, of Ashley Street, Piccadilly, who died suddenly, of apoplectic seizure, at the beginning of 1892, a leaf of manuscript paper was found, covered with pencil jottings. These notes were in Latin, much abbreviated, and had evidently been made in great haste. The MS. was only deciphered with great difficulty, and some words have up to the present time evaded all the efforts of the experts employed. The date, "XXV Jul. 1888," is written on the right-hand corner of the MS. The following is a translation of Dr. Matheson's manuscript.

Whether science would benefit by these brief notes if they could be published, I do not know, but rather doubt. But certainly I shall never take the responsibility of publishing or divulging one word of what is here written, not only on account of my oath freely given to those two persons who were present, but also because the details are too abominable. It is probably that, upon mature consideration, and after weighing the good and evil, I shall one day destroy this paper, or at least leave it under seal to my friend D., trusting in his discretion, to use it or to burn it, as he may think fit.

As was befitting, I did all that my knowledge suggested to make sure that I was suffering under no delusion. At first astounded, I could hardly think, but in a minute's time I was sure that my pulse was steady and regular, and that I was in my real and true senses. I then fixed my eyes quietly on what was before me.

Though horror and revolting nausea rose up within me, and an odour of corruption choked my breath, I remained firm. I was then privileged or accursed, I dare not say which, to see that which was on the bed, lying there black like ink, transformed before my eyes. The skin, and the flesh, and the muscles, and the bones, and the firm structure of the human body that I had thought to be unchangeable, and permanent as adamant, began to melt and dissolve.

I knew that the body may be separated into its elements by external agencies, but I should have refused to believe what I saw. For here there was some internal force, of which I knew nothing, that caused dissolution and change.

Here too was all the work by which man had been made repeated before my eyes. I saw the form waver from sex to sex, dividing itself from itself, and then again reunited. Then I saw the body descend to the beasts whence it ascended, and that which was on the heights go down to the depths, even to the abyss of all being. The principle of life, which makes organism, always remained, while the outward form changed.

The light within the room had turned to blackness, not the darkness of night, in which objects are seen dimly, for I could see clearly and without difficulty. But it was the negation of light; objects were presented to my eyes, if I may say so, without any medium, in such a manner that if there had been a prism in the room I should have seen no colours represented in it.

I watched, and at last I saw nothing but a substance as jelly. Then the ladder was ascended again . . . [here the MS. is illegible] . . . for one instant I saw a Form, shaped in dimness before me, which I will not farther describe. But the symbol of this form may be seen in ancient sculptures, and in paintings which survived beneath the lava, too foul to be spoken of . . . as a horrible and unspeakable shape, neither man nor beast, was changed into human form, there came finally death.

I who saw all this, not without great horror and loathing of soul, here write my name, declaring all that I have set on this paper to be true.

Robert Matheson, Med. Dr.

. . . Such, Raymond, is the story of what I know and what I have seen. The burden of it was too heavy for me to bear alone, and yet I could tell it to none but you. Villiers, who was with me at the last, knows nothing of that awful secret of the wood, of how what we both saw die, lay upon the smooth, sweet turf amidst the summer flowers, half in sun and half in shadow, and holding the girl Rachel's hand, called and summoned those companions, and shaped in solid form, upon the earth we tread on, the horror which we can but hint at, which we can only name under a figure. I would not tell Villiers of this, nor of that resemblance, which struck me as with a blow upon my heart, when I saw the portrait, which filled the cup of terror at the end. What this can mean I dare not guess. I know that what I saw perish was not Mary, and yet in the last agony Mary's eyes looked into mine. Whether there be anyone who can show the last link in this chain of awful mystery, I do not know, but if there be anyone who can do this, you, Raymond, are the man. And if you know the secret, it rests with you to tell it or not, as you please.

I am writing this letter to you immediately on my getting back to town. I have been in the country for the last few days; perhaps you may be able to guess in what part. While the horror and wonder of London was at its height—"Mrs. Beaumont," as I have told you, was well known in society—I wrote to my friend Dr. Phillips, giving some brief outline, or rather hint, of what had happened, and asking him to tell me the name of the village where the events he had related to me occurred. He gave me the name, as he said with the less hesitation, because Rachel's father and mother were dead, and the rest of the family had gone to a relative in the state of Washington six months before. The parents, he said, had undoubtedly died of grief and horror caused by the terrible death of their daughter, and by what had gone before that death. On the evening of the day on which I received Phillips's letter I was at Caermaen, and standing beneath the mouldering Roman walls, white with the winters of seventeen hundred years, I looked over the meadow where once had stood the older temple of the "God of the Deeps," and saw a house gleaming in the sunlight. It was the house where Helen had lived. I stayed at Caermaen for several days. The people of the place, I found, knew little and had guessed less. Those whom I spoke to on the matter seemed surprised that an antiquarian (as I professed myself to be) should trouble about a village tragedy, of which they gave a very commonplace version, and, as you may imagine, I told nothing of what I knew. Most of my time was spent in the great wood that rises just above the village and climbs the hillside, and goes down to the river in the valley; such another long lovely valley, Raymond, as that on which we looked one summer night, walking to and fro before your house. For many an hour I strayed through the maze of the forest, turning now to right and now to left, pacing slowly down long alleys of undergrowth, shadowy and chill, even under the midday sun, and halting beneath great oaks; lying on the short turf of a clearing where the faint sweet scent of wild roses came to me on the wind and mixed with the heavy perfume of the elder, whose mingled odour is like the odour of the room of the dead, a vapour of incense and corruption. I stood at the edges of the wood, gazing at all the pomp and procession of the foxgloves towering amidst the bracken and shining red in the broad sunshine, and beyond them into deep thickets of close undergrowth where springs boil up from the rock and nourish the water-weeds, dank and evil. But in all my wanderings I avoided one part of the wood; it was not till yesterday that I climbed to the summit of the hill, and stood upon the ancient Roman road that threads the highest ridge of the wood. Here they had walked, Helen and Rachel, along this quiet causeway, upon the pavement of green turf, shut in on either side by high banks of red earth, and tall hedges of shining beech, and here I followed in their steps, looking out, now and again, through partings in the boughs, and seeing on one side the sweep of the wood stretching far to right and left, and sinking into the broad level, and beyond, the yellow sea, and the land over the sea. On the other side was the valley and the river and hill following hill as wave on wave, and wood and meadow, and cornfield, and white houses gleaming, and a great wall of mountain, and far blue peaks in the north. And so at last I came to the place. The track went up a gentle slope, and widened out into an open space with a wall of thick undergrowth around it, and then, narrowing again, passed on into the distance and the faint blue mist of summer heat. And into this pleasant summer glade Rachel passed a girl, and left it, who shall say what? I did not stay long there.

In a small town near Caermaen there is a museum, containing for the most part Roman remains which had been found in the neighbourhood at various times. On the day after my arrival at Caermaen I walked over to the town in question, and took the opportunity of inspecting the museum. After I had seen most of the sculptured stones, the coffins, rings, coins, and fragments of tessellated pavement which the place contains, I was shown a small square pillar of white stone, which had been recently discovered in the wood of which I have been speaking, and, as I found on inquiry, in that open space where the Roman road broadens out. On one side of the pillar was an inscription, of which I took a note. Some of the letters have been defaced, but I do not think there can be any doubt as to those which I supply. The inscription is as follows:

DEVOMNODENTi
FLAVIVSSENILISPOSSvit
PROPTERNVPtias
quasVIDITSVBVMBra

"To the great god Nodens (the god of the Great Deep or Abyss) Flavius Senilis has erected this pillar on account of the marriage which he saw beneath the shade."

The custodian of the museum informed me that local antiquaries were much puzzled, not by the inscription, or by any difficulty in translating it, but as to the circumstance or rite to which allusion is made.

. . . And now, my dear Clarke, as to what you tell me about Helen Vaughan, whom you say you saw die under circumstances of the utmost and almost incredible horror. I was interested in your account, but a good deal, nay all, of what you told me I knew already. I can understand the strange likeness you remarked both in the portrait and in the actual face; you have seen Helen's mother. You remember that still summer night so many years ago, when I talked to you of the world beyond the shadows, and of the god Pan. You remember Mary. She was the mother of Helen Vaughan, who was born nine months after that night.

Mary never recovered her reason. She lay, as you saw her, all the while upon her bed, and a few days after the child was born she died. I fancy that just at the last she knew me; I was standing by the bed, and the old look came into her eyes for a second, and then she shuddered and groaned and died. It was an ill work I did that night when you were present; I broke open the door of the house of life, without knowing or caring what might pass forth or enter in. I recollect your telling me at the time, sharply enough, and rightly enough too, in one sense, that I had ruined the reason of a human being by a foolish experiment, based on an absurd theory. You did well to blame me, but my theory was not all absurdity. What I said Mary would see, she saw, but I forgot that no human eyes could look on such a vision with impunity. And I forgot, as I have just said, that when the house of life is thus thrown open, there may enter in that for which we have no name, and human flesh may become the veil of a horror one dare not express. I played with energies which I did not understand, and you have seen the ending of it. Helen Vaughan did well to bind the cord about her neck and die, though the death was horrible. The blackened face, the hideous form upon the bed, changing and melting before your eyes from woman to man, from man to beast, and from beast to worse than beast, all the strange horror that you witnessed, surprises me but little. What you say the doctor whom you sent for saw and shuddered at I noticed long ago; I knew what I had done the moment the child was born, and when it was scarcely five years old I surprised it, not once or twice but several times with a playmate, you may guess of what kind. It was for me a constant, an incarnate horror, and after a few years I felt I could bear it no longer, and I sent Helen Vaughan away. You know now what frightened the boy in the wood. The rest of the strange story, and all else that you tell me, as discovered by your friend, I have contrived to learn from time to time, almost to the last chapter. And now Helen is with her companions. . . .

The Willows

ALGERNON BLACKWOOD

[1869–1951]

Algernon Blackwood was one of the very greatest and most prolific supernatural writers of our century. Although Blackwood's tales are quite diverse within the confines of the mystical tradition—ranging from the bizarre earthy horror of "The Transfer" *to the eerie remoteness of* "The Other Wing"*—his most popular works have always been what are termed (rather irreverently) his "nature stories."* "The Wendigo" *and* "The Willows" *are the most famous of this type, and* "The Willows" *itself remains one of the (if not* the*) most frightening tales ever written.*

After leaving Vienna, and long before you come to Buda-Pesth, the Danube enters a region of singular loneliness and desolation, where its waters spread away on all sides regardless of a main channel, and the country becomes a swamp for miles upon miles, covered by a vast sea of low willow bushes. On the big maps this deserted area is painted in a fluffy blue, growing fainter in colour as it leaves the banks, and across it may be seen in large straggling letters the word *Sümpfe,* meaning marshes.

In high flood this great acreage of sand, shingle-beds, and willow-grown islands is almost topped by the water, but in normal seasons the bushes bend and rustle in the free winds, showing their silver leaves to the sunshine in an ever-moving plain of bewildering beauty. These willows never attain to the dignity of trees; they have no rigid trunks; they remain humble bushes, with rounded tops and soft outline, swaying on slender stems that answer to the least pressure of the wind; supple as grasses, and so continually shifting that they somehow give the impression that the entire plain is moving and *alive.* For the wind sends waves rising and falling over the whole surface, waves of leaves instead of waves of water, green swells like the sea, too, until the branches turn and lift, and then silvery white as their under-side turns to the sun.

Happy to slip beyond the control of the stern banks, the Danube here wanders about at will among the intricate network of channels intersecting the islands everywhere with broad avenues down which the waters pour with a shouting sound; making whirlpools, eddies, and foaming rapids; tearing at the sandy banks; carrying away masses of shore and willow-clumps; and forming new islands innumerable which shift daily in size and shape and possess at best an impermanent life, since the flood-time obliterates their very existence.

Properly speaking, this fascinating part of the river's life begins soon after leaving Pressburg, and we, in our Canadian canoe, with gipsy tent and frying-pan on board, reached it on the crest of a rising flood about mid-July. That very same morning, when the sky was reddening before sunrise, we had slipped swiftly through still-sleeping Vienna, leaving it a couple of hours later a mere patch of smoke against the blue hills of the Wienerwald on the horizon; we had breakfasted below Fischeramend under a grove of birch trees roaring in the wind; and had then swept on the tearing current past Orth, Hainburg, Petronell (the old Roman Carnuntum of Marcus Aurelius,) and so under the frowning heights of Theben on a spur of the Carpathians, where the March steals in quietly from the left and the frontier is crossed between Austria and Hungary.

Racing along at twelve kilometres an hour soon took us well into Hungary, and the muddy waters—sure sign of flood—sent us aground on many a shingle-bed, and twisted us like a cork in many a sudden belching whirlpool before the towers of Pressburg (Hungarian, Poszóny) showed against the sky; and then the canoe, leaping like a spirited horse, flew at top speed under the grey walls, negotiated safely the sunken chain of the Fliegende Brücke ferry, turned the corner sharply to the left, and plunged on yellow foam into the wilderness of islands, sand-banks, and swampland beyond—the land of the willows.

The change came suddenly, as when a series of bioscope pictures snaps down on the streets of a town and shifts without warning into the scenery of lake and forest. We entered the land of desolation on wings, and in less than half an hour there was neither boat nor fishing-hut nor red roof, nor any single sign of human habitation and civilisation within sight. The sense of remoteness from the world of human kind, the utter isolation, the fascination of this singular world of willows, winds, and waters, instantly laid its spell upon us both, so that we allowed laughingly to one another that we ought by rights to have held some special kind of passport to admit us, and that we had, somewhat audaciously, come without asking leave into a separate little kingdom of wonder and magic—a kingdom that was reserved for the use of others who had a right to it, with everywhere unwritten warnings to trespassers for those who had the imagination to discover them.

Though still early in the afternoon, the ceaseless buffetings of a most tempestuous wind made us feel weary, and we at once began casting about for a suitable camping-ground for the night. But the bewildering character of the islands made landing difficult; the swirling flood carried us in-shore and then swept us out again; the willow branches tore our hands as we seized them to stop the canoe, and we pulled many a yard of sandy bank into the water before at length we shot with a great sideways blow from the wind into a backwater and managed to beach the bows in a cloud of spray. Then we lay panting and laughing after our exertions on hot yellow sand, sheltered from the wind, and in the full blaze of a scorching sun, a cloudless blue sky above, and an immense army of dancing, shouting willow bushes, closing in from all sides, shining with spray and clapping their thousand little hands as though to applaud the success of our efforts.

"What a river!" I said to my companion, thinking of all the way we had travelled from the source in the Black Forest, and how he had often been obliged to wade and push in the upper shallows at the beginning of June.

"Won't stand much nonsense now, will it?" he said, pulling the canoe a little farther into safety up the sand, and then composing himself for a nap.

I lay by his side, happy and peaceful in the bath of the elements —water, wind, sand, and the great fire of the sun—thinking of the long journey that lay behind us, and of the great stretch before us to the Black Sea, and how lucky I was to have such a delightful and charming travelling companion as my friend, the Swede.

We had made many similar journeys together, but the Danube, more than any other river I knew, impressed us from the very beginning with its *aliveness.* From its tiny bubbling entry into the world among the pinewood gardens of Donaueschingen, until this moment when it began to play the great river-game of losing itself among the deserted swamps, unobserved, unrestrained, it had seemed to us like following the growth of some living creature. Sleepy at first, but later developing violent desires as it became conscious of its deep soul, it rolled, like some huge fluid being, through all the countries we had passed, holding our little craft on its mighty shoulders, playing roughly with us sometimes, yet always friendly and well-meaning, till at length we had come inevitably to regard it as a Great Personage.

How, indeed, could it be otherwise, since it told us so much of its secret life? At night we heard it singing to the moon as we lay in our tent, uttering that odd sibilant note peculiar to itself and said to be caused by the rapid tearing of the pebbles along its bed, so great is its hurrying speed. We knew, too, the voice of its gurgling whirlpools, suddenly bubbling up on a surface previously quite calm; the roar of its shallows and swift rapids; its constant steady thundering below all mere surface sounds; and that ceaseless tearing of its icy waters at the banks. How it stood up and shouted when the rains fell flat upon its face! And how its laughter roared out when the wind blew upstream and tried to stop its growing speed! We knew all its sounds and voices, its tumblings and foamings, its unnecessary splashing against the bridges; that self-conscious chatter when there were hills to look on; the affected dignity of its speech when it passed through the little towns, far too important to laugh; and all these faint, sweet whisperings when the sun caught it fairly in some slow curve and poured down upon it till the steam rose.

It was full of tricks, too, in its early life before the great world knew it. There were places in the upper reaches among the Swabian forests, when yet the first whispers of its destiny had not reached it, where it elected to disappear through holes in the ground, to appear again on the other side of the porous limestone hills and start a new river with another name; leaving, too, so little water in its own bed that we had to climb out and wade and push the canoe through miles of shallows.

And a chief pleasure, in those early days of its irresponsible youth, was to lie low, like Brer Fox, just before the little turbulent tributaries came to join it from the Alps, and to refuse to acknowledge them when in, but to run for miles side by side, the dividing line well marked, the very levels different, the Danube utterly declining to recognise the newcomer. Below Passau, however, it gave up this particular trick, for there the Inn comes in with a thundering power impossible to ignore, and so pushes and incommodes the parent river that there is hardly room for them in the long twisting gorge that follows, and the Danube is shoved this way and that against the cliffs, and forced to hurry itself with great waves and much dashing to and fro in order to get through in time. And during the fight our canoe slipped down from its shoulder to its breast, and had the time of its life among the struggling waves. But the Inn taught the old river a lesson, and after Passau it no longer pretended to ignore new arrivals.

This was many days back, of course, and since then we had come to know other aspects of the great creature, and across the Bavarian wheat plain of Straubing she wandered so slowly under the blazing June sun that we could well imagine only the surface inches were water, while below there moved, concealed as by a silken mantle, a whole army of Undines, passing silently and unseen down to the sea, and very leisurely too, lest they be discovered.

Much, too, we forgave her because of her friendliness to the birds and animals that haunted the shores. Cormorants lined the banks in lonely places in rows like short black palings; grey crows crowded the shingle-beds; storks stood fishing in the vistas of shallower water that opened up between the islands, and hawks, swans, and marsh birds of all sorts filled the air with glinting wings and singing, petulant cries. It was impossible to feel annoyed with the river's vagaries after seeing a deer leap with a splash into the water at sunrise and swim past the bows of the canoe; and often we saw fawns peering at us from the underbrush, or looked straight into the brown eyes of a stag as we charged full tilt round a corner and entered another reach of the river. Foxes, too, everywhere haunted the banks, tripping daintily among the driftwood and disappearing so suddenly that it was impossible to see how they managed it.

But now, after leaving Pressburg, everything changed a little, and the Danube became more serious. It ceased trifling. It was halfway to the Black Sea, within scenting distance almost of other, stranger countries where no tricks would be permitted or understood. It became suddenly grown-up, and claimed our respect and even our awe. It broke out into three arms, for one thing, that only met again a hundred kilometres farther down, and for a canoe there were no indications which one was intended to be followed.

"If you take a side channel," said the Hungarian officer we met in the Pressburg shop while buying provisions, "you may find yourselves, when the flood subsides, forty miles from anywhere, high and dry, and you may easily starve. There are no people, no farms, no fishermen. I warn you not to continue. The river, too, is still rising, and this wind will increase."

The rising river did not alarm us in the least, but the matter of being left high and dry by a sudden subsidence of the waters might be serious, and we had consequently laid in an extra stock of provisions. For the rest, the officer's prophecy held true, and the wind, blowing down a perfectly clear sky, increased steadily till it reached the dignity of a westerly gale.

It was earlier than usual when we camped, for the sun was a good hour or two from the horizon, and leaving my friend still asleep on the hot sand, I wandered about in desultory examination of our hotel. The island, I found, was less than an acre in extent, a mere sandy bank standing some two or three feet above the level of the river. The far end, pointing into the sunset, was covered with flying spray which the tremendous wind drove off the crests of the broken waves. It was triangular in shape, with the apex up stream.

I stood there for several minutes, watching the impetuous crimson flood bearing down with a shouting roar, dashing in waves against the bank as though to sweep it bodily away, and then swirling by in two foaming streams on either side. The ground seemed to shake with the shock and rush, while the furious movement of the willow bushes as the wind poured over them increased the curious illusion that the island itself actually moved. Above, for a mile or two, I could see the great river descending upon me: it was like looking up the slope of a sliding hill, white with foam, and leaping up everywhere to show itself to the sun.

The rest of the island was too thickly grown with willows to make walking pleasant, but I made the tour, nevertheless. From the lower end the light, of course, changed, and the river looked dark and angry. Only the backs of the flying waves were visible, streaked with foam, and pushed forcibly by the great puffs of wind that fell upon them from behind. For a short mile it was visible, pouring in and out among the islands, and then disappearing with a huge sweep into the willows, which closed about it like a herd of monstrous antediluvian creatures crowding down to drink. They made me think of gigantic sponge-like growths that sucked the river up into themselves. They caused it to vanish from sight. They herded there together in such overpowering numbers.

Altogether it was an impressive scene, with its utter loneliness, its bizarre suggestion; and as I gazed, long and curiously, a singular emotion began to stir somewhere in the depths of me. Midway in my delight of the wild beauty, there crept, unbidden and unexplained, a curious feeling of disquietude, almost of alarm.

A rising river, perhaps, always suggests something of the ominous: many of the little islands I saw before me would probably have been swept away by the morning; this resistless, thundering flood of water touched the sense of awe. Yet I was aware that my uneasiness lay deeper far than the emotions of awe and wonder. It was not that I felt. Nor had it directly to do with the power of the driving wind —this shouting hurricane that might almost carry up a few acres of willows into the air and scatter them like so much chaff over the landscape. The wind was simply enjoying itself, for nothing rose out of the flat landscape to stop it, and I was conscious of sharing its great game with a kind of pleasurable excitement. Yet this novel emotion had nothing to do with the wind. Indeed, so vague was the sense of distress I experienced, that it was impossible to trace it to its source and deal with it accordingly, though I was aware somehow that it had to do with my realisation of our utter insignificance before this unrestrained power of the elements about me. The huge-grown river had something to do with it too—a vague, unpleasant idea that we had somehow trifled with these great elemental forces in whose power we lay helpless every hour of the day and night. For here, indeed, they were gigantically at play together, and the sight appealed to the imagination.

But my emotion, so far as I could understand it, seemed to attach itself more particularly to the willow bushes, to these acres and acres of willows, crowding, so thickly growing there, swarming everywhere the eye could reach, pressing upon the river as though to suffocate it, standing in dense array mile after mile beneath the sky, watching, waiting, listening. And, apart quite from the elements, the willows connected themselves subtly with my malaise, attacking the mind insidiously somehow by reason of their vast numbers, and contriving in some way or other to represent to the imagination a new and mighty power, a power, moreover, not altogether friendly to us.

Great revelations of nature, of course, never fail to impress in one way or another, and I was no stranger to moods of the kind.

Mountains overawe and oceans terrify, while the mystery of great forests exercises a spell peculiarly its own. But all these, at one point or another, somewhere link on intimately with human life and human experience. They stir comprehensible, even if alarming, emotions. They tend on the whole to exalt.

With this multitude of willows, however, it was something far different, I felt. Some essence emanated from them that besieged the heart. A sense of awe awakened, true, but of awe touched somewhere by a vague terror. Their serried ranks, growing everywhere darker about me as the shadows deepened, moving furiously yet softly in the wind, woke in me the curious and unwelcome suggestion that we had trespassed here upon the borders of an alien world, a world where we were intruders, a world where we were not wanted or invited to remain—where we ran grave risks perhaps!

The feeling, however, though it refused to yield its meaning entirely to analysis, did not at the time trouble me by passing into menace. Yet it never left me quite, even during the very practical business of putting up the tent in a hurricane of wind and building a fire for the stew-pot. It remained, just enough to bother and perplex, and to rob a most delightful camping-ground of a good portion of its charm. To my companion, however, I said nothing, for he was a man I considered devoid of imagination. In the first place, I could never have explained to him what I meant, and in the second, he would have laughed stupidly at me if I had.

There was a slight depression in the centre of the island, and here we pitched the tent. The surrounding willows broke the wind a bit.

"A poor camp," observed the imperturbable Swede when at last the tent stood upright; "no stones and precious little firewood. I'm for moving on early to-morrow—eh? This sand won't hold anything."

But the experience of a collapsing tent at midnight had taught us many devices, and we made the cosy gipsy house as safe as possible, and then set about collecting a store of wood to last till bed-time. Willow bushes drop no branches, and driftwood was our only source of supply. We hunted the shores pretty thoroughly. Everywhere the banks were crumbling as the rising flood tore at them and carried away great portions with a splash and a gurgle.

"The island's much smaller than when we landed," said the

accurate Swede. "It won't last long at this rate. We'd better drag the canoe close to the tent, and be ready to start at a moment's notice. *I* shall sleep in my clothes."

He was a little distance off, climbing along the bank, and I heard his rather jolly laugh as he spoke.

"By Jove!" I heard him call, a moment later, and turned to see what had caused his exclamation. But for the moment he was hidden by the willows, and I could not find him.

"What in the world's this?" I heard him cry again, and this time his voice had become serious.

I ran up quickly and joined him on the bank. He was looking over the river, pointing at something in the water.

"Good heavens, it's a man's body!" he cried excitedly. "Look!"

A black thing, turning over and over in the foaming waves, swept rapidly past. It kept disappearing and coming up to the surface again. It was about twenty feet from the shore, and just as it was opposite to where we stood it lurched round and looked straight at us. We saw its eyes reflecting the sunset, and gleaming an odd yellow as the body turned over. Then it gave a swift, gulping plunge, and dived out of sight in a flash.

"An otter, by gad!" we exclaimed in the same breath, laughing.

It *was* an otter, alive, and out on the hunt; yet it had looked exactly like the body of a drowned man turning helplessly in the current. Far below it came to the surface once again, and we saw its black skin, wet and shining in the sunlight.

Then, too, just as we turned back, our arms full of driftwood, another thing happened to recall us to the river bank. This time it really was a man, and what was more, a man in a boat. Now a small boat on the Danube was an unusual sight at any time, but here in this deserted region, and at flood time, it was so unexpected as to constitute a real event. We stood and stared.

Whether it was due to the slanting sunlight, or the refraction from the wonderfully illumined water, I cannot say, but, whatever the cause, I found it difficult to focus my sight properly upon the flying apparition. It seemed, however, to be a man standing upright in a sort of flat-bottomed boat, steering with a long oar, and being carried down the opposite shore at a tremendous pace. He apparently was looking across in our direction, but the distance was too great and the light too uncertain for us to make out very plainly what he was about. It seemed to me that he was gesticulating and making signs at us. His voice came across the water to us shouting something furiously, but the wind drowned it so that no single word was audible. There was something curious about the whole appearance—man, boat, signs, voice—that made an impression on me out of all proportion to its cause.

"He's crossing himself!" I cried. "Look, he's making the sign of the Cross!"

"I believe you're right," the Swede said, shading his eyes with his hand and watching the man out of sight. He seemed to be gone in a moment, melting away down there into the sea of willows where the sun caught them in the bend of the river and turned them into a great crimson wall of beauty. Mist, too, had begun to rise, so that the air was hazy.

"But what in the world is he doing at nightfall on this flooded river?" I said, half to myself. "Where is he going at such a time, and what did he mean by his signs and shouting? D'you think he wished to warn us about something?"

"He saw our smoke, and thought we were spirits probably," laughed my companion. "These Hungarians believe in all sorts of rubbish: you remember the shopwoman at Pressburg warning us that no one ever landed here because it belonged to some sort of beings outside man's world! I suppose they believe in fairies and elementals, possibly demons too. That peasant in the boat saw people on the islands for the first time in his life," he added, after a slight pause, "and it scared him, that's all."

The Swede's tone of voice was not convincing, and his manner lacked something that was usually there. I noted the change instantly while he talked, though without being able to label it precisely.

"If they had enough imagination," I laughed loudly—I remember trying to make as much *noise* as I could—"they might well people a place like this with the old gods of antiquity. The Romans must have haunted all this region more or less with their shrines and sacred groves and elemental deities."

The subject dropped and we returned to our stew-pot, for my friend was not given to imaginative conversation as a rule. Moreover, just then I remember feeling distinctly glad that he was not imaginative; his stolid, practical nature suddenly seemed to me welcome and comforting. It was an admirable temperament, I felt: he could steer down rapids like a red Indian, shoot dangerous bridges and whirlpools better than any white man I ever saw in a canoe. He was a grand fellow for an adventurous trip, a tower of strength when untoward things happened. I looked at his strong face and light curly hair as he staggered along under his pile of driftwood (twice the size of mine!), and I experienced a feeling of relief. Yes, I was distinctly glad just then that the Swede was—what he was, and that he never made remarks that suggested more than they said.

"The river's still rising, though," he added, as if following out some thoughts of his own, and dropping his load with a gasp. "This island will be under water in two days if it goes on."

"I wish the *wind* would go down," I said. "I don't care a fig for the river."

The flood, indeed, had no terrors for us; we could get off at ten minutes' notice, and the more water the better we liked it. It meant an increasing current and the obliteration of the treacherous shingle-beds that so often threatened to tear the bottom out of our canoe.

Contrary to our expectations, the wind did not go down with the sun. It seemed to increase with the darkness, howling overhead and shaking the willows round us like straws. Curious sounds accompanied it sometimes, like the explosion of heavy guns, and it fell upon the water and the island in great flat blows of immense power. It made me think of the sounds a planet must make, could we only hear it, driving along through space.

But the sky kept wholly clear of clouds, and soon after supper the full moon rose up in the east and covered the river and the plain of shouting willows with a light like the day.

We lay on the sandy patch beside the fire, smoking, listening to the noises of the night round us, and talking happily of the journey we had already made, and of our plans ahead. The map lay spread in the door of the tent, but the high wind made it hard to study, and presently we lowered the curtain and extinguished the lantern. The firelight was enough to smoke and see each other's faces by, and the sparks flew about overhead like fireworks. A few yards beyond, the river gurgled and hissed, and from time to time a heavy splash announced the falling away of further portions of the bank.

Our talk, I noticed, had to do with the far-away scenes and incidents of our first camps in the Black Forest, or of other subjects altogether remote from the present setting, for neither of us spoke of the actual moment more than was necessary—almost as though we had agreed tacitly to avoid discussion of the camp and its incidents. Neither the otter nor the boatman, for instance, received the honour of a single mention, though ordinarily these would have furnished discussion for the greater part of the evening. They were, of course, distinct events in such a place.

The scarcity of wood made it a business to keep the fire going, for the wind, that drove the smoke in our faces wherever we sat, helped at the same time to make a forced draught. We took it in turn to make foraging expeditions into the darkness, and the quantity the Swede brought back always made me feel that he took an absurdly long time finding it; for the fact was I did not care much about being left alone, and yet it always seemed to be my turn to grub about among the bushes or scramble along the slippery banks in the moonlight. The long day's battle with wind and water—such wind and such water!—had tired us both, and an early bed was the obvious programme. Yet neither of us made the move for the tent. We lay there, tending the fire, talking in desultory fashion, peering about us into the dense willow bushes, and listening to the thunder of wind and river. The loneliness of the place had entered our very bones, and silence seemed natural, for after a bit the sound of our voices became a trifle unreal and forced; whispering would have been the fitting mode of communication, I felt, and the human voice, always rather absurd amid the roar of the elements, now carried with it something almost illegitimate. It was like talking out loud in church, or in some place where it was not lawful, perhaps not quite *safe,* to be overheard.

The eeriness of this lonely island, set among a million willows, swept by a hurricane, and surrounded by hurrying deep waters, touched us both, I fancy. Untrodden by man, almost unknown to man, it lay there beneath the moon, remote from human influence, on the frontier of another world, an alien world, a world tenanted by willows only and the souls of willows. And we, in our rashness, had dared to invade it, even to make use of it! Something more than the power of its mystery stirred in me as I lay on the sand, feet to fire, and peered up through the leaves at the stars. For the last time I rose to get firewood.

"When this has burnt up," I said firmly, "I shall turn in," and my companion watched me lazily as I moved off into the surrounding shadows.

For an unimaginative man I thought he seemed unusually receptive that night, unusually open to suggestion of things other than sensory. He too was touched by the beauty and loneliness of the place. I was not altogether pleased, I remember, to recognise this slight change in him, and instead of immediately collecting sticks, I made my way to the far point of the island where the moonlight on plain and river could be seen to better advantage. The desire to be alone had come suddenly upon me; my former dread returned in force; there was a vague feeling in me I wished to face and probe to the bottom.

When I reached the point of sand jutting out among the waves, the spell of the place descended upon me with a positive shock. No mere "scenery" could have produced such an effect. There was something more here, something to alarm.

I gazed across the waste of wild waters; I watched the whispering willows; I heard the ceaseless beating of the tireless wind; and, one and all, each in its own way, stirred in me this sensation of a strange distress. But the *willows* especially: for ever they went on chattering and talking among themselves, laughing a little, shrilly crying out, sometimes sighing—but what it was they made so much to-do about belonged to the secret life of the great plain they inhabited. And it was utterly alien to the world I knew, or to that of the wild yet kindly elements. They made me think of a host of beings from another plane of life, another evolution altogether, perhaps, all discussing a mystery known only to themselves. I watched them moving busily together, oddly shaking their big bushy heads, twirling their myriad leaves even when there was no wind. They moved of their own will as though alive, and they touched, by some incalculable method, my own keen sense of the *horrible.*

There they stood in the moonlight, like a vast army surrounding our camp, shaking their innumerable silver spears defiantly, formed all ready for an attack.

The psychology of places, for some imaginations at least, is very vivid; for the wanderer, especially, camps have their "note" either of welcome or rejection. At first it may not always be apparent, because the busy preparations of tent and cooking prevent, but with the first pause—after supper usually—it comes and announces itself. And the note of this willow-camp now became unmistakably plain to me: we were interlopers, trespassers; we were not welcomed. The sense of unfamiliarity grew upon me as I stood there watching. We touched the frontier of a region where our presence was resented. For a night's lodging we might perhaps be tolerated; but for a prolonged and inquisitive stay—No! by all the gods of the trees and the wilderness, no! We were the first human influences upon this island, and we were not wanted. *The willows were against us.*

Strange thoughts like these, bizarre fancies, borne I know not whence, found lodgment in my mind as I stood listening. What, I thought, if, after all, these crouching willows proved to be alive; if suddenly they should rise up, like a swarm of living creatures, marshalled by the gods whose territory we had invaded, sweep towards us off the vast swamps, booming overhead in the night—and then *settle down!* As I looked it was so easy to imagine they actually moved, crept nearer, retreated a little, huddled together in masses, hostile, waiting for the great wind that should finally start them a-running. I could have sworn their aspect changed a little, and their ranks deepened and pressed more closely together.

The melancholy shrill cry of a night-bird sounded overhead, and suddenly I nearly lost my balance as the piece of bank I stood upon fell with a great splash into the river, undermined by the flood. I stepped back just in time, and went on hunting for firewood again, half laughing at the odd fancies that crowded so thickly into my mind and cast their spell upon me. I recalled the Swede's remark about moving on next day, and I was just thinking that I fully agreed with him, when I turned with a start and saw the subject of my thoughts standing immediately in front of me. He was quite close. The roar of the elements had covered his approach.

"You've been gone so long," he shouted above the wind, "I thought something must have happened to you."

But there was that in his tone, and a certain look in his face as well, that conveyed to me more than his actual words, and in a flash I understood the real reason for his coming. It was because the spell of the place had entered his soul too, and he did not like being alone.

"River still rising," he cried, pointing to the flood in the moonlight, "and the wind's simply awful."

He always said the same things, but it was the cry for companionship that gave the real importance to his words.

"Lucky," I cried back, "our tent's in the hollow. I think it'll hold all right." I added something about the difficulty of finding wood, in order to explain my absence, but the wind caught my words and flung them across the river, so that he did not hear, but just looked at me through the branches, nodding his head.

"Lucky if we get away without disaster!" he shouted, or words to that effect; and I remember feeling half angry with him for putting the thought into words, for it was exactly what I felt myself. There was disaster impending somewhere, and the sense of presentiment lay unpleasantly upon me.

We went back to the fire and made a final blaze, poking it up with our feet. We took a last look round. But for the wind the heat would have been unpleasant. I put this thought into words, and I remember my friend's reply struck me oddly: that he would rather have the heat, the ordinary July weather, than this "diabolical wind."

Everything was snug for the night; the canoe lying turned over beside the tent, with both yellow paddles beneath her; the provision sack hanging from a willow-stem, and the washed-up dishes removed to a safe distance from the fire, all ready for the morning meal.

We smothered the embers of the fire with sand, and then turned in. The flap of the tent door was up, and I saw the branches and the stars and the white moonlight. The shaking willows and the heavy buffetings of the wind against our taut little house were the last things I remembered as sleep came down and covered all with its soft and delicious forgetfulness.

Suddenly I found myself lying awake, peering from my sandy mattress through the door of the tent. I looked at my watch pinned against the canvas, and saw by the bright moonlight that it was past twelve o'clock—the threshold of a new day—and I had therefore slept a couple of hours. The Swede was asleep still beside me; the wind howled as before; something plucked at my heart and made me feel afraid. There was a sense of disturbance in my immediate neighbourhood.

I sat up quickly and looked out. The trees were swaying violently to and fro as the gusts smote them, but our little bit of green canvas lay snugly safe in the hollow, for the wind passed over it without meeting enough resistance to make it vicious. The feeling of disquietude did not pass, however, and I crawled quietly out of the tent to see if our belongings were safe. I moved carefully so as not to waken my companion. A curious excitement was on me.

I was half-way out, kneeling on all fours, when my eye first took in that the tops of the bushes opposite, with their moving tracery of leaves, made shapes against the sky. I sat back on my haunches and stared. It was incredible, surely, but there, opposite and slightly above me, were shapes of some indeterminate sort among the willows, and as the branches swayed in the wind they seemed to group themselves about these shapes, forming a series of monstrous outlines that shifted rapidly beneath the moon. Close, about fifty feet in front of me, I saw these things.

My first instinct was to waken my companion, that he too might see them, but something made me hesitate—the sudden realisation, probably, that I should not welcome corroboration; and meanwhile I crouched there staring in amazement with smarting eyes. I was wide awake. I remember saying to myself that I was *not* dreaming.

They first became properly visible, these huge figures, just within the tops of the bushes—immense, bronze-coloured, moving, and wholly independent of the swaying of the branches. I saw them plainly and noted, now I came to examine them more calmly, that they were very much larger than human, and indeed that something in their appearance proclaimed them to be *not human* at all. Certainly they were not merely the moving tracery of the branches against the moonlight. They shifted independently. They rose upwards in a continuous stream from earth to sky, vanishing utterly as soon as they reached the dark of the sky. They were interlaced one with another, making a great column, and I saw their limbs and huge bodies melting in and out of each other, forming this serpentine line that bent and swayed and twisted spirally with the contortions of the wind-tossed trees. They were nude, fluid shapes, passing up the bushes, *within* the leaves almost—rising up in a living column into the heavens. Their faces I never could see. Unceasingly they poured upwards, swaying in great bending curves, with a hue of dull bronze upon their skins.

I stared, trying to force every atom of vision from my eyes. For a long time I thought they *must* every moment disappear and resolve themselves into the movements of the branches and prove to be an optical illusion. I searched everywhere for a proof of reality, when all the while I understood quite well that the standard of reality had changed. For the longer I looked the more certain I became that these figures were real and living, though perhaps not according to the standards that the camera and the biologist would insist upon.

Far from feeling fear, I was possessed with a sense of awe and wonder such as I have never known. I seemed to be gazing at the personified elemental forces of this haunted and primeval region. Our intrusion had stirred the powers of the place into activity. It was we who were the cause of the disturbance, and my brain filled to bursting with stories and legends of the spirits and deities of places that have been acknowledged and worshipped by men in all ages of the world's history. But, before I could arrive at any possible explanation, something impelled me to go farther out, and I crept forward on to the sand and stood upright. I felt the ground still warm under my bare feet; the wind tore at my hair and face; and the sound of the river burst upon my ears with a sudden roar. These things, I knew, were real, and proved that my senses were acting normally. Yet the figures still rose from earth to heaven, silent, majestically, in a great spiral of grace and strength that overwhelmed me at length with a genuine deep emotion of worship. I felt that I must fall down and worship—absolutely worship.

Perhaps in another minute I might have done so, when a gust of wind swept against me with such force that it blew me sideways, and I nearly stumbled and fell. It seemed to shake the dream violently out of me. At least it gave me another point of view somehow. The figures still remained, still ascended into heaven from the heart of the night, but my reason at last began to assert itself. It must be a subjective experience, I argued—none the less real for that, but still subjective. The moonlight and the branches combined to work out these pictures upon the mirror of my imagination, and for some reason I projected them outwards and made them appear objective. I knew this must be the case, of course. I was the subject of a vivid and interesting hallucination. I took courage, and began to move forward across the open patches of sand. By Jove, though, was it all hallucination? Was it merely subjective? Did not my reason argue in the old futile way from the little standard of the known?

I only know that great column of figures ascended darkly into the sky for what seemed a very long period of time, and with a very complete measure of reality as most men are accustomed to gauge reality. Then suddenly they were gone!

And, once they were gone and the immediate wonder of their great presence had passed, fear came down upon me with a cold rush. The esoteric meaning of this lonely and haunted region suddenly flamed up within me, and I began to tremble dreadfully. I took a quick look round—a look of horror that came near to panic—calculating vainly ways of escape; and then, realising how helpless I was to achieve anything really effective, I crept back silently into the tent and lay down again upon my sandy mattress, first lowering the door-curtain to shut out the sight of the willows in the moonlight, and then burying my head as deeply as possible beneath the blankets to deaden the sound of the terrifying wind.

As though further to convince me that I had not been dreaming, I remember that it was a long time before I fell again into a troubled and restless sleep; and even then only the upper crust of me slept, and underneath there was something that never quite lost consciousness, but lay alert and on the watch.

But this second time I jumped up with a genuine start of terror. It was neither the wind nor the river that woke me, but the slow approach of something that caused the sleeping portion of me to grow smaller and smaller till at last it vanished altogether, and I found myself sitting bolt upright—listening.

Outside there was a sound of multitudinous little patterings. They had been coming, I was aware, for a long time, and in my sleep they had first become audible. I sat there nervously wide awake as though I had not slept at all. It seemed to me that my breathing came with difficulty, and that there was a great weight upon the surface of my body. In spite of the hot night, I felt clammy with cold and shivered. Something surely was pressing steadily against the sides of the tent and weighing down upon it from above. Was it the body of the wind? Was this the pattering rain, the dripping of the leaves? The spray blown from the river by the wind and gathering in big drops? I thought quickly of a dozen things.

Then suddenly the explanation leaped into my mind: a bough from the poplar, the only large tree on the island, had fallen with the wind. Still half caught by the other branches, it would fall with the next gust and crush us, and meanwhile its leaves brushed and tapped upon the tight canvas surface of the tent. I raised the loose flap and rushed out, calling to the Swede to follow.

But when I got out and stood upright I saw that the tent was free. There was no hanging bough; there was no rain or spray; nothing approached.

A cold, grey light filtered down through the bushes and lay on the faintly gleaming sand. Stars still crowded the sky directly overhead, and the wind howled magnificently, but the fire no longer gave out any glow, and I saw the east reddening in streaks through the trees. Several hours must have passed since I stood there before watching the ascending figures, and the memory of it now came back to me horribly, like an evil dream. Oh, how tired it made me feel, that ceaseless raging wind! Yet, though the deep lassitude of a sleepless night was on me, my nerves were tingling with the activity of an equally tireless apprehension, and all idea of repose was out of the question. The river I saw had risen further. Its thunder filled the air, and a fine spray made itself felt through my thin sleeping shirt.

Yet nowhere did I discover the slightest evidences of anything to cause alarm. This deep, prolonged disturbance in my heart remained wholly unaccounted for.

My companion had not stirred when I called him, and there was no need to waken him now. I looked about me carefully, noting everything: the turned-over canoe; the yellow paddles—two of them, I'm certain; the provision sack and the extra lantern hanging together from the tree; and, crowding everywhere about me, enveloping all, the willows, those endless, shaking willows. A bird uttered its morning cry, and a string of duck passed with whirring flight overhead in the twilight. The sand whirled, dry and stinging, about my bare feet in the wind.

I walked round the tent and then went out a little way into the bush, so that I could see across the river to the farther landscape, and the same profound yet indefinable emotion of distress seized upon me again as I saw the interminable sea of bushes stretching to the horizon, looking ghostly and unreal in the wan light of dawn. I walked softly here and there, still puzzling over that odd sound of infinite pattering, and of that pressure upon the tent that had wakened me. It *must* have been the wind, I reflected—the wind beating upon the loose, hot sand, driving the dry particles smartly against the taut canvas—the wind dropping heavily upon our fragile roof.

Yet all the time my nervousness and malaise increased appreciably.

I crossed over to the farther shore and noted how the coast-line had altered in the night, and what masses of sand the river had torn away. I dipped my hands and feet into the cool torrent, and bathed my forehead. Already there was a glow of sunrise in the sky and the exquisite freshness of coming day. On my way back I passed purposely beneath the very bushes where I had seen the column of figures rising into the air, and midway among the clumps I suddenly found myself overtaken by a sense of vast terror. From the shadows a large figure went swiftly by. Someone passed me, as sure as ever man did. . . .

It was a great staggering blow from the wind that helped me

forward again, and once out in the more open space, the sense of terror diminished strangely. The winds were about and walking, I remember saying to myself; for the winds often move like great presences under the trees. And altogether the fear that hovered about me was such an unknown and immense kind of fear, so unlike anything I had ever felt before, that it woke a sense of awe and wonder in me that did much to counteract its worst effects; and when I reached a high point in the middle of the island from which I could see the wide stretch of river, crimson in the sunrise, the whole magical beauty of it all was so overpowering that a sort of wild yearning woke in me and almost brought a cry up into the throat.

But this cry found no expression, for as my eyes wandered from the plain beyond to the island round me and noted our little tent half hidden among the willows, a dreadful discovery leaped out at me, compared to which my terror of the walking winds seemed as nothing at all.

For a change, I thought, had somehow come about in the arrangement of the landscape. It was not that my point of vantage gave me a different view, but that an alteration had apparently been effected in the relation of the tent to the willows, and of the willows to the tent. Surely the bushes now crowded much closer—unnecessarily, unpleasantly close. *They had moved nearer.*

Creeping with silent feet over the shifting sands, drawing imperceptibly nearer by soft, unhurried movements, the willows had come closer during the night. But had the wind moved them, or had they moved of themselves? I recalled the sound of infinite small patterings and the pressure upon the tent and upon my own heart that caused me to wake in terror. I swayed for a moment in the wind like a tree, finding it hard to keep my upright position on the sandy hillock. There was a suggestion here of personal agency, of deliberate intention, of aggressive hostility, and it terrified me into a sort of rigidity.

Then the reaction followed quickly. The idea was so bizarre, so absurd, that I felt inclined to laugh. But the laughter came no more readily than the cry, for the knowledge that my mind was so receptive to such dangerous imaginings brought the additional terror that it was through our minds and not through our physical bodies that the attack would come, and was coming.

The wind buffeted me about, and, very quickly it seemed, the sun came up over the horizon, for it was after four o'clock, and I must have stood on that little pinnacle of sand longer than I knew, afraid to come down to close quarters with the willows. I returned quietly, creepily, to the tent, first taking another exhaustive look round and —yes, I confess it—making a few measurements. I paced out on the warm sand the distances between the willows and the tent, making a note of the shortest distance particularly.

I crawled stealthily into my blankets. My companion, to all appearances, still slept soundly, and I was glad that this was so. Provided my experiences were not corroborated, I could find strength somehow to deny them, perhaps. With the daylight I could persuade myself that it was all a subjective hallucination, a fantasy of the night, a projection of the excited imagination.

Nothing further came to disturb me, and I fell asleep almost at once, utterly exhausted, yet still in dread of hearing again that weird sound of multitudinous pattering, or of feeling the pressure upon my heart that had made it difficult to breathe.

The sun was high in the heavens when my companion woke me from a heavy sleep and announced that the porridge was cooked and there was just time to bathe. The grateful smell of frizzling bacon entered the tent door.

"River still rising," he said, "and several islands out in mid-stream have disappeared altogether. Our own island's much smaller."

"Any wood left?" I asked sleepily.

"The wood and the island will finish to-morrow in a dead heat," he laughed, "but there's enough to last us till then."

I plunged in from the point of the island, which had indeed altered a lot in size and shape during the night, and was swept down in a moment to the landing-place opposite the tent. The water was icy, and the banks flew by like the country from an express train. Bathing under such conditions was an exhilarating operation, and the terror of the night seemed cleansed out of me by a process of evaporation in the brain. The sun was blazing hot; not a cloud showed itself anywhere; the wind, however, had not abated one little jot.

Quite suddenly then the implied meaning of the Swede's words flashed across me, showing that he no longer wished to leave post-haste, and had changed his mind. "Enough to last till to-morrow"—he assumed we should stay on the island another night. It struck me as odd. The night before he was so positive the other way. How had the change come about?

Great crumblings of the banks occurred at breakfast, with heavy splashings and clouds of spray which the wind brought into our frying-pan, and my fellow-traveller talked incessantly about the difficulty the Vienna-Pesth steamers must have to find the channel in flood. But the state of his mind interested and impressed me far more than the state of the river or the difficulties of the steamers. He had changed somehow since the evening before. His manner was different—a trifle excited, a trifle shy, with a sort of suspicion about his voice and gestures. I hardly know how to describe it now in cold blood, but at the time I remember being quite certain of one thing —that he had become frightened.

He ate very little breakfast, and for once omitted to smoke his pipe. He had the map spread open beside him, and kept studying its markings.

"We'd better get off sharp in an hour," I said presently, feeling for an opening that must bring him indirectly to a partial confession at any rate. And his answer puzzled me uncomfortably: "Rather! If they'll let us."

"Who'll let us? The elements?" I asked quickly, with affected indifference.

"The powers of this awful place, whoever they are," he replied, keeping his eyes on the map. "The gods are here, if they are anywhere at all in the world."

"The elements are always the true immortals," I replied, laughing as naturally as I could manage, yet knowing quite well that my face reflected my true feelings when he looked up gravely at me and spoke across the smoke:

"We shall be fortunate if we get away without further disaster."

This was exactly what I had dreaded, and I screwed myself up to the point of the direct question. It was like agreeing to allow the dentist to extract the tooth; it *had* to come anyhow in the long run, and the rest was all pretence.

"Further disaster! Why, what's happened?"

"For one thing—the steering paddle's gone," he said quietly.

"The steering paddle gone!" I repeated, greatly excited, for this was our rudder, and the Danube in flood without a rudder was suicide. "But what—"

"And there's a tear in the bottom of the canoe," he added, with a genuine little tremor in his voice.

I continued staring at him, able only to repeat the words in his face somewhat foolishly. There, in the heat of the sun, and on this burning sand, I was aware of a freezing atmosphere descending round us. I got up to follow him, for he merely nodded his head gravely and led the way towards the tent a few yards on the other side of the fireplace. The canoe still lay there as I had last seen her in the night, ribs uppermost, the paddles, or rather, *the* paddle, on the sand beside her.

"There's only one," he said, stooping to pick it up. "And here's the rent in the base-board."

It was on the tip of my tongue to tell him that I had clearly noticed *two* paddles a few hours before, but a second impulse made me think better of it, and I said nothing. I approached to see.

There was a long, finely-made tear in the bottom of the canoe where a little slither of wood had been neatly taken clean out; it looked as if the tooth of a sharp rock or snag had eaten down her length, and investigation showed that the hole went through. Had we launched out in her without observing it we must inevitably have foundered. At first the water would have made the wood swell so as to close the hole, but once out in mid-stream the water must have poured in, and the canoe, never more than two inches above the surface, would have filled and sunk very rapidly.

"There, you see an attempt to prepare a victim for the sacrifice," I heard him saying, more to himself than to me, "two victims rather," he added as he bent over and ran his fingers along the slit.

I began to whistle—a thing I always do unconsciously when utterly nonplussed—and purposely paid no attention to his words. I was determined to consider them foolish.

"It wasn't there last night," he said presently, straightening up from his examination and looking anywhere but at me.

"We must have scratched her in landing, of course," I stopped whistling to say. "The stones are very sharp—"

I stopped abruptly, for at that moment he turned round and met my eye squarely. I knew just as well as he did how impossible my explanation was. There were no stones, to begin with.

"And then there's this to explain too," he added quietly, handing me the paddle and pointing to the blade.

A new and curious emotion spread freezingly over me as I took and examined it. The blade was scraped down all over, beautifully scraped, as though someone had sandpapered it with care, making it so thin that the first vigorous stroke must have snapped it off at the elbow.

"One of us walked in his sleep and did this thing," I said feebly, "or—or it has been filed by the constant stream of sand particles blown against it by the wind, perhaps."

"Ah," said the Swede, turning away, laughing a little, "you can explain everything!"

"The same wind that caught the steering paddle and flung it so near the bank that it fell in with the next lump that crumbled," I called out after him, absolutely determined to find an explanation for everything he showed me.

"I see," he shouted back, turning his head to look at me before disappearing among the willow bushes.

Once alone with these perplexing evidences of personal agency, I think my first thought took the form of "One of us must have done this thing, and it certainly was not I." But my second thought decided how impossible it was to suppose, under all the circumstances, that either of us had done it. That my companion, the trusted friend of a dozen similar expeditions, could have knowingly had a hand in it, was a suggestion not to be entertained for a moment. Equally absurd seemed the explanation that this imperturbable and densely practical nature had suddenly become insane and was busied with insane purposes.

Yet the fact remained that what disturbed me most, and kept my fear actively alive even in this blaze of sunshine and wild beauty, was the clear certainty that some curious alteration had come about in his *mind*—that he was nervous, timid, suspicious, aware of goings on he did not speak about, watching a series of secret and hitherto unmentionable events—waiting, in a word, for a climax that he expected, and, I thought, expected very soon. This grew up in my mind intuitively—I hardly knew how.

I made a hurried examination of the tent and its surroundings, but the measurements of the night remained the same. There were deep hollows formed in the sand I now noticed for the first time, basin-shaped and of various depths and sizes, varying from that of a tea-cup to a large bowl. The wind, no doubt, was responsible for these miniature craters, just as it was for lifting the paddle and tossing it towards the water. The rent in the canoe was the only thing that seemed quite inexplicable; and, after all, it *was* conceivable that a sharp point had caught it when we landed. The examination I made of the shore did not assist this theory, but all the same I clung to it with that diminishing portion of my intelligence which I called my "reason." An explanation of some kind was an absolute necessity, just as some working explanation of the universe is necessary—however absurd—to the happiness of every individual who seeks to do his duty in the world and face the problems of life. The simile seemed to me at the time an exact parallel.

I at once set the pitch melting, and presently the Swede joined me at the work, though under the best conditions in the world the canoe could not be safe for travelling till the following day. I drew his attention casually to the hollows in the sand.

"Yes," he said, "I know. They're all over the island. But *you* can explain them, no doubt!"

"Wind, of course," I answered without hesitation. "Have you never watched those little whirlwinds in the street that twist and twirl everything into a circle? This sand's loose enough to yield, that's all."

He made no reply, and we worked on in silence for a bit. I watched him surreptitiously all the time, and I had an idea he was watching me. He seemed, too, to be always listening attentively to something I could not hear, or perhaps for something that he expected to hear, for he kept turning about and staring into the bushes, and up into the sky, and out across the water where it was visible through the openings among the willows. Sometimes he even put his hand to his ear and held it there for several minutes. He said nothing to me, however, about it, and I asked no questions. And meanwhile, as he mended that torn canoe with the skill and address of a red Indian, I was glad to notice his absorption in the work, for there was a vague dread in my heart that he would speak of the changed aspect of the willows. And, if he had noticed *that,* my imagination could no longer be held a sufficient explanation of it.

At length, after a long pause, he began to talk.

"Queer thing," he added in a hurried sort of voice, as though he wanted to say something and get it over. "Queer thing, I mean, about that otter last night."

I had expected something so totally different that he caught me with surprise, and I looked up sharply.

"Shows how lonely this place is. Otters are awfully shy things—"

"I don't mean that, of course," he interrupted. "I mean—do you think—did you think it really *was* an otter?"

"What else, in the name of Heaven, what else?"

"You know, I saw it before you did, and at first it seemed—so *much* bigger than an otter."

"The sunset as you looked up-stream magnified it, or something," I replied.

He looked at me absently a moment, as though his mind were busy with other thoughts.

"It had such extraordinary yellow eyes," he went on half to himself.

"That was the sun too," I laughed, a trifle boisterously. "I suppose you'll wonder next if that fellow in the boat—"

I suddenly decided not to finish the sentence. He was in the act again of listening, turning his head to the wind, and something in the expression of his face made me halt. The subject dropped, and we went on with our caulking. Apparently he had not noticed my unfinished sentence. Five minutes, later, however, he looked at me across the canoe, the smoking pitch in his hand, his face exceedingly grave.

"I *did* rather wonder, if you want to know," he said slowly, "what that thing in the boat was. I remember thinking at the time it was not a man. The whole business seemed to rise quite suddenly out of the water."

I laughed again boisterously in his face, but this time there was impatience, and a strain of anger too, in my feeling.

"Look here now," I cried, "this place is quite queer enough without going out of our way to imagine things! That boat was an ordinary boat, and the man in it was an ordinary man, and they were both going down-stream as fast as they could lick. And that otter *was* an otter, so don't let's play the fool about it!"

He looked steadily at me with the same grave expression. He was not in the least annoyed. I took courage from his silence.

"And, for Heaven's sake," I went on, "don't keep pretending you hear things, because it only gives me the jumps, and there's nothing to hear but the river and this cursed old thundering wind."

"You *fool!*" he answered in a low, shocked voice, "you utter fool. That's just the way all victims talk. As if you didn't understand just as well as I do!" he sneered with scorn in his voice, and a sort of resignation. "The best thing you can do is to keep quiet and try to hold your mind as firm as possible. This feeble attempt at self-deception only makes the truth harder when you're forced to meet it."

My little effort was over, and I found nothing more to say, for

I knew quite well his words were true, and that *I* was the fool, not *he.* Up to a certain stage in the adventure he kept ahead of me easily, and I think I felt annoyed to be out of it, to be thus proved less psychic, less sensitive than himself to these extraordinary happenings, and half ignorant all the time of what was going on under my very nose. *He knew* from the very beginning, apparently. But at the moment I wholly missed the point of his words about the necessity of there being a victim, and that we ourselves were destined to satisfy the want. I dropped all pretence thenceforward, but thenceforward likewise my fear increased steadily to the climax.

"But you're quite right about one thing," he added, before the subject passed, "and that is that we're wiser not to talk about it, or even to think about it, because what one *thinks* finds expression in words, and what one says, happens."

That afternoon, while the canoe dried and hardened, we spent trying to fish, testing the leak, collecting wood, and watching the enormous flood of rising water. Masses of driftwood swept near our shores sometimes, and we fished for them with long willow branches. The island grew perceptibly smaller as the banks were torn away with great gulps and splashes. The weather kept brilliantly fine till about four o'clock, and then for the first time for three days the wind showed signs of abating. Clouds began to gather in the south-west, spreading thence slowly over the sky.

This lessening of the wind came as a great relief, for the incessant roaring, banging, and thundering had irritated our nerves. Yet the silence that came about five o'clock with its sudden cessation was in a manner quite as oppressive. The booming of the river had everything in its own way then: it filled the air with deep murmurs, more musical than the wind noises, but infinitely more monotonous. The wind held many notes, rising, falling, always beating out some sort of great elemental tune; whereas the river's song lay between three notes at most—dull pedal notes, that held a lugubrious quality foreign to the wind, and somehow seemed to me, in my then nervous state, to sound wonderfully well the music of doom.

It was extraordinary, too, how the withdrawal suddenly of bright sunlight took everything out of the landscape that made for cheerfulness; and since this particular landscape had already managed to convey the suggestion of something sinister, the change of course was all the more unwelcome and noticeable. For me, I know, the darkening outlook became distinctly more alarming, and

I found myself more than once calculating how soon after sunset the full moon would get up in the east, and whether the gathering clouds would greatly interfere with her lighting of the little island.

With this general hush of the wind—though it still indulged in occasional brief gusts—the river seemed to me to grow blacker, the willows to stand more densely together. The latter, too, kept up a sort of independent movement of their own, rustling among themselves when no wind stirred, and shaking oddly from the roots upwards. When common objects in this way become charged with the suggestion of horror, they stimulate the imagination far more than things of unusual appearance; and these bushes, crowding huddled about us, assumed for me in the darkness a bizarre *grotesquerie* of appearance that lent to them somehow the aspect of purposeful and living creatures. Their very ordinariness, I felt, masked what was malignant and hostile to us. The forces of the region drew nearer with the coming of night. They were focusing upon our island, and more particularly upon ourselves. For thus, somehow, in the terms of the imagination, did my really indescribable sensations in this extraordinary place present themselves.

I had slept a good deal in the early afternoon, and had thus recovered somewhat from the exhaustion of a disturbed night, but this only served apparently to render me more susceptible than before to the obsessing spell of the haunting. I fought against it, laughing at my feelings as absurd and childish, with very obvious physiological explanations, yet, in spite of every effort, they gained in strength upon me so that I dreaded the night as a child lost in a forest must dread the approach of darkness.

The canoe we had carefully covered with a waterproof sheet during the day, and the one remaining paddle had been securely tied by the Swede to the base of a tree, lest the wind should rob us of that too. From five o'clock onwards I busied myself with the stew-pot and preparations for dinner, it being my turn to cook that night. We had potatoes, onions, bits of bacon fat to add flavour, and a general thick residue from former stews at the bottom of the pot; with black bread broken up into it the result was most excellent, and it was followed by a stew of plums with sugar and a brew of strong tea with dried milk. A good pile of wood lay close at hand, and the absence of wind made my duties easy. My companion sat lazily watching me, dividing his attentions between cleaning his pipe and giving useless advice—an admitted privilege of the off-duty man. He had been very quiet all the afternoon, engaged in re-caulking the canoe, strengthening the tent ropes, and fishing for driftwood while I slept. No more talk about undesirable things had passed between us, and I think his only remarks had to do with the gradual destruction of the island, which he declared was now fully a third smaller than when we first landed.

The pot had just begun to bubble when I heard his voice calling to me from the bank, where he had wandered away without my noticing. I ran up.

"Come and listen," he said, "and see what you make of it." He held his hand cupwise to his ear, as so often before.

"*Now* do you hear anything?" he asked, watching me curiously.

We stood there, listening attentively together. At first I heard only the deep note of the water and the hissings rising from its turbulent surface. The willows, for once, were motionless and silent. Then a sound began to reach my ears faintly, a peculiar sound—something like the humming of a distant gong. It seemed to come across to us in the darkness from the waste of swamps and willows opposite. It was repeated at regular intervals, but it was certainly neither the sound of a bell nor the hooting of a distant steamer. I can liken it to nothing so much as to the sound of an immense gong, suspended far up in the sky, repeating incessantly its muffled metallic note, soft and musical, as it was repeatedly struck. My heart quickened as I listened.

"I've heard it all day," said my companion. "While you slept this afternoon it came all round the island. I hunted it down, but could never get near enough to see—to localise it correctly. Sometimes it was overhead, and sometimes it seemed under the water. Once or twice, too, I could have sworn it was not outside at all, but *within myself* —you know—the way a sound in the fourth dimension is supposed to come."

I was too much puzzled to pay much attention to his words. I listened carefully, striving to associate it with any known familiar sound I could think of, but without success. It changed in the direction, too, coming nearer, and then sinking utterly away into remote distance. I cannot say that it was ominous in quality, because to me it seemed distinctly musical, yet I must admit it set going a distressing feeling that made me wish I had never heard it.

"The wind blowing in those sand-funnels," I said determined to find an explanation, "or the bushes rubbing together after the storm perhaps."

"It comes off the whole swamp," my friend answered. "It comes from everywhere at once." He ignored my explanations. "It comes from the willow bushes somehow—"

"But now the wind has dropped," I objected. "The willows can hardly make a noise by themselves, can they?"

His answer frightened me, first because I had dreaded it, and secondly, because I knew intuitively it was true.

"It is *because* the wind has dropped we now hear it. It was drowned before. It is the cry, I believe, of the—"

I dashed back to my fire, warned by a sound of bubbling that the stew was in danger, but determined at the same time to escape further conversation. I was resolute, if possible, to avoid the exchanging of views. I dreaded, too, that he would begin about the gods, or the elemental forces, or something else disquieting, and I wanted to keep myself well in hand for what might happen later. There was another night to be faced before we escaped from this distressing place, and there was no knowing yet what it might bring forth.

"Come and cut up bread for the pot," I called to him, vigorously stirring the appetising mixture. That stew-pot held sanity for us both, and the thought made me laugh.

He came over slowly and took the provision sack from the tree, fumbling in its mysterious depths, and then emptying the entire contents upon the ground-sheet at his feet.

"Hurry up!" I cried; "it's boiling."

The Swede burst out into a roar of laughter that startled me. It was forced laughter, not artificial exactly, but mirthless.

"There's nothing here!" he shouted, holding his sides.

"Bread, I mean."

"It's gone. There is no bread. They've taken it!"

I dropped the long spoon and ran up. Everything the sack had contained lay upon the ground-sheet, but there was no loaf.

The whole dead weight of my growing fear fell upon me and shook me. Then I burst out laughing too. It was the only thing to do: and the sound of my laughter also made me understand his. The strain of psychical pressure caused it—this explosion of unnatural laughter in both of us; it was an effort of repressed forces to seek relief; it was a temporary safety-valve. And with both of us it ceased quite suddenly.

"How criminally stupid of me!" I cried, still determined to be consistent and find an explanation. "I clean forgot to buy a loaf at

Pressburg. That chattering woman put everything out of my head, and I must have left it lying on the counter or—"

"The oatmeal, too, is much less than it was this morning," the Swede interrupted.

Why in the world need he draw attention to it? I thought angrily.

"There's enough for to-morrow," I said, stirring vigorously, "and we can get lots more at Komorn or Gran. In twenty-four hours we shall be miles from here."

"I hope so—to God," he muttered, putting the things back into the sack, "unless we're claimed first as victims for the sacrifice," he added with a foolish laugh. He dragged the sack into the tent, for safety's sake, I suppose, and I heard him mumbling on to himself, but so indistinctly that it seemed quite natural for me to ignore his words.

Our meal was beyond question a gloomy one, and we ate it almost in silence, avoiding one another's eyes, and keeping the fire bright. Then we washed up and prepared for the night, and, once smoking, our minds unoccupied with any definite duties, the apprehension I had felt all day long became more and more acute. It was not then active fear, I think, but the very vagueness of its origin distressed me far more than if I had been able to ticket and face it squarely. The curious sound I have likened to the note of a gong became now almost incessant, and filled the stillness of the night with a faint, continuous ringing rather than a series of distinct notes. At one time it was behind and at another time in front of us. Sometimes I fancied it came from the bushes on our left, and then again from the clumps on our right. More often it hovered directly overhead like the whirring of wings. It was really everywhere at once, behind, in front, at our sides and over our heads, completely surrounding us. The sound really defies description. But nothing within my knowledge is like that ceaseless muffled humming rising off the deserted world of swamps and willows.

We sat smoking in comparative silence, the strain growing every minute greater. The worst feature of the situation seemed to me that we did not know what to expect, and could therefore make no sort of preparation by way of defence. We could anticipate nothing. My explanations made in the sunshine, moreover, now came to haunt me with their foolish and wholly unsatisfactory nature, and it was more and more clear to us that some kind of plain talk with my companion was inevitable, whether I liked it or not. After all, we had to spend the night together, and to sleep in the same tent side by side. I saw that I could not get along much longer without the support of his mind, and for that, of course, plain talk was imperative. As long as possible, however, I postponed this little climax, and tried to ignore or laugh at the occasional sentences he flung into the emptiness.

Some of these sentences, moreover, were confoundedly disquieting to me, coming as they did to corroborate much that I felt myself: corroboration, too—which made it so much more convincing—from a totally different point of view. He composed such curious sentences, and hurled them at me in such an inconsequential sort of way, as though his main line of thought was secret to himself, and these fragments were bits he found it impossible to digest. He got rid of them by uttering them. Speech relieved him. It was like being sick.

"There are things about us, I'm sure, that make for disorder, disintegration, destruction, *our* destruction," he said once, while the fire blazed between us. "We've strayed out of a safe line somewhere."

And another time, when the gong sounds had come nearer, ringing much louder than before, and directly over our heads, he said as though talking to himself:

"I don't think a gramophone would show any record of that. The sound doesn't come to me by the ears at all. The vibrations reach me in another manner altogether, and seem to be within me, which is precisely how a fourth dimensional sound might be supposed to make itself heard."

I purposely made no reply to this, but I sat up a little closer to the fire and peered about me into the darkness. The clouds were massed all over the sky, and no trace of moonlight came through. Very still, too, everything was, so that the river and the frogs had things all their own way.

"It has that about it," he went on, "which is utterly out of common experience. It is *unknown.* Only one thing describes it really: it is a non-human sound; I mean a sound outside humanity."

Having rid himself of this indigestible morsel, he lay quiet for a time; but he had so admirably expressed my own feeling that it was a relief to have the thought out, and to have confined it by the limitation of words from dangerous wandering to and fro in the mind.

The solitude of that Danube camping-place, can I ever forget it? The feeling of being utterly alone on an empty planet! My thoughts ran incessantly upon cities and the haunts of men. I would have given my soul, as the saying is, for the "feel" of those Bavarian villages we had passed through by the score; for the normal, human commonplaces: peasants drinking beer, tables beneath the trees, hot sunshine, and a ruined castle on the rocks behind the red-roofed church. Even the tourists would have been welcome.

Yet what I felt of dread was no ordinary ghostly fear. It was infinitely greater, stranger, and seemed to arise from some dim ancestral sense of terror more profoundly disturbing than anything I had known or dreamed of. We had "strayed," as the Swede put it, into some region or some set of conditions where the risks were great, yet unintelligible to us; where the frontiers of some unknown world lay close about us. It was a spot held by the dwellers in some outer space, a sort of peep-hole whence they could spy upon the earth, themselves unseen, a point where the veil between had worn a little thin. As the final result of too long a sojourn here, we should be carried over the border and deprived of what we called "our lives," yet by mental, not physical, processes. In that sense, as he said, we should be the victims of our adventure—a sacrifice.

It took us in different fashion, each according to the measure of his sensitiveness and powers of resistance. I translated it vaguely into a personification of the mightily disturbed elements, investing them with the horror of a deliberate and malefic purpose, resentful of our audacious intrusion into their breeding-place; whereas my friend threw it into the unoriginal form at first of a trespass on some ancient shrine, some place where the old gods still held sway, where the emotional forces of former worshippers still clung, and the ancestral portion of him yielded to the old pagan spell.

At any rate, here was a place unpolluted by men, kept clean by the winds from coarsening human influences, a place where spiritual agencies were within reach and aggressive. Never, before or since, have I been so attacked by indescribable suggestions of a "beyond region," of another scheme of life, another revolution not parallel to the human. And in the end our minds would succumb under the weight of the awful spell, and we should be drawn across the frontier into *their* world.

Small things testified to the amazing influence of the place, and now in the silence round the fire they allowed themselves to be noted by the mind. The very atmosphere had proved itself a magnifying medium to distort every indication: the otter rolling in the current, the hurrying boatman making signs, the shifting willows, one and all had been robbed of its natural character, and revealed in something of its other aspect—as it existed across the border in that other region. And this changed aspect I felt was new not merely to me, but to the race. The whole experience whose verge we touched was unknown to humanity at all. It was a new order of experience, and in the true sense of the word *unearthly*.

"It's the deliberate, calculating purpose that reduces one's courage to zero," the Swede said suddenly, as if he had been actually following my thoughts. "Otherwise imagination might count for much. But the paddle, the canoe, the lessening food—"

"Haven't I explained all that once?" I interrupted viciously.

"You have," he answered dryly; "you have indeed."

He made other remarks too, as usual, about what he called the "plain determination to provide a victim"; but, having now arranged my thoughts better, I recognised that this was simply the cry of his frightened soul against the knowledge that he was being attacked in a vital part, and that he would be somehow taken or destroyed. The situation called for a courage and calmness of reasoning that neither of us could compass, and I have never before been so clearly conscious of two persons in me—the one that explained everything, and the other that laughed at such foolish explanations, yet was horribly afraid.

Meanwhile, in the pitchy night the fire died down and the wood pile grew small. Neither of us moved to replenish the stock, and the darkness consequently came up very close to our faces. A few feet beyond the circle of firelight it was inky black. Occasionally a stray puff of wind set the willows shivering about us, but apart from this not very welcome sound a deep and depressing silence reigned, broken only by the gurgling of the river and the humming in the air overhead.

We both missed, I think, the shouting company of the winds.

At length, at a moment when a stray puff prolonged itself as though the wind were about to rise again, I reached the point for me of saturation, the point where it was absolutely necessary to find relief in plain speech, or else to betray myself by some hysterical extravagance that must have been far worse in its effect upon both of us. I kicked the fire into a blaze, and turned to my companion abruptly. He looked up with a start.

"I can't disguise it any longer," I said; "I don't like this place, and the darkness, and the noises, and the awful feelings I get. There's something here that beats me utterly. I'm in a blue funk, and that's the plain truth. If the other shore was—different, I swear I'd be inclined to swim for it!"

The Swede's face turned very white beneath the deep tan of sun and wind. He stared straight at me and answered quietly, but his voice betrayed his huge excitement by its unnatural calmness. For the moment, at any rate, he was the strong man of the two. He was more phlegmatic, for one thing.

"It's not a physical condition we can escape from by running away," he replied, in the tone of a doctor diagnosing some grave disease; "we must sit tight and wait. There are forces close here that could kill a herd of elephants in a second as easily as you or I could squash a fly. Our only chance is to keep perfectly still. Our insignificance perhaps may save us."

I put a dozen questions into my expression of face, but found no words. It was precisely like listening to an accurate description of a disease whose symptoms had puzzled me.

"I mean that so far, although aware of our disturbing presence, they have not *found* us—not 'located' us, as the Americans say," he went on. "They're blundering about like men hunting for a leak of gas. The paddle and canoe and provisions prove that. I think they *feel* us, but cannot actually see us. We must keep our minds quiet—it's our minds they feel. We must control our thoughts, or it's all up with us."

"Death, you mean?" I stammered, icy with the horror of his suggestion.

"Worse—by far," he said. "Death, according to one's belief, means either annihilation or release from the limitations of the senses, but it involves no change of character. *You* don't suddenly alter just because the body's gone. But this means a radical alteration, a complete change, a horrible loss of oneself by substitution—far worse than death, and not even annihilation. We happen to have camped in a spot where their region touches ours, where the veil between has worn thin"—horrors! he was using my very own phrase, my actual words—"so that they are aware of our being in their neighbourhood."

"But *who* are aware?" I asked.

I forgot the shaking of the willows in the windless calm, the humming overhead, everything except that I was waiting for an answer that I dreaded more than I can possibly explain.

He lowered his voice at once to reply, leaning forward a little over the fire, an indefinable change in his face that made me avoid his eyes and look down upon the ground.

"All my life," he said, "I have been strangely, vividly conscious of another region—not far removed from our own world in one sense, yet wholly different in kind—where great things go on unceasingly, where immense and terrible personalities hurry by, intent on vast purposes compared to which earthly affairs, the rise and fall of nations, the destinies of empires, the fate of armies and continents, are all as dust in the balance; vast purposes, I mean, that deal directly with the soul, and not indirectly with mere expressions of the soul—"

"I suggest just now—" I began, seeking to stop him, feeling as though I was face to face with a madman. But he instantly overbore me with his torrent that *had* to come.

"You think," he said, "it is the spirits of the elements, and I thought perhaps it was the old gods. But I tell you now it is—*neither*. These would be comprehensible entities, for they have relations with men, depending upon them for worship or sacrifice, whereas these beings who are now about us have absolutely nothing to do with mankind, and it is mere chance that their space happens just at this spot to touch our own."

The mere conception, which his words somehow made so convincing, as I listened to them there in the dark stillness of that lonely island, set me shaking a little all over. I found it impossible to control my movements.

"And what do you propose?" I began again.

"A sacrifice, a victim, might save us by distracting them until we could get away," he went on, "just as the wolves stop to devour the dogs and give the sleigh another start. But—I see no chance of any other victim now."

I stared blankly at him. The gleam in his eyes was dreadful. Presently he continued.

"It's the willows, of course. The willows *mask* the others, but the others are feeling about for us. If we let our minds betray our fear, we're lost, lost utterly." He looked at me with an expression so calm, so determined, so sincere, that I no longer had any doubts as to his sanity. He was as sane as any man ever was. "If we can hold out through the night," he added, "we may get off in the daylight unnoticed, or rather, *undiscovered*."

"But you really think a sacrifice would—"

That gong-like humming came down very close over our heads as I spoke, but it was my friend's scared face that really stopped my mouth.

"Hush!" he whispered, holding up his hand. "Do not mention them more than you can help. Do not refer to them *by name.* To name is to reveal: it is the inevitable clue, and our only hope lies in ignoring them, in order that they may ignore us."

"Even in thought?" He was extraordinarily agitated.

"Especially in thought. Our thoughts make spirals in their world. We must keep them *out of our minds* at all costs if possible."

I raked the fire together to prevent the darkness having everything its own way. I never longed for the sun as I longed for it then in the awful blackness of that summer night.

"Were you awake all last night?" he went on suddenly.

"I slept badly a little after dawn," I replied evasively, trying to follow his instructions, which I knew instinctively were true, "but the wind, of course—"

"I know. But the wind won't account for all the noises."

"Then you heard it too?"

"The multiplying countless little footsteps I heard," he said, adding, after a moment's hesitation, "and that other sound—"

"You mean above the tent, and the pressing down upon us of something tremendous, gigantic?"

He nodded significantly.

"It was like the beginning of a sort of inner suffocation." I said.

"Partly, yes. It seemed to me that the weight of the atmosphere had been altered—had increased enormously, so that we should be crushed."

"And *that,*" I went on, determined to have it all out, pointing upwards where the gong-like note hummed ceaselessly, rising and falling like wind. "What do you make of that?"

"It's *their* sound," he whispered gravely. "It's the sound of their world, the humming in their region. The division here is so thin that it leaks through somehow. But, if you listen carefully, you'll find it's not above so much as around us. It's in the willows. It's the willows themselves humming, because here the willows have been made symbols of the forces that are against us."

I could not follow exactly what he meant by this, yet the thought and idea in my mind were beyond question the thought and idea in his. I realised what he realised, only with less power of analysis than his. It was on the tip of my tongue to tell him at last about my hallucination of the ascending figures and the moving bushes, when he suddenly thrust his face again close into mine across the firelight and began to speak in a very earnest whisper. He amazed me by his calmness and pluck, his apparent control of the situation. This man I had for years deemed unimaginative, stolid!

"Now listen," he said. "The only thing for us to do is to go on as though nothing had happened, follow our usual habits, go to bed, and so forth; pretend we feel nothing and notice nothing. It is a question wholly of the mind, and the less we think about them the better our chance of escape. Above all, don't *think,* for what you think happens!"

"All right," I managed to reply, simply breathless with his words and the strangeness of it all; "all right, I'll try, but tell me one thing more first. Tell me what you make of those hollows in the ground all about us, those sand-funnels?"

"No!" he cried, forgetting to whisper in his excitement. "I dare not, simply dare not, put the thought into words. If you have not guessed I am glad. Don't try to. *They* have put it into my mind; try your hardest to prevent their putting it into yours."

He sank his voice again to a whisper before he finished, and I did not press him to explain. There was already just about as much horror in me as I could hold. The conversation came to an end, and we smoked our pipes busily in silence.

Then something happened, something unimportant apparently, as the way is when the nerves are in a very great state of tension, and this small thing for a brief space gave me an entirely different point of view. I chanced to look down at my sand-shoe—the sort we used for the canoe—and something to do with the hole at the toe suddenly recalled to me the London shop where I had bought them, the difficulty the man had in fitting me, and other details of the uninteresting but practical operation. At once, in its train, followed a wholesome view of the modern sceptical world I was accustomed to move in at home. I thought of roast beef and ale, motor-cars, policemen, brass bands, and a dozen other things that proclaimed the soul of ordinariness or utility. The effect was immediate and astonishing even to myself. Psychologically, I suppose, it was simply a sudden and violent reaction after the strain of living in an atmosphere of things that to the normal consciousness must seem impossible and incredible. But, whatever the cause, it momentarily lifted the spell from my heart, and left me for the short space of a minute feeling free and utterly unafraid. I looked up at my friend opposite.

"You damned old pagan!" I cried, laughing aloud in his face. "You imaginative idiot! You superstitious idolator! You—"

I stopped in the middle, seized anew by the old horror. I tried to smother the sound of my voice as something sacrilegious. The Swede, of course, heard it too—the strange cry overhead in the darkness—and that sudden drop in the air as though something had come nearer.

He had turned ashen white under the tan. He stood bolt upright in front of the fire, stiff as a rod, staring at me.

"After that," he said in a sort of helpless, frantic way, "we must go! We can't stay now; we must strike camp this very instant and go on—down the river."

He was talking, I saw, quite wildly, his words dictated by abject terror—the terror he had resisted so long, but which had caught him at last.

"In the dark?" I exclaimed, shaking with fear after my hysterical outburst, but still realising our position better than he did. "Sheer madness! The river's in flood, and we've only got a single paddle. Besides, we only go deeper into their country! There's nothing ahead for fifty miles but willows, willows, willows!"

He sat down again in a state of semi-collapse. The positions, by one of those kaleidoscopic changes nature loves, were suddenly reversed, and the control of our forces passed over into my hands. His mind at last had reached the point where it was beginning to weaken.

"What on earth possessed you to do such a thing?" he whispered with the awe of genuine terror in his voice and face.

I crossed round to his side of the fire. I took both his hands in mine, kneeling down beside him and looking straight into his frightened eyes.

"We'll make one more blaze," I said firmly, "and then turn in for the night. At sunrise we'll be off full speed for Komorn. Now, pull yourself together a bit, and remember your own advice about *not thinking fear!*"

He said no more, and I saw that he would agree and obey. In some measure, too, it was a sort of relief to get up and make an excursion into the darkness for more wood. We kept close together, almost touching, groping among the bushes and along the bank.

The humming overhead never ceased, but seemed to me to grow louder as we increased our distance from the fire. It was shivery work!

We were grubbing away in the middle of a thickish clump of willows where some driftwood from a former flood had caught high among the branches, when my body was seized in a grip that made me half drop upon the sand. It was the Swede. He had fallen against me, and was clutching me for support. I heard his breath coming and going in short gasps.

"Look! By my soul!" he whispered, and for the first time in my experience I knew what it was to hear tears of terror in a human voice. He was pointing to the fire, some fifty feet away. I followed the direction of his finger, and I swear my heart missed a beat.

There, in front of the dim glow, *something was moving.*

I saw it through a veil that hung before my eyes like the gauze drop-curtain used at the back of a theatre—hazily a little. It was neither a human figure nor an animal. To me it gave the strange impression of being as large as several animals grouped together, like horses, two or three, moving slowly. The Swede, too, got a similar result, though expressing it differently, for he thought it was shaped and sized like a clump of willow bushes, rounded at the top, and moving all over upon its surface—"coiling upon itself like smoke," he said afterwards.

"I watched it settle downwards through the bushes," he sobbed at me. "Look, by God! It's coming this way! Oh, oh!"—he gave a kind of whistling cry. *"They've found us."*

I gave one terrified glance, which just enabled me to see that the shadowy form was swinging towards us through the bushes, and then I collapsed backwards with a crash into the branches. These failed, of course, to support my weight, so that with the Swede on the top of me we fell in a struggling heap upon the sand. I really hardly knew what was happening. I was conscious only of a sort of enveloping sensation of icy fear that plucked the nerves out of their fleshly covering, twisted them this way and that, and replaced them quivering. My eyes were tightly shut; something in my throat choked me; a feeling that my consciousness was expanding, extending out into space, swiftly gave way to another feeling that I was losing it altogether, and about to die.

An acute spasm of pain passed through me, and I was aware that the Swede had hold of me in such a way that he hurt me abominably. It was the way he caught at me in falling.

But it was the pain, he declared afterwards, that saved me: it caused me to *forget them* and think of something else at the very instant when they were about to find me. It concealed my mind from them at the moment of discovery, yet just in time to evade their terrible seizing of me. He himself, he says, actually swooned at the same moment, and that was what saved him.

I only know that at a later date, how long or short is impossible to say, I found myself scrambling up out of the slippery network of willow branches, and saw my companion standing in front of me holding out a hand to assist me. I stared at him in a dazed way, rubbing the arm he had twisted for me. Nothing came to me to say, somehow.

"I lost consciousness for a moment or two," I heard him say. "That's what saved me. It made me stop thinking about them."

"You nearly broke my arm in two," I said, uttering my only connected thought at the moment. A numbness came over me.

"That's what saved *you!*" he replied. "Between us, we've managed to set them off on a false tack somewhere. The humming has ceased. It's gone—for the moment at any rate!"

A wave of hysterical laughter seized me again, and this time spread to my friend too—great healing gusts of shaking laughter that brought a tremendous sense of relief in their train. We made our way back to the fire and put the wood on so that it blazed at once. Then we saw that the tent had fallen over and lay in a tangled heap upon the ground.

We picked it up, and during the process tripped more than once and caught our feet in sand.

"It's those sand-funnels," exclaimed the Swede, when the tent was up again and the firelight lit up the ground for several yards about us. "And look at the size of them!"

All round the tent and about the fireplace where we had seen the moving shadows there were deep funnel-shaped hollows in the sand, exactly similar to the ones we had already found over the island, only far bigger and deeper, beautifully formed, and wide enough in some instances to admit the whole of my foot and leg.

Neither of us said a word. We both knew that sleep was the safest thing we could do, and to bed we went accordingly without further delay, having first thrown sand on the fire and taken the provision sack and the paddle inside the tent with us. The canoe, too, we propped in such a way at the end of the tent that our feet touched it, and the least motion would disturb and wake us.

In case of emergency, too, we again went to bed in our clothes, ready for a sudden start.

It was my firm intention to lie awake all night and watch, but the exhaustion of nerves and body decreed otherwise, and sleep after a while came over me with a welcome blanket of oblivion. The fact that my companion also slept quickened its approach. At first he fidgeted and constantly sat up, asking me if I "heard this" or "heard that." He tossed about on his cork mattress, and said the tent was moving and the river had risen over the point of the island; but each time I went out to look I returned with the report that all was well, and finally he grew calmer and lay still. Then at length his breathing became regular and I heard unmistakable sounds of snoring—the first and only time in my life when snoring has been a welcome and calming influence.

This, I remember, was the last thought in my mind before dozing off.

A difficulty in breathing woke me, and I found the blanket over my face. But something else besides the blanket was pressing upon me, and my first thought was that my companion had rolled off his mattress on to my own in his sleep. I called to him and sat up, and at the same moment it came to me that the tent was *surrounded.* That sound of multitudinous soft pattering was again audible outside, filling the night with horror.

I called again to him, louder than before. He did not answer, but I missed the sound of his snoring, and also noticed that the flap of the tent door was down. This was the unpardonable sin. I crawled out in the darkness to hook it back securely, and it was then for the first time I realised positively that the Swede was not there. He had gone.

I dashed out in a mad run, seized by a dreadful agitation, and the moment I was out I plunged into a sort of torrent of humming that surrounded me completely and came out of every quarter of the heavens at once. It was that same familiar humming—gone mad! A swarm of great invisible bees might have been about me in the air. The sound seemed to thicken the very atmosphere, and I felt that my lungs worked with difficulty.

But my friend was in danger, and I could not hesitate.

The dawn was just about to break, and a faint whitish light spread upwards over the clouds from a thin strip of clear horizon. No wind stirred. I could just make out the bushes and river beyond, and the pale sandy patches. In my excitement I ran frantically to and fro about the island, calling him by name, shouting at the top of my voice the first words that came into my head. But the willows smothered my voice, and the humming muffled it, so that the sound only travelled a few feet round me. I plunged among the bushes, tripping headlong, tumbling over roots, and scraping my face as I tore this way and that among the preventing branches.

Then, quite unexpectedly, I came out upon the island's point and saw a dark figure outlined between the water and the sky. It was the Swede. And already he had one foot in the river! A moment more and he would have taken the plunge.

I threw myself upon him, flinging my arms about his waist and dragging him shorewards with all my strength. Of course he struggled furiously, making a noise all the time just like that cursed humming, and using the most outlandish phrases in his anger about "going *inside* to Them," and "taking the way of the water and the wind," and God only knows what more besides, that I tried in vain to recall afterwards, but which turned me sick with horror and amazement as I listened. But in the end I managed to get him into the comparative safety of the tent, and flung him breathless and cursing upon the mattress where I held him until the fit had passed.

I think the suddenness with which it all went and he grew calm, coinciding as it did with the equally abrupt cessation of the humming and pattering outside—I think this was almost the strangest part of the whole business perhaps. For he just opened his eyes and turned his tired face up to me so that the dawn threw a pale light upon it through the doorway, and said, for all the world just like a frightened child:

"My life, old man—it's my life I owe you. But it's all over now anyhow. They've found a victim in our place!"

Then he dropped back upon his blankets and went to sleep literally under my eyes. He simply collapsed, and began to snore again as healthily as though nothing had happened and he had never tried to offer his own life as a sacrifice by drowning. And when the sunlight woke him three hours later—hours of ceaseless vigil for me—it became so clear to me that he remembered absolutely nothing of what he had attempted to do, that I deemed it wise to hold my peace and ask no dangerous questions.

He woke naturally and easily, as I have said, when the sun was already high in a windless hot sky, and he at once got up and set about the preparation of the fire for breakfast. I followed him anxiously at bathing, but he did not attempt to plunge in, merely dipping his head and making some remark about the extra coldness of the water.

"River's falling at last," he said, "and I'm glad of it."

"The humming has stopped too," I said.

He looked up at me quietly with his normal expression. Evidently he remembered everything except his own attempt at suicide.

"Everything has stopped," he said, "because—"

He hesitated. But I knew some reference to that remark he had made just before he fainted was in his mind, and I was determined to know it.

"Because 'They've found another victim'?" I said, forcing a little laugh.

"Exactly," he answered, "exactly! I feel as positive of it as though—as though—I feel quite safe again, I mean," he finished.

He began to look curiously about him. The sunlight lay in hot patches on the sand. There was no wind. The willows were motionless. He slowly rose to his feet.

"Come," he said; "I think if we look, we shall find it."

He started off on a run, and I followed him. He kept to the banks, poking with a stick among the sandy bays and caves and little backwaters, myself always close on his heels.

"Ah!" he exclaimed presently, "ah!"

The tone of his voice somehow brought back to me a vivid sense of the horror of the last twenty-four hours, and I hurried up to join him. He was pointing with his stick at a large black object that lay half in the water and half on the sand. It appeared to be caught by some twisted willow roots so that the river could not sweep it away. A few hours before the spot must have been under water.

"See," he said quietly, "the victim that made our escape possible!"

And when I peered across his shoulder I saw that his stick rested on the body of a man. He turned it over. It was the corpse of a peasant, and the face was hidden in the sand. Clearly the man had been drowned but a few hours before, and his body must have been swept down upon our island somewhere about the hour of the dawn —*at the very time the fit had passed.*

"We must give it a decent burial, you know."

"I suppose so," I replied. I shuddered a little in spite of myself, for there was something about the appearance of that poor drowned man that turned me cold.

The Swede glanced up sharply at me, an undecipherable expression on his face, and began clambering down the bank. I followed him more leisurely. The current, I noticed, had torn away much of the clothing from the body, so that the neck and part of the chest lay bare.

Half-way down the bank my companion suddenly stopped and held up his hand in warning; but either my foot slipped, or I had gained too much momentum to bring myself quickly to a halt, for I bumped into him and sent him forward with a sort of leap to save himself. We tumbled together on to the hard sand so that our feet splashed into the water. And, before anything could be done, we had collided a little heavily against the corpse.

The Swede uttered a sharp cry. And I sprang back as if I had been shot.

At the moment we touched the body there rose from its surface the loud sound of humming—the sound of several hummings—which passed with a vast commotion as of winged things in the air about us and disappeared upwards into the sky, growing fainter and fainter till they finally ceased in the distance. It was exactly as though we had disturbed some living yet invisible creatures at work.

My companion clutched me, and I think I clutched him, but before either of us had time properly to recover from the unexpected shock, we saw that a movement of the current was turning the corpse round so that it became released from the grip of the willow roots. A moment later it had turned completely over, the dead face uppermost, staring at the sky. It lay on the edge of the main stream. In another moment it would be swept away.

The Swede started to save it, shouting again something I did not catch about a "proper burial"—and then abruptly dropped upon his knees on the sand and covered his eyes with his hands. I was beside him in an instant.

I saw what he had seen.

For just as the body swung round to the current the face and the exposed chest turned full towards us, and showed plainly how the skin and flesh were indented with small hollows, beautifully formed, and exactly similar in shape and kind to the sand-funnels that we had found all over the island.

"Their mark!" I heard my companion mutter under his breath. "Their awful mark!"

And when I turned my eyes again from his ghastly face to the river, the current had done its work, and the body had been swept away into mid-stream and was already beyond our reach and almost out of sight, turning over and over on the waves like an otter.

The Beckoning Fair One

OLIVER ONIONS

[1873–1961]

"The Beckoning Fair One" *appeared originally in Onions's first book of ghost stories,* Widdershins *(1911). It was the best in the book; the best story Onions wrote; and, some say, the best ghost story ever written. This tale of a novelist's fatal absorption with his own creation is so carefully developed, and the realism of the setting and situation so painstakingly maintained, that the ghostly element within* "The Beckoning Fair One" *has a verisimilitude unique in supernatural fiction.*

I

The three or four "To Let" boards had stood within the low paling as long as the inhabitants of the little triangular "Square" could remember, and if they had ever been vertical it was a very long time ago. They now overhung the palings each at its own angle, and resembled nothing so much as a row of wooden choppers, ever in the act of falling upon some passer-by, yet never cutting off a tenant for the old house from the stream of his fellows. Not that there was ever any great "stream" through the square; the stream passed a furlong and more away, beyond the intricacy of tenements and alleys and byways that had sprung up since the old house had been built, hemming it in completely; and probably the house itself was only suffered to stand pending the falling-in of a lease or two, when doubtless a clearance would be made of the whole neighbourhood.

It was of bloomy old red brick, and built into its walls were the crowns and clasped hands and other insignia of insurance companies long since defunct. The children of the secluded square had swung upon the low gate at the end of the entrance-alley until little more than the solid top bar of it remained, and the alley itself ran past boarded basement windows on which tramps had chalked their cryptic marks. The path was washed and worn uneven by the spilling of water from the eaves of the encroaching next house, and cats and dogs had made the approach their own. The chances of a tenant did not seem such as to warrant the keeping of the "To Let" boards in a state of legibility and repair, and as a matter of fact they were not so kept.

For six months Oleron had passed the old place twice a day or oftener, on his way from his lodgings to the room, ten minutes' walk away, he had taken to work in; and for six months no hatchet-like notice-board had fallen across his path. This might have been due to the fact that he usually took the other side of the square. But he chanced one morning to take the side that ran past the broken gate and the rain-worn entrance alley, and to pause before one of the inclined boards. The board bore, besides the agent's name, the announcement, written apparently about the time of Oleron's own early youth, that the key was to be had at Number Six.

Now Oleron was already paying, for his separate bedroom and workroom, more than an author who, without private means, habitually disregards his public, can afford; and he was paying in addition a small rent for the storage of the greater part of his grandmother's furniture. Moreover, it invariably happened that the book he wished to read in bed was at his working-quarters half a mile or more away, while the note or letter he had sudden need of during the day was as likely as not to be in the pocket of another coat hanging behind his bedroom door. And there were other inconveniences in having a divided domicile. Therefore Oleron, brought suddenly up by the hatchet-like noticeboard, looked first down through some scanty privet-bushes at the boarded basement windows, then up at the blank and grimy windows of the first floor, and so up to the second floor and the flat stone coping of the leads. He stood for a minute thumbing his lean and shaven jaw; then, with another glance at the board, he walked slowly across the square to Number Six.

He knocked, and waited for two or three minutes, but, although the door stood open, received no answer. He was knocking again when a long-nosed man in shirt-sleeves appeared.

"I was arsking a blessing on our food," he said in severe explanation.

Oleron asked if he might have the key of the old house; and the long-nosed man withdrew again.

Oleron waited for another five minutes on the step; then the man, appearing again and masticating some of the food of which he had spoken, announced that the key was lost.

"But you won't want it," he said. "The entrance door isn't closed, and a push 'll open any of the others. I'm a agent for it, if you're thinking of taking it—"

Oleron recrossed the square, descended the two steps at the broken gate, passed along the alley, and turned in at the old wide doorway. To the right, immediately within the door, steps descended to the roomy cellars, and the staircase before him had a carved rail, and was broad and handsome and filthy. Oleron ascended it, avoiding contact with the rail and wall, and stopped at the first landing. A door facing him had been boarded up, but he pushed at that on his right hand, and an insecure bolt or staple yielded. He entered the empty first floor.

He spent a quarter of an hour in the place, and then came out again. Without mounting higher, he descended and recrossed the square to the house of the man who had lost the key.

"Can you tell me how much the rent is?" he asked.

The man mentioned a figure, the comparative lowness of which seemed accounted for by the character of the neighbourhood and the abominable state of unrepair of the place.

"Would it be possible to rent a single floor?"

The long-nosed man did not know; they might. . . .

"Who are they?"

The man gave Oleron the name of a firm of lawyers in Lincoln's Inn.

"You might mention my name—Barrett," he added.

Pressure of work prevented Oleron from going down to Lincoln's Inn that afternoon, but he went on the morrow, and was instantly offered the whole house as a purchase for fifty pounds down, the remainder of the purchase-money to remain on mortgage. It took him half an hour to disabuse the lawyer's mind of the idea that he wished anything more of the place than to rent a single floor of it. This made certain hums and haws of a difference, and the lawyer was by no means certain that it lay within his power to do as Oleron suggested; but it was finally extracted from him that, provided the notice-boards were allowed to remain up, and that, provided it was agreed that in the event of the whole house letting, the arrangement should terminate automatically without further notice, something might be done. That the old place should suddenly let over his head seemed to Oleron the slightest of risks to take, and he promised a decision within a week. On the morrow he visited the house again, went through it from top to bottom, and then went home to his lodgings to take a bath.

He was immensely taken with that portion of the house he had already determined should be his own. Scraped clean and repainted, and with that old furniture of Oleron's grandmother's, it ought to be entirely charming. He went to the storage warehouse to refresh his memory of his half-forgotten belongings, and to take the measurements; and thence he went to a decorator's. He was very busy with his regular work, and could have wished that the notice-board had caught his attention either a few months earlier or else later in the year; but the quickest way would be to suspend work entirely until after his removal. . . .

A fortnight later his first floor was painted throughout in a tender, elder-flower white, the paint was dry, and Oleron was in the middle of his installation. He was animated, delighted; and he rubbed his hands as he polished and made disposals of his grandmother's effects—the tall lattice-paned china cupboard with its Derby and Mason and Spode, the large folding Sheraton table, the long, low bookshelves (he had had two of them "copied"), the chairs, the Sheffield candlesticks, the riveted rose-bowls. These things he set against his newly painted elder-white walls—walls of wood panelled in the happiest proportions, and moulded and coffered to the low-seated window-recesses in a mood of gaiety and rest that the builders of rooms no longer know. The ceilings were lofty, and faintly painted with an old pattern of stars; even the tapering mouldings of his iron fireplace were as delicately designed as jewellery; and Oleron walked about rubbing his hands, frequently stopping for the mere pleasure of the glimpses from white room to white room. . . .

"Charming, charming!" he said to himself. "I wonder what Elsie Bengough will think of this!"

He bought a bolt and a Yale lock for his door, and shut off his quarters from the rest of the house. If he now wanted to read in bed, his book could be had for stepping into the next room. All the time, he thought how exceedingly lucky he was to get the place. He put up a hat-rack in the little square hall, and hung up his hats and caps and coats; and passers through the small triangular square late at night, looking up over the little serried row of wooden "To Let" hatchets, could see the light within Oleron's red blinds, or else the sudden darkening of one blind and the illumination of another, as Oleron, candlestick in hand, passed from room to room, making final settlings of his furniture, or preparing to resume the work that his removal had interrupted.

II

As far as the chief business of his life—his writing—was concerned, Paul Oleron treated the world a good deal better than he was treated by it; but he seldom took the trouble to strike a balance, or to compute how far, at forty-four years of age, he was behind his points on the handicap. To have done so wouldn't have altered matters, and it might have depressed Oleron. He had chosen his path, and was committed to it beyond possibility of withdrawal. Perhaps he had chosen it in the days when he had been easily swayed by something a little disinterested, a little generous, a little noble; and had he ever thought of questioning himself he would still have held to it that a life without nobility and generosity and disinterestedness was no life for him. Only quite recently, and rarely, had he even vaguely suspected that there was more in it than this; but it was no good anticipating the day when, he supposed, he would reach that maximum point of his powers beyond which he must inevitably decline, and be left face to face with the question whether it would not have profited him better to have ruled his life by less exigent ideals.

In the meantime, his removal into the old house with the insurance marks built into its brick merely interrupted *Romilly Bishop* at the fifteenth chapter.

As this tall man with the lean, ascetic face moved about his new abode, arranging, changing, altering, hardly yet into his working-stride again, he gave the impression of almost spinster-like precision and nicety. For twenty years past, in a score of lodgings, garrets, flats, and rooms furnished and unfurnished, he had been accustomed to do many things for himself, and he had discovered that it saves time and temper to be methodical. He had arranged with the wife of the long-nosed Barrett, a stout Welsh woman with a falsetto voice, the Merionethshire accent of which long residence in London had not perceptibly modified, to come across the square each morning to prepare his breakfast, and also to "turn the place out" on Saturday mornings; and for the rest, he even welcomed a little housework as a relaxation from the strain of writing.

His kitchen, together with the adjoining strip of an apartment into which a modern bath had been fitted, overlooked the alley at the side of the house; and at one end of it was a large closet with a door, and a square sliding hatch in the upper part of the door. This had been a powder-closet, and through the hatch the elaborately dressed head had been thrust to receive the click and puff of the powder-pistol. Oleron puzzled a little over this closet; then, as its use occurred to him, he smiled faintly, a little moved, he knew not by what. . . . He would have to put it to a very different purpose from its original one; it would probably have to serve as his larder. . . . It was in this closet that he made a discovery. The back of it was shelved, and, rummaging on an upper shelf that ran deeply into the wall, Oleron found a couple of mushroom-shaped old wooden wig-stands. He did not know how they had come to be there. Doubtless the painters had turned them up somewhere or other, and had put them there. But his five rooms, as a whole, were short of cupboard and closet-room; and it was only by the exercise of some ingenuity that he was able to find places for the bestowal of his household linen, his boxes, and his seldom-used but not-to-be-destroyed accumulation of papers.

It was in early spring that Oleron entered on his tenancy, and he was anxious to have *Romilly* ready for publication in the coming autumn. Nevertheless, he did not intend to force its production. Should it demand longer in the doing, so much the worse; he realised its importance, its crucial importance, in his artistic development, and it must have its own length and time. In the workroom he had recently left he had been making excellent progress; *Romilly* had begun, as the saying is, to speak and act of herself; and he did not doubt she would continue to do so the moment the distraction of his removal was over. This distraction was almost over; he told himself it was time he pulled himself together again; and on a March morning he went out, returned again with two great bunches of yellow daffodils, placed one bunch on his mantelpiece between the Sheffield sticks and the other on the table before him, and took out the half-completed manuscript of *Romilly Bishop.*

But before beginning work he went to a small rosewood cabinet and took from a drawer his cheque-book and passbook. He totted them up, and his monk-like face grew thoughtful. His installation had cost him more than he had intended it should, and his balance was rather less than fifty pounds, with no immediate prospect of more.

"Hm! I'd forgotten rugs and chintz curtains and so forth mounted up so," said Oleron. "But it would have been a pity to spoil the place for the want of ten pounds or so. . . . Well, *Romilly* simply *must* be out for the autumn, that's all. So here goes—"

He drew his papers towards him.

But he worked badly; or, rather, he did not work at all. The square outside had its own noises, frequent and new, and Oleron could only hope that he would speedily become accustomed to these. First came hawkers, with their carts and cries; at midday the children, returning from school, trooped into the square and swung on Oleron's gate; and when the children had departed again for afternoon school, an itinerant musician with a mandoline posted himself beneath Oleron's window and began to strum. This was a not unpleasant distraction, and Oleron, pushing up his window, threw the man a penny. Then he returned to his table again. . . .

But it was no good. He came to himself, at long intervals, to find that he had been looking about his room and wondering how it had formerly been furnished—whether a settee in buttercup or petunia satin had stood under the farther window, whether from the centre moulding of the light lofty ceiling had depended a glimmering crystal chandelier, or where the tambour-frame or the picquet-table had stood. . . . No, it was no good; he had far better be frankly doing nothing than getting fruitlessly tired; and he decided that he would take a walk, but, chancing to sit down for a moment, dozed in his chair instead.

"This won't do," he yawned when he awoke at half-past four in the afternoon; "I must do better than this tomorrow—"

And he felt so deliciously lazy that for some minutes he even contemplated the breach of an appointment he had for the evening.

The next morning he sat down to work without even permitting himself to answer one of his three letters—two of them tradesmen's accounts, the third a note from Miss Bengough, forwarded from his old address. It was a jolly day of white and blue, with a gay noisy wind and a subtle turn in the colour of growing things; and over and over again, once or twice a minute, his room became suddenly light and then subdued again, as the shining white clouds rolled north-eastwards over the square. The soft fitful illumination was reflected in the polished surface of the table and even in the footworn old floor; and the morning noises had begun again.

Oleron made a pattern of dots on the paper before him, and then broke off to move the jar of daffodils exactly opposite the centre of a creamy panel. Then he wrote a sentence that ran continuously for a couple of lines, after which it broke off into notes and jottings. For a time he succeeded in persuading himself that in making these memoranda he was really working; then he rose and began to pace his room. As he did so, he was struck by an idea. It was that the place might possibly be a little better for more positive colour. It was, perhaps, a thought *too* pale—mild and sweet as a kind old face, but a little devitalised, even wan. . . . Yes, decidedly it would bear a robuster note—more and richer flowers, and possibly some warm and gay stuff for cushions for the window-seats. . . .

"Of course, I really can't afford it," he muttered, as he went for a two-foot and began to measure the width of the window recesses. . . .

In stooping to measure a recess, his attitude suddenly changed to one of interest and attention. Presently he rose again, rubbing his hands with gentle glee.

"Oho, oho!" he said. "These look to me very much like window-boxes, nailed up. We must look into this! Yes, those are boxes, or I'm . . . oho, this is an adventure!"

On that wall of his sitting-room there were two windows (the third was in another corner), and, beyond the open bedroom door, on the same wall, was another. The seats of all had been painted, repainted, and painted again; and Oleron's investigating finger had barely detected the old nailheads beneath the paint. Under the ledge over which he stooped an old keyhole also had been puttied up. Oleron took out his penknife.

He worked carefully for five minutes, and then went into the kitchen for a hammer and chisel. Driving the chisel cautiously under the seat, he started the whole lid slightly. Again using the penknife, he cut along the hinged edge and outward along the ends; and then he fetched a wedge and a wooden mallet.

"Now for our little mystery—" he said.

The sound of the mallet on the wedge seemed, in that sweet and pale apartment, somehow a little brutal—nay, even shocking. The panelling rang and rattled and vibrated to the blows like a sounding-board. The whole house seemed to echo; from the roomy cellarage to the garrets above a flock of echoes seemed to awake; and the sound got a little on Oleron's nerves. All at once he paused, fetched a duster, and muffled the mallet. . . . When the edge was sufficiently raised he put his fingers under it and lifted. The paint flaked and starred a little; the rusty old nails squeaked and grunted; and the lid came up, laying open the box beneath. Oleron looked into it. Save for a couple of inches of scurf and mould and old cobwebs it was empty.

"No treasure there," said Oleron, a little amused that he should have fancied there might have been. "*Romilly* will still have to be out by the autumn. Let's have a look at the others."

He turned to the second window.

The raising of the two remaining seats occupied him until well into the afternoon. That of the bedroom, like the first, was empty; but from the second seat of his sitting-room he drew out something yielding and folded and furred over an inch thick with dust. He carried the object into the kitchen, and having swept it over a bucket, took a duster to it.

It was some sort of a large bag, of an ancient frieze-like material, and when unfolded it occupied the greater part of the small kitchen floor. In shape it was an irregular, a very irregular, triangle, and it had a couple of wide flaps, with the remains of straps and buckles. The patch that had been uppermost in the folding was of a faded yellowish brown; but the rest of it was of shades of crimson that varied according to the exposure of the parts of it.

"Now whatever can that have been?" Oleron mused as he stood surveying it. . . . "I give it up. Whatever it is, it's settled my work for to-day, I'm afraid—"

He folded the object up carelessly and thrust it into a corner of the kitchen; then, taking pans and brushes and an old knife, he returned to the sitting-room and began to scrape and to wash and to line with paper his newly discovered receptacles. When he had finished, he put his spare boots and books and papers into them; and he closed the lids again, amused with his little adventure, but also a little anxious for the hour to come when he should settle fairly down to his work again.

III

It piqued Oleron a little that his friend, Miss Bengough, should dismiss with a glance the place he himself had found so singularly winning. Indeed she scarcely lifted her eyes to it. But then she had always been more or less like that—a little indifferent to the graces of life, careless of appearances, and perhaps a shade more herself when she ate biscuits from a paper bag than when she dined with greater observance of the convenances. She was an unattached journalist of thirty-four, large, showy, fair as butter, pink as a dog-rose, reminding one of a florist's picked specimen bloom, and given to sudden and ample movements and moist and explosive utterances. She "pulled a better living out of the pool" (as she expressed it) than Oleron did; and by cunningly disguised puffs of drapers and haberdashers she "pulled" also the greater part of her very varied wardrobe. She left small whirlwinds of air behind her when she moved, in which her veils and scarves fluttered and spun.

Oleron heard the flurry of her skirts on his staircase and her single loud knock at his door when he had been a month in his new abode. Her garments brought in the outer air, and she flung a bundle of ladies' journals down on a chair.

"Don't knock off for me," she said across a mouthful of large-headed hatpins as she removed her hat and veil. "I didn't know whether you were straight yet, so I've brought some sandwiches for lunch. You've got coffee, I suppose?—No, don't get up—I'll find the kitchen—"

"Oh, that's all right, I'll clear these things away. To tell the truth, I'm rather glad to be interrupted," said Oleron.

He gathered his work together and put it away. She was already in the kitchen; he heard the running of water into the kettle. He joined her, and ten minutes later followed her back to the sitting-room with the coffee and sandwiches on a tray. They sat down, with the tray on a small table between them.

"Well, what do you think of the new place?" Oleron asked as she poured out coffee.

"Hm! . . . Anybody'd think you were going to get married, Paul."

He laughed.

"Oh no. But it's an improvement on some of them, isn't it?"

"Is it? I suppose it is; I don't know. I liked the last place, in spite of the black ceiling and no watertap. How's *Romilly?*"

Oleron thumbed his chin.

"Hm! I'm rather ashamed to tell you. The fact is, I've not got on very well with it. But it will be all right on the night, as you used to say."

"Stuck?"

"Rather stuck."

"Got any of it you care to read to me? . . ."

Oleron had long been in the habit of reading portions of his work to Miss Bengough occasionally. Her comments were always quick and practical, sometimes directly useful, sometimes indirectly suggestive. She, in return for his confidence, always kept all mention of her own work sedulously from him. His, she said, was "real work"; hers merely filled space, not always even grammatically.

"I'm afraid there isn't," Oleron replied, still meditatively dry-shaving his chin. Then he added, with a little burst of candour, "The fact is, Elsie, I've not written—not actually written—very much more of it—*any* more of it, in fact. But, of course, that doesn't mean I haven't progressed. I've progressed, in one sense, rather alarmingly. I'm now thinking of reconstructing the whole thing."

Miss Bengough gave a gasp. "Reconstructing!"

"Making Romilly herself a different type of woman. Somehow, I've begun to feel that I'm not getting the most out of her. As she stands, I've certainly lost interest in her to some extent."

"But—but—" Miss Bengough protested, "you had her so real, so *living,* Paul!"

Oleron smiled faintly. He had been quite prepared for Miss Bengough's disapproval. He wasn't surprised that she liked Romilly as she at present existed; she would. Whether she realised it or not, there was much of herself in his fictitious creation. Naturally Romilly would seem "real," "living," to her. . . .

"But are you really serious, Paul?" Miss Bengough asked presently, with a round-eyed stare.

"Quite serious."

"You're really going to scrap those fifteen chapters?"

"I didn't exactly say that."

"That fine, rich love-scene?"

"I should only do it reluctantly, and for the sake of something I thought better."

"And that beautiful, *beau*tiful description of Romilly on the shore?"

"It wouldn't necessarily be wasted," he said a little uneasily.

But Miss Bengough made a large and windy gesture, and then let him have it.

"Really, you are *too* trying!" she broke out. "I do wish sometimes you'd remember you're human, and live in a world! You know I'd be the *last* to wish you to lower your standard one inch, but it wouldn't be lowering it to bring it within human comprehension. Oh, you're sometimes altogether too godlike! . . . Why, it would be a wicked, criminal waste of your powers to destroy those fifteen chapters! Look at it reasonably, now. You've been working for nearly twenty years; you've now got what you've been working for almost within your grasp; your affairs are at a most critical stage (oh, don't tell me; I know you're about at the end of your money); and here you are, deliberately proposing to withdraw a thing that will probably make your name, and to substitute for it something that ten to one nobody on earth will ever want to read—and small blame to them! Really, you try my patience!"

Oleron had shaken his head slowly as she had talked. It was an old story between them. The noisy, able, practical journalist was an admirable friend—up to a certain point; beyond that . . . well, each of us knows that point beyond which we stand alone. Elsie Bengough sometimes said that had she had one-tenth part of Oleron's genius there were few things she could not have done—thus making that genius a quantitatively divisible thing, a sort of ingredient, to be added to or to subtracted from in the admixture of his work. That it was a qualitative thing, essential, indivisible, informing, passed her comprehension. Their spirits parted company at that point. Oleron knew it. She did not appear to know it.

"Yes, yes, yes," he said a little wearily, by-and-by, "practically you're quite right, entirely right, and I haven't a word to say. If I could only turn *Romilly* over to you you'd make an enormous success of her. But that can't be, and I, for my part, am seriously doubting whether she's worth my while. You know what that means."

"What does it mean?" she demanded bluntly.

"Well," he said, smiling wanly, "what *does* it mean when you're convinced a thing isn't worth doing? You simply don't do it."

Miss Bengough's eyes swept the ceiling for assistance against this impossible man.

"What utter rubbish!" she broke out at last. "Why, when I saw you last you were simply oozing *Romilly;* you were turning her off at the rate of four chapters a week; if you hadn't moved you'd have had her three-parts done by now. What on earth possessed you to move right in the middle of your most important work?"

Oleron tried to put her off with a recital of inconveniences, but she wouldn't have it. Perhaps in her heart she partly suspected the reason. He was simply mortally weary of the narrow circumstances of his life. He had had twenty years of it—twenty years of garrets and roof-chambers and dingy flats and shabby lodgings, and he was tired of dinginess and shabbiness. The reward was as far off as ever—or if it was not, he no longer cared as once he would have cared to put out his hand and take it. It is all very well to tell a man who is at the point of exhaustion that only another effort is required of him; if he cannot make it he is as far off as ever. . . .

"Anyway," Oleron summed up, "I'm happier here than I've been for a long time. That's some sort of a justification."

"And doing no work," said Miss Bengough pointedly.

At that a trifling petulance that had been gathering in Oleron came to a head.

"And why should I do nothing but work?" he demanded. "How much happier am I for it? I don't say I don't love my work—when it's done; but I hate doing it. Sometimes it's an intolerable burden that I simply long to be rid of. Once in many weeks it has a moment, one moment, of glow and thrill for me; I remember the days when it was all glow and thrill; and now I'm forty-four, and it's becoming drudgery. Nobody wants it; I'm ceasing to want it myself; and if any ordinary sensible man were to ask me whether I didn't think I was a fool to go on, I think I should agree that I was."

Miss Bengough's comely pink face was serious.

"But you knew all that, many, many years ago, Paul—and still you chose it," she said in a low voice.

"Well, and how should I have known?" he demanded. "I didn't know. I was told so. My heart, if you like, told me so, and I thought I knew. Youth always thinks it knows; then one day it discovers that it is nearly fifty—"

"Forty-four, Paul—"

"—forty-four, then—and it finds that the glamour isn't in front, but behind. Yes, I knew and chose, if *that's* knowing and choosing . . . but it's a costly choice we're called on to make when we're young!"

Miss Bengough's eyes were on the floor. Without moving them she said, "You're not regretting it, Paul?"

"Am I not?" he took her up. "Upon my word, I've lately thought I am! What *do* I get in return for it all?"

"You know what you get," she replied.

He might have known from her tone what else he could have had for the holding up of a finger—herself. She knew, but could not tell him, that he could have done no better thing for himself. Had he, any time these ten years, asked her to marry him, she would have replied quietly, "Very well; when?" He had never thought of it. . . .

"Yours is the real work," she continued quietly. "Without you we jackals couldn't exist. You and a few like you hold everything upon your shoulders."

For a minute there was a silence. Then it occurred to Oleron that this was common vulgar grumbling. It was not his habit. Suddenly he rose and began to stack cups and plates on the tray.

"Sorry you catch me like this, Elsie," he said, with a little laugh. . . . "No, I'll take them out; then we'll go for a walk, if you like. . . ."

He carried out the tray, and then began to show Miss Bengough round his flat. She made few comments. In the kitchen she asked what an old faded square of reddish frieze was, that Mrs. Barrett used as a cushion for her wooden chair.

"That? I should be glad if you could tell *me* what it is," Oleron replied as he unfolded the bag and related the story of its finding in the window-seat.

"I think I know what it is," said Miss Bengough. "It's been used to wrap up a harp before putting it into its case."

"By Jove, that's probably just what it was," said Oleron. "I could make neither head nor tail of it. . . ."

They finished the tour of the flat, and returned to the sitting-room.

"And who lives in the rest of the house?" Miss Bengough asked.

"I dare say a tramp sleeps in the cellar occasionally. Nobody else."

"Hm! . . . Well, I'll tell you what I think about it, if you like."

"I should like."

"You'll never work here."

"Oh?" said Oleron quickly. "Why not?"

"You'll never finish *Romilly* here. Why, I don't know, but you won't. I know it. You'll have to leave before you get on with that book."

He mused for a moment, and then said:

"Isn't that a little—prejudiced, Elsie?"

"Perfectly ridiculous. As an argument it hasn't a leg to stand on. But there it is," she replied, her mouth once more full of the large-headed hat pins.

Oleron was reaching down his hat and coat. He laughed.

"I can only hope you're entirely wrong," he said, "for I shall be in a serious mess if *Romilly* isn't out in the autumn."

IV

As Oleron sat by his fire that evening, pondering Miss Bengough's prognostication that difficulties awaited him in his work, he came to the conclusion that it would have been far better had she kept her beliefs to herself. No man does a thing better for having his confidence damped at the outset, and to speak of difficulties is in a sense to make them. Speech itself becomes a deterrent act, to which other discouragements accrete until the very event of which warning is given is as likely as not to come to pass. He heartily confounded her. An influence hostile to the completion of *Romilly* had been born.

And in some illogical, dogmatic way women seem to have, she had attached this antagonistic influence to his new abode. Was ever anything so absurd! "You'll never finish *Romilly* here." . . . Why not? Was this her idea of the luxury that saps the springs of action and brings a man down to indolence and dropping out of the race? The place was well enough—it was entirely charming, for that matter—but it was not so demoralising as all that! No; Elsie had missed the mark that time. . . .

He moved his chair to look round the room that smiled, positively smiled, in the firelight. He too smiled, as if pity was to be entertained for a maligned apartment. Even that slight lack of robust colour he had remarked was not noticeable in the soft glow. The drawn chintz curtains—they had a flowered and trellised pattern, with baskets and oaten pipes—fell in long quiet folds to the window-seats; the rows of bindings in old book cases took the light richly; the last trace of sallowness had gone with the daylight; and, if the truth must be told, it had been Elsie herself who had seemed a little out of the picture.

That reflection struck him a little, and presently he returned to it. Yes, the room had, quite accidentally, done Miss Bengough a disservice that afternoon. It had, in some subtle but unmistakable way, placed her, marked a contrast of qualities. Assuming for the sake of argument the slightly ridiculous proposition that the room in which Oleron sat *was* characterised by a certain sparsity and lack of vigour; so much the worse for Miss Bengough; she certainly erred on the side of redundancy and general muchness. And if one must contrast abstract qualities, Oleron inclined to the austere in taste. . . .

Yes, here Oleron had made a distinct discovery; he wondered he had not made it before. He pictured Miss Bengough again as she had appeared that afternoon—large, showy, moistly pink, with that quality of the prize bloom exuding, as it were from her; and instantly she suffered in his thought. He even recognised now that he had noticed something odd at the time, and that unconsciously his attitude, even while she had been there, had been one of criticism. The mechanism of her was a little obvious; her melting humidity was the result of analysable processes; and behind her there had seemed to lurk some dim shape emblematic of mortality. He had never, during the ten years of their intimacy, dreamed for a moment of asking her to marry him; none the less, he now felt for the first time a thankfulness that he had not done so. . . .

Then, suddenly and swiftly, his face flamed that he should be thinking thus of his friend. What! Elsie Bengough, with whom he had spent weeks and weeks of afternoons—she, the good chum, on whose help he would have counted had all the rest of the world failed him—she, whose loyalty to him would not, he knew, swerve as long as there was breath in her—Elsie to be even in thought dissected thus! He was an ingrate and a cad. . . .

Had she been there in that moment he would have abased himself before her.

For ten minutes and more he sat, still gazing into the fire, with that humiliating red fading slowly from his cheeks. All was still within and without, save for a tiny musical tinkling that came from his kitchen—the dripping of water from an imperfectly turned-off tap into the vessel beneath it. Mechanically he began to beat with his fingers to the faintly heard falling of the drops; the tiny regular movement seemed to hasten that shameful withdrawal from his face. He grew cool once more; and when he resumed his meditation he was all unconscious that he took it up again at the same point. . . .

It was not only her florid superfluity of build that he had approached in the attitude of criticism; he was conscious also of the wide differences between her mind and his own. He felt no thankfulness that up to a certain point their natures had ever run companionably side by side; he was now full of questions beyond that point. Their intellects diverged; there was no denying it; and, looking back, he was inclined to doubt whether there had been any real coincidence. True, he had read his writings to her and she had appeared to speak comprehendingly and to the point; but what can a man do who, having assumed that another sees as he does, is suddenly brought up sharp by something that falsifies and discredits all that has gone before? He doubted all now. . . . It did for a moment occur to him that the man who demands of a friend more than can be given to him is in danger of losing that friend, but he put the thought aside.

Again he ceased to think, and again moved his finger to the distant dripping of the tap. . . .

And now (he resumed by-and-by), if these things were true of Elsie Bengough, they were also true of the creation of which she was the prototype—Romilly Bishop. And since he could say of Romilly what for very shame he could not say of Elsie, he gave his thoughts rein. He did so in that smiling, fire-lighted room, to the accompaniment of the faintly heard tap.

There was no longer any doubt about it; he hated the central character of his novel. Even as he had described her physically she overpowered the senses; she was coarse-fibred, over-coloured, rank. It became true the moment he formulated his thought; Gulliver had described the Brobdingnagian maids-of-honour thus: and mentally and spiritually she corresponded—was unsensitive, limited, common. The model (he closed his eyes for a moment)—the model stuck out through fifteen vulgar and blatant chapters to such a pitch that, without seeing the reason, he had been unable to begin the sixteenth. He marvelled that it had only just dawned upon him.

And *this* was to have been his Beatrice, his vision! As Elsie she was to have gone into the furnace of his art, and she was to have come out the Woman all men desire! Her thoughts were to have been culled from his own finest, her form from his dearest dreams, and her setting wherever he could find one fit for her worth. He had brooded long before making the attempt; then one day he had felt her stir within him as a mother feels a quickening, and he had begun to write; and so he had added chapter to chapter. . . .

And those fifteen sodden chapters were what he had produced!

Again he sat, softly moving his finger. . . .

Then he bestirred himself.

She must go, all fifteen chapters of her. That was settled. For what was to take her place his mind was a blank; but one thing at a time; a man is not excused from taking the wrong course because the right one is not immediately revealed to him. Better would come if it was to come; in the meantime—

He rose, fetched the fifteen chapters, and read them over before he should drop them into the fire.

But instead of putting them into the fire he let them fall from his hand. He became conscious of the dripping of the tap again. It had a tinkling gamut of four or five notes, on which it rang irregular changes, and it was foolishly sweet and dulcimer-like. In his mind Oleron could see the gathering of each drop, its little tremble on the lip of the tap, and the tiny percussion of its fall "Plink—plunk," minimised almost to inaudibility. Following the lowest note there seemed to be a brief phrase, irregularly repeated; and presently Oleron found himself waiting for the recurrence of this phrase. It was quite pretty. . . .

But it did not conduce to wakefulness, and Oleron dozed over his fire.

When he awoke again the fire had burned low and the flames of the candles were licking the rims of the Sheffield sticks. Sluggishly he rose, yawned, went his nightly round of door-locks, and window-fastenings, and passed into his bedroom. Soon, he slept soundly.

But a curious little sequel followed on the morrow. Mrs. Barrett usually tapped, not at his door, but at the wooden wall beyond which lay Oleron's bed; and then Oleron rose, put on his dressing-gown, and admitted her. He was not conscious that as he did so that morning he hummed an air; but Mrs. Barrett lingered with her hand on the door-knob and her face a little averted and smiling.

"De-ar me!" her soft falsetto rose. "But that will be a very o-ald tune, Mr. Oleron! I will not have heard it this for-ty years!"

"What tune?" Oleron asked.

"The tune, indeed, that you was humming, sir."

Oleron had his thumb in the flap of a letter. It remained there.

"*I* was humming? . . . Sing it, Mrs. Barrett."

Mrs. Barrett prut-prutted.

"I have no voice for singing, Mr. Oleron; it was Ann Pugh was the singer of our family; but the tune will be very o-ald, and it is called 'The Beckoning Fair One.' "

"Try to sing it," said Oleron, his thumb still in the envelope; and Mrs. Barrett, with much dimpling and confusion, hummed the air.

"They do say it was sung to a harp, Mr. Oleron, and it will be very o-ald," she concluded.

"And *I* was singing that?"

"Indeed you was. I would not be likely to tell you lies."

With a "Very well—let me have breakfast," Oleron opened his letter; but the trifling circumstance struck him as more odd than he would have admitted to himself. The phrase he had hummed had been that which he had associated with the falling from the tap on the evening before.

V

Even more curious than that the commonplace dripping of an ordinary water-tap should have tallied so closely with an actually existing air was another result it had, namely, that it awakened, or seemed to awaken, in Oleron an abnormal sensitiveness to other noises of the old house. It has been remarked that silence obtains its fullest and most impressive quality when it is broken by some minute sound; and, truth to tell, the place was never still. Perhaps the mildness of the spring air operated on its torpid old timbers; perhaps Oleron's fires caused it to stretch its old anatomy; and certainly a whole world of insect life bored and burrowed in its baulks and joists. At any rate Oleron had only to sit quiet in his chair and to wait for a minute or two in order to become aware of such a change in the auditory scale as comes upon a man who, conceiving the mid-summer woods to be motionless and still, all at once finds his ear sharpened to the crepitation of a myriad insects.

And he smiled to think of man's arbitrary distinction between that which has life and that which has not. Here, quite apart from such recognisable sounds as the scampering of mice, the falling of plaster behind his panelling, and the popping of purses or coffins from his fire, was a whole house talking to him had he but known its language. Beams settled with a tired sigh into their old mortices; creatures ticked in the walls; joints cracked, boards complained; with no palpable stirring of the air window-sashes changed their positions with a soft knock in their frames. And whether the place had life in this sense or not, it had at all events a winsome personality. It needed but an hour of musing for Oleron to conceive the idea that, as his own body stood in friendly relation to his soul, so, by an extension and an attenuation, his habitation might fantastically be supposed to stand in some relation to himself. He even amused himself with the far-fetched fancy that he might so identify himself with the place that some future tenant, taking possession, might regard it as in a sense haunted. It would be rather a joke if he, a perfectly harmless author, with nothing on his mind worse than a novel he had discovered he must begin again, should turn out to be laying the foundation of a future ghost! . . .

In proportion, however, as he felt this growing attachment to the fabric of his abode, Elsie Bengough, from being merely unattracted, began to show a dislike of the place that was more and more marked. And she did not scruple to speak of her aversion.

"It doesn't belong to to-day at all, and for you especially it's bad," she said with decision. "You're only too ready to let go your hold on actual things and to slip into apathy; *you* ought to be in a place with concrete floors and a patent gas-meter and a tradesman's lift. And it would do you all the good in the world if you had a job that made you scramble and rub elbows with your fellow-men. Now, if I could get you a job, for, say, two or three days a week, one that would allow you heaps of time for your proper work—would you take it?"

Somehow, Oleron resented a little being diagnosed like this. He thanked Miss Bengough, but without a smile.

"Thank you, but I don't think so. After all each of us has his own life to live," he could not refrain from adding.

"His own life to live! . . . How long is it since you were out, Paul?"

"About two hours."

"I don't mean to buy stamps or to post a letter. How long is it since you had anything like a stretch?"

"Oh, some little time perhaps. I don't know."

"Since I was here last?"

"I haven't been out much."

"And has *Romilly* progressed much better for your being cooped up?"

"I think she has. I'm laying the foundations of her. I shall begin the actual writing presently."

It seemed as if Miss Bengough had forgotten their tussle about the first *Romilly.* She frowned, turned half away, and then quickly turned again.

"Ah! . . . So you've still got that ridiculous idea in your head?"

"If you mean," said Oleron slowly, "that I've discarded the old *Romilly,* and am at work on a new one, you're right. I have still got that idea in my head."

Something uncordial in his tone struck her; but she was a fighter. His own absurd sensitiveness hardened her. She gave a "Pshaw!" of impatience.

"Where is the old one?" she demanded abruptly.

"Why?" asked Oleron.

"I want to see it. I want to show some of it to you. I want, if you're not wool-gathering entirely, to bring you back to your senses."

This time it was he who turned his back. But when he turned round again he spoke more gently.

"It's no good, Elsie. I'm responsible for the way I go, and you must allow me to go it—even if it should seem wrong to you. Believe me, I am giving thought to it. . . . The manuscript? I was on the point of burning it, but I didn't. It's in that window-seat, if you must see it."

Miss Bengough crossed quickly to the window-seat, and lifted the lid. Suddenly she gave a little exclamation, and put the back of her hand to her mouth. She spoke over her shoulder:

"You ought to knock those nails in, Paul," she said.

He strode to her side.

"What? What is it? What's the matter?" he asked. "I did knock them in—or, rather, pulled them out."

"You left enough to scratch with," she replied, showing her hand. From the upper wrist to the knuckle of the little finger a welling red wound showed.

"Good—Gracious!" Oleron ejaculated. . . . "Here, come to the bathroom and bathe it quickly—"

He hurried her to the bathroom, turned on warm water, and bathed and cleansed the bad gash. Then, still holding the hand, he turned cold water on it, uttering broken phrases of astonishment and concern.

"Good Lord, how did that happen! As far as I knew I'd . . . is this water too cold? Does that hurt? I can't imagine how on earth . . . there; that'll do—"

"No—one moment longer—I can bear it," she murmured, her eyes closed. . . .

Presently he led her back to the sitting-room and bound the hand in one of his handkerchiefs; but his face did not lose its expression of perplexity. He had spent half a day in opening and making serviceable the three window-boxes, and he could not conceive how he had come to leave an inch and a half of rusty nail standing in the wood. He himself had opened the lids of each of them a dozen times and had not noticed any nail; but there it was. . . .

"It shall come out now, at all events," he muttered, as he went for a pair of pincers. And he made no mistake about it that time.

Elsie Bengough had sunk into a chair, and her face was rather white; but in her hand was the manuscript of *Romilly.* She had not finished with *Romilly* yet. Presently she returned to the charge.

"Oh, Paul, it will be the greatest mistake you ever, *ever* made if you do not publish this!" she said.

He hung his head, genuinely distressed. He couldn't get that incident of the nail out of his head, and *Romilly* occupied a second place in his thoughts for the moment. But still she insisted; and when presently he spoke it was almost as if he asked her pardon for something.

"What can I say, Elsie? I can only hope that when you see the new version, you'll see how right I am. And if in spite of all you *don't* like her, well . . ." he made a hopeless gesture. "Don't you see that I *must* be guided by my own lights?"

She was silent.

"Come, Elsie," he said gently. "We've got along well so far; don't let us split on this."

The last words had hardly passed his lips before he regretted them. She had been nursing her injured hand, with her eyes once more closed; but her lips and lids quivered simultaneously. Her voice shook as she spoke.

"I can't help saying it, Paul, but you are so greatly changed."

"Hush, Elsie," he murmured soothingly; "you've had a shock; rest for a while. How could I change?"

"I don't know, but you are. You've not been yourself ever since you came here. I wish you'd never seen the place. It's stopped your work, it's making you into a person I hardly know, and it's made me horribly anxious about you. . . . Oh, how my hand is beginning to throb!"

"Poor child!" he murmured. "Will you let me take you to a doctor and have it properly dressed?"

"No—I shall be all right presently—I'll keep it raised—"

She put her elbow on the back of her chair, and the bandaged hand rested lightly on his shoulder.

At that touch an entirely new anxiety stirred suddenly within him. Hundreds of times previously, on their jaunts and excursions, she had slipped her hand within his arm as she might have slipped it into the arm of a brother, and he had accepted the little affectionate gesture as a brother might have accepted it. But now, for the first time, there rushed into his mind a hundred startling questions. Her eyes were still closed, and her head had fallen pathetically back; and there was a lost and ineffable smile on her parted lips. The truth broke in upon him. Good God! . . . And he had never divined it!

And stranger than all was that, now that he did see that she was lost in love of him, there came to him, not sorrow and humility and abasement, but something else that he struggled in vain against—something entirely strange and new, that, had he analysed it, he would have found to be petulance and irritation and resentment and ungentleness. The sudden selfish prompting mastered him before he was aware. He all but gave it words. What was she doing there at all? Why was she not getting on with her own work? Why was she here interfering with his? Who had given her this guardianship over him that lately she had put forward so assertively?—"Changed?" It was she, not himself, who had changed. . . .

But by the time she had opened her eyes again he had overcome his resentment sufficiently to speak gently, albeit with reserve.

"I wish you would let me take you to a doctor."

She rose.

"No, thank you, Paul," she said. "I'll go now. If I need a dressing I'll get one; take the other hand, please. Good-bye—"

He did not attempt to detain her. He walked with her to the foot of the stairs. Half-way along the narrow alley she turned.

"It would be a long way to come if you happened not to be in," she said; "I'll send you a postcard the next time."

At the gate she turned again.

"Leave here, Paul," she said, with a mournful look. "Everything's wrong with this house."

Then she was gone.

Oleron returned to his room. He crossed straight to the window-box. He opened the lid and stood long looking at it. Then he closed it again and turned away.

"That's rather frightening," he muttered. "It's simply not possible that I should not have removed that nail. . . ."

VI

Oleron knew very well what Elsie had meant when she had said that her next visit would be preceded by a postcard. She, too, had realised that at last, at last he knew—knew, and didn't want her. It gave him a miserable, pitiful pang, therefore, when she came again within a week, knocking at the door unannounced. She spoke from the landing; she did not intend to stay, she said; and he had to press her before she would so much as enter.

Her excuse for calling was that she had heard of an inquiry for short stories that he might be wise to follow up. He thanked her. Then, her business over, she seemed anxious to get away again. Oleron did not seek to detain her; even he saw through the pretext of the stories; and he accompanied her down the stairs.

But Elsie Bengough had no luck whatever in that house. A second accident befell her. Half-way down the staircase there was the sharp sound of splintering wood, and she checked a loud cry. Oleron knew the woodwork to be old, but he himself had ascended and descended frequently enough without mishap. . . .

Elsie had put her foot through one of the stairs.

He sprang to her side in alarm.

"Oh, I say! My poor girl!"

She laughed hysterically.

"It's my weight—I know I'm getting fat—"

"Keep still—let me clear these splinters away," he muttered between his teeth.

She continued to laugh and sob that it was her weight—she was getting fat—

He thrust downwards at the broken boards. The extrication was no easy matter, and her torn boot showed him how badly the foot and ankle within it must be abraded.

"Good God—good God!" he muttered over and over again.

"I shall be too heavy for anything soon," she sobbed and laughed.

But she refused to reascend and to examine her hurt.

"No, let me go quickly—let me go quickly," she repeated.

"But it's a frightful gash!"

"No—not so bad—let me get away quickly—I'm—I'm not wanted."

At her words, that she was not wanted, his head dropped as if she had given him a buffet.

"Elsie!" he choked, brokenly and shocked.

But she too made a quick gesture, as if she put something violently aside.

"Oh, Paul, not *that*—not *you*—of course I do mean that too in a sense—oh, you know what I mean! . . . But if the other can't be, spare me this now! I—I wouldn't have come, but—but oh, I did, I *did* try to keep away!"

It was intolerable, heartbreaking; but what could he do—what could he say? He did not love her. . . .

"Let me go—I'm not wanted—let me take away what's left of me—"

"Dear Elsie—you are very dear to me—"

But again she made the gesture, as of putting something violently aside.

"No, not that—not anything less—don't offer me anything less—leave me a little pride—"

"Let me get my hat and coat—let me take you to a doctor," he muttered.

But she refused. She refused even the support of his arm. She gave another unsteady laugh.

"I'm sorry I broke your stairs, Paul. . . . You will go and see about the short stories, won't you?"

He groaned.

"Then if you won't see a doctor, will you go across the square and let Mrs. Barrett look at you? Look, there's Barrett passing now—"

The long-nosed Barrett was looking curiously down the alley, but as Oleron was about to call him he made off without a word. Elsie seemed anxious for nothing so much as to be clear of the place, and finally promised to go straight to a doctor, but insisted on going alone.

"Good-bye," she said.

And Oleron watched her until she was past the hatchet-like "To Let" boards, as if he feared that even they might fall upon her and maim her.

That night Oleron did not dine. He had far too much on his mind. He walked from room to room of his flat, as if he could have walked away from Elsie Bengough's haunting cry that still rang in his ears. "I'm not wanted—don't offer me anything less—let me take away what's left of me—"

Oh, if he could only have persuaded himself that he loved her!

He walked until twilight fell, then, without lighting candles, he stirred up the fire and flung himself into a chair.

Poor, poor Elsie! . . .

But even while his heart ached for her, it was out of the question. If only he had known! If only he had used common observation! But those walks, those sisterly takings of the arm—what a fool he had been! . . . Well, it was too late now. It was she, not he, who must now act—act by keeping away. He would help her all he could. He himself would not sit in her presence. If she came, he would hurry her out again as fast as he could. . . . Poor, poor Elsie!

His room grew dark; the fire burned dead; and he continued to sit, wincing from time to time as a fresh tortured phrase rang again in his ears.

Then suddenly, he knew not why, he found himself anxious for her in a new sense—uneasy about her personal safety. A horrible fancy that even then she might be looking over an embankment down into dark water, that she might even now be glancing up at the hook on the door, took him. Women had been known to do those things. . . . Then there would be an inquest, and he himself would be called upon to identify her, and would be asked how she had come by an ill-healed wound on the hand and a bad abrasion of the ankle. Barrett would say that he had seen her leaving his house. . . .

Then he recognised that his thoughts were morbid. By an effort of will he put them aside, and sat for a while listening to the faint creakings and tickings and rappings within his panelling. . . .

If only he could have married her! . . . But he couldn't. Her face had risen before him again as he had seen it on the stairs, drawn with pain and ugly and swollen with tears. Ugly—yes, positively blubbered; if tears were women's weapons, as they were said to be, such tears were weapons turning against themselves . . . suicide again. . . .

Then all at once he found himself attentively considering her two accidents.

Extraordinary they had been, both of them. He *could not* have left that old nail standing in the wood; why, he had fetched tools specially from the kitchen; and he was convinced that that step that had broken beneath her weight had been as sound as the others. It was inexplicable. If these things could happen, anything could happen. There was not a beam nor a jamb in the place that might not fall without warning, not a plank that might not crash inwards, not a nail that might not become a dagger. The whole place was full of life even now; as he sat there in the dark he heard its crowds of noises as if the house had been one great microphone. . . .

Only half conscious that he did so, he had been sitting for some time identifying these noises, attributing to each crack or creak or knock its material cause; but there was one noise which, again not fully conscious of the omission, he had not sought to account for. It had last come some minutes ago; it came again now—a sort of soft sweeping rustle that seemed to hold an almost inaudible minute crackling. For half a minute or so it had Oleron's attention; then his heavy thoughts were of Elsie Bengough again.

He was nearer to loving her in that moment than he had ever been. He thought how to some men their loved ones were but the dearer for those poor mortal blemishes that tell us we are but sojourners on earth, with a common fate not far distant that makes it hardly worth while to do anything but love for the time remaining. Strangling sobs, blearing tears, bodies buffeted by sickness, hearts and mind callous and hard with the rubs of the world—how little love there would be were these things a barrier to love! In that sense he did love Elsie Bengough. What her happiness had never moved in him her sorrow almost awoke. . . .

Suddenly his meditation went. His ear had once more become conscious of that soft and repeated noise—the long sweep with the almost inaudible crackle in it. Again and again it came, with a curious insistence and urgency. It quickened a little as he became increasingly attentive . . . it seemed to Oleron that it grew louder. . . .

All at once he started bolt upright in his chair, tense and listening. The silky rustle came again; he was trying to attach it to something. . . .

The next moment he had leapt to his feet, unnerved and terrified. His chair hung poised for a moment, and then went over, setting the fire-irons clattering as it fell. There was only one noise in the world like that which had caused him to spring thus to his feet. . . .

The next time it came Oleron felt behind him at the empty air with his hand, and backed slowly until he found himself against the wall.

"God in Heaven!" The ejaculation broke from Oleron's lips. The sound had ceased.

The next moment he had given a high cry.

"What is it? What's there? *Who's* there?"

A sound of scuttling caused his knees to bend under him for a moment; but that, he knew, was a mouse. That was not something that his stomach turned sick and his mind reeled to entertain. That other sound, the like of which was not in the world, had now entirely ceased; and again he called. . . .

He called and continued to call; and then another terror, a terror of the sound of his own voice, seized him. He did not dare to call again. His shaking hand went to his pocket for a match, but found none. He thought there might be matches on the mantelpiece—

He worked his way to the mantelpiece round a little recess, without for a moment leaving the wall. Then his hand encountered the mantelpiece, and groped along it. A box of matches fell to the hearth. He could just see them in the firelight, but his hand could not pick them up until he had cornered them inside the fender.

Then he rose and struck a light.

The room was as usual. He struck a second match. A candle stood on the table. He lighted it, and the flame sank for a moment and then burned up clear. Again he looked round.

There was nothing.

There was nothing; but there had been something, and might still be something. Formerly, Oleron had smiled at the fantastic thought that, by a merging and interplay of identities between himself and his beautiful room, he might be preparing a ghost for the future; it had not occurred to him *that there might have been a similar merging and coalescence in the past.* Yet with this staggering impossibility he was now face to face. Something did persist in the house; it had a tenant other than himself; and that tenant, whatsoever or whosoever, had appalled Oleron's soul by producing the sound of a woman brushing her hair.

VII

Without quite knowing how he came to be there Oleron found himself striding over the loose board he had temporarily placed on the step broken by Miss Bengough. He was hatless, and descending the stairs. Not until later did there return to him a hazy memory that he had left the candle burning on the table, had opened the door no wider than was necessary to allow the passage of his body, and had sidled out, closing the door softly behind him. At the foot of the stairs another shock awaited him. Something dashed with a flurry up from the disused cellars and disappeared out of the door. It was only a cat, but Oleron gave a childish sob.

He passed out of the gate, and stood for a moment under the "To Let" boards, plucking foolishly at his lip and looking up at the glimmer of light behind one of his red blinds. Then, still looking over his shoulder, he moved stumblingly up the square. There was a small public-house round the corner; Oleron had never entered it; but he entered it now, and put down a shilling that missed the counter by inches.

"B—b—bran—brandy," he said, and then stooped to look for the shilling.

He had the little sawdusted bar to himself; what company there was—carters and labourers and the small tradesmen of the neighbourhood—was gathered in the farther compartment, beyond the space where the white-haired landlady moved among her taps and bottles. Oleron sat down on a hardwood settee with a perforated seat, drank half his brandy, and then, thinking he might as well drink it as spill it, finished it.

Then he fell to wondering which of the men whose voices he heard across the public-house would undertake the removal of his effects on the morrow.

In the meantime he ordered more brandy.

For he did not intend to go back to that room where he had left the candle burning. Oh no! He couldn't have faced even the entry and the staircase with the broken step—certainly not that pith-white, fascinating room. He would go back for the present to his old arrangement, of work-room and separate sleeping-quarters; he would go to his old landlady at once—presently—when he had finished his brandy—and see if she could put him up for the night. His glass was empty now. . . .

He rose, had it refilled, and sat down again.

And if anybody asked his reason for removing again? Oh, he had reason enough—reason enough! Nails that put themselves back into wood again and gashed people's hands, steps that broke when you trod on them, and women who came into a man's place and brushed their hair in the dark, were reasons enough! He was querulous and injured about it all. He had taken the place for himself, not for invisible women to brush their hair in; that lawyer fellow in Lincoln's Inn should be told so, too, before many hours were out; it was outrageous, letting people in for agreements like that!

A cut-glass partition divided the compartment where Oleron sat from the space where the white-haired landlady moved; but it stopped seven or eight inches above the level of the counter. There was no partition at the further bar. Presently Oleron, raising his eyes, saw that faces were watching him through the aperture. The faces disappeared when he looked at them.

He moved to a corner where he could not be seen from the other bar; but this brought him into line with the white-haired landlady.

She knew him by sight—had doubtless seen him passing and repassing; and presently she made a remark on the weather. Oleron did not know what he replied, but it sufficed to call forth the further remark that the winter had been a bad one for influenza, but that the spring weather seemed to be coming at last. . . . Even this slight contact with the commonplace steadied Oleron a little; an idle, nascent wonder whether the landlady brushed her hair every night, and, if so, whether it gave out those little electric cracklings, was shut down with a snap; and Oleron was better. . . .

With his next glass of brandy he was all for going back to his flat. Not go back? Indeed, he would go back! They should very soon see whether he was to be turned out of his place like that! He began to wonder why he was doing the rather unusual thing he was doing at that moment, unusual for him—sitting hatless, drinking brandy, in a public-house. Suppose he were to tell the white-haired landlady all about it—to tell her that a caller had scratched her hand on a nail, had later had the bad luck to put her foot through a rotten stair, and that he himself, in an old house full of squeaks and creaks and whispers, had heard a minute noise and had bolted from it in fright—what would she think of him? That he was mad, of course. . . .

Pshaw! The real truth of the matter was that he hadn't been doing enough work to occupy him. He had been dreaming his days away, filling his head with a lot of moonshine about a new *Romilly* (as if the old one was not good enough), and now he was surprised that the devil should enter an empty head!

Yes, he would go back. He would take a walk in the air first—he hadn't walked enough lately—and then he would take himself in hand, settle the hash of that sixteenth chapter of *Romilly* (fancy, he had actually been fool enough to think of destroying fifteen chapters!) and thenceforward he would remember that he had obligations to his fellow men and work to do in the world. There was the matter in a nutshell.

He finished his brandy and went out.

He had walked for some time before any other bearing of the matter than that on himself occurred to him. At first, the fresh air had increased the heady effect of the brandy he had drunk; but afterwards his mind grew clearer than it had been since morning. And the clearer it grew, the less final did his boastful self-assurances become, and the firmer his conviction that, when all explanations had been made, there remained something that could not be explained. His hysteria of an hour before had passed; he grew steadily calmer; but the disquieting conviction remained. A deep fear took possession of him. It was a fear for Elsie.

For something in his place was inimical to her safety. Of themselves, her two accidents might not have persuaded him of this; but she herself had said it. *"I'm not wanted here. . . ."* And she had declared that there was something wrong with the place. She had seen it before he had. Well and good. One thing stood out clearly: namely, that if this was so, she must be kept away for quite another reason than that which had so confounded and humiliated Oleron. Luckily she had expressed her intention of staying away; she must be held to that intention. He must see to it.

And he must see to it all the more that he now saw his first example, never to set foot in the place again, was absurd. People did not do that kind of thing. With Elsie made secure, he could not with any respect to himself suffer himself to be turned out by a shadow, nor even by a danger merely because it was a danger. He had to live somewhere, and he would live there. He must return.

He mastered the faint chill of fear that came with the decision, and turned in his walk abruptly. Should fear grow on him again he would, perhaps, take one more glass of brandy. . . .

But by the time he reached the short street that led to the square he was too late for more brandy. The little public-house was still lighted, but closed, and one or two men were standing talking on the kerb. Oleron noticed that a sudden silence fell on them as he passed, and he noticed further that the long-nosed Barrett, whom he passed a little lower down, did not return his good-night. He turned in at the broken gate, hesitated merely an instant in the alley, and then mounted his stairs again.

Only an inch of candle remained in the Sheffield stick, and Oleron did not light another one. Deliberately he forced himself to take it up and to make the tour of his five rooms before retiring. It was as he returned from the kitchen across his little hall that he noticed that a letter lay on the floor. He carried it into his sitting-room, and glanced at the envelope before opening it.

It was unstamped, and had been put into the door by hand. Its handwriting was clumsy, and it ran from beginning to end without comma or period. Oleron read the first line, turned to the signature, and then finished the letter.

It was from the man Barrett, and it informed Oleron that he, Barrett, would be obliged if Mr. Oleron would make other arrangements for the preparing of his breakfasts and the cleaning-out of his place. The sting lay in the tail, that is to say, the postscript. This consisted of a text of Scripture. It embodied an allusion that could only be to Elsie Bengough. . . .

A seldom-seen frown had cut deeply into Oleron's brow. So! That was it! Very well; they would see about that on the morrow. . . . For the rest, this seemed merely another reason why Elsie should keep away. . . .

Then his suppressed rage broke out. . . .

The foul-minded lot! The devil himself could not have given a leer at anything that had ever passed between Paul Oleron and Elsie Bengough, yet this nosing rascal must be prying and talking! . . .

Oleron crumpled the paper up, held it in the candle flame, and then ground the ashes under his heel.

One useful purpose, however, the letter had served: it had created in Oleron a wrathful blaze that effectually banished pale shadows. Nevertheless, one other puzzling circumstance was to close the day. As he undressed, he chanced to glance at his bed. The coverlets bore an impress as if somebody had lain on them. Oleron could not remember that he himself had lain down during the day —off-hand, he would have said that certainly he had not; but after all he could not be positive. His indignation for Elsie, acting possibly with the residue of the brandy in him, excluded all other considerations; and he put out his candle, lay down, and passed immediately into a deep and dreamless sleep, which, in the absence of Mrs. Barrett's morning call, lasted almost once round the clock.

VIII

To the man who pays heed to that voice within him which warns him that twilight and danger are settling over his soul, terror is apt to appear an absolute thing, against which his heart must be safeguarded in a twink unless there is to take place an alteration in the whole range and scale of his nature. Mercifully, he has never far to look for safeguards. Of the immediate and small and common and momentary things of life, of usages and observances and modes and conventions, he builds up fortifications against the powers of darkness. He is even content that, not terror only, but joy also, should for working purposes be placed in the category of the absolute things; and the last treason he will commit will be that breaking down of terms and limits that strikes, not at one man, but at the welfare of the souls of all.

In his own person, Oleron began to commit this treason. He began to commit it by admitting the inexplicable and horrible to an increasing familiarity. He did it insensibly, unconsciously, by a neglect of the things that he now regarded it as an impertinence in Elsie Bengough to have prescribed. Two months before, the words "a haunted house," applied to his lovely bemusing dwelling, would have chilled his marrow; now, his scale of sensation becoming depressed, he could ask "Haunted by what?" and remain unconscious that horror, when it can be proved to be relative, by so much loses its proper quality. He was setting aside the landmarks. Mists and confusion had begun to enwrap him.

And he was conscious of nothing so much as of a voracious inquisitiveness. He wanted *to know.* He was resolved to know. Nothing but the knowledge would satisfy him; and craftily he cast about for means whereby he might attain it.

He might have spared his craft. The matter was the easiest imaginable. As in time past he had known, in his writing, moments when his thoughts had seemed to rise of themselves and to embody themselves in words not to be altered afterwards, so now the question he put himself seemed to be answered even in the moment of their asking. There was exhilaration in the swift, easy processes. He had known no such joy in his own power since the days when his writing had been a daily freshness and a delight to him. It was almost as if the course he must pursue was being dictated to him.

And the first thing he must do, of course, was to define the problem. He defined it in terms of mathematics. Granted that he had not the place to himself; granted that the old house had inexpressibly caught and engaged his spirit; granted that, by virtue of the common denominator of the place, this unknown co-tenant stood in some relation to himself: what next? Clearly, the nature of the other numerator must be ascertained.

And how? Ordinarily this would not have seemed simple, but to Oleron it was now pellucidly clear. The key, *of course,* lay in his half-written novel—or rather, in both *Romilly*s, the old and the proposed new one.

A little while before Oleron would have thought himself mad to have embraced such an opinion; now he accepted the dizzying hypothesis without a quiver.

He began to examine the first and second *Romilly*s.

From the moment of his doing so the thing advanced by leaps and bounds. Swiftly he reviewed the history of the *Romilly* of the fifteen chapters. He remembered clearly now that he had found her insufficient on the very first morning on which he had sat down to work in his new place. Other instances of his aversion leaped up to confirm his obscure investigation. There had come the night when he had hardly forborne to throw the whole thing into the fire; and the next morning he had begun the planning of the new *Romilly.* It had been on that morning that Mrs. Barrett, overhearing him humming a brief phrase that the dripping of a tap the night before had suggested, had informed him that he was singing some air he had never in his life heard before, called "The Beckoning Fair One." . . .

The Beckoning Fair One! . . .

With scarcely a pause in thought he continued:

The first *Romilly* having been definitely thrown over, the second had instantly fastened herself upon him, clamouring for birth in his brain. He even fancied now, looking back, that there had been something like passion, hate almost, in the supplanting, and that more than once a stray thought given to his discarded creation had—(it was astonishing how credible Oleron found the almost unthinkable idea)—had offended the supplanter.

Yet that a malignancy almost homicidal should be extended to his fiction's poor mortal prototype. . . .

In spite of his inuring to a scale in which the horrible was now a thing to be fingered and turned this way and that, a "Good God!" broke from Oleron.

This intrusion of the first *Romilly's* prototype into his thought again was a factor that for the moment brought his inquiry into the nature of his problem to a termination; the mere thought of Elsie was fatal to anything abstract. For another thing, he could not yet think of that letter of Barrett's, nor of a little scene that had followed it, without a mounting of colour and a quick contraction of the brow. For, wisely or not, he had had that argument out at once. Striding across the square on the following morning, he had bearded Barrett on his own doorstep. Coming back again a few minutes later, he had been strongly of opinion that he had only made matters worse. The man had been vagueness itself. He had not been able to be either challenged or brow-beaten into anything more definite than a muttered farrago in which the words "Certain things . . . Mrs. Barrett . . . respectable house . . . if the cap fits . . . proceedings that shall be nameless," had been constantly repeated.

"Not that I make any charge—" he had concluded.

"Charge!" Oleron had cried.

"I 'ave my idears of things, as I don't doubt you 'ave yours—"

"Ideas—mine!" Oleron had cried wrathfully, immediately dropping his voice as heads had appeared at windows of the square. "Look you here, my man; you've an unwholesome mind, which probably you can't help, but a tongue which you can help, and shall! If there is a breath of this repeated . . ."

"I'll not be talked to on my own doorstep like this by anybody. . . ." Barrett had blustered. . . .

"You shall, and I'm doing it . . ."

"Don't you forget there's a Gawd above all, Who 'as said . . ."

"You're a low scandalmonger! . . ."

And so forth, continuing badly what was already badly begun. Oleron had returned wrathfully to his own house, and thenceforward, looking out of his windows, had seen Barrett's face at odd times, lifting blinds or peering round curtains, as if he sought to put himself in possession of Heaven knew what evidence, in case it should be required of him.

The unfortunate occurrence made certain minor differences in Oleron's domestic arrangements. Barrett's tongue, he gathered, had already been busy; he was looked at askance by the dwellers of the square; and he judged it better, until he should be able to obtain other help, to make his purchases of provisions a little farther afield rather than at the small shops of the immediate neighbourhood. For the rest, housekeeping was no new thing to him, and he would resume his old bachelor habits. . . .

Besides, he was deep in certain rather abstruse investigations, in which it was better that he should not be disturbed.

He was looking out of his window one midday rather tired, not very well, and glad that it was not very likely he would have to stir out of doors, when he saw Elsie Bengough crossing the square towards his house. The weather had broken; it was a raw and gusty day; and she had to force her way against the wind that set her ample skirts bellying about her opulent figure and her veil spinning and streaming behind her.

Oleron acted swiftly and instinctively. Seizing his hat, he sprang to the door and descended the stairs at a run. A sort of panic had seized him. She must be prevented from setting foot in the place. As he ran along the alley he was conscious that his eyes went up to the eaves as if something drew them. He did not know that a slate might not accidentally fall. . . .

He met her at the gate, and spoke with curious volubleness.

"This is really too bad, Elsie! Just as I'm urgently called away! I'm afraid it can't be helped though, and that you'll have to think me an inhospitable beast." He poured it out just as it came into his head.

She asked if he was going to town.

"Yes, yes—to town," he replied. "I've got to call on—on Chambers. You know Chambers, don't you? No, I remember you don't; a big man you once saw me with. . . . I ought to have gone yesterday, and—" this he felt to be a brilliant effort—"and he's going out of town this afternoon. To Brighton. I had a letter from him this morning."

He took her arm and led her up the square. She had to remind him that his way to town lay in the other direction.

"Of course—how stupid of me!" he said, with a little loud laugh. "I'm so used to going the other way with you—of course; it's the other way to the bus. Will you come along with me? I am so awfully sorry it's happened like this. . . ."

They took the street to the bus terminus.

This time Elsie bore no signs of having gone through interior struggles. If she detected anything unusual in his manner she made no comment, and he, seeing her calm, began to talk less recklessly through silences. By the time they reached the bus terminus, nobody, seeing the pallid-faced man without an overcoat and the large ample-skirted girl at his side, would have supposed that one of them was ready to sink on his knees for thankfulness that he had, as he believed, saved the other from a wildly unthinkable danger.

They mounted to the top of the bus, Oleron protesting that he should not miss his overcoat, and that he found the day, if anything, rather oppressively hot. They sat down on a front seat.

Now that this meeting was forced upon him, he had something else to say that would make demands upon his tact. It had been on his mind for some time, and was, indeed, peculiarly difficult to put. He revolved it for some minutes, and then, remembering the success of his story of a sudden call to town, cut the knot of his difficulty with another lie.

"I'm thinking of going away for a little while, Elsie," he said.

She merely said, "Oh?"

"Somewhere for a change. I need a change. I think I shall go to-morrow, or the day after. Yes, to-morrow, I think."

"Yes," she replied.

"I don't quite know how long I shall be," he continued. "I shall have to let you know when I am back."

"Yes, let me know," she replied in an even tone.

The tone was, for her, suspiciously even. He was a little uneasy.

"You don't ask me where I'm going," he said, with a little cumbrous effort to rally her.

She was looking straight before her, past the bus-driver.

"I know," she said.

He was startled. "How, you know?"

"You're not going anywhere," she replied.

He found not a word to say. It was a minute or so before she continued, in the same controlled voice she had employed from the start.

"You're not going anywhere. You weren't going out this morning. You only came out because I appeared; don't behave as if we were strangers, Paul."

A flush of pink had mounted to his cheeks. He noticed that the wind had given her the pink of early rhubarb. Still he found nothing to say.

"Of course, you ought to go away," she continued. "I don't know whether you look at yourself often in the glass, but you're rather noticeable. Several people have turned to look at you this morning. So, of course, you ought to go away. But you won't, and I know why."

He shivered, coughed a little, and then broke silence.

"Then if you know, there's no use in continuing this discussion," he said curtly.

"Not for me, perhaps, but there is for you," she replied. "Shall I tell you what I know?"

"No," he said in a voice slightly raised.

"No?" she asked, her round eyes earnestly on him.

"No."

Again he was getting out of patience with her; again he was conscious of the strain. Her devotion and fidelity and love plagued him; she was only humiliating both herself and him. It would have been bad enough had he ever, by word or deed, given her cause for thus fastening herself on him . . . but there; that was the worst of that kind of life for a woman. Women such as she, business women, in and out of offices all the time, always, whether they realised it or not, made comradeship a cover for something else. They accepted the unconventional status, came and went freely, as men did, were honestly taken by men at their own valuation—and then it turned out to be the other thing after all, and they went and fell in love. No wonder there was gossip in shops and squares and public-houses! In a sense the gossipers were in the right of it. Independent, yet not efficient; with some of womanhood's graces forgone, and yet with all the woman's hunger and need; half sophisticated, yet not wise; Oleron was tired of it all. . . .

And it was time he told her so.

"I suppose," he said tremblingly, looking down between his knees, "I suppose the real trouble is in the life women who earn their own living are obliged to lead."

He could not tell in what sense she took the lame generality; she merely replied, "I suppose so."

"It can't be helped," he continued, "but you do sacrifice a good deal."

She agreed: a good deal; and then she added after a moment, "What, for instance?"

"You may or may not be gradually attaining a new status, but you're in a false position to-day."

It was very likely, she said; she hadn't thought of it much in that light—

"And," he continued desperately, "you're bound to suffer. Your most innocent acts are misunderstood; motives you never dreamed of are attributed to you; and in the end it comes to"—he hesitated a moment and then took the plunge—"to the sidelong look and the leer."

She took his meaning with perfect ease. She merely shivered a little as she pronounced the name.

"Barrett?"

His silence told her the rest.

Anything further that was to be said must come from her. It came as the bus stopped at a stage and fresh passengers mounted the stairs.

"You'd better get down here and go back, Paul," she said. "I understand perfectly—perfectly. It isn't Barrett. You'd be able to deal with Barrett. It's merely convenient for you to say it's Barrett. I know what it is . . . but you said I wasn't to tell you that. Very well. But before you go let me tell you why I came up this morning."

In a dull tone he asked her why. Again she looked straight before her as she replied:

"I came to force your hand. Things couldn't go on as they have been going, you know; and now that's all over."

"All over," he repeated stupidly.

"All over. I want you now to consider yourself, as far as I'm concerned, perfectly free. I make only one reservation."

He hardly had the spirit to ask her what that was.

"If *I* merely need *you,*" she said, "please don't give that a thought; that's nothing; I shan't come near for that. But," she dropped her voice, "if *you're* in need of *me,* Paul—I shall know if you are, *and you will be*—then I shall come at no matter what cost. You understand that?"

He could only groan.

"So that's understood," she concluded. "And I think that's all.

Now go back. I should advise you to walk back, for you're shivering —good-bye—"

She gave him a cold hand, and he descended. He turned on the edge of the kerb as the bus started again. For the first time in all the years he had known her she parted from him with no smile and no wave of her long arm.

IX

He stood on the kerb plunged in misery, looking after her as long as she remained in sight; but almost instantly with her disappearance he felt the heaviness lift a little from his spirit. She had given him his liberty; true, there was a sense in which he had never parted with it, but now was no time for splitting hairs; he was free to act, and all was clear ahead. Swiftly the sense of lightness grew on him: it became a positive rejoicing in his liberty; and before he was half-way home he had decided what must be done next.

The vicar of the parish in which his dwelling was situated lived within ten minutes of the square. To his house Oleron turned his steps. It was necessary that he should have all the information he could get about this old house with the insurance marks and the sloping "To Let" boards, and the vicar was the person most likely to be able to furnish it. This last preliminary out of the way, and—aha! Oleron chuckled—things might be expected to happen!

But he gained less information than he had hoped for. The house, the vicar said, was old—but there needed no vicar to tell Oleron that; it was reputed (Oleron pricked up his ears) to be haunted—but there were few old houses about which some such rumour did not circulate among the ignorant; and the deplorable lack of Faith of the modern world, the vicar thought, did not tend to dissipate these superstitions. For the rest, his manner was the soothing manner of one who prefers not to make statements without knowing how they will be taken by his hearer. Oleron smiled as he perceived this.

"You may leave my nerves out of the question," he said. "How long has the place been empty?"

"A dozen years, I should say," the vicar replied.

"And the last tenant—did you know him—or her?" Oleron was conscious of a tingling of his nerves as he offered the vicar the alternative of sex.

"Him," said the vicar. "A man. If I remember rightly, his name was Madley; an artist. He was a great recluse; seldom went out of the place, and"—the vicar hesitated and then broke into a little gush of candour—"and since you appear to have come for this information, and since it is better that the truth should be told than that garbled versions should get about, I don't mind saying that this man Madley died there, under somewhat unusual circumstances. It was ascertained at the post-mortem that there was not a particle of food in his stomach, although he was found to be not without money. And his frame was simply worn out. Suicide was spoken of, but you'll agree with me that deliberate starvation is, to say the least, an uncommon form of suicide. An open verdict was returned."

"Ah!" said Oleron. . . . "Does there happen to be any comprehensive history of this parish?"

"No; partial ones only. I myself am not guiltless of having made a number of notes on its purely ecclesiastical history, its registers and so forth, which I shall be happy to show you if you would care to see them; but it is a large parish, I have only one curate, and my leisure, as you will readily understand . . ."

The extent of the parish and the scantiness of the vicar's leisure occupied the remainder of the interview, and Oleron thanked the vicar, took his leave, and walked slowly home.

He walked slowly for a reason, twice turning away from the house within a stone's-throw of the gate and taking another turn of twenty minutes or so. He had a very ticklish piece of work now before him; it required the greatest mental concentration; it was nothing less than to bring his mind, if he might, into such a state of unpreoccupation and receptivity that he should see the place as he had seen it on that morning when, his removal accomplished, he had sat down to begin the sixteenth chapter of the first *Romilly*.

For, could he recapture that first impression, he now hoped for far more from it. Formerly, he had carried no end of mental lumber. Before the influence of the place had been able to find him out at all, it had had the inertia of those dreary chapters to overcome. No results had shown. The process had been one of slow saturation, charging, filling up to a brim. But now he was light, unburdened, rid at last both of that *Romilly* and of her prototype. Now for the new unknown, coy, jealous, bewitching, Beckoning Fair! . . .

At half-past two of the afternoon he put his key into the Yale lock, entered, and closed the door behind him. . . .

His fantastic attempt was instantly and astonishingly successful.

He could have shouted with triumph as he entered the room; it was as if he had *escaped* into it. Once more, as in the days when his writing had had a daily freshness and wonder and promise for him, he was conscious of that new ease and mastery and exhilaration and release. The air of the place seemed to hold more oxygen; as if his own specific gravity had changed, his very tread seemed less ponderable. The flowers in the bowls, the fair proportions of the meadowsweet-coloured panels and mouldings, the polished floor, and the lofty and faintly starred ceiling, fairly laughed their welcome. Oleron actually laughed back, and spoke aloud.

"Oh, you're pretty, pretty!" he flattered it.

Then he lay down on his couch.

He spent that afternoon as a convalescent who expected a dear visitor might have spent it—in a delicious vacancy, smiling now and then as if in his sleep, and ever lifting drowsy and contented eyes to his alluring surroundings. He lay thus until darkness came, and, with darkness, the nocturnal noises of the old house. . . .

But if he waited for any specific happening, he waited in vain.

He waited similarly in vain on the morrow, maintaining, though with less ease, that sensitised-platelike condition of his mind. Nothing occurred to give it an impression. Whatever it was which he so patiently wooed, it seemed to be both shy and exacting.

Then on the third day he thought he understood. A look of gentle drollery and cunning came into his eyes, and he chuckled.

"Oho, oho! . . . Well, if the wind sits in *that* quarter we must see what else there is to be done. What is there, now? . . . No, I won't send for Elsie; we don't need a wheel to break the butterfly on; we won't go to those lengths, my butterfly. . . ."

He was standing musing, thumbing his lean jaw, looking aslant; suddenly he crossed to his hall, took down his hat, and went out.

"My lady is coquettish, is she? Well, we'll see what a little neglect will do," he chuckled as he went down the stairs.

He sought a railway station, got into a train, and spent the rest of the day in the country. Oh, yes: Oleron thought *he* was the man to deal with Fair Ones who beckoned, and invited, and then took refuge in shyness and hanging back!

He did not return until after eleven that night.

"*Now,* my Fair Beckoner!" he murmured as he walked along the alley and felt in his pocket for his keys. . . .

Inside his flat, he was perfectly composed, perfectly deliberate, exceedingly careful not to give himself away. As if to intimate that he intended to retire immediately, he lighted only a single candle; and as he set out with it on his nightly round he affected to yawn. He went first into his kitchen. There was a full moon, and a lozenge of moonlight, almost peacock-blue by contrast with his candle-frame, lay on the floor. The window was uncurtained, and he could see the reflection of the candle, and, faintly, that of his own face, as he moved about. The door of the powder-closet stood a little ajar, and he closed it before sitting down to remove his boots on the chair with the cushion made of the folded harpbag. From the kitchen he passed to the bathroom. There, another slant of blue moonlight cut the windowsill and lay across the pipes on the wall. He visited his seldom-used study, and stood for a moment gazing at the silvered roofs across the square. Then, walking straight through his sitting-room, his stockinged feet making no noise, he entered his bedroom and put the candle on the chest of drawers. His face all this time wore no expression save that of tiredness. He had never been wilier nor more alert.

His small bedroom fireplace was opposite the chest of drawers on which the mirror stood, and his bed and the window occupied the remaining sides of the room. Oleron drew down his blind, took off his coat, and then stooped to get his slippers from under the bed.

He could have given no reason for the conviction, but that the manifestation that for two days had been withheld was close at hand he never for an instant doubted. Nor, though he could not form the faintest guess of the shape it might take, did he experience fear. Startling or surprising it might be; he was prepared for that; but that was all; his scale of sensation had become depressed. His hand moved this way and that under the bed in search of his slippers. . . .

But for all his caution and method and preparedness, his heart all at once gave a leap and a pause that was almost horrid. His hand had found the slippers, but he was still on his knees; save for this circumstance he would have fallen. The bed was a low one; the groping for the slippers accounted for the turn of his head to one side; and he was careful to keep the attitude until he had partly recovered his self-possession. When presently he rose there was a drop of blood on his lower lip where he had caught at it with his teeth, and his watch had jerked out of the pocket of his waistcoat and was dangling at the end of its short leather guard. . . .

Then, before the watch had ceased its little oscillation, he was himself again.

In the middle of his mantelpiece there stood a picture, a portrait of his grandmother; he placed himself before this picture, so that he could see in the glass of it the steady flame of the candle that burned behind him on the chest of drawers. He could see also in the picture-glass the little glancings of light from the bevels and facets of the objects about the mirror and candle. But he could see more. These twinklings and reflections and re-reflections did not change their position; but there was one gleam that had motion. It was fainter than the rest, and it moved up and down through the air. It was the reflection of the candle on Oleron's black vulcanite comb, and each of its downward movements was accompanied by a silky and crackling rustle.

Oleron, watching what went on in the glass of his grandmother's portrait, continued to play his part. He felt for his dangling watch and began slowly to wind it up. Then, for a moment ceasing to watch, he began to empty his trousers pockets and to place methodically in a little row on the mantelpiece the pennies and halfpennies he took from them. The sweeping, minutely electric noise filled the whole bedroom, and had Oleron altered his point of observation he could have brought the dim gleam of the moving comb so into position that it would almost have outlined his grandmother's head.

Any other head of which it might have been following the outline was invisible.

Oleron finished the emptying of his pockets; then, under cover of another simulated yawn, not so much summoning his resolution as overmastered by an exorbitant curiosity, he swung suddenly round. That which was being combed was still not to be seen, but the comb did not stop. It had altered its angle a little, and had moved a little to the left. It was passing, in fairly regular sweeps, from a point rather more than five feet from the ground, in a direction roughly vertical, to another point a few inches below the level of the chest of drawers.

Oleron continued to act to admiration. He walked to his little washstand in the corner, poured out water, and began to wash his hands. He removed his waistcoat, and continued his preparations for bed. The combing did not cease, and he stood for a moment in thought. Again his eyes twinkled. The next was very cunning—

"Hm! . . . *I think I'll read for a quarter of an hour,*" he said aloud. . . .

He passed out of the room.

He was away a couple of minutes; when he returned again the room was suddenly quiet. He glanced at the chest of drawers; the comb lay still, between the collar he had removed and a pair of gloves. Without hesitation Oleron put out his hand and picked it up. It was an ordinary eighteen-penny comb, taken from a card in a chemist's shop, of a substance of a definite specific gravity, and no more capable of rebellion against the Laws by which it existed than are the worlds that keep their orbits through the void. Oleron put it down again; then he glanced at the bundle of papers he held in his hand. What he had gone to fetch had been the fifteen chapters of the original *Romilly*.

"Hm!" he muttered as he threw the manuscript into a chair. . . . "As I thought. . . . She's just blindly, ragingly, murderously jealous."

On the night after that, and on the following night, and for many nights and days, so many that he began to be uncertain about the count of them, Oleron, courting, cajoling, neglecting, threatening, beseeching, eaten out with unappeased curiosity and regardless that his life was becoming one consuming passion and desire, continued his search for the unknown co-numerator of his abode.

X

As time went on, it came to pass that few except the postman mounted Oleron's stairs; and since men who do not write letters receive few, even the postman's tread became so infrequent that it was not heard more than once or twice a week. There came a letter from Oleron's publishers, asking when they might expect to receive the manuscript of his new book; he delayed for some days to answer it, and finally forgot it. A second letter came, which also he failed to answer. He received no third.

The weather grew bright and warm. The privet bushes among the chopper-like notice-boards flowered, and in the streets where Oleron did his shopping the baskets of flower-women lined the kerbs. Oleron purchased flowers daily; his room clamoured for flowers, fresh and continually renewed; and Oleron did not stint its demands. Nevertheless, the necessity for going out to buy them began to irk him more and more, and it was with a greater and ever greater sense of relief that he returned home again. He began to be conscious that again his scale of sensation had suffered a subtle change—a change that was not restoration to its former capacity, but an extension and enlarging that once more included terror. It admitted it in an entirely new form. *Lux orco, tenebræ Jovi.* The name of this terror was agoraphobia. Oleron had begun to dread air and space and the horror that might pounce upon the unguarded back.

Presently he so contrived it that his food and flowers were delivered daily at his door. He rubbed his hands when he had hit upon this expedient. That was better! Now he could please himself whether he went out or not. . . .

Quickly he was confirmed in his choice. It became his pleasure to remain immured.

But he was not happy—or, if he was, his happiness took an extraordinary turn. He fretted discontentedly, could sometimes have wept for mere weakness and misery; and yet he was dimly conscious that he would not have exchanged his sadness for all the noisy mirth of the world outside. And speaking of noise: noise, much noise, now caused him the acutest discomfort. It was hardly more to be endured than that new-born fear that kept him, on the increasingly rare occasions when he did go out, sidling close to walls and feeling friendly railings with his hand. He moved from room to room softly and in slippers, and sometimes stood for many seconds closing a door so gently that not a sound broke the stillness that was in itself a delight. Sunday now became an intolerable day to him, for, since the coming of the fine weather, there had begun to assemble in the square under his windows each Sunday morning certain members of the sect to which the long-nosed Barrett adhered. These came with a great drum and large brass-bellied instruments; men and women uplifted anguished voices, struggling with their God; and Barrett himself, with upraised face and closed eyes and working brows, prayed that the sound of his voice might penetrate the ears of all unbelievers—as it certainly did Oleron's. One day, in the middle of one of these rhapsodies, Oleron sprang to his blind and pulled it down, and heard as he did so, his own name made the object of a fresh torrent of outpouring.

And sometimes, but not as expecting a reply, Oleron stood still and called softly. Once or twice he called "Romilly!" and then waited; but more often his whispering did not take the shape of a name.

There was one spot in particular of his abode that he began to haunt with increasing persistency. This was just within the opening of his bedroom door. He had discovered one day that by opening every door in his place (always excepting the outer one, which he only opened unwillingly) and by placing himself on this particular spot, he could actually see to a greater or less extent into each of his five rooms without changing his position. He could see the whole of his sitting-room, all of his bedroom except the part hidden by the open door, and glimpses of his kitchen, bathroom, and of his rarely used study. He was often in this place, breathless and with his finger on his lip. One day, as he stood there, he suddenly found himself wondering whether this Madley, of whom the vicar had spoken, had ever discovered the strategic importance of the bedroom entry.

Light, moreover, now caused him greater disquietude than did darkness. Direct sunlight, of which, as the sun passed daily round the house, each of his rooms had now its share, was like a flame in his brain; and even diffused light was a dull and numbing ache. He began, at successive hours of the day, one after another, to lower his crimson blinds. He made short and daring excursions in order to do this; but he was ever careful to leave his retreat open, in case he should have sudden need of it. Presently this lowering of the blinds had become a daily methodical exercise, and his rooms, when he had been his round, had the blood-red half-light of a photographer's dark-room.

One day, as he drew down the blind of his little study and backed in good order out of the room again, he broke into a soft laugh.

"*That* bilks Mr. Barrett!" he said; and the baffling of Barrett continued to afford him mirth for an hour.

But on another day, soon after, he had a fright that left him trembling also for an hour. He had seized the cord to darken the window over the seat in which he had found the harp-bag, and was standing with his back well protected in the embrasure, when he thought he saw the tail of a black-and-white check skirt disappear round the corner of the house. He could not be sure—had he run to the window of the other wall, which was blinded, the skirt must have been already past—but he was *almost* sure that it was Elsie. He listened in an agony of suspense for her tread on the stairs. . . .

But no tread came, and after three or four minutes he drew a long breath of relief.

"By Jove, but that would have compromised me horribly!" he muttered. . . .

And he continued to mutter from time to time, "Horribly compromising . . . *no* woman would stand that . . . not *any* kind of woman . . . oh, compromising in the extreme!"

Yet he was not happy. He could not have assigned the cause of the fits of quiet weeping which took him sometimes; they came and went, like the fitful illumination of the clouds that travelled over the square; and perhaps, after all, if he was not happy, he was not unhappy. Before he could be unhappy something must have been withdrawn, and nothing had been granted. He was waiting for that granting, in that flower-laden, frightfully enticing apartment of his, with the pith-white walls tinged and subdued by the crimson blinds to a blood-like gloom.

He paid no heed to it that his stock of money was running perilously low, nor that he had ceased to work. Ceased to work? He had not ceased to work. They knew very little about it who supposed that Oleron had ceased to work! He was in truth only now beginning to work. He was preparing such a work . . . such a work . . . such a Mistress was a-making in the gestation of his Art . . . let him but get this period of probation and poignant waiting over and men should see. . . . How *should* men know her, this Fair One of Oleron's, until Oleron himself knew her? Lovely radiant creations are not thrown off like How-d'ye-do's. The men to whom it is committed to father them must weep wretched tears, as Oleron did, must swell with vain presumptuous hopes, as Oleron did, must pursue, as Oleron pursued, the capricious, fair, mocking, slippery, eager Spirit that, ever eluding, ever sees to it that the chase does not slacken. Let Oleron but hunt this Huntress a little longer . . . he would have her sparkling and panting in his arms yet. . . . Oh no: they were very far from the truth who supposed that Oleron had ceased to work!

And if all else was falling away from Oleron, gladly he was letting it go. So do we all when our Fair Ones beckon. Quite at the beginning we wink, and promise ourselves that we will put Her Ladyship through her paces, neglect her for a day, turn her own jealous wiles against her, flout and ignore her when she comes wheedling; perhaps there lurks within us all the time a heartless sprite who is never fooled; but in the end all falls away. She beckons, beckons, and all goes. . . .

And so Oleron kept his strategic post within the frame of his bedroom door, and watched, and waited, and smiled, with his finger on his lips. . . . It was his duteous service, his worship, his troth-plighting, all that he had ever known of Love. And when he found himself, as he now and then did, hating the dead man Madley, and wishing that he had never lived, he felt that that, too, was an acceptable service. . . .

But, as he thus prepared himself, as it were, for a Marriage, and moped and chafed more and more that the Bride made no sign, he made a discovery that he ought to have made weeks before.

It was through a thought of the dead Madley that he made it. Since that night when he had thought in his greenness that a little studied neglect would bring the lovely Beckoner to her knees, and had made use of her own jealousy to banish her, he had not set eyes on those fifteen discarded chapters of *Romilly.* He had thrown them back into the window-seat, forgotten their very existence. But his own jealousy of Madley put him in mind of hers of her jilted rival of flesh and blood, and he remembered them. . . . Fool that he had been! Had he, then, expected his Desire to manifest herself while there still existed the evidence of his divided allegiance? What, and she with a passion so fierce and centred that it had not hesitated at the destruction, twice attempted, of her rival? Fool that he had been! . . .

But if *that* was all the pledge and sacrifice she required she should have it—ah, yes, and quickly!

He took the manuscript from the window-seat, and brought it to the fire.

He kept his fire always burning now; the warmth brought out the last vestige of odour of the flowers with which his room was banked. He did not know what time it was; long since he had allowed his clock to run down—it had seemed a foolish measurer of time in regard to the stupendous things that were happening to Oleron; but he knew it was late. He took the *Romilly* manuscript and knelt before the fire.

But he had not finished removing the fastening that held the sheets together before he suddenly gave a start, turned his head over his shoulder, and listened intently. The sound he had heard had not been loud—it had been, indeed, no more than a tap, twice or thrice repeated—but it had filled Oleron with alarm. His face grew dark as it came again.

He heard a voice outside on his landing.

"Paul! . . . Paul! . . ."

It was Elsie's voice.

"Paul! . . . I know you're in . . . I want to see you. . . ."

He cursed her under his breath, but kept perfectly still. He did not intend to admit her.

"Paul! . . . You're in trouble. . . . I believe you're in danger . . . at least come to the door! . . ."

Oleron smothered a low laugh. It somehow amused him that she, in such danger herself, should talk to him of *his* danger! . . . Well, if she was, serve her right; she knew, or said she knew, all about it. . . .

"Paul! . . . Paul! . . ."

"Paul! . . . Paul! . . ." He mimicked her under his breath.

"Oh, Paul, it's *horrible! . . .*"

Horrible was it? thought Oleron. Then let her get away. . . .

"I only want to help you, Paul. . . . I didn't promise not to come if you needed me. . . ."

He was impervious to the pitiful sob that interrupted the low cry. The devil take the woman! Should he shout to her to go away and not come back? No: let her call and knock and sob. She had a gift for sobbing; she mustn't think her sobs would move him. They irritated him, so that he set his teeth and shook his fist at her, but that was all. Let her sob.

"Paul! . . . Paul! . . ."

With his teeth hard set, he dropped the first page of *Romilly* into the fire. Then he began to drop the rest in, sheet by sheet.

For many minutes the calling behind his door continued; then suddenly it ceased. He heard the sound of feet slowly descending the stairs. He listened for the noise of a fall or a cry or the crash of a piece of the handrail of the upper landing; but none of these things came. She was spared. Apparently her rival suffered her to crawl abject and beaten away. Oleron heard the passing of her steps under his window; then she was gone.

He dropped the last page into the fire, and then, with a low laugh rose. He looked fondly round his room.

"Lucky to get away like that," he remarked. "She wouldn't have got away if I'd given her as much as a word or a look! What devils these women are! . . . But no; I oughtn't to say that; one of 'em showed forbearance. . . ."

Who showed forbearance? And what was forborne? Ah, Oleron knew! . . . Contempt, no doubt, had been at the bottom of it, but that didn't matter: the pestering creature had been allowed to go unharmed. Yes, she was lucky; Oleron hoped she knew it. . . .

And now, now, now for his reward!

Oleron crossed the room. All his doors were open; his eyes shone as he placed himself within that of his bedroom.

Fool that he had been, not to think of destroying the manuscript sooner! . . .

How, in a houseful of shadows, should he know his own Shadow? How, in a houseful of noises, distinguish the summons he felt to be at hand? Ah, trust him! He would know! The place was full of a jugglery of dim lights. The blind at his elbow that allowed the light of a street lamp to struggle vaguely through—the glimpse of greeny blue moonlight seen through the distant kitchen door—the sulky glow of the fire under the black ashes of the burnt manuscript—the glimmering of the tulips and the moon-daisies and narcissi in the bowls and jugs and jars—these did not so trick and bewilder his eyes that he would not know his Own! It was he, not she, who had been delaying the shadowy Bridal; he hung his head for a moment in mute acknowledgment; then he bent his eyes on the deceiving, puzzling gloom again. He would have called her name had he known it—but now he would not ask her to share even a name with the other. . . .

His own face, within the frame of the door, glimmered white as the narcissi in the darkness. . . .

A shadow, light as fleece, seemed to take shape in the kitchen (the time had been when Oleron would have said that a cloud had passed over the unseen moon). The low illumination on the blind at his elbow grew dimmer (the time had been when Oleron would have concluded that the lamplighter going his rounds had turned low the flame of the lamp). The fire settled, letting down the black and charred papers; a flower fell from a bowl, and lay indistinct upon the floor; all was still; and then a stray draught moved through the old house, passing before Oleron's face. . . .

Suddenly, inclining his head, he withdrew a little from the door-jamb. The wandering draught caused the door to move a little on its hinges. Oleron trembled violently, stood for a moment longer, and then, putting his hand out to the knob, softly drew the door to, sat down on the nearest chair, and waited, as a man might await the calling of his name that should summon him to some weighty, high and privy Audience. . . .

XI

One knows not whether there can be human compassion for anæmia of the soul. When the pitch of Life is dropped, and the spirit is so put over and reversed that that only is horrible which before was sweet and worldly and of the day, the human relation disappears. The sane soul turns appalled away, lest not merely itself, but sanity should suffer. We are not gods. We cannot drive out devils. We must see selfishly to it that devils do not enter into ourselves.

And this we must do even though Love so transfuse us that we may well deem our nature to be half divine. We shall but speak of honour and duty in vain. The letter dropped within the dark door will lie unregarded, or, if regarded for a brief instant between two unspeakable lapses, left and forgotten again. The telegram will be undelivered, nor will the whistling messenger (wiselier guided than he knows to whistle) be conscious as he walks away of the drawn blind that is pushed aside an inch by a finger and then fearfully replaced again. No: let the miserable wrestle with his own shadows; let him, if indeed he be so mad, clip and strain and enfold and couch the succubus; but let him do so in a house into which not an air of Heaven penetrates, nor a bright finger of the sun pierces the filthy twilight. The lost must remain lost. Humanity has other business to attend to.

For the handwriting of the two letters that Oleron, stealing noiselessly one June day into his kitchen to rid his sitting-room of an armful of fœtid and decaying flowers, had seen on the floor within his door, had had no more meaning for him than if it had belonged to some dim and far-away dream. And at the beating of the telegraph-boy upon the door, within a few feet of the bed where he lay, he had gnashed his teeth and stopped his ears. He had pictured the lad standing there, just beyond his partition, among packets of provisions and bundles of dead and dying flowers. For his outer landing was littered with these. Oleron had feared to open his door to take them in. After a week, the errand lads had reported that there must be some mistake about the order, and had left no more. Inside, in the red twilight, the old flowers turned brown and fell and decayed where they lay.

Gradually his power was draining away. The Abomination fastened on Oleron's power. The steady sapping sometimes left him for many hours of prostration gazing vacantly up at his red-tinged ceiling, idly suffering such fancies as came of themselves to have their way with him. Even the strongest of his memories had no more than a precarious hold upon his attention. Sometimes a flitting half-memory, of a novel to be written, a novel it was important that he should write, tantalised him for a space before vanishing again; and sometimes whole novels, perfect, splendid, established to endure, rose magically before him. And sometimes the memories were absurdly remote and trivial, of garrets he had inhabited and lodgings that had sheltered him, and so forth. Oleron had known a good deal about such things in his time, but all that was now past. He had at last found a place which he did not intend to leave until they fetched him out—a place that some might have thought a little on the green-sick side, that others might have considered to be a little too redolent of long-dead and morbid things for a living man to be mewed up in, but ah, so irresistible, with such an authority of its own, with such an associate of its own, and a place of such delights when once a man had ceased to struggle against its inexorable will! A novel? Somebody ought to write a novel about a place like that! There must be lots to write about in a place like that if one could but get to the bottom of it! It had probably already been painted, by a man called Madley who had lived there . . . but Oleron had not known this Madley—had a strong feeling that he wouldn't have liked him—would rather he had lived somewhere else—really couldn't stand the fellow—hated him, Madley, in fact. (Aha! That was a joke!) He seriously doubted whether the man had led the life he ought; Oleron was in two minds sometimes whether he wouldn't tell that long-nosed guardian of the public morals across the way about him; but probably he knew, and had made his praying hullabaloos for him also. That was his line. Why, Oleron himself had had a dust-up with him about something or other . . . some girl or other . . . Elsie Bengough her name was, he remembered. . . .

Oleron had moments of deep uneasiness about this Elsie Bengough. Or rather, he was not so much uneasy about her as restless about the things she did. Chief of these was the way in which she persisted in thrusting herself into his thoughts; and, whenever he was quick enough, he sent her packing the moment she made her appearance there. The truth was that she was not merely a bore; she had always been that; it had now come to the pitch when her very presence in his fancy was inimical to the full enjoyment of certain experiences. . . . She had no tact; really ought to have known that people are not at home to the thoughts of everybody all the time; ought in mere politeness to have allowed him certain seasons quite to himself; and was monstrously ignorant of things if she did not know, as she appeared not to know, that there were certain special hours when a man's veins ran with fire and daring and power, in which . . . well, in which he had a reasonable right to treat folk as he had treated that prying Barrett—to shut them out completely. . . . But no, up she popped: the thought of her, and ruined all. Bright towering fabrics, by the side of which even those perfect, magical novels of which he dreamed were dun and grey, vanished utterly at her intrusion. It was as if a fog should suddenly quench some fair-beaming star, as if at the threshold of some golden portal prepared for Oleron a pit should suddenly gape, as if a bat-like shadow should turn the growing dawn to mirk and darkness again. . . . Therefore, Oleron strove to stifle even the nascent thought of her.

Nevertheless, there came an occasion on which this woman Bengough absolutely refused to be suppressed. Oleron could not have told exactly when this happened; he only knew by the glimmer of the street lamp on his blind that it was some time during the night, and that for some time she had not presented herself.

He had no warning, none, of her coming; she just came—was there. Strive as he would, he could not shake off the thought of her nor the image of her face. She haunted him.

But for her to come at *that* moment of all moments! . . . Really, it was past belief! How *she* could endure it, Oleron could not conceive! Actually, to look on, as it were, at the triumph of a Rival. . . . Good God! It was monstrous! Tact—reticence—he had never credited her with an overwhelming amount of either: but he had never attributed mere—oh, there was no word for it! Monstrous—monstrous! Did she intend thenceforward. . . . Good God! To look on! . . .

Oleron felt the blood rush up to the roots of his hair with anger against her.

"Damnation take her!" he choked. . . .

But the next moment his heat and resentment had changed to

a cold sweat of cowering fear. Panic-stricken, he strove to comprehend what he had done. For though he knew not what, he knew he had done something, something fatal, irreparable, blasting. Anger he had felt, but not *this* blaze of ire that suddenly flooded the twilight of his consciousness with a white infernal light. *That* appalling flash was not his—not his *that* open rift of bright and searing Hell—not his, not his! His had been the hand of a child, preparing a puny blow; but what was *this other* horrific hand that was drawn back to strike in the same place? Had *he* set that in motion? Had *he* provided the spark that had touched off the whole accumulated power of that formidable and relentless place? He did not know. He only knew that that poor igniting particle in himself was blown out, that—Oh, impossible!—a clinging kiss (how else to express it?) had changed on his very lips to a gnashing and a removal, and that for very pity of the awful odds he must cry out to her against whom he had lately raged to guard herself . . . guard herself. . . .

"Look out!" he shrieked aloud. . . .

The revulsion was instant. As if a cold slow billow had broken over him, he came to to find that he was lying in his bed, that the mist and horror that had for so long enwrapped him had departed, that he was Paul Oleron, and that he was sick, naked, helpless, and unutterably abandoned and alone. His faculties, though weak, answered at last to his calls upon them; and he knew that it must have been a hideous nightmare that had left him sweating and shaking thus.

Yes, he was himself, Paul Oleron, a tired novelist, already past the summit of his best work, and slipping downhill again empty-handed from it all. He had struck short in his life's aim. He had tried too much, had over-estimated his strength, and was a failure, a failure. . . .

It all came to him in the single word, enwrapped and complete; it needed no sequential thought; he was a failure. He had missed. . . .

And he had missed not one happiness, but two. He had missed the ease of this world, which men love, and he had missed also that other shining prize for which men forgo ease, the snatching and holding and triumphant bearing up aloft of which is the only justification of the mad adventurer who hazards the enterprise. And there was no second attempt. Fate has no morrow. Oleron's morrow must be to sit down to profitless, ill-done, unrequired work again, and so on the morrow after that, and the morrow after that, and as many morrows as there might be. . . .

He lay there, weakly yet sanely considering it. . . .

And since the whole attempt had failed, it was hardly worth while to consider whether a little might not be saved from the general wreck. No good would ever come of that half-finished novel. He had intended that it should appear in the autumn; was under contract that it should appear; no matter; it was better to pay forfeit to his publishers than to waste what days were left. He was spent; age was not far off; and paths of wisdom and sadness were the properest for the remainder of the journey. . . .

If only he had chosen the wife, the child, the faithful friend at the fireside, and let them follow an *ignis fatuus* that list! . . .

In the meantime it began to puzzle him exceedingly why he should be so weak, that his room should smell so overpoweringly of decaying vegetable matter, and that his hand, chancing to stray to his face in the darkness, should encounter a beard.

"Most extraordinary!" he began to mutter to himself. "Have I been ill? Am I ill now? And if so, why have they left me alone? . . . Extraordinary! . . ."

He thought he heard a sound from the kitchen or bathroom. He rose a little on his pillow, and listened. . . . Ah! He was not alone, then! It certainly would have been extraordinary if they had left him ill and alone— Alone? Oh no. He would be looked after. He wouldn't be left, ill, to shift for himself. If everybody else had forsaken him, he could trust Elsie Bengough, the dearest chum he had, for that . . . bless her faithful heart!

But suddenly a short, stifled, spluttering cry rang sharply out: *"Paul!"*

It came from the kitchen.

And in the same moment it flashed upon Oleron, he knew not how, that two, three, five, he knew not how many minutes before, another sound, unmarked at the time but suddenly transfixing his attention now, had striven to reach his intelligence. This sound had been the slight touch of metal on metal—just such a sound as Oleron made when he put his key into the lock.

"Hallo! . . . Who's that?" he called sharply from his bed.

He had no answer.

He called again. "Hallo! . . . Who's there? . . . Who is it?"

This time he was sure he heard noises, soft and heavy, in the kitchen.

"This is a queer thing altogether," he muttered. "By Jove, I'm as weak as a kitten too. . . . Hallo, there! Somebody called, didn't they? . . . Elsie! Is that you? . . ."

Then he began to knock with his hand on the wall at the side of his bed.

"Elsie! . . . Elsie! . . . You called, didn't you? . . . Please come here, whoever it is! . . .

There was a sound as of a closing door, and then silence. Oleron began to get rather alarmed.

"It may be a nurse," he muttered; "Elsie'd have to get me a nurse, of course. She'd sit with me as long as she could spare the time, brave lass, and she'd get a nurse for the rest. . . . But it was awfully like her voice. . . . Elsie, or whoever it is! . . . I can't make this out at all. I must go and see what's the matter. . . ."

He put one leg out of bed. Feeling its feebleness, he reached with his hand for the additional support of the wall. . . .

But before putting out the other leg he stopped and considered, picking at his new-found beard. He was suddenly wondering whether he *dared* go into the kitchen. It was such a frightfully long way; no man knew what horror might not leap and huddle on his shoulders if he went so far; when a man has an overmastering impulse to get back into bed he ought to take heed of the warning and obey it. Besides, why should he go? What was there to go for? If it was that Bengough creature again, let her look after herself; Oleron was not going to have things cramp themselves on his defenceless back for the sake of such a spoilsport as *she!* . . . If she was in, let her let herself out again, and the sooner the better for her! Oleron simply couldn't be bothered. He had his work to do. On the morrow, he must set about the writing of a novel with a heroine so winsome, capricious, adorable, jealous, wicked, beautiful, inflaming, and altogether evil, that men should stand amazed. She was coming over him now; he knew by the alteration of the very air of the room when she was near him; and that soft thrill of bliss that had begun to stir in him never came unless she was beckoning, beckoning. . . .

He let go the wall and fell back into bed again as—oh, unthinkable!—the other half of that kiss that a gnash had interrupted was placed (how else convey it?) on his lips, robbing him of very breath. . . .

XII

In the bright June sunlight a crowd filled the square, and looked up at the windows of the old house with the antique insurance marks in its walls of red brick and the agents' notice-boards hanging like wooden choppers over the paling. Two constables stood at the broken gate of the narrow entrance-alley, keeping folk back. The women kept to the outskirts of the throng, moving now and then as if to see the drawn red blinds of the old house from a new angle, and talking in whispers. The children were in the houses, behind closed doors.

A long-nosed man had a little group about him, and he was telling some story over and over again; and another man, little and fat and wide-eyed, sought to capture the long-nosed man's audience with some relation in which a key figured.

". . . and it was revealed to me that there'd been something that very afternoon," the long-nosed man was saying. "I was standing there, where Constable Saunders is—or rather, I was passing about my business, when they came out. There was no deceiving me, oh, no deceiving *me! I* saw her face. . . ."

"What was it like, Mr. Barrett?" a man asked.

"It was like hers whom our Lord said to, 'Woman, doth any man accuse thee?'—white as paper, and no mistake! Don't tell *me!* . . . And so I walks straight across to Mrs. Barrett, and 'Jane,' I says, 'this must stop, and stop at once; we are commanded to avoid evil,' I says, 'and it must come to an end now; let him get help elsewhere.' And she says to me, 'John,' she says, 'it's four-and-sixpence a week'—them was her words. 'Jane,' I says, 'if it was forty-six thousand pounds it should stop' . . . and from that day to this she hasn't set foot inside that gate."

There was a short silence: then,

"Did Mrs. Barrett ever . . . *see* anythink, like?" somebody vaguely inquired.

Barrett turned austerely on the speaker.

"What Mrs. Barrett saw and Mrs. Barrett didn't see shall not pass these lips; even as it is written, keep thy tongue from speaking evil," he said.

Another man spoke.

"He was pretty near canned up in the Waggon and Horses that night, weren't he, Jim?"

"Yes, 'e 'adn't 'alf copped it. . . ."

"Not standing treat much, neither; he was in the bar, all on his own. . . ."

"So 'e was; we talked about it. . . ."

The fat, scared-eyed man made another attempt.

"She got the key off of me—she 'ad the number of it—she came into my shop of a Tuesday evening. . . ."

Nobody heeded him.

"Shut your heads," a heavy labourer commented gruffly, "she hasn't been found yet. 'Ere's the inspectors; we shall know more in a bit."

Two inspectors had come up and were talking to the constables who guarded the gate. The little fat man ran eagerly forward, saying that she had bought the key off him. "I remember the number, because of its being three one's and three three's—111333!" he exclaimed excitedly.

An inspector put him aside.

"Nobody's been in?" he asked of one of the constables.

"No, sir."

"Then you, Brackley, come with us; you, Smith, keep the gate. There's a squad on its way."

The two inspectors and the constable passed down the alley and entered the house. They mounted the wide carved staircase.

"This don't look as if he'd been out much lately," one of the inspectors muttered as he kicked aside a litter of dead leaves and paper that lay outside Oleron's door. "I don't think we need knock—break a pane, Brackley."

The door had two glazed panels; there was a sound of shattered glass; and Brackley put his hand through the hole his elbow had made and drew back the latch.

"Faugh!" . . . choked one of the inspectors as they entered. "Let some light and air in, quick. It stinks like a hearse—"

The assembly out in the square saw the red blinds go up and the windows of the old house flung open.

"That's better," said one of the inspectors, putting his head out of a window and drawing a deep breath. . . . "That seems to be the bedroom in there; will you go in, Simms, while I go over the rest? . . ."

They had drawn up the bedroom blind also, and the waxy-white, emaciated man on the bed had made a blinker of his hand against the torturing flood of brightness. Nor could he believe that his hearing was not playing tricks with him, for there were two policemen in his room, bending over him and asking where "she" was. He shook his head.

"This woman Bengough . . . goes by the name of Miss Elsie Bengough . . . d'ye hear? Where is she? . . . No good, Brackley; get him up; be careful with him; I'll just shove *my* head out of the window, I think. . . ."

The other inspector had been through Oleron's study and had found nothing, and was now in the kitchen, kicking aside an ankle-deep mass of vegetable refuse that cumbered the floor. The kitchen window had no blind, and was overshadowed by the blank end of the house across the alley. The kitchen appeared to be empty.

But the inspector, kicking aside the dead flowers, noticed that a shuffling track that was not of his making had been swept to a cupboard in the corner. In the upper part of the door of the cupboard was a square panel that looked as if it slid on runners. The door itself was closed.

The inspector advanced, put out his hand to the little knob, and slid the hatch along its groove.

Then he took an involuntary step back again.

Framed in the aperture, and falling forward a little before it jammed again in its frame, was something that resembled a large lumpy pudding, done up in a pudding-bag of faded browny red frieze.

"Ah!" said the inspector.

To close the hatch again he would have had to thrust that pudding back with his hand; and somehow he did not quite like the idea of touching it. Instead, he turned the handle of the cupboard itself. There was weight behind it, so much weight that, after opening the door three or four inches and peering inside, he had to put his shoulder to it in order to close it again. In closing it he left sticking out, a few inches from the floor, a triangle of black and white check skirt.

He went into the small hall.

"All right!" he called.

They had got Oleron into his clothes. He still used his hands as blinkers, and his brain was very confused. A number of things were happening that he couldn't understand. He couldn't understand the extraordinary mess of dead flowers there seemed to be everywhere; he couldn't understand why there should be police officers in his room; he couldn't understand why one of these should be sent for a four-wheeler and a stretcher; and he couldn't understand what heavy article they seemed to be moving about in the kitchen—his kitchen. . . .

"What's the matter?" he muttered sleepily. . . .

Then he heard a murmur in the square, and the stopping of a four-wheeler outside. A police officer was at his elbow again, and Oleron wondered why, when he whispered something to him, he should run off a string of words—something about "used in evidence against you." They had lifted him to his feet, and were assisting him towards the door. . . .

No, Oleron couldn't understand it at all.

They got him down the stairs and along the alley. Oleron was aware of confused angry shoutings; he gathered that a number of people wanted to lynch somebody or other. Then his attention became fixed on a little fat frightened-eyed man who appeared to be making a statement that an officer was taking down in a notebook.

"I'd seen her with him . . . they was often together . . . she came into my shop and said it was for him . . . I thought it was all right . . . 111333 the number was," the man was saying.

The people seemed to be very angry; many police were keeping them back; but one of the inspectors had a voice that Oleron thought quite kind and friendly. He was telling somebody to get somebody else into the cab before something or other was brought out; and Oleron noticed that a four-wheeler was drawn up at the gate. It appeared that it was himself who was to be put into it; and as they lifted him up he saw that the inspector tried to stand between him and something that stood behind the cab, but was not quick enough to prevent Oleron seeing that this something was a hooded stretcher. The angry voices sounded like a sea; something hard, like a stone, hit the back of the cab; and the inspector followed Oleron in and stood with his back to the window nearer the side where the people were. The door they had put Oleron in at remained open, apparently till the other inspector should come; and through the opening Oleron had a glimpse of the hatchet-like "To Let" boards among the privet-trees. One of them said that the key was at Number Six. . . .

Suddenly the raging of voices was hushed. Along the entrance-alley shuffling steps were heard, and the other inspector appeared at the cab door.

"Right away," he said to the driver.

He entered, fastened the door after him, and blocked up the second window with his back. Between the two inspectors Oleron slept peacefully. The cab moved down the square, the other vehicle went up the hill. The mortuary lay that way.

The Voice in the Night

WILLIAM HOPE HODGSON

[1877–1918]

William Hope Hodgson, by far the greatest writer to use the sea as a vehicle for horror, was born in Essex, England, and died in the trenches of the French front near Ypres. He left behind a distinguished legacy of supernatural fiction, including the sea novels The Boats of the Glen Carrig *and* The Ghost Pirates, *and the eerie, apocalyptic* The House on the Borderland. *Although his finest short story is undeniably* "The Voice in the Night," *he wrote many others that are remarkable for their weird atmosphere and unusual vision.*

It was a dark, starless night. We were becalmed in the Northern Pacific. Our exact position I do not know; for the sun had been hidden during the course of a weary, breathless week, by a thin haze which had seemed to float above us, about the height of our mastheads, at whiles descending and shrouding the surrounding sea.

With there being no wind, we had steadied the tiller, and I was the only man on deck. The crew, consisting of two men and a boy, were sleeping forrard in their den; while Will—my friend, and the master of our little craft—was aft in his bunk on the port side of the little cabin.

Suddenly, from out of the surrounding darkness, there came a hail:

"Schooner, ahoy!"

The cry was so unexpected that I gave no immediate answer, because of my surprise.

It came again—a voice curiously throaty and inhuman, calling from somewhere upon the dark sea away on our port broadside:

"Schooner, ahoy!"

"Hullo!" I sung out, having gathered my wits somewhat. "What are you? What do you want?"

"You need not be afraid," answered the queer voice, having probably noticed some trace of confusion in my tone. "I am only an old—man."

The pause sounded oddly; but it was only afterwards that it came back to me with any significance.

"Why don't you come alongside, then?" I queried somewhat snappishly; for I liked not his hinting at my having been a trifle shaken.

"I—I—can't. It wouldn't be safe. I—" The voice broke off, and there was silence.

"What do you mean?" I asked, growing more and more astonished. "Why not safe? Where are you?"

I listened for a moment; but there came no answer. And then, a sudden indefinite suspicion, of I knew not what, coming to me, I stepped swiftly to the binnacle, and took out the lighted lamp. At the same time, I knocked on the deck with my heel to waken Will. Then I was back at the side, throwing the yellow funnel of light out into the silent immensity beyond our rail. As I did so, I heard a slight, muffled cry, and then the sound of a splash, as though someone had dipped oars abruptly. Yet I cannot say that I saw anything with certainty; save, it seemed to me, that with the first flash of the light, there had been something upon the waters, where now there was nothing.

"Hullo, there!" I called. "What foolery is this!"

But there came only the indistinct sounds of a boat being pulled away into the night.

Then I heard Will's voice, from the direction of the after scuttle:

"What's up, George?"

"Come here, Will!" I said.

"What is it?" he asked, coming across the deck.

I told him the queer things which had happened. He put several questions; then, after a moment's silence, he raised his hands to his lips, and hailed:

"Boat, ahoy!"

From a long distance away, there came back to us a faint reply, and my companion repeated his call. Presently, after a short period of silence, there grew on our hearing the muffled sound of oars; at which Will hailed again.

This time there was a reply:

"Put away the light."

"I'm damned if I will," I muttered; but Will told me to do as the voice bade, and I shoved it down under the bulwarks.

"Come nearer," he said, and the oar-strokes continued. Then, when apparently some half-dozen fathoms distant, they again ceased.

"Come alongside," exclaimed Will. "There's nothing to be frightened of aboard here!"

"Promise that you will not show the light?"

"What's to do with you," I burst out, "that you're so infernally afraid of the light?"

"Because—" began the voice, and stopped short.

"Because what?" I asked, quickly.

Will put his hand on my shoulder.

"Shut up a minute, old man," he said, in a low voice. "Let me tackle him."

He leant more over the rail.

"See here, Mister," he said, "this is a pretty queer business, you coming upon us like this, right out in the middle of the blessed Pacific. How are we to know what sort of a hanky-panky trick you're up to? You say there's only one of you. How are we to know, unless we get a squint at you—eh? What's your objection to the light, anyway?"

As he finished, I heard the noise of the oars again, and then the voice came; but now from a greater distance, and sounding extremely hopeless and pathetic.

"I am sorry—sorry! I would not have troubled you, only I am hungry, and—so is she."

The voice died away, and the sound of the oars, dipping irregularly, was borne to us.

"Stop!" sung out Will. "I don't want to drive you away. Come back! We'll keep the light hidden, if you don't like it."

He turned to me:

"It's a damned queer rig, this; but I think there's nothing to be afraid of?"

There was a question in his tone, and I replied.

"No, I think the poor devil's been wrecked around here, and gone crazy."

The sound of the oars drew nearer.

"Shove that lamp back in the binnacle," said Will; then he leaned over the rail, and listened. I replaced the lamp, and came back to his side. The dipping of the oars ceased some dozen yards distant.

"Won't you come alongside now?" asked Will in an even voice. "I have had the lamp put back in the binnacle."

"I—I cannot," replied the voice. "I dare not come nearer. I dare not even pay you for the—the provisions."

"That's all right," said Will, and hesitated. "You're welcome to as much grub as you can take—" Again he hesitated.

"You are very good," exclaimed the voice. "May God, Who understands everything, reward you—" It broke off huskily.

"The—the lady?" said Will, abruptly. "Is she—"

"I have left her behind upon the island," came the voice.

"What island?" I cut in.

"I know not its name," returned the voice. "I would to God—!" it began, and checked itself as suddenly.

"Could we not send a boat for her?" asked Will at this point.

"No!" said the voice, with extraordinary emphasis. "My God! No!" There was a moment's pause; then it added, in a tone which seemed a merited reproach:

"It was because of our want I ventured—Because her agony tortured me."

"I am a forgetful brute," exclaimed Will. "Just wait a minute, whoever you are, and I will bring you up something at once."

In a couple of minutes he was back again, and his arms were full of various edibles. He paused at the rail.

"Can't you come alongside for them?" he asked.

"No—I *dare not,*" replied the voice, and it seemed to me that in its tones I detected a note of stifled craving—as though the owner hushed a mortal desire. It came to me then in a flash, that the poor old creature out there in the darkness, was *suffering* for actual need of that which Will held in his arms; and yet, because of some unintelligible dread, refraining from dashing to the side of our little schooner, and receiving it. And with the lightning-like conviction, there came the knowledge that the Invisible was not mad; but sanely facing some intolerable horror.

"Damn it, Will!" I said, full of many feelings, over which predominated a vast sympathy. "Get a box. We must float off the stuff to him in it."

This we did—propelling it away from the vessel, out into the darkness, by means of a boat-hook. In a minute, a slight cry from the Invisible came to us, and we knew that he had secured the box.

A little later, he called out a farewell to us, and so heartful a blessing, that I am sure we were the better for it. Then, without more ado, we heard the ply of oars across the darkness.

"Pretty soon off," remarked Will, with perhaps just a little sense of injury.

"Wait," I replied. "I think somehow he'll come back. He must have been badly needing that food."

"And the lady," said Will. For a moment he was silent; then he continued:

"It's the queerest thing ever I've tumbled across, since I've been fishing."

"Yes," I said, and fell to pondering.

And so the time slipped away—an hour, another, and still Will stayed with me; for the queer adventure had knocked all desire for sleep out of him.

The third hour was three parts through, when we heard again the sound of oars across the silent ocean.

"Listen!" said Will, a low note of excitement in his voice.

"He's coming, just as I thought," I muttered.

The dipping of the oars grew nearer, and I noted that the strokes were firmer and longer. The food had been needed.

They came to a stop a little distance off the broadside, and the queer voice came again to us through the darkness:

"Schooner, ahoy!"

"That you?" asked Will.

"Yes," replied the voice. "I left you suddenly; but—but there was great need."

"The lady?" questioned Will.

"The—lady is grateful now on earth. She will be more grateful soon in—in heaven."

Will began to make some reply, in a puzzled voice; but became confused, and broke off short. I said nothing. I was wondering at the curious pauses, and, apart from my wonder, I was full of a great sympathy.

The voice continued:

"We—she and I, have talked, as we shared the result of God's tenderness and yours—"

Will interposed; but without coherence.

"I beg of you not to—to belittle your deed of Christian charity this night," said the voice. "Be sure that it has not escaped His notice."

It stopped, and there was a full minute's silence. Then it came again:

"We have spoken together upon that which—which has befallen us. We had thought to go out, without telling any, of the terror which has come into our—lives. She is with me in believing that tonight's happenings are under a special ruling, and that it is God's wish that we should tell you all that we have suffered since —since—"

"Yes?" said Will, softly.

"Since the sinking of the *Albatross.*"

"Ah!" I exclaimed, involuntarily. "She left Newcastle for 'Frisco some six months ago, and hasn't been heard of since."

"Yes," answered the voice. "But some few degrees to the North of the line she was caught in a terrible storm, and dismasted. When the day came, it was found that she was leaking badly, and, presently, it falling to a calm, the sailors took to the boats, leaving—leaving a young lady—my fiancée—and myself upon the wreck.

"We were below, gathering together a few of our belongings, when they left. They were entirely callous, through fear, and when we came up upon the decks, we saw them only as small shapes afar off upon the horizon. Yet we did not despair, but set to work and constructed a small raft. Upon this we put such few matters as it would hold, including a quantity of water and some ship's biscuit. Then, the vessel being very deep in the water, we got ourselves on to the raft, and pushed off.

"It was later, when I observed that we seemed to be in the way of some tide or current, which bore us from the ship at an angle; so that in the course of three hours, by my watch, her hull became invisible to our sight, her broken masts remaining in view for a somewhat longer period. Then, towards evening, it grew misty, and so through the night. The next day we were still encompassed by the mist, the weather remaining quiet.

"For four days, we drifted through this strange haze, until, on the evening of the fourth day, there grew upon our ears the murmur of breakers at a distance. Gradually it became plainer, and, somewhat after midnight, it appeared to sound upon either hand at no very great space. The raft was raised upon a swell several times, and then we were in smooth water, and the noise of the breakers was behind.

"When the morning came, we found that we were in a sort of great lagoon; but of this we noticed little at the time; for close before us, through the enshrouding mist, loomed the hull of a large sailing-vessel. With one accord, we fell upon our knees and thanked God; for we thought that here was an end to our perils. We had much to learn.

"The raft drew near to the ship, and we shouted on them, to take us aboard; but none answered. Presently, the raft touched the side of the vessel, and, seeing a rope hanging downwards, I seized it and began to climb. Yet I had much ado to make my way up, because of a kind of grey, lichenous fungus, which had seized upon the rope, and which blotched the side of the ship, lividly.

"I reached the rail, and clambered over it, on to the deck. Here, I saw that the decks were covered, in great patches, with the grey masses, some of them rising into nodules several feet in height; but at the time, I thought less of this matter than of the possibility of there being people aboard the ship. I shouted; but none answered. Then I went to the door below the poop deck. I opened it, and peered in. There was a great smell of staleness, so that I knew in a moment that nothing living was within, and with the knowledge, I shut the door quickly; for I felt suddenly lonely.

"I went back to the side, where I had scrambled up. My—my sweetheart was still sitting quietly upon the raft. Seeing me look down, she called up to know whether there were any aboard of the ship. I replied that the vessel had the appearance of having been long deserted; but that if she would wait a little I would see whether there was anything in the shape of a ladder, by which she could ascend to the deck. Then we would make a search through the vessel together. A little later, on the opposite side of the decks, I found a rope side-ladder. This I carried across, and a minute afterwards, she was beside me.

"Together, we explored the cabins and apartments in the after-part of the ship; but nowhere was there any sign of life. Here and there, within the cabins themselves, we came across odd patches of that queer fungus; but this, as my sweetheart said, could be cleansed away.

"In the end, having assured ourselves that the after portion of the vessel was empty, we picked our ways to the bows, between the ugly grey nodules of that strange growth; and here we made a further search, which told us that there was indeed none aboard but ourselves.

"This being now beyond any doubt, we returned to the stern of the ship, and proceeded to make ourselves as comfortable as possible. Together, we cleared out and cleaned two of the cabins; and after that, I made examination whether there was anything eatable in the ship. This I soon found was so, and thanked God in my heart for His goodness. In addition to this, I discovered the whereabouts of the freshwater pump, and having fixed it, I found the water drinkable, though somewhat unpleasant to the taste.

"For several days, we stayed aboard the ship, without attempting to get to the shore. We were busily engaged in making the place habitable. Yet even thus early, we became aware that our lot was even less to be desired than might have been imagined; for though, as a first step, we scraped away the odd patches of growth that studded the floors and walls of the cabins and saloon, yet they returned almost to their original size within the space of twenty-four hours, which not only discouraged us, but gave us a feeling of vague unease.

"Still, we would not admit ourselves beaten, so set to work afresh, and not only scraped away the fungus, but soaked the places where it had been, with carbolic, a can-full of which I had found in the pantry. Yet, by the end of the week, the growth had returned in full strength, and, in addition, it had spread to other places, as though our touching it had allowed germs from it to travel elsewhere.

"On the seventh morning, my sweetheart woke to find a small patch of it growing on her pillow, close to her face. At that, she came to me, so soon as she could get her garments upon her. I was in the galley at the time, lighting the fire for breakfast.

" 'Come here, John,' she said, and led me aft. When I saw the thing upon her pillow, I shuddered, and then and there we agreed to go right out of the ship and see whether we could not fare to make ourselves more comfortable ashore.

"Hurriedly, we gathered together our few belongings, and even among these, I found that the fungus had been at work; for one of her shawls had a little lump of it growing near one edge. I threw the whole thing over the side, without saying anything to her.

"The raft was still alongside; but it was too clumsy to guide, and I lowered down a small boat that hung across the stern, and in this we made our way to the shore. Yet, as we drew near to it, I became gradually aware that here the vile fungus, which had driven us from the ship, was growing riot. In places it rose into horrible, fantastic mounds, which seemed almost to quiver, as with a quiet life, when the wind blew across them. Here and there, it took on the forms of vast fingers, and in others it just spread out flat and smooth and treacherous. Odd places, it appeared as grotesque stunted trees, seeming extraordinarily kinked and gnarled—The whole quaking vilely at times.

"At first, it seemed to us that there was no single portion of the surrounding shore which was not hidden beneath the masses of the hideous lichen; yet, in this, I found we were mistaken; for somewhat later, coasting along the shore at a little distance, we descried a smooth white patch of what appeared to be fine sand, and there we landed. It was not sand. What it was, I do not know. All that I have observed, is that upon it, the fungus will not grow; while everywhere else, save where the sand-like earth wanders oddly, path-wise, amid the grey desolation of the lichen, there is nothing but that loathsome greyness.

"It is difficult to make you understand how cheered we were to find one place that was absolutely free from the growth, and here we deposited our belongings. Then we went back to the ship for such things as it seemed to us we should need. Among other matters, I managed to bring ashore with me one of the ship's sails, with which I constructed two small tents, which, though exceedingly rough-shaped, served the purposes for which they were intended. In these, we lived and stored our various necessities, and thus for a matter of some four weeks, all went smoothly and without particular unhappiness. Indeed, I may say with much of happiness—for—for we were together.

"It was on the thumb of her right hand, that the growth first showed. It was only a small circular spot, much like a little grey mole. My God! how the fear leapt to my heart when she showed me the place. We cleaned it, between us, washing it with carbolic and water. In the morning of the following day, she showed her hand to me again. The grey warty thing had returned. For a little while, we looked at one another in silence. Then, still wordless, we started again to remove it. In the midst of the operation, she spoke suddenly.

" 'What's that on the side of your face, Dear!' Her voice was sharp with anxiety. I put my hand up to feel.

" 'There! Under the hair by your ear.—A little to the front a bit.' My finger rested upon the place, and then I knew.

" 'Let us get your thumb done first,' I said. And she submitted, only because she was afraid to touch me until it was cleansed. I finished washing and disinfecting her thumb, and then she turned to my face. After it was finished, we sat together and talked awhile of many things; for there had come into our lives sudden, very terrible thoughts. We were, all at once, afraid of something worse than death. We spoke of loading the boat with provisions and water, and making our way out on to the sea; yet we were helpless, for many causes, and —and the growth had attacked us already. We decided to stay. God would do with us what was His will. We would wait.

"A month, two months, three months passed, and the places grew somewhat, and there had come others. Yet we fought so strenuously with the fear, that its headway was but slow, comparatively speaking.

"Occasionally, we ventured off to the ship for such stores as we needed. There, we found that the fungus grew persistently. One of the nodules on the maindeck became soon as high as my head.

"We had now given up all thought or hope of leaving the island. We had realised that it would be unallowable to go among healthy humans with the thing from which we were suffering.

"With this determination and knowledge in our minds, we knew that we should have to husband our food and water; for we did not know, at that time, but that we should possibly live for many years.

"This reminds me that I have told you that I am an old man. Judged by years this is not so. But—but—"

He broke off; then continued somewhat abruptly:

"As I was saying, we knew that we should have to use care in the matter of food. But we had no idea then how little food there was left, of which to take care. It was a week later, that I made the discovery that all the other bread tanks—which I had supposed full —were empty, and that (beyond odd tins of vegetables and meat, and some other matters) we had nothing on which to depend, but the bread in the tank which I had already opened.

"After learning this, I bestirred myself to do what I could, and set to work at fishing in the lagoon; but with no success. At this, I was somewhat inclined to feel desperate, until the thought came to me to try outside the lagoon, in the open sea.

"Here, at times, I caught odd fish; but, so infrequently, that they proved of but little help in keeping us from the hunger which threatened. It seemed to me that our deaths were likely to come by hunger, and not by the growth of the thing which had seized upon our bodies.

"We were in this state of mind when the fourth month wore out.

Then I made a very horrible discovery. One morning, a little before midday, I came off from the ship, with a portion of the biscuits which were left. In the mouth of her tent, I saw my sweetheart sitting, eating something.

" 'What is it, my dear?' I called out as I leapt ashore. Yet, on hearing my voice, she seemed confused, and, turning, slyly threw something towards the edge of the little clearing. It fell short, and, a vague suspicion having arisen within me, I walked across and picked it up. It was a piece of the grey fungus.

"As I went to her, with it in my hand, she turned deadly pale; then a rose red.

"I felt strangely dazed and frightened.

" 'My dear! My dear!' I said, and could say no more. Yet, at my words, she broke down and cried bitterly. Gradually, as she calmed, I got from her the news that she had tried it the preceding day, and —and liked it. I got her to promise on her knees not to touch it again, however great our hunger. After she had promised, she told me that the desire for it had come suddenly, and that, until the moment of desire, she had experienced nothing towards it, but the most extreme repulsion.

"Later in the day, feeling strangely restless, and much shaken with the thing which I had discovered, I made my way along one of the twisted paths—formed by the white, sand-like substance—which led among the fungoid growth. I had, once before, ventured along there; but not to any great distance. This time, being involved in perplexing thought, I went much further than hitherto.

"Suddenly, I was called to myself, by a queer hoarse sound on my left. Turning quickly, I saw that there was movement among an extraordinarily shaped mass of fungus, close to my elbow. It was swaying uneasily, as though it possessed life of its own. Abruptly, as I stared, the thought came to me that the thing had a grotesque resemblance to the figure of a distorted human creature. Even as the fancy flashed into my brain, there was a slight, sickening noise of tearing, and I saw that one of the branch-like arms was detaching itself from the surrounding grey masses, and coming towards me. The head of the thing—a shapeless grey ball, inclined in my direction. I stood stupidly, and the vile arm brushed across my face. I gave out a frightened cry, and ran back a few paces. There was a sweetish taste upon my lips, where the thing had touched me. I licked them, and was immediately filled with an inhuman desire. I turned and seized a mass of the fungus. Then more, and—more. I was insatiable. In the midst of devouring, the remembrance of the morning's discovery swept into my mazed brain. It was sent by God. I dashed the fragment I held to the ground. Then, utterly wretched and feeling a dreadful guiltiness, I made my way back to the little encampment.

"I think she knew, by some marvellous intuition which love must have given, so soon as she set eyes on me. Her quiet sympathy made it easier for me, and I told her of my sudden weakness; yet omitted to mention the extraordinary thing which had gone before. I desired to spare her all unnecessary terror.

"But, for myself, I had added an intolerable knowledge, to breed an incessant terror in my brain; for I doubted not but that I had seen the end of one of those men who had come to the island in the ship in the lagoon; and in that monstrous ending, I had seen our own.

"Thereafter, we kept from the abominable food, though the desire for it had entered into our blood. Yet, our drear punishment was upon us; for, day by day, with monstrous rapidity, the fungoid growth took hold of our poor bodies. Nothing we could do would check it materially, and so—and so—we who had been human, became—Well, it matters less each day. Only—only we had been man and maid!

"And day by day, the fight is more dreadful, to withstand the hunger-lust for the terrible lichen.

"A week ago we ate the last of the biscuit, and since that time I have caught three fish. I was out here fishing tonight, when your schooner drifted upon me out of the mist. I hailed you. You know the rest, and may God, out of His great heart, bless you for your goodness to a—a couple of poor outcast souls."

There was the dip of an oar—another. Then the voice came again, and for the last time, sounding through the slight surrounding mist, ghostly and mournful.

"God bless you! Good-bye!"

"Good-bye," we shouted together, hoarsely, our hearts full of many emotions.

I glanced about me. I became aware that the dawn was upon us.

The sun flung a stray beam across the hidden sea; pierced the mist dully, and lit up the receding boat with a gloomy fire. Indistinctly, I saw something nodding between the oars. I thought of a sponge—a great, grey nodding sponge—The oars continued to ply. They were grey—as was the boat—and my eyes searched a moment vainly for the conjunction of hand and oar. My gaze flashed back to the—head. It nodded forward as the oars went backward for the stroke. Then the oars were dipped, the boat shot out of the patch of light, and the—the thing went nodding into the mist.

The Shadow Out of Time

H. P. LOVECRAFT

[1890–1937]

The greatest American writer of ghostly horror since Poe was a retiring, eccentric, and ultimately sickly individual who never lived to see his stories reach the wide audience they have today. The tales and novellas that once brought in barely enough money to keep Lovecraft alive are now constantly reprinted and continually praised. "The Shadow Out of Time," *one of his very best, is a cornerstone in the elaborate "Cthulhu mythos" that became Lovecraft's primary contribution to the genre. This story displays Lovecraft's highly effective method of advancing supernatural material under the guise of an empirical, scientific approach—a method that makes things all the more terrifying for readers of a century perhaps less affected by haunted castles and parlor ghosts.*

I

After twenty-two years of nightmare and terror, saved only by a desperate conviction of the mythical source of certain impressions, I am unwilling to vouch for the truth of that which I think I found in Western Australia on the night of July 17–18, 1935. There is reason to hope that my experience was wholly or partly an hallucination—for which, indeed, abundant causes existed. And yet, its realism was so hideous that I sometimes find hope impossible.

If the thing did happen, then man must be prepared to accept notions of the cosmos, and of his own place in the seething vortex of time, whose merest mention is paralyzing. He must, too, be placed on guard against a specific, lurking peril which, though it will never engulf the whole race, may impose monstrous and unguessable horrors upon certain venturesome members of it.

It is for this latter reason that I urge, with all the force of my being, a final abandonment of all the attempts at unearthing those fragments of unknown, primordial masonry which my expedition set out to investigate.

Assuming that I was sane and awake, my experience on that night was such as has befallen no man before. It was, moreover, a frightful confirmation of all I had sought to dismiss as myth and dream. Mercifully there is no proof, for in my fright I lost the awesome object which would—if real and brought out of that noxious abyss—have formed irrefutable evidence.

When I came upon the horror I was alone—and I have up to now told no one about it. I could not stop the others from digging in its direction, but chance and the shifting sand have so far saved them from finding it. Now I must formulate some definite statement—not only for the sake of my own mental balance, but to warn such others as may read it seriously.

These pages—much in whose earlier parts will be familiar to close readers of the general and scientific press—are written in the cabin of the ship that is bringing me home. I shall give them to my son, Professor Wingate Peaslee of Miskatonic University—the only member of my family who stuck to me after my queer amnesia of long ago, and the man best informed on the inner facts of my case. Of all living persons, he is least likely to ridicule what I shall tell of that fateful night.

I did not enlighten him orally before sailing, because I think he had better have the revelation in written form. Reading and rereading at leisure will leave with him a more convincing picture than my confused tongue could hope to convey.

He can do anything that he thinks best with this account—showing it, with suitable comment, in any quarters where it will be likely to accomplish good. It is for the sake of such readers as are unfamiliar with the earlier phases of my case that I am prefacing the revelation itself with a fairly ample summary of its background.

My name is Nathaniel Wingate Peaslee, and those who recall the newspaper tales of a generation back—or the letters and articles in psychological journals six or seven years ago—will know who and what I am. The press was filled with the details of my strange amnesia in 1908–13, and much was made of the traditions of horror, madness, and witchcraft which lurked behind the ancient Massachusetts town then and now forming my place of residence. Yet I would have it known that there is nothing whatever of the mad or sinister in my heredity and early life. This is a highly important fact in view of the shadow which fell so suddenly upon me from *outside* sources.

It may be that centuries of dark brooding had given to crumbling, whisper-haunted Arkham a peculiar vulnerability as regards such shadows—though even this seems doubtful in the light of those other cases which I later came to study. But the chief point is that my own ancestry and background are altogether normal. What came, came from *somewhere else*—where, I even now hesitate to assert in plain words.

I am the son of Jonathan and Hannah (Wingate) Peaslee, both of wholesome old Haverhill stock. I was born and reared in Haverhill—at the old homestead in Boardman Street near Golden Hill—and did not go to Arkham till I entered Miskatonic University as instructor of political economy in 1895.

For thirteen years more my life ran smoothly and happily. I married Alice Keezar of Haverhill in 1896, and my three children, Robert, Wingate and Hannah were born in 1898, 1900, and 1903, respectively. In 1898 I became an associate professor, and in 1902 a full professor. At no time had I the least interest in either occultism or abnormal psychology.

It was on Thursday, May 14, 1908, that the queer amnesia came. The thing was quite sudden, though later I realized that certain brief, glimmering visions of several hours previous—chaotic visions which disturbed me greatly because they were so unprecedented—must have formed premonitory symptoms. My head was aching, and I had a singular feeling—altogether new to me—that some one else was trying to get possession of my thoughts.

The collapse occurred about 10:20 A.M., while I was conducting a class in Political Economy VI—history and present tendencies of economics—for juniors and a few sophomores. I began to see strange shapes before my eyes, and to feel that I was in a grotesque room other than the classroom.

My thoughts and speech wandered from my subject, and the students saw that something was gravely amiss. Then I slumped down, unconscious, in my chair, in a stupor from which no one could arouse me. Nor did my rightful faculties again look out upon the daylight of our normal world for five years, four months, and thirteen days.

It is, of course, from others that I have learned what followed. I showed no sign of consciousness for sixteen and a half hours, though removed to my home at 27 Crane Street, and given the best of medical attention.

At 3 A.M. May 15th my eyes opened and I began to speak, but

before long the doctor and my family were thoroughly frightened by the trend of my expression and language. It was clear that I had no remembrance of my identity and my past, though for some reason I seemed anxious to conceal this lack of knowledge. My eyes gazed strangely at the persons around me, and the flections of my facial muscles were altogether unfamiliar.

Even my speech seemed awkward and foreign. I used my vocal organs clumsily and gropingly, and my diction had a curiously stilted quality, as if I had laboriously learned the English language from books. The pronunciation was barbarously alien, whilst the idiom seemed to include both scraps of curious archaism and expressions of a wholly incomprehensible cast.

Of the latter, one in particular was very potently—even terrifiedly—recalled by the youngest of the physicians twenty years afterward. For at that late period such a phrase began to have an actual currency—first in England and then in the United States—and though of much complexity and indisputable newness, it reproduced in every least particular the mystifying words of the strange Arkham patient of 1908.

Physical strength returned at once, although I required an odd amount of reeducation in the use of my hands, legs, and bodily apparatus in general. Because of this and other handicaps inherent in the mnemonic lapse, I was for some time kept under strict medical care.

When I saw that my attempts to conceal the lapse had failed, I admitted it openly, and became eager for information of all sorts. Indeed, it seemed to the doctors that I lost interest in my proper personality as soon as I found the case of amnesia accepted as a natural thing.

They noticed that my chief efforts were to master certain points in history, science, art, language, and folklore—some of them tremendously abstruse, and some childishly simple—which remained, very oddly in many cases, outside my consciousness.

At the same time they noticed that I had an inexplicable command of many almost unknown sorts of knowledge—a command which I seemed to wish to hide rather than display. I would inadvertently refer, with casual assurance, to specific events in dim ages outside of the range of accepted history—passing off such references as a jest when I saw the surprise they created. And I had a way of speaking of the future which two or three times caused actual fright.

These uncanny flashes soon ceased to appear, though some observers laid their vanishment more to a certain furtive caution on my part than to any waning of the strange knowledge behind them. Indeed, I seemed anomalously avid to absorb the speech, customs, and perspectives of the age around me; as if I were a studious traveler from a far, foreign land.

As soon as permitted, I haunted the college library at all hours; and shortly began to arrange for those odd travels, and special courses at American and European Universities, which evoked so much comment during the next few years.

I did not at any time suffer from a lack of learned contacts, for my case had a mild celebrity among the psychologists of the period. I was lectured upon as a typical example of secondary personality—even though I seemed to puzzle the lecturers now and then with some bizarre symptoms or some queer trace of carefully veiled mockery.

Of real friendliness, however, I encountered little. Something in my aspect and speech seemed to excite vague fears and aversions in every one I met, as if I were a being infinitely removed from all that is normal and healthful. This idea of a black, hidden horror connected with incalculable gulfs of some sort of *distance* was oddly widespread and persistent.

My own family formed no exception. From the moment of my strange waking my wife had regarded me with extreme horror and loathing, vowing that I was some utter alien usurping the body of her husband. In 1910 she obtained a legal divorce, nor would she ever consent to see me even after my return to normality in 1913. These feelings were shared by my elder son and my small daughter, neither of whom I have ever seen since.

Only my second son, Wingate, seemed able to conquer the terror and repulsion which my change aroused. He indeed felt that I was a stranger, but though only eight years old held fast to a faith that my proper self would return. When it did return he sought me out, and the courts gave me his custody. In succeeding years he helped me with the studies to which I was driven, and today, at thirty-five, he is a professor of psychology at Miskatonic.

But I do not wonder at the horror I caused—for certainly, the mind, voice, and facial expression of the being that awakened on May 15, 1908, were not those of Nathaniel Wingate Peaslee.

I will not attempt to tell much of my life from 1908 to 1913, since readers may glean all the outward essentials—as I largely had to do—from files of old newspapers and scientific journals.

I was given charge of my funds, and spent them slowly and on the whole wisely, in travel and in study at various centers of learning. My travels, however, were singular in extreme, involving long visits to remote and desolate places.

In 1909 I spent a month in the Himalayas, and in 1911 aroused much attention through a camel trip into the unknown deserts of Arabia. What happened on those journeys I have never been able to learn.

During the summer of 1912 I chartered a ship and sailed in the Arctic, north of Spitzbergen, afterward showing signs of disappointment.

Later in that year I spent weeks alone beyond the limits of previous or subsequent exploration in the vast limestone cavern systems of western Virginia—black labyrinths so complex that no retracing of my steps could even be considered.

My sojourns at the universities were marked by abnormally rapid assimilation, as if the secondary personality had an intelligence enormously superior to my own. I have found, also, that my rate of reading and solitary study was phenomenal. I could master every detail of a book merely by glancing over it as fast as I could turn the leaves; while my skill at interpreting complex figures in an instant was veritably awesome.

At times there appeared almost ugly reports of my power to influence the thoughts and acts of others, though I seemed to have taken care to minimize displays of this faculty.

Other ugly reports concerned my intimacy with leaders of occultist groups, and scholars suspected of connection with nameless bands of abhorrent elder-world hierophants. These rumors, though never proved at the time, were doubtless stimulated by the known tenor of some of my reading—for the consultation of rare books at libraries cannot be effected secretly.

There is tangible proof—in the form of marginal notes—that I went minutely through such things as the Comte d'Erlette's *Cultes des Goules,* Ludvig Prinn's *De Vermis Mysteriis,* the *Unaussprechlichen Kulten* of von Junzt, the surviving fragments of the puzzling *Book of Eibon,* and the dreaded *Necronomicon* of the mad Arab Abdul Alhazred. Then, too, it is undeniable that a fresh and evil wave of underground cult activity set in about the time of my odd mutation.

In the summer of 1913 I began to display signs of ennui and flagging interest, and to hint to various associates that a change might soon be expected in me. I spoke of returning memories of my earlier life—though most auditors judged me insincere, since all the recollections I gave were casual, and such as might have been learned from my old private papers.

About the middle of August I returned to Arkham and reopened my long-closed house in Crane Street. Here I installed a mechanism of the most curious aspect, constructed piecemeal by different makers of scientific apparatus in Europe and America, and guarded carefully from the sight of any one intelligent enough to analyze it.

Those who did see it—a workman, a servant, and the new housekeeper—say that it was a queer mixture of rods, wheels, and mirrors, though only about two feet tall, one foot wide, and one foot thick. The central mirror was circular and convex. All this is borne out by such makers of parts as can be located.

On the evening of Friday, September 26, I dismissed the housekeeper and the maid until noon of the next day. Lights burned in the house till late, and a lean, dark, curiously foreign-looking man called in an automobile.

It was about one A.M. that the lights were last seen. At 2:15 A.M. a policeman observed the place in darkness, but the stranger's motor still at the curb. By four o'clock the motor was certainly gone.

It was at six o'clock that a hesitant, foreign voice on the telephone asked Dr. Wilson to call at my house and bring me out of a peculiar faint. This call—a long-distance one—was later traced to a public booth in the North Station in Boston, but no sign of the lean foreigner was ever unearthed.

When the doctor reached my house he found me unconscious in the sitting room—in an easy-chair with a table drawn up before it. On the polished top were scratches showing where some heavy object had rested. The queer machine was gone, nor was anything afterward heard of it. Undoubtedly the dark, lean foreigner had taken it away.

In the library grate were abundant ashes, evidently left from the burning of every remaining scrap of paper on which I had written since the advent of the amnesia. Dr. Wilson found my breathing very peculiar, but after a hypodermic injection it became more regular.

At 11:15 A.M., September 27th, I stirred vigorously, and my hitherto masklike face began to show signs of expression. Dr. Wilson remarked that the expression was not that of my secondary personality, but seemed much like that of my normal self. About 11:30 I muttered some very curious syllables—syllables which seemed unrelated to any human speech. I appeared, too, to struggle against something. Then, just after noon—the housekeeper and the maid having meanwhile returned—I began to mutter in English.

"—of the orthodox economists of that period, Jevons typifies the prevailing trend toward scientific correlation. His attempt to link the commercial cycle of prosperity and depression with the physical cycle of the solar spots forms perhaps the apex of—"

Nathaniel Wingate Peaslee had come back—a spirit in whose time scale it was still Thursday morning in 1908, with the economics class gazing up at the battered desk on the platform.

II

My reabsorption into normal life was a painful and difficult process. The loss of over five years creates more complications than can be imagined, and in my case there were countless matters to be adjusted.

What I heard of my actions since 1908 astonished and disturbed me, but I tried to view the matter as philosophically as I could. At last, regaining custody of my second son, Wingate, I settled down with him in the Crane Street house and endeavored to resume my teaching—my old professorship having been kindly offered me by the college.

I began work with the February, 1914, term, and kept at it just a year. By that time I realized how badly my experience had shaken me. Though perfectly sane—I hoped—and with no flaw in my original personality, I had not the nervous energy of the old days. Vague dreams and queer ideas continually haunted me, and when the outbreak of the World War turned my mind to history I found myself thinking of periods and events in the oddest possible fashion.

My conception of *time*—my ability to distinguish between consecutiveness and simultaneousness—seemed subtly disordered; so that I formed chimerical notions about living in one age and casting one's mind all over eternity for knowledge of past and future ages.

The War gave me strange impressions of remembering some of its far-off consequences—as if I knew how it was coming out and could look *back* upon it in the light of future information. All such quasi-memories were attended with much pain, and with a feeling that some artificial psychological barrier was set against them.

When I diffidently hinted to others about my impressions, I met with varied responses. Some persons looked uncomfortably at me, but men in the mathematics department spoke of new developments in those theories of relativity—then discussed only in learned circles—which were later to become so famous. Dr. Albert Einstein, they said, was rapidly reducing time to the status of a mere dimension.

But the dreams and disturbed feelings gained on me, so that I had to drop my regular work in 1915. Certain of the impressions were taking an annoying shape—giving me the persistent notion that my amnesia had formed some unholy sort of exchange; that the secondary personality had indeed been an intruding force from unknown regions, and that my own personality had suffered displacement.

Thus I was driven to vague and frightful speculations concerning the whereabouts of my true self during the years that another had held my body. The curious knowledge and strange conduct of my body's late tenant troubled me more and more as I learned further details from persons, papers, and magazines.

Queerness that had baffled others seemed to harmonize terribly with some background of black knowledge which festered in the chasms of my subconsciousness. I began to search feverishly for every scrap of information bearing on the studies and travels of that other one during the dark years.

Not all of my troubles were as semi-abstract as this. There were the dreams—and these seemed to grow in vividness and concreteness. Knowing how most would regard them, I seldom mentioned them to any one but my son or certain trusted psychologists, but eventually I commenced a scientific study of other cases in order to see how typical or nontypical such visions might be among amnesia victims.

My results, aided by psychologists, historians, anthropologists, and mental specialists of wide experience, and by a study that included all records of split personalities from the days of demoniac-possession legends to the medically realistic present, at first bothered me more than they consoled me.

I soon found that my dreams had, indeed, no counterpart in the overwhelming bulk of true amnesia cases. There remained, however, a tiny residue of accounts which for years baffled and shocked me with their parallelism to my own experience. Some of them were bits of ancient folklore; others were case histories in the annals of medicine; one or two were anecdotes obscurely buried in standard histories.

It thus appeared that, while my special kind of affliction was prodigiously rare, instances of it had occurred at long intervals ever since the beginning of men's annals. Some centuries might contain one, two, or three cases, others none—or at least none whose record survived.

The essence was always the same—a person of keen thoughtfulness seized with a strange secondary life and leading for a greater or lesser period an utterly alien existence typified at first by vocal and bodily awkwardness, and later by a wholesale acquisition of scientific, historic, artistic, and anthropological knowledge; an acquisition carried on with feverish zest and with a wholly abnormal absorptive power. Then a sudden return of the rightful consciousness, intermittently plagued ever after with vague unplaceable dreams suggesting fragments of some hideous memory elaborately blotted out.

And the close resemblance of those nightmares to my own—even in some of the smallest particulars—left no doubt in my mind of their significantly typical nature. One or two of the cases had an added ring of faint, blasphemous familiarity, as if I had heard of them before through some cosmic channel too morbid and frightful to contemplate. In three instances there was specific mention of such an unknown machine as had been in my house before the second change.

Another thing that worried me during my investigation was the somewhat greater frequency of cases where a brief, elusive glimpse of the typical nightmares was afforded to persons not visited with well-defined amnesia.

These persons were largely of mediocre mind or less—some so primitive that they could scarcely be thought of as vehicles for abnormal scholarship and preternatural mental acquisitions. For a second they would be fired with alien force—then a backward lapse, and a thin, swift-fading memory of unhuman horrors.

There had been at least three such cases during the past half century—one only fifteen years before. Had something been groping blindly through time from some unsuspected abyss in nature? Were these faint cases monstrous, sinister experiments of a kind and authorship utterly beyond sane belief?

Such were a few of the formless speculations of my weaker hours—fancies abetted by myths which my studies uncovered. For I could not doubt but that certain persistent legends of immemorial antiquity apparently unknown to the victims and physicians connected with recent amnesia cases, formed a striking and awesome elaboration of memory lapses such as mine.

Of the nature of the dreams and impressions which were growing so clamorous I still almost fear to speak. They seemed to savor of madness, and at times I believed I was indeed going mad. Was there a special type of delusion afflicting those who had suffered lapses of memory? Conceivably, the efforts of the subconscious mind to fill up a perplexing blank with pseudomemories might give rise to strange imaginative vagaries.

This, indeed—though an alternative folklore theory finally seemed to me more plausible—was the belief of many of the alienists who helped me in my search for parallel cases, and who shared my puzzlement at the exact resemblances sometimes discovered.

They did not call the condition pure insanity, but classed it rather among neurotic disorders. My course in trying to track down and analyse it, instead of vainly seeking to dismiss or forget it, they heartily endorsed as correct according to the best psychological principles. I especially valued the advice of such physicians as had studied me during my possession by the other personality.

My first disturbances were not visual at all, but concerned the more abstract matters which I have mentioned. There was, too, a feeling of profound and inexplicable horror concerning myself. I developed a queer fear of seeing my own form, as if my eyes would find it something utterly alien and inconceivably abhorrent.

When I did glance down and behold the familiar human shape in quiet gray or blue clothing, I always felt a curious relief, though in order to gain this relief I had to conquer an infinite dread. I shunned mirrors as much as possible, and was always shaved at the barber's.

It was a long time before I correlated any of these disappointed feelings with the fleeting visual impressions which began to develop. The first such correlation had to do with the odd sensation of an external, artificial restraint on my memory.

I felt that the snatches of sight I experienced had a profound and terrible meaning, and a frightful connection with myself, but that some purposeful influence held me from grasping that meaning and that connection. Then came that queerness about the element of time, and with it desperate efforts to place the fragmentary dream glimpses in the chronological and spatial pattern.

The glimpses themselves were at first merely strange rather than horrible. I would seem to be in an enormous vaulted chamber whose lofty stone groinings were well nigh lost in the shadows overhead. In whatever time or place the scene might be, the principle of the arch was known as fully and used as extensively as by the Romans.

There were colossal, round windows and high, arched doors, and pedestals or tables each as tall as the height of an ordinary room. Vast shelves of dark wood lined the walls, holding what seemed to be volumes of immense size with strange hieroglyphs on their backs.

The exposed stonework held curious carvings, always in curvilinear mathematical designs, and there were chiseled inscriptions in the same characters that the huge books bore. The dark granite masonry was of a monstrous megalithic type, with lines of convex-topped blocks fitting the concave-bottomed courses which rested upon them.

There were no chairs, but the tops of the vast pedestals were littered with books, papers, and what seemed to be writing materials —oddly figured jars of a purplish metal, and rods with stained tips. Tall as the pedestals were, I seemed at times able to view them from above. On some of them were great globes of luminous crystal serving as lamps, and inexplicable machines formed of vitreous tubes and metal rods.

The windows were glazed, and latticed with stout-looking bars. Though I dared not approach and peer out them, I could see from where I was the waving tops of singular fernlike growths. The floor was of massive octagonal flagstones, while rugs and hangings were entirely lacking.

Later, I had visions of sweeping through cyclopean corridors of stone, and up and down gigantic inclined planes of the same monstrous masonry. There were no stairs anywhere, nor was any passageway less than thirty feet wide. Some of the structures through which I floated must have towered in the sky for thousands of feet.

There were multiple levels of black vaults below, and never-opened trap-doors, sealed down with metal bands and holding dim suggestions of some special peril.

I seemed to be a prisoner, and horror hung broodingly over everything I saw. I felt that the mocking curvilinear hieroglyphs on the walls would blast my soul with their message were I not guarded by a merciful ignorance.

Still later my dreams included vistas from the great round windows, and from the titanic flat roof, with its curious gardens, wide barren area, and high, scalloped parapet of stone, to which the topmost of the inclined planes led.

There were almost endless leagues of giant buildings, each in its garden, and ranged along paved roads fully two hundred feet wide. They differed greatly in aspect, but few were less than five hundred feet square or a thousand feet high. Many seemed so limitless that they must have had a frontage of several thousand feet, while some shot up to mountainous altitudes in the gray, steamy heavens.

They seemed to be mainly of stone or concrete, and most of them embodied the oddly curvilinear type of masonry noticeable in the building that held me. Roofs were flat and garden-covered, and tended to have scalloped parapets. Sometimes there were terraces and higher levels, and wide, cleared spaces amidst the gardens. The great roads held hints of motion, but in the earlier visions I could not resolve this impression into details.

In certain places I beheld enormous dark cylindrical towers which climbed far above any of the other structures. These appeared to be of a totally unique nature and showed signs of prodigious age and dilapidation. They were built of a bizarre type of square-cut basalt masonry, and tapered slightly toward their rounded tops. Nowhere in any of them could the least traces of windows or other apertures save huge doors be found. I noticed also some lower buildings—all crumbling with the weathering of aeons—which resembled these dark, cylindrical towers in basic architecture. Around all these aberrant piles of square-cut masonry there hovered an inexplicable aura of menace and concentrated fear, like that bred by the sealed trapdoors.

The omnipresent gardens were almost terrifying in their strangeness, with bizarre and unfamiliar forms of vegetation nodding over broad paths lined with curiously carven monoliths. Abnormally vast fernlike growths predominated—some green, and some of a ghastly, fungoid pallor.

Among them rose great spectral things resembling calamites, whose bamboo-like trunks towered to fabulous heights. Then there were tufted forms like fabulous cycades, and grotesque dark-green shrubs and trees of coniferous aspect.

Flowers were small, colorless, and unrecognizable, blooming in geometrical beds and at large among the greenery.

In a few of the terrace and roof-top gardens were larger and more vivid blossoms of almost offensive contours and seeming to suggest artificial breeding. Fungi of inconceivable size, outlines, and colors speckled the scene in patterns bespeaking some unknown but well-established horticultural tradition. In the larger gardens on the ground there seemed to be some attempt to preserve the irregularities of nature, but on the roofs there was more selectiveness, and more evidences of the topiary art.

The skies were almost always moist and cloudy, and sometimes I would seem to witness tremendous rains. Once in a while, though, there would be glimpses of the sun—which looked abnormally large—and of the moon, whose markings held a touch of difference from the normal that I could never quite fathom. When—very rarely—the night sky was clear to any extent, I beheld constellations which were nearly beyond recognition. Known outlines were sometimes approximated, but seldom duplicated; and from the position of the few groups I could recognize, I felt I must be in the earth's southern hemisphere, near the Tropic of Capricorn.

The far horizon was always steamy and indistinct, but I could see that great jungles of unknown tree ferns, Calamites, Lepidodendro, and Sigillaria lay outside the city, their fantastic frondage waving mockingly in the shifting vapors. Now and then there would be suggestions of motion in the sky, but these my early visions never resolved.

By the autumn of 1914 I began to have infrequent dreams of strange floatings over the city and through the regions around it. I saw interminable roads through forests of fearsome growths with mottled, fluted, and banded trunks, and past other cities as strange as the one which persistently haunted me.

I saw monstrous constructions of black or iridescent stone in glades and clearings where perpetual twilight reigned, and traversed long causeways over swamps so dark that I could tell but little of their moist, towering vegetation.

Once I saw an area of countless miles strewn with age-blasted basaltic ruins whose architecture had been like that of the few windowless, round-topped towers in the haunting city.

And once I saw the sea—a boundless, steamy expanse beyond the colossal stone piers of an enormous town of domes and arches. Great shapeless suggestions of shadow moved over it, and here and there its surface was vexed with anomalous spoutings.

III

As I have said, it was not immediately that these wild visions began to hold their terrifying quality. Certainly, many persons have dreamed intrinsically stranger things—things compounded of unrelated scraps of daily life, pictures, and reading, and arranged in fantastically novel forms by the unchecked caprices of sleep.

For some time I accepted the visions as natural, even though I had never before been an extravagant dreamer. Many of the vague anomalies, I argued, must have come from trivial sources too numerous to track down; while others seemed to reflect a common textbook knowledge of the plants and other conditions of the primitive world of a hundred and fifty million years ago—the world of the Permian or Triassic Age.

In the course of some months, however, the element of terror did figure with accumulating force. This was when the dreams began so unfailingly to have the aspect of memories, and when my mind began to link them with my growing abstract disturbances—the feeling of mnemonic restraint, the curious impressions regarding time, the sense of a loathsome exchange with my secondary personality of 1908–13, and, considerably later, the inexplicable loathing of my own person.

As certain definite details began to enter the dreams, their horror increased a thousandfold—until by October, 1915, I felt I must do something. It was then that I began an intensive study of other cases of amnesia and visions, feeling that I might thereby objectivize my trouble and shake clear of its emotional grip.

However, as before mentioned, the result was at first almost exactly opposite. It disturbed me vastly to find that my dreams had been so closely duplicated; especially since some of the accounts were too early to admit of any geological knowledge—and therefore of any idea of primitive landscapes—on the subjects' part.

What is more, many of these accounts supplied very horrible details and explanations in connection with the visions of great buildings and jungle gardens—and other things. The actual sights and vague impressions were bad enough, but what was hinted or asserted by some of the other dreamers savored of madness and blasphemy. Worst of all, my own pseudomemory was aroused to wilder dreams and hints of coming revelations. And yet most doctors deemed my course, on the whole, an advisable one.

I studied psychology systematically, and under the prevailing stimulus my son Wingate did the same—his studies leading eventually to his present professorship. In 1917 and 1918 I took special courses at Miskatonic. Meanwhile, my examination of medical, historical, and anthropological records became indefatigable, involving travels to distant libraries, and finally including even a reading of the hideous books of forbidden lore in which my secondary personality had been so disturbingly interested.

Some of the latter were the actual copies I had consulted in my altered state, and I was greatly disturbed by certain marginal notations and ostensible *corrections* of the hideous text in a script and idiom which somehow seemed oddly unhuman.

These markings were mostly in the respective languages of the various books, all of which the writer seemed to know with equal, though obviously, academic facility. One note appended to von Junzt's *Unaussprechlichen Kulten,* however, was alarmingly otherwise. It consisted of certain curvilinear hieroglyphs in the same ink as that of the German corrections, but following no recognized human pattern. And these hieroglyphs were closely and unmistakably akin to the characters constantly met with in my dreams—characters whose meaning I would sometimes momentarily fancy I knew, or was just on the brink of recalling.

To complete my black confusion, many librarians assured me that, in view of previous examinations and records of consultation of the volumes in question, all of these notations must have been made by myself in my secondary state. This despite the fact that I was and still am ignorant of three of the languages involved. Piecing together the scattered records, ancient and modern, anthropological and medical, I found a fairly consistent mixture of myth and hallucination whose scope and wildness left me utterly dazed. Only one thing consoled me: the fact that the myths were of such early existence. What lost knowledge could have brought pictures of the Paleozoic or Mesozoic landscape into these primitive fables, I could not even guess; but the pictures had been there. Thus, a basis existed for the formation of a fixed type of delusion.

Cases of amnesia no doubt created the general myth pattern—but afterward the fanciful accretions of the myths must have reacted on amnesia sufferers and colored their pseudomemories. I myself had read and heard all the early tales during my memory lapse—my quest had amply proved that. Was it not natural, then, for my subsequent dreams and emotional impressions to become colored and molded by what my memory subtly held over from my secondary state?

A few of the myths had significant connections with other cloudy legends of the prehuman world, especially those Hindu tales involving stupefying gulfs of time and forming part of the lore of modern theosophists.

Primal myth and modern delusion joined in their assumption that mankind is only one—perhaps the least—of the highly evolved and dominant races of this planet's long and largely unknown career. Things of inconceivable shape, they implied, had reared towers to the sky and delved into every secret of nature before the first amphibian forbear of man had crawled out of the hot sea three hundred million years ago.

Some had come down from the stars; a few were as old as the cosmos itself; others had arisen swiftly from terrane germs as far behind the first germs of our life cycle as those germs are behind ourselves. Spans of thousands of millions of years, and linkages of other galaxies and universes, were spoken of. Indeed, there was no such thing as time in its humanly accepted sense.

But most of the tales and impressions concerned a relatively late race, of a queer and intricate shape, resembling no life form known to science, which had lived till only fifty million years before the advent of man. This, they indicated, was the greatest race of all because it alone had conquered the secret of time.

It had learned all things that ever were known or ever would be known on the Earth, through the power of its keener minds to project themselves into the past and future, even through gulfs of millions of years, and study the lore of every age. From the accomplishments of this race arose all legends of prophets, including those in human mythology.

In its vast libraries were volumes of texts and pictures holding the whole of Earth's annals—histories and descriptions of every species that had ever been or that ever would be, with full records of their arts, their achievements, their languages, and their psychologies.

With this aeon-embracing knowledge, the Great Race chose from every era and life form such thoughts, arts, and processes as might suit its own nature and situation. Knowledge of the past, secured through a kind of mindcasting outside the recognized senses, was harder to glean than knowledge of the future.

In the latter case the course was easier and more material. With suitable mechanical aid a mind would project itself forward in time, feeling its dim, extra-sensory way till it approached the desired period. Then, after preliminary trials, it would seize on the best discoverable representative of the highest of that period's life forms. It would enter the organism's brain and set up therein its own vibrations, while the displaced mind would strike back to the period of the displacer, remaining in the latter's body till a reverse process was set up.

The projected mind, in the body of the organism of the future, would then pose as a member of the race whose outward form it wore, learning as quickly as possible all that could be learned of the chosen age and its massed information and techniques.

Meanwhile the displaced mind, thrown back to the displacer's age and body, would be carefully guarded. It would be kept from harming the body it occupied, and would be drained of all its knowledge by trained questioners. Often it could be questioned in its own language, when previous quests into the future had brought back records of that language.

If the mind came from a body whose language the Great Race could not physically reproduce, clever machines would be made, on which the alien speech could be played as on a musical instrument.

The Great Race's members were immense rugose cones ten feet high, and with head and other organs attached to foot-thick distensible limbs spreading from the apexes. They spoke by the clicking or scraping of huge paws or claws attached to the end of two of their four limbs, and walked by the expansion and contraction of a viscous layer attached to their vast, ten-foot bases.

When the captive mind's amazement and resentment had worn off, and when—assuming that it came from a body vastly different from the Great Race's—it had lost its horror at its unfamiliar, temporary form, it was permitted to study its new environment and experience a wonder and wisdom approximating that of its displacer.

With suitable precautions, and in exchange for suitable services, it was allowed to rove all over the habitable world in titan airships or on the huge boat-like atomic-engined vehicles which traversed the great roads, and to delve freely into the libraries containing the records of the planet's past and future.

This reconciled many captive minds to their lot; since none were other than keen, and to such minds the unveiling of hidden mysteries of Earth—closed chapters of inconceivable pasts and dizzying vortices of future time which include the years ahead of their own natural ages—forms always, despite the abysmal horrors often unveiled, the supreme experience of life.

Now and then certain captives were permitted to meet other captive minds seized from the future—to exchange thoughts with consciousnesses living a hundred or a thousand or a million years before or after their own ages. And all were urged to write copiously in their own languages of themselves and their respective periods, such documents to be filed in the great central archives.

It may be added that there was one special type of captive whose privileges were far greater than those of the majority. These were the dying *permanent* exiles, whose bodies in the future had been seized by keen-minded members of the Great Race who, faced with death, sought to escape mental extinction.

Such melancholy exiles were not as common as might be expected, since the longevity of the Great Race lessened its love of life —especially among those superior minds capable of projection. From cases of the permanent projection of elder minds arose many of those lasting changes of personality noticed in later history—including mankind's.

As for the ordinary cases of exploration—when the displacing mind had learned what it wished in the future, it would build an apparatus like that which had started its flight and reverse the process of projection. Once more it would be in its own body in its own age while the lately captive mind would return to that body of the future to which it properly belonged.

Only when one or the other of the bodies had died during the exchange was this restoration impossible. In such cases, of course, the exploring mind had—like those of the death escapers—to live out an alien-bodied life in the future; or else the captive mind—like the dying permanent exiles—had to end its days in the form and past age of the Great Race.

This fate was less horrible when the captive mind was also of the Great Race—a not infrequent occurrence, since in all its periods that race was intensely concerned with its own future. The number of dying permanent exiles of the Great Race was very slight—largely because of the tremendous penalties attached to displacements of future Great Race minds by the moribund.

Through projection, arrangements were made to inflict these penalties on the offending minds in their new future bodies—and sometimes forced reëxchanges were effected.

Complex cases of the displacement of exploring or already captive minds by minds in various regions of the past had been known and carefully rectified. In every age since the discovery of mind projection, a minute but well-recognized element of the population consisted of Great Race minds from past ages, sojourning for a longer or shorter while.

When a captive mind of alien origin was returned to its own

body in the future, it was purged by an intricate mechanical hypnosis of all it had learned in the Great Race's Age—this because of certain troublesome consequences inherent in the general carrying forward of knowledge in large quantities.

The few existing instances of clear transmission had caused, and would cause at known future times, great disasters. And it was largely in consequence of two cases of the kind—said the old myths—that mankind had learned what it had concerning the Great Race.

Of all things surviving physically and directly from that aeon-distant world, there remained only certain ruins of great stones in far places and under the sea, and parts of the text of the frightful Pnakotic Manuscripts.

Thus the returning mind reached its own age with only the faintest and most fragmentary vision of what it had undergone since its seizure. All memories that could be eradicated were eradicated, so that in most cases only a dream-shadowed blank stretched back to the time of the first exchange. Some minds recalled more than others, and the chance joining of memories had at rare times brought hints of the forbidden past to future ages.

There probably never was a time when groups or cults did not secretly cherish certain of these hints. In the *Necronomicon* the presence of such a cult among human beings was suggested—a cult that sometimes gave aid to minds voyaging down the aeons from the days of the Great Race.

And, meanwhile, the Great Race itself waxed well-nigh omniscient, and turned to the task of setting up exchanges with the minds of other planets, and of exploring their pasts and futures. It sought likewise to fathom the past years and origin of that black, aeon-dead orb in far space whence its own mental heritage had come—for the mind of the Great Race was older than its bodily form.

The beings of a dying elder world, wise with the ultimate secrets, had looked ahead for a new world and species wherein they might have long life, and had sent their minds *en masse* into that future race best adapted to house them—the cone-shaped beings that peopled our earth a billion years ago.

Thus the Great Race came to be, while the myriad minds sent backward were left to die in the horror of strange shapes. Later the race would again face death, yet would live through another forward migration of its best minds into the bodies of others who had a longer physical span ahead of them.

Such was the background of intertwined legend and hallucination. When, around 1920, I had my researches in coherent shape, I felt a slight lessening of the tension which their earlier stages had increased. After all, and in spite of the fancies prompted by blind emotions, were not most of my phenomena readily explainable? Any chance might have turned my mind to dark studies during the amnesia—and then I read the forbidden legends and met the members of ancient and ill-regarded cults. That, plainly, supplied the material for the dreams and disturbed feelings which came after the return of memory.

As for the marginal notes in dream hieroglyphs and languages unknown to me, but laid at my door by librarians—I might easily have picked up a smattering of the tongues during my secondary state, while the hieroglyphs were doubtless coined by my fancy from descriptions in old legends, and afterward woven into my dreams. I tried to verify certain points through conversations with known cult leaders, but never succeeded in establishing the right connections.

At times the parallelism of so many cases in so many distant ages continued to worry me as it had at first, but on the other hand I reflected that the excitant folklore was undoubtedly more universal in the past than in the present.

Probably all the other victims whose cases were like mine had had a long and familiar knowledge of the tales I had learned only when in my secondary state. When these victims had lost their memory, they had associated themselves with the creatures of their household myths—the fabulous invaders supposed to displace men's minds—and had thus embarked upon quests for knowledge which they thought they could take back to a fancied, nonhuman past.

Then, when their memory returned, they reversed the associative process and thought of themselves as the former captive minds instead of as the displacers. Hence the dreams and pseudomemories following the conventional myth pattern.

Despite the seeming cumbrousness of these explanations, they came finally to supersede all others in my mind—largely because of the greater weakness of any rival theory. And a substantial number of eminent psychologists and anthropologists gradually agreed with me.

The more I reflected, the more convincing did my reasoning seem; till in the end I had a really effective bulwark against the visions and impressions which still assailed me. Suppose I did see strange things at night? These were only what I had heard and read of. Suppose I did have odd loathings and perspectives and pseudomemories? These, too, were only echoes of myths absorbed in my secondary state. Nothing that I might dream, nothing that I might feel, could be of any actual significance.

Fortified by this philosophy, I greatly improved in nervous equilibrium, even though the visions—rather than the abstract impressions—steadily became more frequent and more disturbingly detailed. In 1922 I felt able to undertake regular work again, and put my newly gained knowledge to practical use by accepting an instructorship in psychology at the university.

My old chair of political economy had long been adequately filled—besides which, methods of teaching economics had changed greatly since my heyday. My son was at this time just entering on the post-graduate studies leading to his present professorship, and we worked together a great deal.

IV

I continued however, to keep a careful record of the *outré* dreams which crowded upon me so thickly and vividly. Such a record, I argued, was of genuine value as a psychological document. The glimpses still seemed damnably like memories, though I fought off this impression with a goodly measure of success.

In writing, I treated the phantasmata as things seen; but at all other times I brushed them aside like any gossamer illusions of the night. I had never mentioned such matters in common conversation; though reports of them, filtering out as such things will, had aroused sundry rumors regarding my mental health. It is amusing to reflect that these rumors were confined wholly to laymen, without a single champion among physicians or psychologists.

Of my visions after 1914 I will here mention only a few, since fuller accounts and records are at the disposal of the serious student. It is evident that with time the curious inhibitions somewhat waned, for the scope of my visions vastly increased. They have never, though, become other than disjointed fragments seemingly without clear motivation.

Within the dreams I seemed gradually to acquire a greater and greater freedom of wandering. I floated through many strange buildings of stone, going from one to the other along mammoth underground passages which seemed to form the common avenues of transit. Sometimes I encountered those gigantic sealed trapdoors in the lowest level, around which such an aura of fear and forbiddenness clung.

I saw tremendous tessellated pools, and rooms of curious and inexplicable utensils of myriad sorts. Then there were colossal caverns of intricate machinery whose outlines and purpose were wholly strange to me, and whose sound manifested itself only after many years of dreaming. I may here remark that sight and sound are the only senses I have ever exercised in the visionary world.

The real horror began in May, 1915, when I first saw the living things. This was before my studies had taught me what, in view of the myths and case histories, to expect. As mental barriers wore down, I beheld great masses of thin vapor in various parts of the building and in the streets below.

These steadily grew more solid and distinct, till at last I could trace their monstrous outlines with uncomfortable ease. They seemed to be enormous, iridescent cones, about ten feet high and ten feet wide at the base, and made up of some ridgy, scaly, semi-elastic matter. From their apexes projected four flexible, cylindrical members, each a foot thick, and of a ridgy substance like that of the cones themselves.

These members were sometimes contracted almost to nothing, and sometimes extended to any distance up to about ten feet. Terminating two of them were enormous claws or nippers. At the end of a third were four red, trumpetlike appendages. The fourth terminated in an irregular yellowish globe some two feet in diameter and having three great dark eyes ranged along its central circumference.

Surmounting this head were four slender gray stalks bearing flowerlike appendages, whilst from its nether side dangled eight greenish antennae or tentacles. The great base of the central cone was fringed with a rubbery, gray substance which moved the whole entity through expansion and contraction.

Their actions, though harmless, horrified me even more than their appearance—for it is not wholesome to watch monstrous objects doing what one had known only human beings to do. These objects moved intelligently about the great rooms, getting books from the shelves and taking them to the great tables, or *vice versa,* and sometimes writing diligently with a peculiar rod gripped in the greenish head tentacles. The huge nippers were used in carrying books and in conversation—speech consisting of a kind of clicking.

The objects had no clothing, but wore satchels or knapsacks suspended from the top of the conical trunk. They commonly carried their head and its supporting member at the level of the cone top, though it was frequently raised or lowered.

The other three great members tended to rest downward at the sides of the cone, contracted to above five feet each, when not in use. From their rate of reading, writing, and operating their machines—those on the tables seemed somehow connected with thought—I concluded that their intelligence was enormously greater than man's.

Afterward I saw them everywhere; swarming in all the great chambers and corridors, tending monstrous machines in vaulted crypts, and racing along the vast roads in gigantic, boat-shaped cars. I ceased to be afraid of them, for they seemed to form supremely natural parts of their environment.

Individual differences amongst them began to be manifest, and a few appeared to be under some kind of restraint. These latter, though showing no physical variation, had a diversity of gestures and habits which marked them off not only from the majority, but very largely from one another.

They wrote a great deal in what seemed to my cloudy vision a vast variety of characters—never the typical curvilinear hieroglyphs of the majority. A few, I fancied, used our own familiar alphabet. Most of them worked much more slowly than the general mass of the entities.

All this time my own part in the dreams seemed to be that of a disembodied consciousness with a range of vision wider than the normal, floating freely about, yet confined to the ordinary avenues and speeds of travel. Not until August, 1915, did any suggestions of bodily existence begin to harass me. I say harass, because the first phase was a purely abstract, though infinitely terrible, association of my previously noted body-loathing with the scenes of my visions.

For a while my chief concern during dreams was to avoid looking down at myself, and I recall how grateful I was for the total absence of large mirrors in the strange rooms. I was mightily troubled by the fact that I always saw the great tables—whose height could not be under ten feet—from a level not below that of their surfaces.

And then the morbid temptation to look down at myself became greater and greater, till one night I could not resist it. At first my downward glance revealed nothing whatever. A moment later I perceived that this was because my head lay at the end of a flexible neck of enormous length. Retracting this neck and gazing down very sharply, I saw the scaley, rugose, iridescent bulk of a vast cone ten feet tall and ten feet wide at the base. That was when I waked half of Arkham with my screaming as I plunged madly up from the abyss of sleep.

Only after weeks of hideous repetition did I grow half reconciled to these visions of myself in monstrous form. In the dreams I now moved bodily among the other unknown entities, reading terrible books from the endless shelves and writing for hours at the great tables with a stylus managed by the green tentacles that hung down from my head.

Snatches of what I read and wrote would linger in my memory. There were horrible annals of other worlds and other universes, and of stirrings of formless life outside of all universes. There were records of strange orders of beings which had peopled the world in forgotten pasts, and frightful chronicles of grotesque-bodied intelligences which would people it millions of years after the death of the last human being.

I learned of chapters in human history whose existence no scholar of today has ever suspected. Most of these writings were in the language of the hieroglyphs, which I studied in a queer way with the aid of droning machines, and which was evidently an agglutinative speech with root systems utterly unlike any found in human languages.

Other volumes were in other unknown tongues learned in the same queer way. A very few were in languages I knew. Extremely clever pictures, both inserted in the records and forming separate collections, aided me immensely. And all the time I seemed to be setting down a history of my own age in English. On waking, I could recall only minute and meaningless scraps of the unknown tongues which my dream self had mastered, though whole phrases of the history stayed with me.

I learned—even before my waking self had studied the parallel cases or the old myths from which the dreams doubtless sprang—that the entities around me were of the world's greatest race, which had conquered time and had sent exploring minds into every age. I knew, too, that I had been snatched from my age, while another used my body in that age, and that a few of the other strange forms housed similarly captured minds. I seemed to talk, in some odd language of claw clicking, with exiled intellects from every corner of the solar system.

There was a mind from the planet we know as Venus, which would live incalculable epochs to come, and one from an outer moon of Jupiter six million years in the past. Of earthly minds there were some from the winged, star-headed, half-vegetable race of paleogean Antarctica; one from the reptile people of fabled Valusia; three from the furry prehuman Hyperborean worshippers of Tsathoggua; one from the wholly abominable Tcho-Tchos; two from the Arachnid denizens of earth's last age; five from the hardy Coleopterous species immediately following mankind, to which the Great Race was some day to transfer its keenest minds *en masse* in the face of horrible peril; and several from different branches of humanity.

I talked with the mind of Yiang-Li, a philosopher from the cruel empire of Tsan-Chan, which is to come in 5,000 A.D.; with that of a general of the great-headed brown people who held South Africa in 50,000 B.C.; with that of a twelfth-century Florentine monk named Bartolomeo Corsi; with that of a king of Lomar who had ruled that terrible polar land one hundred thousand years before the squat, yellow Inutos came from the west to engulf it.

I talked with the mind of Nug-Soth, a magician of the dark conquerors of 16,000 A.D.; with that of a Roman named Titus Sempronius Blaesus, who had been a quaestor in Sulla's time; with that of Khephnes, an Egyptian of the 14th Dynasty, who told me the hideous secret of Nyarlathotep; with that of a priest of Atlantis' middle kingdom; with that of a Suffolk gentleman of Cromwell's day, James Woodville; with that of a court astronomer of pre-Inca Peru; with that of the Australian physicist Nevel Kingston-Brown, who will die in 2,518 A.D.; with that of an archimage of vanished Yhe in the Pacific; with that of Theodotides, a Graeco-Bactrian official of 200 B.C.; with that of an aged Frenchman of Louis XIII's time named Pierre-Louis Montagny; with that of Crom-Ya, a Cimmerian chieftain of 15,000 B.C.; and with so many others that my brain can not hold the shocking secrets and dizzying marvels I learned from them.

I awakened each morning in a fever, sometimes frantically trying to verify or discredit such information as fell within the range of modern human knowledge. Traditional facts took on new and doubtful aspects, and I marveled at the dream fancy which could invent such surprising addenda to history and science.

I shivered at the mysteries the past may conceal, and trembled at the menaces the future may bring forth. What was hinted in the speech of post-human entities of the fate of mankind produced such an effect on me that I will not set it down here.

After man there would be the mighty beetle civilization, the bodies of whose members the cream of the Great Race would seize when the monstrous doom overtook the elder world. Later, as the earth's span closed, the transferred minds would again migrate through time and space—to another stopping place in the bodies of the bulbous vegetable entities of Mercury. But there would be races after them, clinging pathetically to the cold planet and burrowing to its horror-filled core, before the utter end.

Meanwhile, in my dreams, I wrote endlessly in that history of my own age which I was preparing—half voluntarily and half through promises of increased library and travel opportunities—for the Great Race's central archives. The archives were in a colossal subterranean structure near the city's center, which I came to know well through frequent labors and consultations. Meant to last as long as the race, and to withstand the fiercest of earth's convulsions, this titan repository surpassed all other buildings in the massive, mountainlike firmness of its construction.

The records, written or printed on great sheets of a curiously tenacious cellulose fabric, were bound into books that opened from the top, and were kept in individual cases of a strange, extremely light rustless metal of grayish hue, decorated with mathematical designs and bearing the title in the Great Race's curvilinear hieroglyphs.

These cases were stored in tiers of rectangular vaults—like closed, locked shelves—wrought of the same rustless metal and fastened by knobs with intricate turnings. My own history was assigned a specific place in the vaults of the lowest or vertebrate level—the section devoted to the cultures of mankind and of the furry and reptilian races immediately preceding it in terrestrial dominance.

But none of the dreams ever gave me a full picture of daily life. All were the merest misty, disconnected fragments, and it is certain that these fragments were not unfolded in their rightful sequence. I have, for example, a very imperfect idea of my own living arrangements in the dream world; though I seem to have possessed a great stone room of my own. My restrictions as a prisoner gradually disappeared, so that some of the visions included vivid travels over the mighty jungle roads, sojourns in strange cities, and explorations of some of the vast, dark, windowless ruins from which the Great Race shrank in curious fear. There were also long sea voyages in enormous, many-decked boats of incredible swiftness, and trips over wild regions in closed projectilelike airships lifted and moved by electrical repulsion.

Beyond the wide, warm ocean were other cities of the Great Race, and on one far continent I saw the crude villages of the black-snouted, winged creatures who would evolve as a dominant stock after the Great Race had sent its foremost minds into the future to escape the creeping horror. Flatness and exuberant green life were always the keynote of the scene. Hills were low and sparse, and usually displayed signs of volcanic forces.

Of the animals I saw, I could write volumes. All were wild; for the Great Race's mechanized culture had long since done away with domestic beasts, while food was wholly vegetable or synthetic. Clumsy reptiles of great bulk floundered in steaming morasses, fluttered in the heavy air, or spouted in the seas and lakes; and among these I fancied I could vaguely recognize lesser, archaic prototypes of many forms—dinosaurs, pterodactyls, ichthyosaurs, labyrinthodonts, plesiosaurs, and the like—made familiar through paleontology. Of birds or mammals there were none that I could discover.

The ground and swamps were constantly alive with snakes, lizards, and crocodiles, while insects buzzed incessantly among the lush vegetation. And far out at sea, unspied and unknown monsters spouted mountainous columns of foam into the vaporous sky. Once I was taken under the ocean in a gigantic submarine vessel with searchlights, and glimpsed some living horrors of awesome magnitude. I saw also the ruins of incredible sunken cities, and the wealth of crinoid, brachiopod, coral, and ichthyic life which everywhere abounded.

Of the physiology, psychology, folkways, and detailed history of the Great Race my visions preserved but little information, and many of the scattered points I here set down were gleaned from my study of old legends and other cases rather than from my own dreaming.

For in time, of course, my reading and research caught up with and passed the dreams in many phases, so that certain dream fragments were explained in advance and formed verifications of what I had learned. This consolingly established my belief that similar reading and research, accomplished by my secondary self, had formed the source of the whole terrible fabric of pseudomemories.

The period of my dreams, apparently, was one somewhat less than 150,000,000 years ago, when the Paleozoic Age was giving place to the Mesozoic. The bodies occupied by the Great Race represented no surviving—or even scientifically known—line of terrestrial evolution, but were of a peculiar, closely homogeneous, and highly specialized organic type inclining as much to the vegetable as to the animal state.

Cell action was of an unique sort almost precluding fatigue, and wholly eliminating the need of sleep. Nourishment, assimilated through the red trumpetlike appendages on one of the great flexible limbs, was always semifluid and in many aspects wholly unlike the food of existing animals.

The beings had but two of the senses which we recognize—sight and hearing, the latter accomplished through the flowerlike appendages on the gray stalks above their heads. Of other and incomprehensible senses—not, however, well utilizable by alien captive minds inhabitating their bodies—they possessed many. Their three eyes were so situated as to give them a range of vision wider than the normal. Their blood was a sort of deep-greenish ichor of great thickness.

They had no sex, but reproduced through seeds or spores which clustered on their bases and could be developed only under water. Great, shallow tanks were used for the growth of their young—which were, however, reared only in small numbers on account of the longevity of individuals—four or five thousand years being the common life span.

Markedly defective individuals were quickly disposed of as soon as their defects were noticed. Disease and the approach of death were, in the absence of a sense of touch or of physical pain, recognized by purely visual symptoms.

The dead were incinerated with dignified ceremonies. Once in a while, as before mentioned, a keen mind would escape death by forward projection in time; but such cases were not numerous. When one did occur, the exiled mind from the future was treated with the utmost kindness till the dissolution of its unfamiliar tenement.

The Great Race seemed to form a single, loosely knit nation or league, with major institutions in common, though there were four definite divisions. The political and economic system of each unit was a sort of fascistic socialism, with major resources rationally distributed, and power delegated to a small governing board elected by the votes of all able to pass certain educational and psychological tests. Family organization was not overstressed, though ties among persons of common descent were recognized, and the young were generally reared by their parents.

Resemblances to human attitudes and institutions were, of course, most marked in those fields where on the one hand highly abstract elements were concerned, or, where on the other hand there was a dominance of the basic, unspecialized urges common to all organic life. A few added likenesses came through conscious adoption as the Great Race probed the future and copied what it liked.

Industry, highly mechanized, demanded but little time from each citizen; and the abundant leisure was filled with intellectual and aesthetic activities of various sorts.

The sciences were carried to an unbelievable height of development, and art was a vital part of life, though at the period of my dreams it had passed its crest and meridian. Technology was enormously stimulated through the constant struggle to survive, and to keep in existence the physical fabric of great cities, imposed by the prodigious geologic upheavals of those primal days.

Crime was surprisingly scant, and was dealt with through highly efficient policing. Punishments ranged from privilege deprivation and imprisonment to death or major emotion wrenching, and were never administered without a careful study of the criminal's motivations.

Warfare, largely civil for the last few millennia though sometimes waged against the winged, star-headed Old Ones who centered in the antarctic, was infrequent though infinitely devastating. An enormous army, using cameralike weapons which produced tremendous electrical effects, was kept on hand for purposes seldom mentioned, but obviously connected with the ceaseless fear of the dark, windowless elder ruins and of the great sealed trapdoors in the lowest subterranean levels.

This fear of the basalt ruins and trapdoors was largely a matter of unspoken suggestion—or, at most, of furtive quasi-whispers. Everything specific which bore on it was significantly absent from such books as were on the common shelves. It was the one subject lying altogether under a taboo among the Great Race, and seemed to be connected alike with horrible bygone struggles, and with that future peril which would some day force the race to send its keener minds ahead *en masse* in time.

Imperfect and fragmentary as were the other things presented by dreams and legends, this matter was still more bafflingly shrouded. The vague old myths avoided it—or perhaps all allusions had for some reason been excised. And in the dreams of myself and others, the hints were peculiarly few. Members of the Great Race never intentionally referred to the matter, and what could be gleaned came only from some of the more sharply observant captive minds.

According to these scraps of information, the basis of the fear was a horrible elder race of half polypous, utterly alien entities which had come through space from immeasurably distant universes and had dominated the earth and three other solar planets about six hundred million years ago. They were only partly material—as we understand matter—and their type of consciousness and media of perception differed widely from those of terrestrial organisms. For example, their senses did not include that of sight; their mental world being a strange, nonvisual pattern of impressions.

They were, however, sufficiently material to use implements of normal matter when in cosmic areas containing it; and they required housing—albeit of a peculiar kind. Though their senses could penetrate all material barriers, their substance could not; and certain forms of electrical energy could wholly destroy them. They had the power of aërial motion, despite the absence of wings or any other visible means of levitation. Their minds were of such texture that no exchange with them could be effected by the Great Race.

When these things had come to the Earth they had built mighty basalt cities of windowless towers, and had preyed horribly upon the beings they found. Thus it was when the minds of the Great Race sped across the void from that obscure, transgalactic world known in the disturbing and debatable Eltdown Shards as Yith.

The newcomers, with the instruments they created, had found it easy to subdue the predatory entities and drive them down to those caverns of inner earth which they had already joined to their abodes and begun to inhabit.

Then they had sealed the entrances and left them to their fate, afterward occupying most of their great cities and preserving certain important buildings for reasons connected more with superstition than with indifference, boldness, or scientific and historical zeal.

But as the aeons passed, there came vague, evil signs that the elder things were growing strong and numerous in the inner world. There were sporadic irruptions of a particularly hideous character in certain small and remote cities of the Great Race, and in some of the deserted elder cities which the Great Race had not peopled—places where the paths to the gulfs below had not been properly sealed or guarded.

After that greater precautions were taken, and many of the paths were closed forever—though a few were left with sealed trapdoors for strategic use in fighting the elder things if ever they broke forth in unexpected places.

The irruptions of the elder things must have been shocking beyond all description, since they had permanently colored the psychology of the Great Race. Such was the fixed mood of horror that the very aspect of the creatures was left unmentioned. At no time was I able to gain a clear hint of what they looked like.

There were veiled suggestions of a monstrous plasticity, and of temporary lapses of visibility, while other fragmentary whispers referred to their control and military use of great winds. Singular whistling noises, and colossal footprints made up of five circular toe marks, seemed also to be associated with them.

It was evident that the coming doom so desperately feared by the Great Race—the doom that was one day to send millions of keen minds across the chasm of time to strange bodies in the safer future—had to do with a final successful irruption of the elder beings.

Mental projections down the ages had clearly foretold such a horror, and the Great Race had resolved that none who could escape should face it. That the foray would be a matter of vengeance, rather than an attempt to reoccupy the outer world, they knew from the planet's later history—for their projections showed the coming and going of subsequent races untroubled by the monstrous entities.

Perhaps these entities had come to prefer Earth's inner abysses to the variable, storm-ravaged surface, since light meant nothing to them. Perhaps, too, they were slowly weakening with the aeons. Indeed, it was known that they would be quite dead in the time of the post-human beetle race which the fleeing minds would tenant.

Meanwhile, the Great Race maintained its cautious vigilance, with potent weapons ceaselessly ready despite the horrified banishing of the subject from common speech and visible records. And always the shadow of nameless fear hung about the sealed trapdoors and the dark, windowless elder towers.

V

That is the world of which my dreams brought me dim, scattered echoes every night. I cannot hope to give any true idea of the horror and dread contained in such echoes, for it was upon a wholly intangible quality—the sharp sense of pseudomemory—that such feelings mainly depended.

As I have said, my studies gradually gave me a defense against these feelings in the form of rational psychological explanations; and this saving influence was augmented by the subtle touch of accustomedness which comes with the passage of time. Yet in spite of everything the vague, creeping terror would return momentarily now and then. It did not, however, engulf me as it had before; and after 1922 I lived a very normal life of work and recreation.

In the course of years I began to feel that my experience—together with the kindred cases and the related folklore—ought to be definitely summarized and published for the benefit of serious students; hence, I prepared a series of articles briefly covering the whole ground and illustrated with crude sketches of some of the shapes, scenes, decorative motifs, and hieroglyphs remembered from the dreams.

These appeared at various times during 1928 and 1929 in the *Journal of the American Psychological Society,* but did not attract much attention. Meanwhile, I continued to record my dreams with the minutest care, even though the growing stack of reports attained troublesomely vast proportions.

On July 10, 1934, there was forwarded to me by the Psychological Society the letter which opened the culminating and most horrible phase of the whole mad ordeal. It was postmarked Pilbarra, Western Australia, and bore the signature of one whom I found, upon inquiry, to be a mining engineer of considerable prominence. Inclosed were some very curious snapshots. I will reproduce the text in its entirety, and no reader can fail to understand how tremendous an effect it and the photographs had upon me.

I was, for a time, almost stunned and incredulous; for, although I had often thought that some basis of fact must underlie certain phases of the legends which had colored my dreams, I was none the less unprepared for anything like a tangible survival from a lost world remote beyond all imagination. Most devastating of all were the photographs—for here, in cold, incontrovertible realism, there stood out against a background of sand certain worn-down, water-ridged, storm-weathered blocks of stone whose slightly convex tops and slightly concave bottoms told their own story.

And when I studied them with a magnifying glass I could see all too plainly, amidst the batterings and pittings, the traces of those vast curvilinear designs and occasional hieroglyphs whose significance had become so hideous to me. But here is the letter, which speaks for itself:

49 Dampier St.,
Pilbarra, W. Australia,
May 18, 1934.

Prof. N. W. Peaslee,
c/o Am. Psychological Society,
30 E. 41st St.,
New York City, U.S.A.

My Dear Sir:

A recent conversation with Dr. E. M. Boyle of Perth, and some papers with your articles which he has just sent me, make it advisable for me to tell you about certain things I have seen in the Great Sandy Desert east of our gold field here. It would seem, in view of the peculiar legends about old cities with huge stonework and strange designs and hieroglyphs which you describe, that I have come upon something very important.

The blackfellows have always been full of talk about "great stones with marks on them," and seem to have a terrible fear of such things. They connect them in some way with their common racial legends about Buddai, the gigantic old man who lies asleep for ages underground with his head on his arm, and who will some day awake and eat up the world.

There are some very old and half-forgotten tales of enormous underground huts of great stones, where passages lead down and down, and where horrible things have happened. The blackfellows claim that once some warriors, fleeing in battle, went down into one and never came back, but that frightful winds began to blow from the place soon after they went down. However, there usually isn't much in what these natives say.

But what I have to tell is more than this. Two years ago, when I was prospecting about five hundred miles east in the desert, I came on a lot of queer pieces of dressed stone perhaps 3 × 2 × 2 feet in size, and weathered and pitted to the very limit.

At first I couldn't find any of the marks the blackfellows told about, but when I looked close enough I could make out some deeply carved lines in spite of the weathering. There were peculiar curves, just like what the blackfellows had tried to describe. I imagine there must have been thirty or forty blocks, some nearly buried in the sand, and all within a circle perhaps a quarter of a mile in diameter.

When I saw some, I looked around closely for more, and made a careful reckoning of the place with my instruments. I also took pictures of ten or twelve of the most typical blocks, and will inclose the prints for you to see.

I turned my information and pictures over to the government at Perth, but they have done nothing about them.

Then I met Dr. Boyle, who had read your articles in the *Journal of the American Psychological Society,* and, in time, happened to mention the stones. He was enormously interested and became quite excited when I showed him my snapshots, saying that the stones and the markings were just like those of the masonry you had dreamed about and seen described in legends.

He meant to write you, but was delayed. Meanwhile, he sent me most of the magazines with your articles and I saw at once, from your drawings and descriptions, that my stones are certainly the kind you mean. You can appreciate this from the inclosed prints. Later on you will hear directly from Dr. Boyle.

Now I can understand how important all this will be to you. Without question we are faced with the remains of an unknown civilization older than any dreamed of before, and forming a basis for your legends.

As a mining engineer I have some knowledge of geology, and can tell you that these blocks are so ancient they frighten me. They are mostly sandstone and granite, though one is almost certainly made of a queer sort of cement or concrete.

They bear evidence of water action, as if this part of the world had been submerged and come up again after long ages—all since those blocks were made and used. It is a matter of hundreds of thousands of years—or Heaven knows how much more. I don't like to think about it.

In view of your previous diligent work in tracking down the legends and everything connected with them, I cannot doubt but that you will want to lead an expedition to the desert and make some archaeological excavations. Both Dr. Boyle and I are prepared to coöperate in such work if you—or organizations known to you—can furnish the funds.

I can get together a dozen miners for the heavy digging—the blackfellows would be of no use, for I've found that they have an almost maniacal fear of this particular spot. Boyle and I are saying nothing to others, for you very obviously ought to have precedence in any discoveries or credit.

The place can be reached from Pilbarra in about four days by motor tractor—which we'd need for our apparatus. It is somewhat west and south of Warburton's path of 1873, and one hundred miles southeast of Joanna Spring. We could float things up the De Grey River instead of starting from Pilbarra—but all that can be talked over later.

Roughly the stones lie at a point about 22° 3′ 14″ South Latitude, 125° 0′ 39″ East Longitude. The climate is tropical, and the desert conditions are trying.

I shall welcome further correspondence upon this subject, and am indeed keenly eager to assist in any plan you may devise. After studying your articles I am deeply impressed with the profound significance of the whole matter. Dr. Boyle will write later. When rapid communication is needed, a cable to Perth can be relayed by wireless.

Hoping profoundly for an early message,

Believe me,
Most faithfully yours,
Robert B. F. Mackenzie

Of the immediate aftermath of this letter, much can be learned from the press. My good fortune in securing the backing of Miskatonic University was great, and both Mr. Mackenzie and Dr. Boyle proved invaluable in arranging matters at the Australian end. We were not too specific with the public about our objects, since the whole matter would have lent itself unpleasantly to sensational and jocose treatment by the cheaper newspapers. As a result, printed reports were sparing; but enough appeared to tell of our quest for reported Australian ruins and to chronicle our various preparatory steps.

Professor William Dyer of the college's geology department—leader of the Miskatonic Antarctic Expedition of 1930–31, Ferdinand C. Ashley of the department of ancient history, and Tyler M. Freeborn of the department of anthropology—together with my son Wingate—accompanied me.

My correspondent, Mackenzie, came to Arkham early in 1935 and assisted in our final preparations. He proved to be a tremendously competent and affable man of about fifty, admirably well-read, and deeply familiar with all the conditions of Australian travel.

He had tractors waiting at Pilbarra, and we chartered a tramp steamer sufficiently small to get up the river to that point. We were prepared to excavate in the most careful and scientific fashion, sifting every particle of sand, and disturbing nothing which might seem to be in or near its original situation.

Sailing from Boston aboard the wheezy *Lexington* on March 28, 1935, we had a leisurely trip across the Atlantic and Mediterranean, through the Suez Canal, down the Red Sea, and across the Indian Ocean to our goal. I need not tell how the sight of the low, sandy West Australian coast depressed me, and how I detested the crude mining town and dreary gold fields where the tractors were given their last loads.

Dr. Boyle, who met us, proved to be elderly, pleasant and intelligent—and his knowledge of psychology led him into many long discussions with my son and me.

Discomfort and expectancy were oddly mingled in most of us when at length our party of eighteen rattled forth over the arid leagues of sand and rock. On Friday, May 31, we forded a branch of the De Grey and entered the realm of utter desolation. A certain positive terror grew on me as we advanced to this actual site of the elder world behind the legends—a terror, of course, abetted by the fact that my disturbing dreams and pseudomemories still beset me with unabated force.

It was on Monday, June 3, that we saw the first of the half-buried blocks. I cannot describe the emotions with which I actually touched—in objective reality—a fragment of cyclopean masonry in every respect like the blocks in the walls of my dream buildings. There was a distinct trace of carving—and my hands trembled as I recognized part of a curvilinear decorative scheme made hellish to me through years of tormenting nightmare and baffling research.

A month of digging brought a total of some 1250 blocks in varying stages of wear and disintegration. Most of these were carven megaliths with curved tops and bottoms. A minority were smaller, flatter, plain-surfaced, and square or octagonally cut—like those of the floors and pavements in my dreams—while a few were singularly massive and curved or slanted in such a manner as to suggest use in vaulting or groining, or as parts of arches or round window casings.

The deeper—and the farther north and east—we dug, the more

blocks we found—though we still failed to discover any trace of arrangement among them. Professor Dyer was appalled at the measureless age of the fragments, and Freeborn found traces of symbols which fitted darkly into certain Papuan and Polynesian legends of infinite antiquity. The condition and scattering of the blocks told mutely of vertiginous cycles of time and geologic upheavals of cosmic savagery.

We had an aeroplane with us, and my son Wingate would often go up to different heights and scan the sand-and-rock waste for signs of dim, large-scale outlines—either differences of level or trails of scattered blocks. His results were virtually negative; for whenever he would one day think he had glimpsed some significant trend, he would on his next trip find the impression replaced by another equally insubstantial—a result of the shifting, wind-blown sand.

One or two of these ephemeral suggestions, though, affected me queerly and disagreeably. They seemed, after a fashion, to dovetail horribly with something I had dreamed or read, but which I could no longer remember. There was a terrible familiarity about them—which somehow made me look furtively and apprehensively over the abominable, sterile terrain.

Around the first week in July I developed an unaccountable set of mixed emotions about that general northeasterly region. There was horror, and there was curiosity—but more than that, there was a persistent and perplexing illusion of memory.

I tried all sorts of psychological expedients to get these notions out of my head, but met with no success. Sleeplessness also gained upon me, but I almost welcomed this because of the resultant shortening of my dream periods. I acquired the habit of taking long, lone walks in the desert late at night—usually to the north or northeast, whither the sum of my strange new impulses seemed subtly to pull me.

Sometimes, on these walks, I would stumble over nearly buried fragments of the ancient masonry. Though there were fewer visible blocks here than where we had started, I felt sure that there must be a vast abundance beneath the surface. The ground was less level than at our camp, and the prevailing high winds now and then piled the sand into fantastic temporary hillocks—exposing low traces of the elder stones while it covered other traces.

I was queerly anxious to have the excavations extend to this territory, yet at the same time dreaded what might be revealed.

Obviously, I was getting into a rather bad state—all the worse because I could not account for it.

An indication of my poor nervous health can be gained from my response to an odd discovery which I made on one of my nocturnal rambles. It was on the evening of July 11, when the moon flooded the mysterious hillocks with a curious pallor.

Wandering somewhat beyond my usual limits, I came upon a great stone which seemed to differ markedly from any we had yet encountered. It was almost wholly covered, but I stooped and cleared away the sand with my hands, later studying the object carefully and supplementing the moonlight with my electric torch.

Unlike the other very large rocks, this one was perfectly square-cut, with no convex or concave surface. It seemed, too, to be of a dark basaltic substance, wholly dissimilar to the granite and sandstone and occasional concrete of the now familiar fragments.

Suddenly I rose, turned, and ran for the camp at top speed. It was a wholly unconscious and irrational flight, and only when I was close to my tent did I fully realize why I had run. Then it came to me. The queer dark stone was something which I had dreamed and read about, and which was linked with the uttermost horrors of the aeon-old legendry.

It was one of the blocks of that basaltic elder masonry which the fabled Great Race held in such fear—the tall, windowless ruins left by those brooding, half-material, alien things that festered in earth's nether abysses and against whose windlike, invisible forces the trapdoors were sealed and the sleepless sentinels posted.

I remained awake all night, but by dawn realized how silly I had been to let the shadow of a myth upset me. Instead of being frightened, I should have had a discoverer's enthusiasm.

The next forenoon I told the others about my find, and Dyer, Freeborn, Boyle, my son, and I set out to view the anomalous block. Failure, however, confronted us. I had formed no clear idea of the stone's location and a late wind had wholly altered the hillocks of shifting sand.

VI

I come now to the crucial and most difficult part of my narrative —all the more difficult because I cannot be quite certain of its reality. At times I feel uncomfortably sure that I was not dreaming or deluded; and it is this feeling—in view of the stupendous implications which the objective truth of my experience would raise—which impels me to make this record.

My son—a trained psychologist with the fullest and most sympathetic knowledge of my whole case—shall be the primary judge of what I have to tell.

First let me outline the externals of the matter, as those at the camp know them: On the night of July 17–18, after a windy day, I retired early but could not sleep. Rising shortly before eleven and afflicted as usual with that strange feeling regarding the northeastward terrain, I set out on one of my typical nocturnal walks, seeing and greeting only one person—an Australian miner named Tupper—as I left our precincts.

The moon, slightly past full, shone from a clear sky, and drenched the ancient sands with a white, leprous radiance which seemed to me somehow infinitely evil. There was no longer any wind, nor did any return for nearly five hours, as amply attested by Tupper and others who saw me walking rapidly across the pallid, secret-guarding hillocks toward the northeast.

About 3:30 A.M., a violent wind blew up, waking every one in camp and felling three of the tents. The sky was unclouded, and the desert still blazed with that leprous moonlight. As the party saw to the tents my absence was noted, but in view of my previous walks this circumstance gave no one alarm. And yet, as many as three men—all Australians—seemed to feel something sinister in the air.

Mackenzie explained to Professor Freeborn that this was a fear picked up from blackfellow folklore—the natives having woven a curious fabric of malignant myth about the high winds which at long intervals sweep across the sands under a clear sky. Such winds, it is whispered, blow out of the great stone huts under the ground, where terrible things have happened—and are never felt except near places where the big marked stones are scattered. Close to four the gale subsided as suddenly as it had begun, leaving the sand hills in new and unfamiliar shapes.

It was just past five, with the bloated, fungoid moon sinking in the west, when I staggered into camp—hatless, tattered, features scratched and ensanguined, and without my electric torch. Most of the men had returned to bed, but Professor Dyer was smoking a pipe in front of his tent. Seeing my winded and almost frenzied state, he called Dr. Boyle, and the two of them got me on my cot and made me comfortable. My son, roused by the stir, soon joined them, and they all tried to force me to lie still and attempt sleep.

But there was no sleep for me. My psychological state was very extraordinary—different from anything I had previously suffered. After a time I insisted upon talking—nervously and elaborately explaining my condition.

I told them I had become fatigued, and had lain down in the sand for a nap. There had, I said, been dreams even more frightful than usual—and when I was awaked by the sudden high wind my overwrought nerves had snapped. I had fled in panic, frequently falling over half-buried stones and thus gaining my tattered and bedraggled aspect. I must have slept long—hence the hours of my absence.

Of anything strange either seen or experienced I hinted absolutely nothing—exercising the greatest self-control in that respect. But I spoke of a change of mind regarding the whole work of the expedition, and urged a halt in all digging toward the northeast.

My reasoning was patently weak—for I mentioned a dearth of blocks, a wish not to offend the superstitious miners, a possible shortage of funds from the college, and other things either untrue or irrelevant. Naturally, no one paid the least attention to my new wishes—not even my son, whose concern for my health was obvious.

The next day I was up and around the camp, but took no part in the excavations. I decided to return home as soon as possible for the sake of my nerves, and my son promised to fly me in the plane to Perth—a thousand miles to the southwest—as soon as he had surveyed the region I wished let alone.

If, I reflected, the thing I had seen was still visible, I might decide to attempt a specific warning even at the cost of ridicule. It was just conceivable that the miners who knew the local folklore might back me up. Humouring me, my son made the survey that very afternoon, flying over all the terrain my walk could possibly have covered. Yet nothing of what I had found remained in sight.

It was the case of the anomalous basalt block all over again—the shifting sand had wiped out every trace. For an instant I half regretted having lost a certain awesome object in my stark fright—but now I know that the loss was merciful. I can still believe my whole experience an illusion—especially if, as I devoutly hope, that hellish abyss is never found.

Wingate took me to Perth on July 20, though declining to abandon the expedition and return home. He stayed with me until the 25th, when the steamer for Liverpool sailed. Now, in the cabin of the

Empress, I am pondering long and frantically upon the entire matter, and have decided that my son, at least, must be informed. It shall rest with him whether to diffuse the matter more widely.

In order to meet any eventuality I have prepared this summary of my background—as already known in a scattered way to others —and will now tell as briefly as possible what seemed to happen during my absence from the camp that hideous night.

Nerves on edge, and whipped into a kind of perverse eagerness by that inexplicable, dread-mingled, mnemonic urge toward the northeast, I plodded on beneath the evil, burning moon. Here and there I saw, half shrouded by sand, those primal cyclopean blocks left from nameless and forgotten aeons.

The incalculable age and brooding horror of this monstrous waste began to oppress me as never before, and I could not keep from thinking of my maddening dreams, of the frightful legends which lay behind them, and of the present fears of natives and miners concerning the desert and its carven stones.

And yet I plodded on as if to some eldritch rendezvous—more and more assailed by bewildering fancies, compulsions, and pseudomemories. I thought of some of the possible contours of the lines of stones as seen by my son from the air, and wondered why they seemed at once so ominous and so familiar. Something was fumbling and rattling at the latch of my recollection, while another unknown force sought to keep the portal barred.

The night was windless, and the pallid sand curved upward and downward like frozen waves of the sea. I had no goal, but somehow plowed along as if with fate-bound assurance. My dreams welled up into the waking world, so that each sand-embedded megalith seemed part of endless rooms and corridors of prehuman masonry, carved and hieroglyphed with symbols that I knew too well from years of custom as a captive mind of the Great Race.

At moments I fancied I saw those omniscient, conical horrors moving about at their accustomed tasks, and I feared to look down lest I find myself one with them in aspect. Yet all the while I saw the sand-covered blocks as well as the rooms and corridors; evil, burning moon as well as the lamps of luminous crystal; the endless desert as well as the waving ferns beyond the windows. I was awake and dreaming at the same time.

I do not know how long or how far—or indeed, in just what direction—I had walked when I first spied the heap of blocks bared by the day's wind. It was the largest group in one place that I ha seen so far, and so sharply did it impress me that the visions of fabulous aeons faded suddenly away.

Again there were only the desert and the evil moon and the shards of an unguessed past. I drew close and paused, and cast the added light of my electric torch over the tumbled pile. A hillock had blown away, leaving a low, irregularly round mass of megaliths and smaller fragments some forty feet across and from two to eight feet high.

From the very outset I realized that there was some utterly unprecedented quality about those stones. Not only was the mere number of them quite without parallel, but something in the sand-worn traces of design arrested me as I scanned them under the mingled beams of the moon and my torch.

Not that any one differed essentially from the earlier specimens we had found. It was something subtler than that. The impression did not come when I looked at one block alone, but only when I ran my eye over several almost simultaneously.

Then, at last, the truth dawned upon me. The curvilinear patterns on many of those blocks were closely related—parts of one vast decorative conception. For the first time in this aeon-shaking waste I had come upon a mass of masonry in its old position—tumbled and fragmentary, it is true, but none the less existing in a very definite sense.

Mounting at a low place, I clambered laboriously over the heap; here and there clearing away the sand with my fingers, and constantly striving to interpret varieties of size, shape, and style, and relationships of design.

After a while I could vaguely guess at the nature of the bygone structure, and at the designs which had once stretched over the vast surfaces of the primal masonry. The perfect identity of the whole with some of my dream glimpses appalled and unnerved me.

This was once a cyclopean corridor thirty feet wide and thirty feet tall, paved with octagonal blocks and solidly vaulted overhead. There would have been rooms opening off on the right, and at the farther end one of those strange inclined planes would have wound down to still lower depths.

I started violently as these conceptions occurred to me, for there was more in them than the blocks themselves had supplied. How did I know that this level should have been far underground? How did

I know that the plane leading upward should have been behind me? How did I know that the long subterrane passage to the Square of Pillars ought to lie on the left one level above me?

How did I know that the room of machines and the rightward-leading tunnel to the central archives ought to lie two levels below? How did I know that there would be one of those horrible metal-banded trapdoors at the very bottom four levels down? Bewildered by this intrusion from the dream world, I found myself shaking and bathed in a cold perspiration.

Then, as a last, intolerable touch, I felt that faint, insidious stream of cool air trickling upward from a depressed place near the center of the huge heap. Instantly, as once before, my visions faded, and I saw again only the evil moonlight, the brooding desert, and the spreading tumulus of paleogean masonry. Something real and tangible, yet fraught with infinite suggestions of nighted mystery, now confronted me. For that stream of air could argue but one thing—a hidden gulf of great size beneath the disordered blocks on the surface.

My first thought was of the sinister blackfellow legends of vast underground huts among the megaliths where horrors happen and great winds are born. Then thoughts of my own dreams came back, and I felt dim pseudomemories tugging at my mind. What manner of place lay below me? What primal, inconceivable source of age-old myth cycles and haunting nightmares might I be on the brink of uncovering?

It was only for a moment that I hesitated, for more than curiosity and scientific zeal was driving me on and working against my growing fear.

I seemed to move almost automatically, as if in the clutch of some compelling fate. Pocketing my torch, and struggling with a strength that I had not thought I possessed, I wrenched aside first one titan fragment of stone and then another, till there welled up a strong draft whose dampness contrasted oddly with the desert's dry air. A black rift began to yawn, and at length—when I had pushed away every fragment small enough to budge—the leprous moonlight blazed on an aperture of ample width to admit me.

I drew out my torch and cast a brilliant beam into the opening. Below me was a chaos of tumbled masonry, sloping roughly down toward the north at an angle of about forty-five degrees, and evidently the result of some bygone collapse from above.

Between its surface and the ground level was a gulf of impenetrable blackness at whose upper edge were signs of gigantic, stress-heaved vaulting. At this point, it appeared, the desert's sands lay directly upon a floor of some titan structure of earth's youth—how preserved through aeons of geologic convulsion I could not then and cannot now even attempt to guess.

In retrospect, the barest idea of a sudden lone descent into such a doubtful abyss—and at a time when one's whereabouts were unknown to any living soul—seems like the utter apex of insanity. Perhaps it was—yet that night I embarked without hesitancy upon such a descent.

Again there was manifest that lure and driving of fatality which had all along seemed to direct my course. With torch flashing intermittently to save the battery, I commenced a mad scramble down the sinister, cyclopean incline below the opening—sometimes facing forward as I found good hand and foot holds, and at other times turning to face the heap of megaliths as I clung and fumbled more precariously.

In two directions beside me, distant walls of carven, crumbling masonry loomed dimly under the direct beams of my torch. Ahead, however, was darkness.

I kept no track of time during my downward scramble. So seething with baffling hints and images was my mind that all objective matters seemed withdrawn to incalculable distances. Physical sensation was dead, and even fear remained as a wraith-like, inactive gargoyle leering impotently at me.

Eventually I reached a level floor strewn with fallen blocks, shapeless fragments of stone, and sand and detritus of every kind. On either side—perhaps thirty feet apart—rose massive walls culminating in huge groinings. That they were carved I could just discern, but the nature of the carvings was beyond my perception.

What held me most was the vaulting overhead. The beam from my torch could not reach the roof, but the lower parts of the monstrous arches stood out distinctly. And so perfect was their identity with what I had seen in countless dreams of the elder world, that I trembled actively for the first time.

Behind and high above, a faint luminous blur told of the distant moonlight world outside. Some vague shred of caution warned me that I should not let it out of my sight, lest I have no guide for my return.

I now advanced toward the wall at my left, where the traces of carving were plainest. The littered floor was nearly as hard to traverse as the downward heap had been, but I managed to pick my difficult way.

At one place I heaved aside some blocks and kicked away the detritus to see what the pavement was like, and shuddered at the utter, fateful familiarity of the great octagonal stones whose buckled surface still held roughly together.

Reaching a convenient distance from the wall, I cast the searchlight slowly and carefully over its worn remnants of carving. Some bygone influx of water seemed to have acted on the sandstone surface, while there were curious incrustations which I could not explain.

In places the masonry was very loose and distorted, and I wondered how many aeons more this primal, hidden edifice could keep its remaining traces of form amidst earth's heavings.

But it was the carvings themselves that excited me most. Despite their time-crumbled state, they were relatively easy to trace at close range; and the complete, intimate familiarity of every detail almost stunned my imagination. That the major attributes of this hoary masonry should be familiar, was not beyond normal credibility.

Powerfully impressing the weavers of certain myths, they had become embodied in a stream of cryptic lore which, somehow, coming to my notice during the amnesic period, had evoked vivid images in my subconscious mind.

But how could I explain the exact and minute fashion in which each line and spiral of these strange designs tallied with what I had dreamed for more than a score of years? What obscure, forgotten iconography could have reproduced each subtle shading and *nuance* which so persistently, exactly, and unvaryingly besieged my sleeping vision night after night?

For this was no chance or remote resemblance. Definitely and absolutely, the millennially ancient, aeon-hidden corridor in which I stood was the original of something I knew in sleep as intimately as I knew my own house in Crane Street, Arkham. True, my dreams showed the place in its undecayed prime; but the identity was no less real on that account. I was wholly and horribly oriented.

The particular structure I was in was known to me. Known, too, was its place in that terrible elder city of dream. That I could visit unerringly any point in that structure or in that city which had escaped the changes and devastations of uncounted ages, I realized with hideous and instinctive certainty. What in Heaven's name could all this mean? How had I come to know what I knew? And what awful reality could lie behind those antique tales of the beings who had dwelt in this labyrinth of primordial stone?

Words can convey only fractionally the welter of dread and bewilderment which ate at my spirit. I knew this place. I knew what lay below me, and what had lain overhead before the myriad towering stories had fallen to dust and debris and the desert. No need now, I thought with a shudder, to keep that faint blur of moonlight in view.

I was torn betwixt a longing to flee and a feverish mixture of burning curiosity and driving fatality. What had happened to this monstrous megalopolis of old in the millions of years since the time of my dreams? Of the subterrene mazes which had underlain the city and linked all the titan towers, how much had still survived the writhings of earth's crust?

Had I come upon a whole buried world of unholy archaism? Could I still find the house of the writing master, and the tower where S'gg'ha, the captive mind from the star-headed vegetable carnivores of Antarctica, had chiseled certain pictures on the blank spaces of the walls?

Would the passage at the second level down to the hall of the alien minds, be still unchoked and traversable? In that hall the captive mind of an incredible entity—a half-plastic denizen of the hollow interior of an unknown trans-Plutonian planet eighteen million years in the future—had kept a certain thing which it had modeled from clay.

I shut my eyes and put my hand to my head in a vain, pitiful effort to drive these insane dream fragments from my consciousness. Then, for the first time I felt acutely the coolness, motion, and dampness of the surrounding air. Shuddering, I realized that a vast chain of aeon-dead black gulfs must indeed be yawning somewhere beyond and below me.

I thought of the frightful chambers and corridors and inclines as I recalled them from my dreams. Would the way to the central archives still be open? Again that driving fatality tugged insistently at my brain as I recalled the awesome records that once lay cased in those rectangular vaults of rustless metal.

There, said the dreams and legends, had reposed the whole history, past and future, of the cosmic space-time continuum—written by captive minds from every orb and every age in the solar system. Madness, of course—but had I not now stumbled into a nighted world as mad as I?

I thought of the locked metal shelves, and of the curious knob twistings needed to open each one. My own came vividly into my consciousness. How often had I gone through that intricate routine of varied turns and pressures in the terrestrial vertebrate section on the lowest level! Every detail was fresh and familiar.

If there were such a vault as I had dreamed of, I could open it in a moment. It was then that madness took me utterly. An instant later, and I was leaping and stumbling over the rocky debris toward the well-remembered incline to the depths below.

VII

From that point forward my impressions are scarcely to be relied on—indeed, I still possess a final, desperate hope that they all form parts of some demoniac dream or illusion born of delirium. A fever raged in my brain, and everything came to me through a kind of haze—sometimes only intermittently.

The rays of my torch shot feebly into the engulfing blackness, bringing phantasmal flashes of hideously familiar walls and carvings, all blighted with the decay of ages. In one place a tremendous mass of vaulting had fallen, so that I had to clamber over a mighty mound of stones reaching almost to the ragged, grotesquely stalactited roof.

It was all the ultimate apex of nightmare, made worse by that blasphemous tug of pseudomemory. One thing only was unfamiliar, and that was my own size in relation to the monstrous masonry. I felt oppressed by a sense of unwonted smallness, as if the sight of these towering walls from a mere human body was something wholly new and abnormal. Again and again I looked nervously down at myself, vaguely disturbed by the human form I possessed.

Onward through the blackness of the abyss I leaped, plunged and staggered—often falling and bruising myself, and once nearly shattering my torch. Every stone and corner of that demoniac gulf was known to me, and at many points I stopped to cast beams of light through choked and crumbling, yet familiar, archways.

Some rooms had totally collapsed; others were bare, or debris-filled. In a few I saw masses of metal—some fairly intact, some broken, and some crushed or battered—which I recognized as the colossal pedestals or tables of my dreams. What they could in truth have been, I dared not guess.

I found the downward incline and began its descent—though after a time halted by a gaping, ragged chasm whose narrowest point could not be much less than four feet across. Here the stone-work had fallen through, revealing incalculable inky depths beneath.

I knew there were two more cellar levels in this titan edifice, and trembled with fresh panic as I recalled the metal-clamped trapdoor on the lowest one. There could be no guards now—for what had lurked beneath had long since done its hideous work and sunk into its long decline. By the time of the posthuman beetle race it would be quite dead. And yet, as I thought of the native legends, I trembled anew.

It cost me a terrible effort to vault that yawning chasm, since the littered floor prevented a running start—but madness drove me on. I chose a place close to the left-hand wall—where the rift was least wide and the landing spot reasonably clear of dangerous debris—and after one frantic moment reached the other side in safety.

At last, gaining the lower level, I stumbled on past the archway of the room of machines, within which were fantastic ruins of metal, half buried beneath fallen vaulting. Everything was where I knew it would be, and I climbed confidently over the heaps which barred the entrance of a vast transverse corridor. This, I realized, would take me under the city to the central archives.

Endless ages seemed to unroll as I stumbled, leaped, and crawled along that debris-cluttered corridor. Now and then I could make out carvings on the age-stained walls—some familiar, others seemingly added since the period of my dreams. Since this was a subterrene house-connecting highway, there were no archways save when the route led through the lower levels of various buildings.

At some of these intersections I turned aside long enough to look down well-remembered rooms. Twice only did I find any radical changes from what I had dreamed of—and in one of these cases I could trace the sealed-up outlines of the archway I remembered.

I shook violently, and felt a curious surge of retarding weakness as I steered a hurried and reluctant course through the crypt of one of those great windowless, ruined towers whose alien, basalt masonry bespoke a whispered and horrible origin.

This primal vault was round and fully two hundred feet across, with nothing carved upon the dark-hued stonework. The floor was here free from anything save dust and sand, and I could see the apertures leading upward and downward. There were no stairs nor inclines—indeed, my dreams had pictured those elder towers as wholly untouched by the fabulous Great Race. Those who had built them had not needed stairs or inclines.

In the dreams, the downward aperture had been tightly sealed and nervously guarded. Now it lay open—black and yawning, and giving forth a current of cool, damp air. Of what limitless caverns of eternal night might brood below, I would not permit myself to think.

Later, clawing my way along a badly heaped section of the corridor, I reached a place where the roof had wholly caved in. The debris rose like a mountain, and I climbed up over it, passing through a vast, empty space where my torchlight could reveal neither walls nor vaulting. This, I reflected, must be the cellar of the house of the metal purveyors, fronting on the third square not far from the archives. What had happened to it I could not conjecture.

I found the corridor again beyond the mountain of detritus and stone, but after a short distance encountered a wholly choked place where the fallen vaulting almost touched the perilously sagging ceiling. How I managed to wrench and tear aside enough blocks to afford a passage, and how I dared disturb the tightly packed fragments when the least shift of equilibrium might have brought down all the tons of superincumbent masonry to crush me to nothingness, I do not know.

It was sheer madness that impelled and guided me—if, indeed, my whole underground adventure was not—as I hope—a hellish delusion or phase of dreaming. But I did make—or dream that I made—a passage that I could squirm through. As I wriggled over the mound of debris—my torch, switched continuously on, thrust deeply in my mouth—I felt myself torn by the fantastic stalactites of the jagged floor above me.

I was now close to the great underground archival structure which seemed to form my goal. Sliding and clambering down the farther side of the barrier, and picking my way along the remaining stretch of corridor with handheld, intermittently flashing torch, I came at last to a low, circular crypt with arches—still in a marvelous state of preservation—opening off on every side.

The walls, or such parts of them as lay within reach of my torchlight, were densely hieroglyphed and chiseled with typical curvilinear symbols—some added since the period of my dreams.

This, I realized, was my fated destination, and I turned at once through a familiar archway on my left. That I could find a clear passage up and down the incline to all the surviving levels, I had, oddly, little doubt. This vast, earth-protected pile, housing the annals of all the solar system, had been built with supernal skill and strength to last as long as the system itself.

Blocks of stupendous size poised with mathematical genius and bound with cements of incredible toughness had combined to form a mass as firm as the planet's rocky core. Here, after ages more prodigious than I could sanely grasp, its buried bulk stood in all its essential contours, the vast, dust-drifted floors scarce sprinkled with the litter elsewhere so dominant.

The relatively easy walking from this point onward went curiously to my head. All the frantic eagerness hitherto frustrated by obstacles now took itself out in a kind of febrile speed, and I literally raced along the low-roofed, monstrously well-remembered aisles beyond the archway.

I was past being astonished by the familiarity of what I saw. On every hand the great hieroglyphed metal shelf doors loomed monstrously; some yet in place, others sprung open, and still others bent and buckled under bygone geological stresses not quite strong enough to shatter the titan masonry.

Here and there a dust-covered heap beneath a gaping, empty shelf seemed to indicate where cases had been shaken down by earth tremors. On occasional pillars were great symbols and letters proclaiming classes and subclasses of volumes.

Once I paused before an open vault where I saw some of the accustomed metal cases still in position amidst the omnipresent gritty dust. Reaching up, I dislodged one of the thinner specimens with some difficulty, and rested it on the floor for inspection. It was titled in the prevailing curvilinear hieroglyphs, though something in the arrangement of the characters seemed subtly unusual.

The odd mechanism of the hooked fastener was perfectly well known to me, and I snapped up the still rustless and workable lid and drew out the book within. The latter, as expected, was some twenty by fifteen inches in area, and two inches thick; the thin metal covers opening at the top.

Its tough cellulose pages seemed unaffected by the myriad cycles of time they had lived through, and I studied the queerly pigmented, brush-drawn letters of the text—symbols unlike either the usual curved hieroglyphs or any alphabet known to human scholarship—with a haunting, half-aroused memory.

It came to me that this was the language used by a captive mind I had known slightly in my dreams—a mind from a large asteroid on which had survived much of the archaic life and lore of the primal planet whereof it formed a fragment. At the same time I recalled that this level of the archives was devoted to volumes dealing with the nonterrestrial planets.

As I ceased poring over this incredible document, I saw that the light of my torch was beginning to fail, hence quickly inserted the extra battery I always had with me. Then, armed with the stronger radiance, I resumed my feverish racing through unending tangles of aisles and corridors—recognizing now and then some familiar shelf, and vaguely annoyed by the acoustic conditions which made my foot-falls echo incongruously in these catacombs.

The very prints of my shoes behind me in the millennially untrodden dust made me shudder. Never before, if my mad dreams held anything of truth, had human feet pressed upon those immemorial pavements.

Of the particular goal of my insane racing, my conscious mind held no hint. There was, however, some force of evil potency pulling at my dazed will and buried recollection, so that I vaguely felt I was not running at random.

I came to a downward incline and followed it to profound depths. Floors flashed by me as I raced, but I did not pause to explore them. In my whirling brain there had begun to beat a certain rhythm which set my right hand twitching in unison. I wanted to unlock something, and felt that I knew all the intricate twists and pressures needed to do it. It would be like a modern safe with a combination lock.

Dream or not, I had once known and still knew. How any dream—or any scrap of unconsciously absorbed legend—could have taught me a detail so minute, so intricate, and so complex, I did not attempt to explain to myself. I was beyond all coherent thought. For was not this whole experience—this shocking familiarity with a set of unknown ruins, and this monstrously exact identity of everything before me with what only dreams and scraps of myth could have suggested—a horror beyond all reason?

Probably it was my basic conviction then—as it is now during my saner moments—that I was not awake at all, and that the entire buried city was a fragment of febrile hallucination.

Eventually, I reached the lowest level and struck off to the right of the incline. For some shadowy reason I tried to soften my steps, even though I lost speed thereby. There was a space I was afraid to cross on this last, deeply buried floor.

As I drew near it I recalled what thing in that space I feared. It was merely one of the metal-barred and closely guarded trapdoors. There would be no guards now, and on that account I trembled and tiptoed as I had done in passing through that black basalt vault where a similar trapdoor had yawned.

I felt a current of cold damp air, as I had felt there, and wished that my course led in another direction. Why I had to take the particular course I was taking, I did not know.

When I came to the space I saw that the trapdoor yawned wildly open. Ahead, the shelves began again, and I glimpsed on the floor before one of them a heap very thinly covered with dust, where a number of cases had recently fallen. At the same moment a fresh wave of panic clutched me, though for some time I could not discover why.

Heaps of fallen cases were not uncommon, for all through the aeons this lightless labyrinth had been racked by the heavings of earth and had echoed at intervals to the deafening clatter of toppling objects. It was only when I was nearly across the space that I realized why I shook so violently.

Not the heap, but something about the dust of the level floor, was troubling me. In the light of my torch it seemed as if that dust were not as even as it ought to be—there were places where it looked thinner, as if it had been disturbed not many months before. I could not be sure, for even the apparently thinner places were dusty enough; yet a certain suspicion of regularity in the fancied unevenness was highly disquieting.

When I brought the torchlight close to one of the queer places I did not like what I saw—for the illusion of regularity became very great. It was as if there were regular lines of composite impressions—impressions that went in threes, each slightly over a foot square, and consisting of five nearly circular three-inch prints, one in advance of the other four.

These possible lines of foot-square impressions appeared to lead in two directions, as if something had gone somewhere and returned. They were, of course, very faint, and may have been illusions or accidents; but there was an element of dim, fumbling terror about the way I thought they ran. For at one end of them was the heap of cases which must have clattered down not long before, while at the other end was the ominous trapdoor with the cool, damp wind, yawning unguarded down to abysses past imagination.

VIII

That my strange sense of compulsion was deep and overwhelming is shown by its conquest of my fear. No rational motive could have drawn me on after that hideous suspicion of prints and the creeping dream memories it excited. Yet my right hand, even as it shook with fright, still twitched rhythmically in its eagerness to turn a lock it hoped to find. Before I knew it I was past the heap of lately fallen cases and running on tiptoe through aisles of utterly unbroken dust toward a point which I seemed to know morbidly, horribly well.

My mind was asking itself questions whose origin and relevancy I was only beginning to guess. Would the shelf be reachable by a human body? Could my human hand master all the aeon-remembered motions of the lock? Would the lock be undamaged and workable? And what would I do—what dare I do—with what—as I now commenced to realize—I both hoped and feared to find? Would it prove the awesome, brain-shattering truth of something past normal conception, or show only that I was dreaming?

The next I knew I had ceased my tiptoed racing and was standing still, staring at a row of maddeningly familiar hieroglyphed shelves. They were in a state of almost perfect preservation, and only three of the doors in this vicinity had sprung open.

My feelings toward these shelves cannot be described—so utter and insistent was the sense of old acquaintance. I was looking high up at a row near the top and wholly out of my reach, and wondering how I could climb to best advantage. An open door four rows from the bottom would help, and the locks of the closed doors formed possible holds for hands and feet. I would grip the torch between my teeth, as I had in other places where both hands were needed. Above all I must make no noise.

How to get down what I wished to remove would be difficult, but I could probably hook its movable fastener in my coat collar and carry it like a knapsack. Again I wondered whether the lock would be undamaged. That I could repeat each familiar motion I had not the least doubt. But I hoped the thing would not scrape or creak—and that my hand could work it properly.

Even as I thought these things I had taken the torch in my mouth and begun to climb. The projecting locks were poor supports; but, as I had expected, the opened shelf helped greatly. I used both the swinging door and the edge of the aperture itself in my ascent, and managed to avoid any loud creaking.

Balanced on the upper edge of the door, and leaning far to my right, I could just reach the lock I sought. My fingers, half numb from climbing, were very clumsy at first; but I soon saw that they were anatomically adequate. And the memory rhythm was strong in them.

Out of unknown gulfs of time the intricate, secret motions had somehow reached my brain correctly in every detail—for after less than five minutes of trying there came a click whose familiarity was all the more startling because I had not consciously anticipated it. In another instant the metal door was slowly swinging open with only the faintest grating sound.

Dazedly I looked over the row of grayish case ends thus exposed, and felt a tremendous surge of some wholly inexplicable emotion. Just within reach of my right hand was a case whose curving hieroglyphs made me shake with a pang infinitely more complex than one of mere fright. Still shaking, I managed to dislodge it amidst a shower of gritty flakes, and ease it over toward myself without any violent noise.

Like the other case I had handled, it was slightly more than twenty by fifteen inches in size, with curved mathematical designs in low relief. In thickness it just exceeded three inches.

Crudely wedging it between myself and the surface I was climbing, I fumbled with the fastener and finally got the hook free. Lifting the cover, I shifted the heavy object to my back, and let the hook catch hold of my collar. Hands now free, I awkwardly clambered down to the dusty floor and prepared to inspect my prize.

Kneeling in the gritty dust, I swung the case around and rested it in front of me. My hands shook, and I dreaded to draw out the book within almost as much as I longed—and felt compelled—to do so. It had very gradually become clear to me what I ought to find, and this realization nearly paralyzed my faculties.

If the thing were there—and if I were not dreaming—the implications would be quite beyond the power of the human spirit to bear. What tormented me most was my momentary inability to feel that my surroundings were a dream. The sense of reality was hideous—and again becomes so as I recall the scene.

At length I tremblingly pulled the book from its container and stared fascinatedly at the well-known hieroglyphs on the cover. It seemed to be in prime condition, and the curvilinear letters of the title held me in almost as hypnotized a state as if I could read them. Indeed, I cannot swear that I did not actually read them in some transient and terrible access of abnormal memory.

I do not know how long it was before I dared to lift that thin metal cover. I temporized and made excuses to myself. I took the torch from my mouth and shut it off to save the battery. Then, in the dark, I collected my courage—finally lifting the cover without turning on the light. Last of all, I did indeed flash the torch upon the exposed page—steeling myself in advance to suppress any sound no matter what I should find.

I looked for an instant, then collapsed. Clenching my teeth, however, I kept silent. I sank wholly to the floor and put a hand to my forehead amidst the engulfing blackness. What I dreaded and expected was there. Either I was dreaming, or time and space had become a mockery.

I must be dreaming—but I would test the horror by carrying this thing back and showing it to my son if it were indeed a reality. My head swam frightfully, even though there were no visible objects in the unbroken gloom to swirl about me. Ideas and images of the starkest terror—excited by the vistas which my glimpse had opened up—began to throng in upon me and cloud my senses.

I thought of those possible prints in the dust, and trembled at the sound of my own breathing as I did so. Once again I flashed on the light and looked at the page as a serpent's victim may look at his destroyer's eyes and fangs.

Then, with clumsy fingers, in the dark, I closed the book, put it in its container, and snapped the lid and the curious, hooked fastener. This was what I must carry back to the outer world if it truly existed—if the whole abyss truly existed—if I, and the world itself, truly existed.

Just when I tottered to my feet and commenced my return I cannot be certain. It comes to me oddly—as a measure of my sense of separation from the normal world—that I did not even once look at my watch during those hideous hours underground.

Torch in hand, and with the ominous case under one arm, I eventually found myself tiptoeing in a kind of silent panic past the draft-giving abyss and those lurking suggestions of prints. I lessened my precautions as I climbed up the endless inclines, but could not shake off a shadow of apprehension which I had not felt on the downward journey.

I dreaded having to repass through that black basalt crypt that was older than the city itself, where cold drafts welled up from unguarded depths. I thought of that which the Great Race had feared, and of what might still be lurking—be it ever so weak and dying—down there. I thought of those five-circle prints and of what my dreams had told me of such prints—and of strange winds and whistling noises associated with them. And I thought of the tales of the modern blackfellows, wherein the horror of great winds and nameless ruins was dwelt upon.

I knew from a carven wall symbol the right floor to enter, and came at last—after passing that other book I had examined—to the great circular space with the branching archways. On my right, and at once recognizable, was the arch through which I had arrived. This I now entered, conscious that the rest of my course would be harder because of the tumbled state of the masonry outside the archive building. My new metal-cased burden weighed upon me, and I found it harder and harder to be quiet as I stumbled among debris and fragments of every sort.

Then I came to the ceiling-high mound of debris through which I had wrenched a scanty passage. My dread at wriggling through again was infinite, for my first passage had made some noise, and I now—after seeing those possible prints—dreaded sound above all things. The case, too, doubled the problem of traversing the narrow crevice.

But I clambered up the barrier as best I could, and pushed the case through the aperture ahead of me. Then, torch in mouth, I scrambled through myself—my back torn as before by stalactites.

As I tried to grasp the case again, it fell some distance ahead of me down the slope of the debris, making a disturbing clatter and arousing echoes which sent me into a cold perspiration. I lunged for it at once, and regained it without further noise—but a moment afterward the slipping of blocks under my feet raised a sudden and unprecedented din.

That din was my undoing. For, falsely or not, I thought I heard it answered in a terrible way from spaces far behind me. I thought I heard a shrill, whistling sound, like nothing else on Earth, and beyond any adequate verbal description. If so, what followed has a grim irony—save for the panic of this thing, the second thing might never have happened.

As it was, my frenzy was absolute and unrelieved. Taking my torch in my hand and clutching feebly at the case, I leaped and bounded wildly ahead with no idea in my brain beyond a mad desire to race out of these nightmare ruins to the waking world of desert and moonlight which lay so far above.

I hardly knew it when I reached the mountain of debris which towered into the vast blackness beyond the caved-in roof, and bruised and cut myself repeatedly in scrambling up its steep slope of jagged blocks and fragments.

Then came the great disaster. Just as I blindly crossed the summit, unprepared for the sudden dip ahead, my feet slipped utterly and I found myself involved in a mangling avalanche of sliding masonry whose cannon-loud uproar split the black, cavern air in a deafening series of earth-shaking reverberations.

I have no recollection of emerging from this chaos, but a momentary fragment of consciousness shows me as plunging and tripping and scrambling along the corridor amidst the clangor—case and torch still with me.

Then, just as I approached that primal basalt crypt I had so dreaded, utter madness came. For as the echoes of the avalanche died down, there became audible a repetition of that frightful alien whistling I thought I had heard before. This time there was no doubt about it—and what was worse, it came from a point not behind but *ahead of me.*

Probably I shrieked aloud then. I have a dim picture of myself as flying through the hellish basalt vault of the elder things, and hearing that damnable alien sound piping up from the open, unguarded door of limitless nether blacknesses. There was a wind, too —not merely a cool, damp draft, but a violent, purposeful blast belching savagely and frigidly from that abominable gulf whence the obscene whistling came.

There are memories of leaping and lurching over obstacles of every sort, with that torrent of wind and shrieking sound growing moment by moment, and seeming to curl and twist purposefully around me as it struck out wickedly from the spaces behind and beneath.

Though in my rear, that wind had the odd effect of hindering instead of aiding my progress; as if it acted like a noose or lasso thrown around me. Heedless of the noise I made, I clattered over a great barrier of blocks and was again in the structure that led to the surface.

I recall glimpsing the archway to the room of machines and almost crying out as I saw the incline leading down to where one of those blasphemous trapdoors must be yawning two levels below. But instead of crying out I muttered over and over to myself that this was all a dream from which I must soon awake. Perhaps I was in camp—perhaps I was at home in Arkham. As these hopes bolstered up my sanity I began to mount the incline to the higher level.

I knew, of course, that I had the four-foot cleft to recross, yet was too racked by other fears to realize the full horror until I came almost upon it. On my descent, the leap across had been easy—but could I clear the gap as readily when going uphill, and hampered by fright, exhaustion, the weight of the metal case, and the anomalous backward tug of that demon wind? I thought of these things at the last moment, and thought also of the nameless entities which might be lurking in the black abysses below the chasm.

My wavering torch was growing feeble, but I could tell by some obscure memory when I neared the cleft. The chill blasts of wind and the nauseous whistling shrieks behind me were for the moment like a merciful opiate, dulling my imagination to the horror of the yawning gulf ahead. And then I became aware of the added blasts and whistling in front of me—tides of abomination surging up through the cleft itself from depths unimagined and unimaginable.

Now, indeed, the essence of pure nightmare was upon me. Sanity departed—and, ignoring everything except the animal impulse of flight, I merely struggled and plunged upward over the incline's debris as if no gulf had existed. Then I saw the chasm's edge, leaped frenziedly with every ounce of strength I possessed, and was instantly engulfed in a pandemoniac vortex of loathsome sound and utter, materially tangible blackness.

That is the end of my experience, so far as I can recall. Any further impressions belong wholly to the domain of phantasmagoric delirium. Dream, madness, and memory merged wildly together in a series of fantastic, fragmentary delusions which can have no relation to anything real.

There was a hideous fall through incalculable leagues of viscous, sentient darkness, and a babel of noises utterly alien to all that we know of the Earth and its organic life. Dormant, rudimentary senses seemed to start into vitality within me, telling of pits and voids peopled by floating horrors and leading to sunless crags and oceans and teeming cities of windowless, basalt towers upon which no light ever shone.

Secrets of the primal planet and its immemorial aeons flashed through my brain without the aid of sight or sound, and there were known to me things which not even the wildest of former dreams had ever suggested. And all the while cold fingers of damp vapor clutched and picked at me, and that eldritch, damnable whistling shrieked fiendishly above all the alternations of babel and silence in the whirlpools of darkness around.

Afterward there were visions of the cyclopean city of my dreams —not in ruins, but just as I had dreamed of it. I was in my conical, nonhuman body again, and mingled with crowds of the Great Race and the captive minds who carried books up and down the lofty corridors and vast inclines.

Then, superimposed upon these pictures, were frightful, momentary flashes of a nonvisual consciousness involving desperate struggles, a writhing free from clutching tentacles of whistling wind, an insane, batlike flight through half-solid air, a feverish burrowing through the cyclone-whipped dark, and a wild stumbling and scrambling over fallen masonry.

Once there was a curious, intrusive flash of half sight—a faint, diffuse suspicion of bluish radiance far overhead. Then there came a dream of wind-pursued climbing and crawling—of wriggling into a blaze of sardonic moonlight through a jumble of debris which slid and collapsed after me amidst a morbid hurricane. It was the evil, monotonous beating of that maddening moonlight which at last told me of the return of what I had once known as the objective, waking world.

I was clawing prone through the sands of the Australian desert, and around me shrieked such a tumult of wind as I had never before known on our planet's surface. My clothing was in rags, and my whole body was a mass of bruises and scratches.

Full consciousness returned very slowly, and at no time could I tell just where delirious dream left off and true memory began. There had seemed to be a mound of titan blocks, an abyss beneath it, a monstrous revelation from the past, and a nightmare horror at the end—but how much of this was real?

My flashlight was gone, and likewise my metal case I may have discovered. Had there been such a case—or any abyss—or any mound? Raising my head, I looked behind me, and saw only the sterile, undulant sands of the desert.

The demon wind died down, and the bloated, fungoid moon sank reddeningly in the west. I lurched to my feet and began to stagger southwestward toward the camp. What in truth had happened to me? Had I merely collapsed in the desert and dragged a dream-racked body over miles of sand and buried blocks? If not, how could I bear to live any longer?

For, in this new doubt, all my faith in the myth-born unreality of my visions dissolved once more into the hellish older doubting. If that abyss was real, then the Great Race was real—and its blasphemous reachings and seizures in the cosmos-wide vortex of time were no myths or nightmares, but a terrible, soul-shattering actuality.

Had I, in full, hideous fact, been drawn back to a prehuman world of a hundred and fifty million years ago in those dark, baffling days of the amnesia? Had my present body been the vehicle of a frightful alien consciousness from paleogean gulfs of time?

Had I, as the captive mind of those shambling horrors, indeed known that accursed city of stone in its primordial heyday, and wriggled down those familiar corridors in the loathsome shape of my captor? Were those tormenting dreams of more than twenty years the offspring of stark, monstrous memories?

Had I once veritably talked with minds from reachless corners of time and space, learned the universe's secrets, past and to come, and written the annals of my own world for the metal cases of those titan archives? And were those others—those shocking elder things of the mad winds and demon pipings—in truth a lingering, lurking menace, waiting and slowly weakening in black abysses while varied shapes of life drag out their multimillennial courses on the planet's age-racked surface?

I do not know. If that abyss and what it held were real, there is no hope. Then, all too truly, there lies upon this world of man a mocking and incredible shadow out of time. But, mercifully there is no proof that these things are other than fresh phases of my myth-born dreams. I did not bring back the metal case that would have been a proof, and so far those subterrane corridors have not been found.

If the laws of the universe are kind, they will never be found. But I must tell my son what I saw or thought I saw, and let him use his judgment as a psychologist in gauging the reality of my experience, and communicating this account to others.

I have said that the awful truth behind my tortured years of dreaming hinges absolutely upon the actuality of what I thought I saw in those cyclopean, buried ruins. It has been hard for me, literally, to set down that crucial revelation, though no reader can have failed to guess it. Of course, it lay in that book within the metal case —the case which I pried out of its lair amidst the dust of a million centuries.

No eye had seen, no hand had touched that book since the advent of man to this planet. And yet, when I flashed my torch upon it in that frightful abyss, I saw that the queerly pigmented letters on the brittle, aeon-browned cellulose pages were not indeed any nameless hieroglyphs of earth's youth. They were, instead, the letters of our familiar alphabet, spelling out the words of the English language in my own handwriting.